CW01433642

LUCKING OUT

Elle M Thomas

Happy reading,
Sophie

Elle M
x

First published 2019

Cover design and **Editing** by Bookfully Yours

This is an Elle M Thomas mature, contemporary romance. Anyone who has read my work before will know what that means, but if you're new to me then let me explain.
This book includes adult situations including, but not limited to: adult characters that swear, a lot. A leading man who talks dirty, really, really dirty. Sex, lots and lots of hot, steamy, sheet gripping and toe curling sex. Due to the dark and explicit nature of this book, it is recommended for mature audiences only.
If this is not what you want to read about then this might not be the book for you, but if it is then sit back, buckle up and enjoy the ride.

Trigger warning – This story includes references, recollections and descriptions of abusive situations that some might find distressing.

Other titles by Elle M Thomas:

Disaster-in-Waiting
One Night Or Forever
Revealing His Prize

Love in Vegas Series (to be read in order):

Lucky Seven (Book 1)
Pushing His Luck (Book 2)
Lucking Out (Book 3)

ACKNOWLEDGEMENT

Thank you seems awfully inadequate for all of the support and encouragement I have received since first sharing the voices in my head, but thank you.

This trilogy of books has been a very long time in the making. There have been times where I have cast it aside, vowed never to pick it up again, and yet something kept pulling me back.

Jim's and Tasha's voices gave me sleepless nights, haunted me in my dreams whilst awake as well as sleeping. Regardless of the difficulties and unlikeliness of them embarking on a romance and making a future together their connection was too strong. The connection they had from that very first meeting was too much to be denied, their meeting and their love were fate.

So to all of you, I say, when fate intervenes, don't fight it, embrace it and cherish every opportunity it sends your way or you may miss your very own Lucky Seven.

X

Chapter One

Pacing the hall Jim was becoming more and more agitated as he waited for Tasha to return. She'd assured him she was on her way home, but it was taking too long. She had been too long and he was beginning to worry when he heard the sound of a car coming to a standstill outside the house, although the car seemed to be travelling fast, too fast, and the braking seemed too severe, too urgent causing his initial relief at hearing it to be short lived as panic resurfaced. He was standing behind the door, ready to pull on the handle when it seemed to fly open, but rather than coming face to face with Tasha, Jim found Juan looking back at him with the mother of all scared expressions on his face that confirmed he had been right to be concerned by Tasha's delayed arrival.

"What?" Jim asked, his voice raised with concern at the other man's expression, the fear in his eyes.

"There's been a crash," Juan started. "Down the hill. A car. The fire crew are preparing to cut the driver out."

"Juan, who is it?" Jim asked, but knew in his head, heart and gut what the other man was going to say.

"The car looks like Tasha's. I came back up here as fast as I could—"

Jim was already heading through the door and rounding his own car while Juan was calling behind him, something about coming with him, but the truth was if he didn't get in the car quickly he would be left behind because Jim had no intention of hanging around if Tasha was hurt. He needed to see her, to make sure she was okay and she had to be, she just had to be or he

4

would never forgive himself.

It was only a couple of minutes before they were pulling up alongside the broken crash barrier the vehicle had gone through. There were blue lights flashing everywhere; police, ambulance and fire crews and as Juan had suggested the latter were indeed cutting the victim from the vehicle. Moving closer and attempting to push past the police cordon to gain a better look at the vehicle if not the driver, Jim met the full force of a very large uniformed police officer.

"Sir, you need to step back," the officer told Jim who was still trying to at least look past the policeman if not move past him.

"I need to get down there. I think it's my fiancée, in the car. We're getting married, soon, in a couple of weeks," he said, and although he knew he was rambling he was incapable of stopping. "We had a fight earlier and she was coming home, but it was taking too long—"

The officer cut him off as he called to someone else and was quickly joined by a young fire fighter who offered Jim a short and sympathetic smile.

"Jim?" With a confirming nod from Jim, he continued, "She was asking for you, Tasha."

"She's okay?" Jim asked, desperate for reassurance and some kind of sign that Tasha was unhurt.

"The vehicle flipped. We've turned it back. She was conscious earlier, but the medics are with her now, keeping her stable while we cut her free. I should get back but you should be okay to travel to the hospital with her."

Jim nodded, unable to say anything else, barely able to think. With a sick feeling in his stomach and a heavy ache across his chest he momentarily doubled over, dropping to his haunches as Juan dropped to his side.

"I'm sure she'll be okay. Tasha is strong, a fighter," Juan told the older man, his own voice breaking at the thought that she might be anything other than well.

Jim made no reply. Juan was right, Tasha was a fighter, she'd had to be from the day she was born and when he'd met her, known she was his lucky seven he'd vowed she'd never have to fight again and yet here she was, doing precisely that. However, unlike in the past, this time she wouldn't be fighting alone because he was here and had no intention of leaving her to face anything alone ever again.

Another ten minutes or so passed in silence before Juan spoke again, "Should I call anyone, Philip?"

"No, not yet," Jim replied, his eyes never leaving the scene of the crash as Tasha's body was finally lifted from the wreck of her car.

With the police now maintaining a cleared path for the stretcher to be carried along, Jim was finally afforded his first look at Tasha and as much as he imagined it proving to be a reassurance that she was okay, alive, it didn't, because for all intents and purposes she looked as close to death as he imagined she could without actually being dead.

"Baby," he whispered as he watched her pass by, a multitude of leads and tubes attached to her along with a collar holding her neck in a fixed position while the bandages or straps, whatever they were seemed to bind her to the stretcher, preventing any movement which he knew was a bad sign.

Jim was vaguely aware of the fire fighter reappearing beside him and mutely nodded as he said, "You can go with her."

Following behind Tasha, Jim felt numb now, numb and impotent because he really was unable to do anything to make this right. Tasha's wellbeing was in the lap of the gods and in the hands of the doctors who awaited them at the hospital. Juan had already relieved Jim of his car keys and was preparing to follow the ambulance to the hospital, but not before he had called Bobby, just Bobby, because he knew Jim would need someone and his brother was that person.

Once at the hospital, Tasha was rushed through the emergency department and Jim was left to sit and wait. He paced the floor, sat down, stood up, sat back down and tapped his feet nervously and then paced some more. Bobby had arrived shortly after Juan who felt as helpless as Jim, but was also conflicted because he knew he should contact Philip.

After the first hour passed, Juan suggested contacting someone else to Bobby who nodded, but said nothing, meaning he was expecting some opposition from Jim. There were none.

Bobby collected some coffee from the nearby vending machine and whilst there made a couple of calls before returning to his brother who was doing a round of pacing and Juan who was sitting in a corner rocking.

"Jimbo," he called. "I've phoned Lenny, well Sara who passed me over to Lenny. He's coming down, to see if he can pull any strings in getting some answers, okay?"

Jim nodded then took the seat next to his brother and sipped the coffee he was offered.

"The coffee is shit." He winced, making his brother smile.

"You should probably contact Tasha's family. They'll want to know and if any of this hits the news…"

"Yeah, I will. As soon as I know something, anything. Juan," he called now. "You should go. There's no point us all being here."

Juan shook his head. "I'd rather stay. Tasha's my friend, so maybe for a while, until we know something, but I would like to call Phil. He'll be wondering where I am."

Jim nodded but quickly added, "Just Philip, not Lizzie. I do not need either of them here, but I definitely don't need to have to put a brave face on and cajole Lizzie right now."

By the time Lenny arrived, Philip had been informed of Tasha's accident but there was still no news on her condition. Lenny was about to make his way through the department to where Tasha was when a doctor appeared and introduced himself as Stan Marvin. He led Jim and the others towards a small office where he explained that Tasha was now stable, but still had some internal bleeding that would need to be stopped surgically. He briefly tried to offer some reassurances that Tasha was young and fit, but was clear that time was of the essence to maximise the chances of a *positive outcome*.

He left as quickly as he'd arrived leaving Jim to wait again. Lenny went through the possibilities of the surgery, complications and postoperative recovery while Bobby began to filter phone calls and a visit from the police who were investigating the cause of the accident. With Tasha out of the picture in terms of giving the police any information about her accident, the police quickly left but assured Jim that they would be back.

It was another two hours before there was any news on Tasha and then it was a simple message from theatre explaining that things were progressing and that Stan and his team were still working on stopping the internal bleeding. A call from Marc alerted Jim to the fact that news reports were beginning to circulate about a crash and that the victim was an actress meaning Jim was going to have to call Paul and Celia to let them know that Tasha was hurt. Bobby offered to make the call, but Jim refused, knowing it was his responsibility.

The phone rang no more than three times before Paul answered and as quickly and concisely as he could, Jim explained about the accident, that Tasha was hurt and still in surgery. Beyond that he had no more to tell them, nor could he assure them that she was going to be okay because he had no idea if she would be. He promised to get them all on flights as soon as was possible and once he'd hung up, he handed that over to Bobby who simply called Amanda who had flights arranged for the following night.

As the clock hit four in the morning Stan appeared with a short smile for Jim who allowed the longest and deepest breath he'd ever known to be released from his body. The relief was immediate, overwhelming and immense and yet it was at that point that his tears began to fall. She was okay, well, alive, and right now that was all that mattered. He still had her in his life. She had survived, although, as Stan had stressed several times, she was not out of the woods.

Jim kept going over how much she'd been through in her short life and now she was enduring even more suffering and pain, and it was his fault. For all the times he'd blamed her parents, Liam, even her grandparents for not intervening, the only person he held responsible now was himself. Had he never met Mickie and become embroiled in her cancer battle and need for a friend he and Tasha wouldn't have fought and she would have had no cause to run away from him, leading to the accident that was still threatening to take her from him.

Jim became aware of an arm around him, Bobby's. A loving and reassuring arm that wanted to comfort him and yet he found none; his head was full of thoughts of how his life might look without Tasha, how sad and lonely he would be, sad, lonely and alone because she really was his lucky seven, his life and his future.

"Hey, Jimbo, she's holding her own. She's telling the world to go fuck itself. This is good news." Bobby reassured his brother who was shaking with the tears and sobs that wracked his body while Lenny and Juan watched on from a distance.

"I am nothing without her. She came into my life and put me on my ass. I can't go back to my old life without her," Jim cried as Stan returned to explain that Tasha had been moved from recovery to a room upstairs. "Can I see her?" Jim asked, but was already up on his feet and heading towards the lift.

Stan muttered something about, *is there any point in me saying no?* But was nodding his head.

"Five minutes and then she needs to rest."

Jim nodded his agreement as he stepped onto the lift.

Once at the door to Tasha's room, Stan was issuing warnings about the machines, tubes, bruises and dressings Jim would see when he entered the room. He also explained that it would only be Jim who could see her now and then everyone would have to leave. Before entering the room Jim thanked the men around him then instructed them all to leave, to go home and promised to call them if Tasha's condition changed.

"Jim, we all need to go home, including you," Lenny said, a concerned frown creasing his brow before giving Bobby a glance that suggested he expected the older Maybury to direct the younger one to going home.

"I'm going nowhere without my fiancée, so while she is here, I will be here too."

With his composure regained and a strong determination, Jim stood firm until the others all nodded their acquiescence and once he was happy they were leaving, he took a very deep breath to steady his emotions. With the door before him being opened by Stan he braced himself for the sight of Tasha, but nothing could have prepared him for the image that greeted him; a motionless, bruised, battered, swollen and barely recognisable Tasha.

A loud sob of shock and grief left his lips before Stan gave his shoulder a reassuring pat.

"It's a shock, right? But she's doing okay and underneath the bruises, tubes, machines and lines she is still your Tasha."

"My Tasha," he said aloud and with that thought in his mind Jim entered the room fully to take the seat next to the bed, unaware of the door closing behind Stan.

The sound of the machines beeping was almost hypnotic for Jim as he sat in the chair next to Tasha's bed, refusing to be moved. It was just after eight in the morning when Bobby returned on his way to work. After a final and futile attempt to get his brother to go home, even briefly, he left him, but not before calling Sandra and arranging for Mike to drop off some food, toiletries and a change of clothes.

Stan returned and checked on Tasha, along with what seemed like dozens of nurses and other doctors. They all smiled at Jim, a little too sympathetically for his liking. It all seemed too nice, as if preparing him for something bad, something final.

By the time lunchtime arrived Jim had briefly left Tasha's side to speak to the police, Sargent Masterson, who explained they now suspected a second vehicle had been involved in Tasha's *accident* that was looking less accidental with each detail that was uncovered. The police left but promised to keep Jim updated with developments. He managed to brush his teeth, freshen up and quickly got changed into the clothes Sandra had sent him. Stan had just made another visit and introduced himself as Lizzie's boyfriend, Dylan's father, which raised no more than an arched brow from Jim rather than his usual annoyance at the idea of that boy who dated his daughter and ogled his girlfriend.

With a tense headache behind his eyes, Jim pinched the bridge of his nose as the door opened behind him. Turning, he expected to find another nurse or doctor, but it was actually Mickie who stood there.

"Sorry if I'm intruding. How is she?" Mickie asked with a point of her finger in Tasha's direction.

"Not good. She had internal bleeding, a punctured lung, and broken ribs. It seems she was struggling to breathe for herself so they've put a tube in. They're checking on her every fifteen minutes or so and they all keep looking at me with sympathetic smiles and sorry eyes. Look, Mickie," Jim began thinking that the woman before him, his friend, no, his former friend would be the last person Tasha would want here and he had stupidly allowed her to come between them once too often, but no more. Tasha was his priority and would continue to be so, forever, until death he thought and then shuddered at the reality of how imminent those two words might prove.

"I should probably go, I'm intruding," Mickie interrupted and sounded so supportive and understanding that Jim was taken aback. "I know we didn't get off on the right foot, Tasha and I, but I want to be here for you, like you were going to be there for me, me and my cancer diagnosis." She left his support hanging between them. "We're friends Jim, have been for so long and I don't want to lose that so maybe we should focus on that. Look, I have to go, my doctor's appointment."

Jim nodded. He was unsure what was actually happening. Totally unsure what Mickie was saying or suggesting even as she left and the door gently closed behind her. His frazzled mind was at risk of going into overdrive but the sudden sound of alarms stopped it dead in its tracks. Machines were going crazy, one after another sounding panicked and desperate as the room filled with nurses and doctors, more and more surrounding Tasha and pushing him farther and farther away from her until she was completely hidden from his view.

Chapter Two

Jim realised he'd barely closed his eyes never mind slept as he watched Tasha for any sign of life, any sign of anything. She was currently fighting off an infection that had caused her temperature to spike and her heart rate to become erratic which is what triggered all of the alarms and panic the previous day. Stan had warned him that if antibiotics were unsuccessful in treating the infection then they'd have to take her back to theatre to try and stem the spread.

Mike had just dropped off more clothes and food when Jim's message alert sounded with several messages enquiring after Tasha. His children, brother and sister-in-law had visited but there really wasn't anything they could do to help her or offer any comfort to him.

A nurse, Chloe, was caring for Tasha and seemed more concerned each time she checked on her and that is what she was doing while Jim watched on.

"I am going to call for the doctor," she told Jim. "Tasha's temperature is rising again."

Jim nodded and knew what that meant. The infection wasn't under control and his beautiful and very sick fiancée would be going back to theatre.

Within the hour, he watched as Tasha was wheeled down a corridor and through heavy looking doors that led to the operating theatre leaving him to sit on a very uncomfortable chair in a hallway to wait.

The first hour seemed to drag, the second, even more so. The sight of the police appearing at the bottom of the corridor caused

Jim to shake his head at their timing.

There was a younger officer with Masterson now and although he was introduced, Jim didn't really register that information.

"Mr Maybury, I believe Miss Winters is back in theatre?"

"Yes." He glanced down at his watch. "We are just entering the third hour."

"Sir, I'm really sorry to intrude at this time, but…"

"But?"

"But, this can't wait. I can confirm that Miss Winters' collision was not an accident."

"Go on." Jim swallowed down a hard knot of fear. Every time he thought this thing couldn't get worse, it did.

"Our investigations have revealed there was another car on the road. That car drove behind Miss Winters and appears to have forced your fiancée off the road and through the barrier."

"Fuck!" cursed Jim.

"There's more. We have traced Miss Winters' movements and acquired some CCTV images that appear to show her car being tampered with when it was parked outside a convenience store."

"Tampered with?" Nausea washed over him. It was one thing knowing someone else had been involved in her crash, and even if it had been an accident they'd still left her, literally for dead. However, if he was understanding what he was being told, the crash had not been an accident, quite the opposite. Someone had tampered with her car, deliberately wanting to cause her harm.

"Yes, tampered with. We have recently received the report on her car and the brakes were cut."

"Cut? Who? Why? This makes no sense at all. Why would anyone hurt her?" Jim pushed a hand through his unusually unkempt hair.

"Our investigation seems to suggest that the man we are looking for entered the country a few days before your fiancée's accident—"

The sound of a phone ringing halted all conversation. Jim watched on as Masterson picked up his call and within seconds was walking down the corridor, presumably wanting some privacy. Jim's glance flitted between the theatre doors and the

Sargent who was now returning with an expression that could only be described as grim.

"We have apprehended the other driver. He was attempting to leave the country but was infiltrated near the airport. Mr Maybury, I don't know how to say this and I'm hoping my colleague has somehow misunderstood this man's identity," Masterson said with a dark and sad expression on his face. "Are you familiar with a Samuel Bailey?"

Jim was beyond stunned, so much so that he fell back onto the seat behind him. Surely there must be a mistake if he was understanding things correctly. The man suspected of being the driver of the other car, the one that ran Tasha off the road was her father.

"Mr Maybury?" Masterson said, forcing Jim to refocus.

"Sorry, yes, he's Tasha's dad.

The officer nodded sadly. Tasha's dad was behind this and that in turn meant Jim had taken his eye off that particular ball and missed this man still posing a danger to Tasha.

A young man coming out of theatre startled them all, especially when he made for Jim.

"I've been asked to update you. The infection was more advanced than we first thought. We're doing everything we can, but it might take a while…there was also some further internal bleeding which complicated things a little, but she's hanging in there."

With a final half-smile and a pat to the shoulder, the doctor left as quickly as he'd arrived.

"We will be questioning the suspect as soon as we're able to and we'll keep you informed," Masterson said flatly. With a little softness entering his voice added, "I hope she pulls through the surgery."

Alone again, Jim checked his phone hoping for some kind of distraction. He saw several missed calls from Katy Myers amongst others, but was in no mood to speak to anyone so slipped the phone back into his pocket and waited, again.

He was still sitting on the chair in the corridor, waiting for Tasha with his eyes shut and his head resting against the wall when he became aware of someone nearby. Opening his eyes slowly, he was greeted by the site of Mickie carrying a cup of coffee in one hand and a leaflet on ovarian cancer in the other. She was wearing a scarf on her head which seemed a little melodramatic, even for Mickie. She clearly noticed Jim's glance on her covered head.

"I thought I'd get used to it," she said with a tight smile. "How's Tasha?" she asked, but seemed strange, although if she'd been told she had ovarian cancer and would need chemotherapy it was no wonder.

Jim was in no mood to talk so simply shrugged at her questioning of Tasha's wellbeing. Unfortunately, Mickie had no problem talking and was doing enough for the two of them. Jim tuned much of it out but did pick up on references to *whatever happens* and *doctors only being able to do so much* which caused a deep scowl to mar Jim's face but then Mickie seemed to change tack, confusing him further.

"Jim, we have been through so much and I have my own battle ahead, but I will always be here to support you," she told him and then, taking his hand in hers, continued. "You need to go home to take a break from this. I'm worried about you so why don't you let me take you home, back to mine if you can't face yours. Let me take care of you?"

Jim stared wide-eyed and disbelievingly at Mickie's persistence and audacity to intrude and that really was what her presence felt like to him now, an intrusion on his time with Tasha. Whatever time they might have left, whether that was an hour, a day, a week, a month or another thirty or forty years there really was no place for Mickie in any of those scenarios.

"Mickie, this is over, us. We were friends, but I think that was through circumstance more than anything else. I should have cut you off when you and Bobby split and even without doing that I should never have allowed any more to happen between us, certainly not a casual sexual relationship that I knew meant considerably more to you than me and for that I apologise." He needed to leave her in no doubt about his feelings.

"No, it wasn't like that," Mickie protested tearfully.

"It was, for me. You were never more than a very casual friend with benefits. I love Tasha and I need her to be well and happy and you make her unhappy, so we are done. I'm sorry you're sick, I really am, Mickie, but I can't be the person to help you through that, no matter what happens with Tasha."

Before Mickie could offer any other comment, Jim was getting to his feet and walking towards the theatre doors.

"You should go. Goodbye, Mickie," Jim said with real finality as he turned his back on her to wait for news on Tasha.

Eventually, after what seemed like a lifetime, Stan appeared through the double doors Jim still stood before.

"You know you don't have to shadow me quite so closely, don't you?" He smiled before giving Jim some news on Tasha. "She is one tough cookie and has come through relatively unscathed. The infection had spread and we needed to do quite a tidy up in there and some of the work we'd already done needed reworking." He smiled then turned more serious. "Tasha's body has been through a lot and the truth is that it is still in shock and struggling to fight everything which is why she has been sedated and will remain that way for a while. The same with the ventilator, plus her punctured lung is finding it hard to re-inflate and needs the help. We've removed her spleen which you can live without but obviously it's not something we'd do unless it was necessary."

"But she's okay, she'll come round and be okay?" Jim asked a little desperately.

"Like I say, she's been through a lot. Let's get her through tonight and tomorrow then we'll have a better idea how she's fairing, okay?"

Jim nodded and thought if Tasha survived this he might never let her out of his sight again because he couldn't do this again, feel like this again.

"We're going to keep her in recovery for a little while and then we'll take her back to her room in ICU, okay?" Stan asked but no reply was necessary.

Jim's phone began to vibrate almost constantly as Stan left him alone again. Pulling his phone from his pocket he saw more calls from Katy but many more from Amanda and then a text from his former wife too.

<Call me, there's something you need to know, something Katy Myers knows>

Rather than text, he called Amanda and found his call was answered on the first ring.

"Thank goodness you're picking up your messages. How's Tasha?" Amanda asked.

"Not good but hanging on in there, but I thought you had something I needed to know." He bristled.

"I do, but not over the phone. I have Katy with me. We're heading to you at the hospital right now."

Jim quickly cut her off. "Amanda," he snapped but she was unfazed.

"Jim, trust me, you need to hear this but not over the phone." She hung up leaving Jim a little startled and then he laughed, loudly, because not only had Amanda just found her dominant side with him she'd called him Jim, not Mr Maybury. He immediately thought of Tasha and how funny she would find this new, forceful Amanda. Briefly he smiled when he thought Amanda's behaviour was more Tasha like than anything else and wondered if she was also being moulded and influenced by the very sassy, smart and beautiful girl he intended to marry. His smile faltered and became a frown as he realised that their plans to marry were unlikely to materialise.

****

Tasha was back in her room while Jim watched over her and absorbed the details of the last few hours. A nurse came in and offered him a pillow and blanket making him check the time that revealed it was three in the morning. He wondered why time went so slowly here. It felt like a lifetime had passed since they'd first arrived just a few days before. He remembered that first week when Tasha had flown to L.A. from New York. Those days had flown by, but then, isn't that what they said? *Time flies when you're having fun.* And what fun they'd had. He honestly couldn't remember when he'd been as happy or had as much fun as he had that week or any week since and there was only one reason for that, Tasha.

Taking Tasha's hand in his, Jim wondered just how he was

going to tell her everything that had happened when she finally woke up. He assumed she'd know she had been in some kind of accident when she came to in a hospital, but the rest was like the plot from a TV mini-series, not that he'd have commissioned the series because it seemed a little implausible and yet it was real. It had happened to Tasha.

The police had been back to see him, after Amanda and Katy, the latter had been doing what she did best by digging around after meeting with Tasha a few days before. What she had dug up was Mickie's cancer diagnosis, or lack thereof. It had all been a big, fat lie; no cancer, no illness, no nothing and worse still no sign of Mickie, but at least the police were looking for her now. The police had come back asking for information about Mickie who Samuel Bailey had immediately incriminated when questioned. Mickie's investigator, Michael Rose, had made contact with her parents but they had made it clear that they were more than happy to take money for pretty much anything and Mickie had then cut a deal for Tasha's dad to travel to The States on forged documents to intervene with Jim and Tasha's wedding plans. Jim had told the police exactly what he knew in relationship to Mickie and Michael Rose, but without going into detail about Tasha's childhood and relationship with her parents. The police were now hunting Mickie.

Jim squeezed Tasha's hand a little tighter as he questioned why he hadn't suspected some involvement in this from Mickie or at least been suspicious of her illness. If he had, he could have kept her onside, maybe even kept her close by until the police gathered evidence and now she would be behind bars along with Tasha's father. This whole mess was likely to break her heart when she found out about it. He just hoped it didn't break her.

Over the next few days Jim seemed to settle into a routine of sorts. Mike arrived each morning, early, with clothes and food. He would quickly wash and change then attempt to eat something whilst talking to Tasha until Bobby arrived. They spent about half an hour together and then he would head off to work leaving Jim to wait for Stan to arrive with an update, the most recent update being that Tasha was stable and her sedation was being reduced. By lunchtime there had usually been a couple of visitors, Jim's family, Sara, Amanda, Abby, Sandra, Juan, Philip, Lizzie, Pippa, Dan or Celia and Paul. Whoever came in the morning knew they'd had their turn for the day as Jim rotated visitors and then at the end of evening visiting he sent everyone away, settling down for the night shift when it was just the two of them. He even attempted lying next to Tasha a couple of times, just to be close, hoping she could sense his presence and wouldn't feel lonely or alone, but he worried in case he lay on something he shouldn't, so those moments were fleeting.

Everyone had been kind and genuinely concerned for Tasha and Jim, although Paul was clearly holding Jim responsible for Tasha having almost died and in fairness he blamed himself so could understand where the other man was coming from. Having said that, the barbed digs were beginning to piss his off, but for now he was biting his tongue because he knew Tasha wouldn't want him to fight fire with fire where her grandfather was concerned.

The nurse was doing another round of checks on Tasha, possibly the last one of her shift and explained that with the reducing sedation schedule Stan had suggested, Tasha was now at zero sedation which presumably meant she could wake up at any time. Even after the nurse had left and a new one had come onto shift Jim found himself staring at Tasha, more so than usual, hoping and praying to see some sign of consciousness.

The police arrived just before lunchtime, still with no news of Mickie's whereabouts but they seemed to be aware of the change in Tasha's medication, meaning they'd spoken to Stan. Jim assured them she was still unconscious and pointed out that after such a traumatic accident she might not remember anything. Masterson agreed but insisted he'd still need to speak to her, just in case. With irritation at being away from Tasha, Jim found himself giving the police a few pointers on just what they should be doing in their unsuccessful pursuit of Mickie before he saw Stan entering Tasha's room which is when he excused himself and returned to her side.

With everything still stable and all signs looking positive a couple of hours later he continued to watch and wait and then he saw a movement. Tasha's finger moved, he was sure of it, although it wouldn't be the first time he'd imagined movement. The truth was he imagined movements daily, several times a day. If wishing for signs of life produced actual signs then she'd have been moving and talking days ago. Jim stood over her once more, looking down at her apparently lifeless body, desperate for something that suggested she was recovering or at least coming to. Briefly, he closed his eyes and took stock with an internal pep talk for himself that he needed to remain positive because if he didn't he had no clue how he'd get through the minutes, hours and days that would follow. With a final deep, calming breath Jim opened his eyes and focused on Tasha and found her eyelids twitching erratically as if she was dreaming or attempting to open them. Maybe wishing had finally paid off.

Chapter Three

Everything was so bright and loud, noises everywhere when Tasha finally opened her eyes. It seemed to take an eternity for them to fully open and as she attempted to take in her surroundings, she felt overwhelmed by a gagging sensation. She was choking. What was happening? She saw Jim standing over her and questioned if he was choking her, but he couldn't be. His hands were up in the air near his face and he was shouting. She couldn't hear what he was saying, there was too much noise from the electronic sounds that were surrounding her, Jim's voice and the rushing of blood through her ears as she felt her mind and body panicking at her compromised breathing. Jim's face and expression were filled with fright and concern, convincing her that the choking sensation she felt was nothing to do with him. She tried to call out to him, however, she couldn't seem to find her voice to form words or stop gagging.

Suddenly, Jim was pushed out of the way by a stern looking woman, a nurse who began speaking to her in a reassuring tone, but still the words remained unclear as her panic rose further. In the blink of an eye, what seemed to be a dozen others in medical uniforms appeared while the nurse continued to smile and speak to her.

"Tasha, I'm Chloe and we're going to make you more comfortable." She smiled down and reached towards her face. The choking sensation she'd felt quickly disappeared.

Gasping loudly, Tasha felt dry, hoarse, but the choking feeling was replaced with distress and confusion. She was crying, loudly and shaking like a leaf on a windy autumn day. The sound of her distress began to drown out all other sounds and as the volume of it increased so did her confusion, but she had no clue what was happening or why she was reacting in this way. Chloe helped her to sit forward briefly, before settling her back against the pillows. At the same time a junior doctor continued checking her over and reassuring her further that she was okay and doing well, that she was safe and in hospital before finally looking across at Jim, giving him an unspoken cue to step in, a cue he took perfectly, settling himself at Tasha's side, taking her hand in his.

The nurse held back slightly, speaking softly to Tasha, who was calming down slowly. Between Jim's fingers stroking the back of her hand, his reassuring smile and the nurse's words and presence it was just a few minutes before Tasha's breathing returned to normal and her high state of disorientation and anxiety began to pass.

"Your doctor's on his way, but I'll leave you with your guardian angel for a while and maybe you can stop him from being such a difficult relative," Chloe said, smiling, first at Jim and then at Tasha. "But take it easy and not too much talking. Any problems, hit the button," she told Jim before being followed out of the room by the other people in uniform, presumably meaning she was in no immediate danger, that her signs were all good.

"Hey, baby," said Jim, nervously sitting next to her, enclosing her hand more tightly in his.

"Hey, yourself," she replied hoarsely, wincing as she tried to shift up the bed.

"Tasha, are you okay? Should I get a nurse?" he asked, panic struck that she might be in pain or deteriorating.

"No," she replied groggily. "I'm just moving, but I think I really do feel as though I have been run over by a steam roller, twice." She grimaced as a few sparse details emerged in her mind. "What happened?" She coughed a little making her clutch her ribs firmly while Jim brushed the remaining tears from her face.

"Let me get you some water or something." Jim cautiously headed for the door, not really wanting to leave her for even a second. He almost bumped into Chloe who was on her way in carrying a cup of ice.

"You can suck on this, Tasha, and the doctor will be down soon. He has an emergency. I have some pain relief for you." She held up a tray with a syringe on it.

"I'm fine," replied Tasha stubbornly.

"Baby, take the pain relief, you're hurting," Jim told her.

"Will it make me sleep?" Tasha asked Chloe.

"Yes, but you need to rest." The nurse sighed, already sensing an objection.

"I'll have it later, I promise. I would like to talk to Jim for a while first."

They both shook their heads at her making her smile. "Please," she pleaded, her voice no more than a whisper now.

"Ten minutes and then I will be back to check your vitals," said Chloe. "And then you need the meds. I am acting under orders," she said seriously before leaving them alone again.

Jim held the cup of ice up for Tasha to suck on then sat back down taking her hand again.

"These machines look really expensive." Tasha gestured to all the equipment she was attached to.

"You know I only have the best for you, honey." He smiled, stroking the back of her free hand.

"What happened?" she asked again as he pulled her hand to his lips and kissed it tenderly; each finger in turn, from her thumb to her little finger before edging towards her palm and finally coming to rest at her wrist where the pulse hammered away beneath the surface of her skin.

"You were involved in a car crash." He gripped her hand more tightly.

"I remember the fireman talking to me and I couldn't find my phone. I wanted to call you and I thought you'd be mad at me." She choked on her own words, struggling to get them past her swollen throat and the emotional thoughts in her mind.

"For what, for the car? Tasha, all I care about is you." Jim's voice shook with an unmistakable break in it. The idea that when she must have been shocked and in fear for her life, she was most worried that he'd be mad at her for a damned car or anything else.

"That's what the fireman thought I meant. I knew you wouldn't give a stuff about the car, but I ran out on you and I thought you'd be mad because if I hadn't done that I wouldn't have been in the crash," Tasha said, revealing the extent of the details she knew.

"Oh, Tasha, that might be true to a point, but I wasn't mad, not with you. I was worried half to death that I was going to lose you and when Juan came by to say he'd seen a car like yours down the hill after an accident I knew it was you and so did he. We drove down and they were preparing to cut you from the car. I really thought I'd lost you and not because of a fight, but forever."

Tasha looked up and saw tears rolling down Jim's face. Just the sight of her handsome, fierce, alpha, dominant man shedding tears for her made her cry too. The idea that her accident, her being hurt did this to him, the strongest person she knew, brought her to her knees because firstly, it meant she had been hurt badly, but secondly, maybe harder to bear was the fact that he'd been emotionally hurt and was clearly flailing in his attempts to maintain control.

"I'm going nowhere. We're getting married and I'm going to take your name and wear your ring, remember?" She grinned but then the grin suddenly dropped from her face and was replaced with a worried expression. "I will be out of here in time to get married, won't I? Although, I may need a little help with make-up because I reckon I may look a little rough." She laughed briefly then winced again holding her ribs.

"Tasha, do you know what day it is, baby?" He gently stroked her cheek.

"No. I actually have no clue." She realised she was clueless and smiled awkwardly at his sad expression.

"Shit, Tasha. Today is, was, should have been our wedding day. You have been here for the last week and a half and you've been really sick, honey." Jim studied her expression, waiting for what he was saying to resonate in her brain.

"No," she cried and allowed a few tears to flow. "I've missed it? I am so sorry." She cried again, helpless to prevent more tears falling.

Jim got to his feet and held her face between his hands, kissing her lips gently. "Tasha, there is no need to apologise. We missed it today, but we'll rearrange as soon as you are well because we have entered into a verbal contract and now that you've agreed to be Natasha Maybury I won't be letting you back out of it." He smiled, still holding her head between his hands.

"So, what happened?" asked Tasha again, stifling a yawn.

"We can talk later, but you should sleep." He returned to a sitting position, her hand safely back in his larger one again.

"Will you stay with me for a while?"

"Sure thing, baby. I'm going nowhere either." With his free hand Jim brushed the hair back off her face.

"Will you lie with me?" Tasha was eager to feel his closeness and warmth.

"I thought you'd never ask." He smiled, dropped the cot side down and kicked his shoes off before sidling next to her on the bed where she pulled his arm across her middle and fell asleep almost immediately without any further medication.

Unsure how long she'd been asleep for, Tasha reached out to find Jim, but he was sitting back in the chair watching her closely.

"You left me," she complained.

"Not my choice." He glared at the man in scrubs who moved towards her.

"Miss Winters, Tasha. I'm Stan Marvin, your doctor, and the man who evicted your fiancé from the bed. How are you feeling?" He smirked at Jim.

"Sore, really quite sore and I have a bit of a headache," she told him honestly.

"A headache? You didn't say you had a headache before. Where? Have you only just noticed it or is it getting worse?" asked Jim. He leapt to his feet and paced the floor around the bed.

"Jim, please calm down," said the doctor. "I'd be surprised if you didn't have a headache after all you've been through, young lady, but feel free to answer Dr Maybury's questions." Stan's sarcasm made Tasha laugh then instantly regret it as she clutched her ribs.

"My head felt fuzzy before, a bit like a hangover, but it's a definite headache now, not getting worse, but then my whole body hurts."

Jim frowned. "What's wrong? Why has she got a headache? Shouldn't you give her something and run some tests?" Jim sounded seriously worried.

"Dear God, I thought you were a thorn in my side when this beautiful lady was unconscious with your questions and *advice*, but now she's back with us you're actually a complete pain in the ass," sighed the doctor with a smile for Tasha. "I will run a couple more tests, Tasha, but I think your head is just aching like the rest of your body and your vitals are all returning to normal after the shock of coming round. You've been through a lot. It's nice to meet you conscious though, and I can certainly see the attraction of my son's regular visits to your house."

Jim huffed and frowned.

"What?" Tasha was confused by the doctor's words and Jim's reaction to them.

"Dylan, my son, is dating Lizzie," explained the doctor.

"Ah, I see. I think Lizzie is the attraction at our house for Dylan," said Tasha diplomatically.

"I think there's more than one attraction for a teenage boy there." Stan grinned while Jim muttered something to himself.

"Can I get rid of some of these things?" Tasha gestured to the machines and equipment at the other end of the wires and leads that were attached to her.

"Soon. I'll run the tests and if they come back clear we can lose most of them," said the doctor as he turned to leave. "Oh, and don't let him up on the furniture." He laughed, pointing to Jim.

"He seems nice," said Tasha as Stan left.

"Mmm, if you say so, but he is a very good doctor. Your grandparents are on their way over," he suddenly announced.

"From London? They didn't have to do that." Smiled Tasha, hoping against all hopes that her family would not overreact or make a fuss.

"No, not London, from our house. They're staying there, have been since they got here the day after your accident. Dan and Pippa too, but Ryan and Lucy had to go back earlier in the week. Everyone has been so worried about you."

"Are they all okay?" She reached up to stroke his face that felt like sandpaper courtesy of not shaving for what she guessed was several days.

"I think they're all fine. Sandra and Mike are taking care of them," he reassured her.

"And you?" She looked worried for and about him.

"I can look after myself so long as I have you. Mike brings your family in and he brings me a change of clothes and food parcels from Sandra, so I am fine."

"When did you last go home and sleep?" Tasha yawned again, absolutely exhausted once more which was ridiculous considering the short amount of time she'd been awake.

"I haven't been home since you got here, baby. I've slept here with you."

Tasha felt tearful again at his show of love and devotion to her. She could only imagine how difficult the days following her crash had proved to be for her crazy control freak fiancé, when the truth was he would have had no control over anything, least of all her.

"You are so much more than I deserve." Tears escaped and ran down her face again.

"Hey, I'm the one who doesn't deserve you, but I'm not letting you go so we're stuck with each other." He landed a single, delicate kiss to the end of her nose.

Chloe, the nurse, appeared in the doorway. "Tasha, I need to take some bloods, check your vitals again and give you a shot." She smiled and gestured for Jim to leave.

He stood firm and as the two of them locked their sights on each other Tasha laughed a little.

"There's someone you may want to speak to waiting outside," Chloe said to Jim with an air of mystery.

"I'm staying here," he said stubbornly.

"Detective Masterson is outside waiting to speak with Tasha."

"The hell he is! Not today. Stay here with Tasha while I go and tell Masterson where to go." He stormed out leaving a confused Tasha looking at Chloe as she drew some blood.

"Is he always so bossy?" Chloe smiled, probably not needing that question answering or suspicion confirming.

"He hasn't even got out of neutral yet." Laughed Tasha, attempting to do so without it hurting. "I should point out that I usually bring out the worst in him where the bossy, control freak is concerned."

"He has barely left this room since you got here. He has security here too and he checks your visitors in and out, he times them and rotates them then sends them all home and sleeps here, over there in that chair, although I don't think he sleeps all that much because he watches you for any movement or sign of change. He loves you and I hope one day I'll find a guy that loves me half as much as he does you." She smiled, readjusting the sheets as Tasha rolled over slowly and cautiously for her shot.

Tasha smiled up at the nurse as she covered and *tidied* her and decided that the pretty, young blonde nurse with pale blue, almost grey eyes was about twenty-five and quite petite at probably only five feet and one hundred and ten pounds, but happy to stand toe to toe with Jim if need be and looked as though she'd be quite fearsome.

The door flew open, startling Tasha momentarily until she realised it was Pippa running towards her.

"Tash, you're awake. You're okay," she cried as she threw herself across Tasha's chest winding her slightly, but she seemed not to notice, unlike Chloe.

"Shall we let Tasha breathe? Let's get you a seat." She smiled, directing Pippa to a chair as Dan and their grandparents followed Pippa into the room looking as relieved as their youngest granddaughter had.

"God Tash, I thought you were going to die. Your car is a complete wreck and the police are doing their nut out there, but Jim won't let them in." She sounded excited and relieved at the same time. She was clearly preparing to unleash another tirade of musings and thoughts when her grandmother interrupted.

"Philippa, really." Celia shook her head at her youngest granddaughter as she reached the bedside of her oldest one where she bent down to carefully kiss her before hugging her warmly. "It is very good to see you."

Paul was on the opposite side of the bed to his wife and struggled to get past the machines, tubes and wires to get close enough to his granddaughter to hug her. "Oh, my darling, girl. You gave us all such a fright. What am I going to do with you?" he asked as she stretched to reach his open arms.

"You sound like Jim now." She smiled up at her grandfather.

Paul muttered something but hugged her tightly. "I love you very much, Nat."

"Ditto," replied Tasha, noticing Dan standing nervously near the door. "You okay over there, little brother, or are you suffering the after effects of a night out with Travis?" She smiled.

"No, unfortunately not. Are you okay, Tash, really okay?" he asked warily, looking scared and young.

"Course I am." With a wave of her hand, she gestured for her brother to come closer as Jim returned to the room looking harassed.

Tasha glanced across and smiled at him raking a hand through his hair and had a desperate urge to go to him and to hold him, to comfort him, not that she was physically capable of doing that, but she wanted to. He looked like he needed a big hug more than anything else. She loved her family, but right now wished they weren't there, that no one was there other than her and Jim. He looked confused, tormented and anxious and she wanted nothing more than to replace those emotions and expression with happier, more positive ones.

He looked across at her and smiled weakly. "Can I get anyone a drink or anything?"

"No thank you, Jim," replied Celia as Dan and Pippa shook their heads.

Paul muttered a disgruntled, "No."

"Philip and Juan are coming in later and bringing Lizzie," said Jim, seeming to keep his distance from her and ignoring her grandfather's churlish tone and demeanour.

"That's nice. Are they okay?" asked Tasha.

"Yeah, fine. Although they've all been worried about you so they're better now that you're better." Jim smiled at her, but it seemed a little forced and Tasha couldn't quite pinpoint what was off, but something definitely was. Finally, she decided it was probably something to do with his reference to her being better and just how un-better she'd been previously.

Paul muttered something again as Celia glared across their granddaughter at him with a warning expression. Tasha was still unsure what was going on, but it was quite obvious now that Jim and Paul had fallen out about something, most likely her. Tasha was considering how to proceed when an older and larger built smiling nurse appeared in the doorway.

"Tasha, my name is Rhona and I'll be your nurse until ten o'clock. I need to take you down for some tests when the orderly arrives," she said cheerfully as an orderly appeared beside her. "If I can ask you all to wait outside for a moment." She phrased it as a question, but it was more of a directive than anything.

Celia, Dan and Pippa immediately headed for the door while Paul and Jim just stared across the room at each other.

"I'll come with you, Nat." Paul smiled at Jim, but Tasha instantly noticed the insincerity of it and felt it was some kind of a point scoring exercise.

"That won't be necessary." Jim refrained from adding his own *I'll go with Tasha* kind of comment.

"Maybe Tasha would like to do this alone," said Tasha firmly. "Look, I am really tired and am sure that once I've been wherever I'm going all I will want to do is sleep, so maybe you should *all* go home for a while." She emphasised the all, something Jim didn't miss.

"Baby, I am not leaving you alone." Jim still stood near the door.

"Jim, you look wrecked. You should go and get some sleep too and make the most of having the bed to yourself." She offered him an encouraging smile.

"And I have told you before that my bed is far too big without you in it." He looked sad.

"Okay, fine." She laughed, holding her hands up in surrender.

"But would you get me some clothes, pyjamas or something, anything that isn't a hospital gown, please?" She thought that would be an ideal excuse to send him on his way for a while.

"Sure. I'll be back before you know it." Jim turned to leave.

"Gramps," she called to Paul who appeared to be following Jim.

"Yes, Nat?" He turned back to her.

She took her grandfather's hand in hers and held it tightly. "Please don't be mean to Jim. He loves me and has found this very tough."

"None of us have found this easy, but he has to accept some responsibility, we all do," replied Paul mysteriously.

Tasha shook her head, confused by his words, but even without knowing the facts she knew Jim couldn't be held accountable for her accident, not even after their fight that led to her going out that night. "Gramps, I don't know what that means. Jim has said there's some stuff I need to know and I trust him to tell me when the time is right, so please, for me if not him, be nice because I love him and he is going to be my husband and the father of my children eventually."

"For you," he replied and leaned in to land a single kiss to her forehead then left her with Rhona again.

The nurse smiled at her and simply said, "Let's go."

Tasha felt slightly relieved to be back in her room and alone. She'd been for a scan on her head then a different scan on her abdomen before being brought back to her room where Rhona had removed some of the wires and tubes, including the less than glamorous catheter which meant she was allowed to get up to use the bathroom. She lay back against the fresh pillows and waited for Jim to return with real nightwear rather than the hospital gown she was currently wearing and wondered whether her grandparents, specifically her grandfather, would return too. Her eyes closed and she attempted to think of nothing, to empty her mind, but was determined not to fall asleep while she waited for Jim. The opposite of that is precisely what she did.

Voices around her got louder and louder and roused her slightly from her sound sleep, but not enough to open her eyes.

"Paul, will you please back off? I have no desire to fight with you and I feel guilty enough that Tasha was hurt without you trying to make this all my fault," she heard Jim say.

"I'm not making this all your fault—it is all your fault. You and that bloody crazy woman. I told you to take care of my girl and you assured me that you would and yet here we are at the hospital thanking all things holy that she is still here. She almost died, Jim, and I do hold you responsible, you, the one that professes to love her." Anger rolled off Paul in waves.

Tasha was still unable to open her eyes and felt sure she'd been given something whilst asleep.

"I accept that I have to take some responsibility in all of this, but if that's the case then so do you. You take a good, hard look at yourself and your family. Think about what went on, what happened to Tasha on your watch before you try to transfer all of the blame and I would imagine your own guilt onto me. Now, I have been really tolerant of the barbed comments and I have given you some time and space, not to mention the run of my house, but I should warn you that I am running out of patience here. You want to blame me, so be it, but do not try and call into question my feelings for Tasha," warned Jim.

Tasha felt a sense of relief that her grandfather made no come back and although she didn't really understand the details of what had been said she trusted Jim would tell her in time and that this couldn't be his fault.

"You should know that when Nat has recovered I intend to take her home, to London, where she belongs," said Paul who was not quite done yet.

"And you should know that Natasha is going nowhere other than home with me and that we will be getting married. This is where she belongs, with me," replied Jim.

Tasha's eyes finally opened and were full of sadness as she looked at two of the most important men in her life, arguing with each other, apportioning blame and trying to compete for her. Her grandfather still looked as though he was ready to keep going, arguing and scoring points whereas Jim looked tired, almost resigned to more angry words and insinuations being hurled his way. His shoulders sagged slightly as Paul prepared to continue their battle of wills, not that Jim was feeling defeated by the other man, quite the opposite, but if he hoped to make and keep Tasha happy he needed there to be no rifts between him and her family.

"Hey, my two favourite men are back," she said gruffly, wincing at the soreness in her throat that still surprised her every time she woke up causing them both to turn and look at her.

"Are you okay, Nat?" Paul looked guilty that she may have heard their conversation.

Jim picked up a glass of water and held the straw to her mouth.

"Did you bring me some pyjamas or something?" asked Tasha when she'd finished drinking and laughed as she saw the box that proved Jim had phoned a local store and had the nightwear couriered over meaning he had still not left the hospital. "Thank you." She smiled, but refused his offer to help her change immediately.

Eventually, Jim left to use the bathroom and without wasting a second of their time alone Tasha took Paul to task.

"Gramps, you said you'd be nice to Jim and you and he were arguing, I heard you," she told him before he could deny her accusation. "Please don't blame Jim for any of this. No matter what has happened I love him and he loves me more than anything in the world and would never deliberately endanger me. I won't be coming back to London with you, I belong here, with Jim." She stroked her grandfather's head as he rested it on the edge of the bed next to her.

"Sorry, Nat. I just need someone to blame and if you hadn't met him and come out here, met the people he knew, none of this would have happened, so it is his fault, but I will try not to be such a stupid fool and think more rationally because it's not like I kept you safe at home, is it? Your grandma is constantly telling me I'm being stupid by blaming Jim, but I can't help it and maybe when you know the details—" Jim's return interrupted Paul. "I'm going to head back to the house, I think Dan is struggling with all of this and may need to talk." Paul kissed Tasha and prepared to leave.

"Mike is downstairs," Jim flatly called after him.

"Tell me what happened," said Tasha.

"Not tonight. Tomorrow when you've had a good night's sleep."

Tasha prepared to argue when the door burst open to reveal Juan, Philip and Lizzie squealing as they all enveloped her in enthusiastic embraces.

Several days passed and between the constant stream of visitors Jim managed to avoid discussing exactly what had happened on the night of Tasha's crash. He'd also somehow got her doctor to tell the police she wasn't up to seeing them to answer their questions. Jim was still insisting on staying with her at night and despite the staff's objections she managed to get him to snuggle beside her on the bed.

It was during one such moment that Tasha finally took the bull by the horns. "Did I cause the crash? Is that why the police want to see me? Am I in trouble?" She sounded panicked. "I don't remember anything of that journey. I left the store car park and then I remember the fireman talking to me, nothing else."

Jim sat up to allow her to roll over towards him, albeit a little gingerly as her ribs were still sore and caused her some discomfort and pain whenever she tried to move.

He looked down at her worried expression and reassuringly shook his head. "No, you didn't cause the crash and you are not in trouble. I think the police just want to see what you remember and to clarify a couple of points."

"So, what did happen?"

Jim lay down and faced her. "This is a very long and pretty messed up story."

She nodded and waited for him to continue.

With a sigh and several deep breaths, Jim began to explain the events of the night of Tasha's crash. "You left me after accepting that call from Mickie. She was telling me all about her worries and concerns for her health and all I could think about was you and told her we'd had a fight. She suggested letting you go for a while and concentrate on what I really needed and what you needed. She was empathetic and questioned whether we may have rushed into this whole thing, but when she quoted that whole *if you love someone set them free and if they come back then they're really yours* it threw me. She talked about how young you were and how she'd figured that you'd endured a difficult childhood. She suggested I was asking for too much too soon and that rushing you into marriage was wrong for you, that you needed to come to terms with everything."

Tasha nodded, understanding everything Jim was saying and even getting Mickie's perspective, not that she really believed the other woman had ever cared or considered what was or wasn't best for her.

Jim continued, "Her words made sense on some level. I couldn't believe that Mickie of all people wouldn't take the opportunity to take advantage and gain some ground, so maybe she was right." Jim exhaled, a long, loud sigh. He kissed Tasha gently on the forehead. "Anyway, I still wanted us to talk because Mickie was right about us needing to concentrate on what we needed and what I needed, still need, is you. Even with Mickie's words fresh in my mind I refused to accept that you didn't need or want me like I did you."

"You're the one thing I have needed and wanted from the second I met you," Tasha told Jim with a small smile curling her lips.

Instinctively, Jim's lips lowered to hers, a succession of tiny kisses littered from one corner of her mouth to the other.

A big smile broke across Jim's face. "Even in hospital you distract me, baby. But back to that night, I knew at that second that it was you and me, for both of us and so I selfishly decided that we could work things out, just us. That's when I text you and was hugely relieved that you said you were coming home, but you didn't get there. Juan came to say a car that looked a lot like yours had crashed and rolled part way down a hill after flipping over the barrier. He was in a bit of a state and I knew he knew it was you. By the time I got there you were sick and they were preparing to cut you out of the wreckage." He nervously pushed a hand through his hair, a sad expression taking over his face as if reliving that moment. "I have to tell you, honey, I was scared shitless. I thought I'd lost you forever." There was a distinct wobble to his voice now.

Tasha felt guilty for having put him through it, although it appeared that the accident wasn't her fault so she shouldn't feel guilty as such, but still thought he was keeping vital information from her still.

Jim began to explain the physical trauma she'd been through and the treatments and procedures she'd endured before addressing the cause of her crash. "The police hung around on and off for a while until Stan told them that you were going nowhere and would be in no fit state to answer questions for some time. The accident wasn't actually an accident as it turns out; someone cut your brakes, baby. It seems you were followed and may have been forced you off the road—the police stopped him a few days later and he sang like the proverbial canary. He told the police he'd been paid to stop you and me from marrying, *to get rid of you* from my life. He was paid handsomely and named his puppet master too."

"James, I don't understand who would want to hurt me to stop us getting married, except for…but, I don't understand." Tasha hadn't realised she was crying until Jim attempted to wipe the tears from her face. Maybe it was the drugs she was on or the shock of everything that had happened to her. In reality she knew there was more to it than that. She was confused and scared at the idea that somewhere in the world there were people cutting deals and exchanging cash to stop her marrying Jim, to kill her.

Jim pulled her towards him more firmly and held her tight, allowing her to absorb the details of what he'd already said and once she was a little calmer he continued with the really messed up part of the story. "Mickie. Mickie paid someone to do it and he was happy to take her money and this is where it becomes really unpleasant. You remember she hired the P.I. who met with your parents and they wouldn't be drawn on details for fear of legal action?"

Jim continued as soon as Tasha nodded her head in confirmation.

"Well, that was crap because they did indeed take money, but not for information." Jim thought he was explaining clearly, but looking down at the confused expression on Tasha's face he realised he wasn't. "There is no easy way of saying this, honey, so I will just say it. Mickie paid your dad to come over here on false papers to stop you marrying me, *using any means necessary* and he did. He is in police custody, but they're still looking for Mickie. Your mom has sold several stories in the U.K. She's claiming that it must all be a mistake, but no mistake, baby." He held her and rocked her gently as she began to sob, pained, heart wrenching sobs.

"I can't believe anybody would want me dead. Am I that dreadful a person, a daughter? Maybe they've done you a favour by saving you from me," Tasha said, still sobbing and reeling from the information Jim had just shared, grateful that his grip remained, his arms around her tightening.

"You stop that," said Jim firmly. "Nobody has done me any favours where you're concerned. I love you and we are going to get married and you are not dreadful, but Mickie is a complete lunatic and your dad is an animal. I spoke to Mickie when your dad had been arrested, before her involvement was known and she was weird, she made me suspicious. She said things that seemed off like, *I will always be here to support you* and *would you like me to take you home, to take care of you* and then a couple of hours later, after I had told her to leave us alone, the police turned up and questioned me about her and your dad. That's when they told me what they knew, but Mickie had disappeared by then. Your dad received a call from her on the night of your crash, after you and I fought. She told him he'd run out of time and to take you out. Oh, Katy Myers got in touch and told me about your meeting, but after a little research on her part she discovered that Mickie didn't have cancer and that was all part of the plan; get rid of you, support me through it, recover from the non-existent cancer and we could—"

"Live happily ever after," finished Tasha.

"Exactly," replied Jim to a terrified looking Tasha.

"Hence the security," she said in a whisper.

"Yes, baby." For Jim there was no more to say. He hated that she was scared and the fear in her eyes was unmistakable. He hated more the fact that people he had exposed her to were the cause of that fear. Every time she was hurt or at risk of hurt from her family or her past he always assured her that he wouldn't let them close enough to harm her and yet here they were; her in a hospital bed, while Mickie, his friend was God knows were and her father, who had once more hurt her, was sitting in a prison cell.

"Will you stay with me tonight?" Tasha sounded as scared as she looked.

Jim hated hearing that, the confirmation of her fright. More than anyone he had ever met she deserved to always feel safe and he was going to do everything and anything in his power to give her that. "Baby, I keep telling you, I'm going nowhere and neither are security until Mickie is found. Now go to sleep," he ordered, making her smile.

"I've missed Mr Control Freak." She reached up to stroke his face.

"I'll have Mike bring your uniform in." He grinned rakishly but it was the wiggling of his eyebrows that made her laugh then grimace as she held her ribs carefully.

"I can see why you and Gramps are at loggerheads, but neither of you are at fault," she said sincerely. "If I was cut out of my car I am guessing it's a write off."

"A total wreck, honey."

"Shame." She smiled sadly.

"After all the fuss you made when I bought it, you now consider it's passing as a *shame*." He shook his head and arched a slightly disbelieving brow. "Although, I can get you the Spyder now." His grin was reinstated but was smug now.

Tasha smiled, stifling a yawn as she reached up to deliver a single kiss to his cheek before she rolled over and pressed her back against his front where his grip tightened on her, holding her safe. Jim cradled her, desperate for her to sleep soundly and maybe even dream the sweetest of dreams. Tasha closed her eyes, allowed a few tears to fall and even with her inability to process all she'd been told, she somehow managed to drift off to a sleep.

Chapter Four

"No, help me!" Tasha jolted up, covered in a sheen of sweat, her heart feeling as though it was going ten to the dozen, no, it was going ten to the dozen, trying to beat right out of her chest.

She looked around the room, both relieved and fearful to be lying in her hospital bed alone. The need to feel safe, and by safe she meant wrapped in Jim's arms, and the desire to keep this hidden from him were at odds.

Tasha had no idea why this was happening—dreams— memories—bad times, all mixed up in her brain and taunting her in her dreams. If she'd dreamt about the crash she'd understand that as a recent trauma, but these dreams were old traumas not her newest one.

The door opened, breaking her thoughts.

"Hi, Tasha, how you doing?" Stan walked to her side and looked around the room then smirked. "Where's your shadow? You're not hiding him beneath the covers are you?"

They both laughed at his reference to Jim, the doctor's humour lifting her panic and anxiety a little.

Tasha wafted the covers as if checking under them for him. "Nope, no sign."

"Well, I'm sure he'll be back before we know it."

Stan smiled but was already setting about doing his observations and checks on Tasha. He talked her through the possibility of going home soon, but seemed non-committal in terms of when. The list of dos and don'ts seemed never-ending but they didn't concern her because she was in no doubt that Jim would ensure they were all complied with.

"You're running a bit of a temperature," Stan muttered and seemed to be weighing up his options. "I'll run some bloods and start you on a broad spectrum antibiotic, as a precaution."

"Okay," Tasha replied meekly, thinking that her high temperature was understandable after waking up hot and sweaty. She watched the doctor leave only to be replaced a minute later by one of the nurses.

"This is not fucking happening." Jim began to pace the corridor.

Bobby leaned against the wall and allowed his brother to make several more lengths of the corridor before stepping into his path.

"Jimbo, please, you're wearing a groove in the floor."

Jim looked down as if checking for the groove Bobby had mentioned, but he did stop.

"She's in good hands—"

"Do not finish that with a *she's in the best place right now* or a similar platitude," Jim pleaded, knowing that those words would offer no comfort to him, in fact, they would only succeed in pissing him off.

Bobby shrugged. "But she is."

"She was better, getter stronger every day," Jim said, possibly not needing a response, but he got one anyway.

"She was, she still is stronger, but she has an infection—"

"Another fucking infection! I mean, what are they doing here that she has now picked up another infection in the hospital?"

"Jim, this isn't the hospital's fault. This isn't negligence. Tasha has just been unlucky."

Jim scowled but offered no argument.

Bobby took his brother's silence to mean he knew what he was saying was true so continued. "A hospital is full of sick people…it's like infection and illness central, plus anyone who has been in to see Tasha could have brought infections in."

"Yeah, well, she is on a visitor ban until she's home so that won't be happening again."

Bobby shook his head, knowing Jim was worried, but knowing that this, his super control freak, shutting everything and everyone down was not in anyone's best interests, least of all Tasha's, assuming she came out of theatre in one piece. He shut his own thoughts down now, needing to focus on his brother remaining calm and together.

Jim glared at his brother, his irritation rising at his attempts at trying to console and placate him as he stressed about Tasha's wellbeing, again.

Bobby, undeterred, shook his head again.

"Go ahead, shake your head, I mean it. Stan picked up the temperature spiking again and thought she might have picked up a cold or something and then within eight hours she is hot, clammy and has passed out walking to the bathroom because her blood pressure has dropped through the floor. The antibiotics may as well have been vitamins for what use they were because they were never going to treat the internal puss fill abscess the size of a fucking tennis ball."

"But—"

"There is no but! What aren't you getting here?" Jim was beginning to lose his hold on any semblance of control.

"I just—" Bobby began but after just two words found himself cut off again.

"You know what? Don't. Don't think, don't speak, just don't fucking do anything suggesting I am out of line in my attempts to keep her safe or that she shouldn't have been safe from these infections because that is guaranteed to piss me off."

Bobby nodded, his brother had summed up the last eight hours accurately, albeit a little over emotionally but that was completely understandable under the circumstances.

"She's a fighter," he said, the only offer of support he could muster now.

"She is, but she has already fought for so much. She has been through enough, hasn't she? I mean, how much more can she fight for and continue to *win?*"

"Jimbo—"

Bobby never finished the words of comfort he was going to offer.

Stan appeared looking tired and a little grim but softened it with a thumbs up. "Your lady is one tough cookie. She gave us a couple of scares with her blood pressure, but she is through the surgery and signs are good. I want to keep an eye on her for a while longer but she'll be back with you soon."

"I'm banning all visitors," Jim seemed to announce.

Surprisingly, Stan nodded. "I can't say that I blame you with all she's been through, but—"

"No. I need her to be well, to recover without any more problems."

Stan nodded again. "She's been unlucky, but I guess I can see why you might react this way. So long as she remains stable, we'll keep her on IV antibiotics and pain relief for the next few days and then look at letting her home with oral meds, probably in around a week."

****

It was actually eight days later before Tasha was released from hospital. During the drive home she considered the last week. She'd been out of it for a couple of days following her surgery and had struggled to recover as quickly as she had previously. That frustrated her almost as much as having no visitors other than Jim, but she did understand where he was coming from in terms of trying to protect from further infections and setbacks. There were times when she wanted nothing more than to be locked in a cocoon containing just the two of them but the confines of a hospital room wasn't really how she'd ever imagined their cocoon. She smiled to herself as the house came into sight. Although she hadn't been aware of much at all when she was at her worst, there had been days when she'd truly doubted whether she would make it back home, back here with Jim.

The car came to a standstill and while Tasha was struggling with her seat belt and opening the door, Jim had already got out and made his way round to her side. The door swung open and he prepared to help her out.

"If you try and pick me up again I will not be responsible for my actions," snapped Tasha as she slid from the passenger seat of the car that was parked in front of the house.

"Okay, okay." Jim held his arms up as if defending himself. "Will you at least take my arm, please," he said seriously but smiled as Tasha took the arm he offered.

The front door virtually flew open as they got to it and Tasha physically jumped and shrank back at the sight of Lizzie, Juan, Philip, Pippa, Dan and her grandparents standing there to greet her with cries of *welcome home.*

Jim briefly allowed a look of annoyance to sneak across his face. "Can we all get in the house please, Tasha is tired." With a short smile and the addition of a simple *please* everyone stepped back

He ushered her through to the back of the house where an uncomfortable looking Sandra and Mike stood in the kitchen. Sandra was preparing food for everyone.

Mike winked at Tasha then excused himself. "Good to have you back, Tasha, but I'm gonna get off and I'll catch up with you later in the week." He quickly exited through the back door.

Tasha silently wished she was back in the two-person cocoon she'd previously been frustrated by. She wished everyone else would do the same as Mike and leave, but they were there for the duration and once she was settled on the sofa, she found herself flanked by Pippa and Lizzie who were already competing for her attention and time.

Sensing her unease, Philip called to them both with some excuse leaving Juan to sit down next to her. He looked concerned as he took the hand of his friend in his. "Too much?"

Tasha smiled at him and nodded as she whispered, "I was hoping the house would be empty and I could just sit down and relax."

"Jim was hoping for much the same so I think this is a surprise to him, too. Everyone was worried about you and with the visiting ban since your last operation we've all missed you."

Tasha nodded and smiled; her nod understanding her friends and family wanting to see her and her smile for Jim and his desire to take care of her. "Jim did what he thought was best and with my track record with infections it was probably for the best. I did miss you all too, though."

"I get it, but you know what Lizzie is like when she gets an idea in her head. Fortunately, we talked her out of a big welcome home party." He smiled, gripping her hand and giving it a squeeze as Paul sat on the other side of her.

"Nat, I was thinking, Jim will have to go back to work at some point so why don't you come home for a while, with us."

"Gramps, please. We've talked about this already. I'm staying here, this is my home now." She rested her head on her grandfather's shoulder, wanting to offer comfort but no glimmer of hope that she might go anywhere.

He ran a hand over her loose hair that was falling down in waves over her face. "If you change your mind, you'll always have a home with us."

"Ditto," she replied as Lizzie and Pippa returned with Philip.

It was Philip who seemed to announce, "I was thinking we could hit the beach this afternoon, if you fancy it?" Tasha stared at him disbelievingly. He quickly clarified, "Not you, Tash! Jeez, the old man would cut me off for the invitation alone, so, Juan? The girls and Dan are up for it." He grinned before bending down to whisper in her ear, "And then we can all leave you in peace before Dad loses it completely."

"Cool, but no ice-cream," said Juan before kissing Tasha and heading out past a relieved and grateful looking Jim.

Philip and the girls kissed her before following Juan and she was then joined by Dan who sat down briefly and admitted, "This whole thing has freaked me a little, but I am seriously pleased to see you, sis." He hugged her tightly and kissed her until Pippa called for him to hurry up.

Sandra appeared with a cup of tea and a sympathetic smile as Celia sat next to Tasha leaving her flanked by her grandparents. She looked around for Jim and smiled as he returned and chatted with Sandra as she tidied around the kitchen.

Tasha let out a loud and exaggerated yawn that was greeted by her grandmother suggesting, "Maybe you should consider a lie down, Tasha. You look exhausted, darling."

Tasha nodded and was pleased to see Jim standing in front of her waiting to help her up and escort her upstairs where he stayed with her while she slept.

****

Tasha woke in an empty bed the following morning and carefully made her way downstairs where she found Bobby arriving.

"Hey, Tasha," he cried, hugging her gently. "All things considered you look seriously hot."

She laughed. "Thanks, but I think I've looked better," she said as Jim took her hand and escorted her through to the back of the house where Sandra immediately sprang into life making tea.

"What time is Masterson due?" asked Bobby, accepting the coffee Sandra offered him.

"Half past nine," replied Jim.

"Masterson? The policeman?" Tasha was confused, she had no idea the police were due.

"Yes, I can't put him off any longer it would seem." Jim was seriously disgruntled at the idea.

"Is that why you're here?" Tasha addressed Bobby.

"Yes, in my capacity as an attorney."

"But you're a criminal attorney," said Tasha.

"Yes, and the detective is investigating a criminal case, so Bobby will be here for any interviews with Masterson," said Jim with a flatness she didn't quite buy into.

"Where are my grandparents?" Tasha was happy to change the subject.

"Mike has taken them to pick up some things before they go home," replied Jim.

"They're going home?" Tasha wondered if there had been another argument between Jim and Paul.

"Not until the weekend. It seems they have some business stuff to deal with back home and I think your granddad wants to try and stop your mother selling any more ridiculous stories, and now that you're home they feel happy to do that."

"What about Dan and Pippa?"

"They're going too, unless you want me to see if I can get them to stay a little longer," offered Jim.

"No. I'm looking forward to getting back to normal," admitted Tasha as a call came through from the security guards that, for the time being were a fixture at the entrance to their home, announcing the arrival of Detective Masterson and his colleague.

Jim sighed, but authorised the guards to let them through the gates and went to the front door to greet them leaving Tasha alone with Bobby.

"Tasha, don't look so worried. Masterson just needs to check details and I'm only here because you're going to be my sister-in-law and my brother is obsessed with taking care of you." Bobby continued to smile at her nervous expression.

"Taking care of me or controlling my life?"

"Same thing for Jimbo." He laughed as Jim re-entered the room with two other men.

The first was about forty-years-old, shorter than Jim by four or five inches and stocky with dark hair, peppered with grey at the sides and very dark brown eyes that looked around suspiciously. The other man was younger, maybe only twenty-five and taller, almost standing eye to eye with Jim and quite athletic looking with thick sandy coloured hair and big blue eyes. Jim introduced the two men, the older one was Sargent Nick Masterson and the younger man was introduced as Detective Pete Murphy.

"Nice to meet you at last, Miss Winters," said Masterson, giving Jim a sideways glance.

"Sorry I've kept you waiting." Smiled Tasha, extending a hand towards the now smiling Masterson.

"Under the circumstances I think I can forgive you." He smiled warmly then looked to Bobby. "Counsellor."

"Sargent," replied Bobby as the detectives sat down and looked on.

"Would you like a drink, tea, coffee, a soft drink?" offered Tasha attempting to get up.

"Coffee would be great, thanks," said Murphy speaking for the first time.

"Sit down, baby. I'll get it." Jim rushed into the kitchen and returned quickly to find the detectives trying to establish some facts with Tasha.

"Miss Winters, tell us why your father would get involved in Miss Adams' plan to stop you marrying Mr Maybury?" asked Masterson.

"Money, I think," replied Tasha honestly.

"Why though?" he persisted. "I have daughters and I could

never imagine being party to anything that might hurt them, so why would your dad?" asked Masterson.

Tasha could feel panic and bile rising as she wondered how much he already knew and how much she should reveal about her past, her past with her parents and in turn with Liam. Even if she told them, would they believe her? After all, by the older detective's own admission, he was confused by her father wanting to hurt her.

"Why don't you ask him?" Jim was irritated that Tasha was being put in this position but more than that he sensed her unease and wanted to put an end to it.

"We have," replied Murphy curtly. "And now we're asking Tasha, for some background, to establish a motive. That's our job."

Tasha could see that Jim was seething at the young detective's audacity to take such a stand, speaking so dismissively towards Jim and referring to her as Tasha.

Jim first spoke to Masterson, "Sargent, I appreciate the difficult job you have to do, but you must appreciate that my job here is to keep my fiancée safe, physically and emotionally. I know you think I've been uncooperative in giving you access to her, but I won't apologise for that because she almost died, several times, and your interview was very, very low on my list of priorities."

The Sargent nodded his understanding of what Jim was saying as he turned to the younger detective.

"Now, detective, you seem to be under some illusion that whilst I have the utmost respect for the law and its officers, that I am going to allow you to speak to me as though I'm a kid who has just been caught with his hand in the cookie jar. I'm not. My fiancée is my only priority here and I understand what your job is, and I even understand the need for you to establish motive and corroboration, even with a confession, but not at her expense. I'm fairly sure if this case ever gets to trial my fiancée's opinion on why her father would or wouldn't do something and any thoughts she might have on his thinking behind it would be inadmissible," said Jim flatly, holding Murphy's stare. "Oh, and as far as I know you and Tasha are not family, personal friends or colleagues, so that would make her Miss Winters to you."

Tasha wasn't surprised by Jim's comments, but did feel uncomfortable until Bobby spoke.

"Guys, can we get this done, please? Tasha is still recuperating, and I am due in court later this morning."

"Of course," smiled Masterson.

"I should explain that Tasha is happy to answer any questions you have regarding the night of her crash and her whole relationship with Miss Adams. She will take questions about her parents under advisement from me because there are younger siblings involved, minors no less, and there are some legal arrangements already in place in the U.K. So now we have established that, continue." Bobby sounded the consummate professional before turning to Murphy and adding with a smile, "I am personal friends with Miss Winters, in fact, the angry tall guy over there is my brother, so that would make her Tasha to me."

Tasha smiled while Jim rolled his eyes at his brother. She couldn't be certain, but Tasha was fairly certain he'd called Bobby an ass. The young detective blushed slightly as Masterson took control again.

"Sorry if we've ruffled feathers, but it was unintentional to offend so let's get on." He looked down at his notebook and launched into his questions.

"Of course." Tasha smiled weakly.

"So, Miss Adams and you were not on good terms as I understand it," said Masterson softly.

Tasha shook her head and began to explain, "No. She didn't like me and as a consequence I didn't like her."

"Why?" chipped in Murphy.

"Simply? Because she was in love with my fiancé," replied Tasha honestly.

Murphy looked across at Jim and smirked. "Is that so?"

Tasha was irritated by him too now. "Yes, that is so."

She glanced across at Jim who interjected as he placed a tray of coffee down on the table. "I had a very casual relationship with Mickie that started about a year ago and ended when I met

Tasha. Mickie had been a friend for over twenty years since she dated my brother, but after they separated, she made it clear that she had feelings for me. I was married at that time with a baby and had no romantic interest in Mickie and she accepted that, I thought, and we remained friends. However, some twenty years later, last summer when we were on vacation with a group of friends, we got together. For me it was a fling, no more, but for her it was more. We met up fairly regularly, but it was never more than a casual relationship for me. I never viewed Mickie as a potential girlfriend never mind a future wife and as I say I ended my casual relationship with Mickie after meeting Tasha, but we remained friends for a while."

"Was there a cross over in your relationships with Miss Winters and Miss Adams?" asked Murphy, his smirk growing.

"Is that relevant?" asked Jim.

"Yes," replied Masterson.

Shrugging, Jim answered, "I met Tasha on the Friday, in New York and I think we both thought our meeting would be casual, but on the Sunday Tasha flew back to L.A. with me and I told Mickie I'd met someone I thought I could have a permanent future with and that she and I would have to go back to being friends, no more. She'd never liked any of my previous wives, but she and I retained a friendship that was independent of my marriages and I assumed it would be the same with Tasha. But a crossover, no."

"Miss Winters, how would you describe your relationship with Miss Adams?" asked Masterson seriously.

"There wasn't one, not really. I originally believed Mickie was a man, with the name," Tasha began, not adding Jim's deceit in allowing her to believe Mickie was anything other than a man because apart from its irrelevance in this, she didn't need to rake over it again. "She wasn't a regular visitor here and her name probably only came up once before I met her at Jim and Bobby's birthday party where I realised she was a woman. She was unpleasant and made it clear that she didn't like me and when Jim and I first got engaged she was on the wedding guest list, but I had her removed. I figured I was only going to do it once so why have people at my wedding who despised me. She hired a P.I. who followed me when I returned home to London for a couple of weeks and tried to use the information she had against me by showing Jim photos of me with an ex-boyfriend. What she hadn't realised was that my meeting with my ex had been pre-planned and was something Jim was already aware of, rendering her photos useless. It seems it was during this time that her man contacted my parents and also tried to dig dirt from my friends, but to no avail."

"So, there was no dirt to find, is that what you're saying?" asked Masterson making her laugh.

"I guess that depends what your definition of dirt is, but Mickie didn't uncover the kind of dirt she was looking for." Tasha hoped she'd managed to remain cool, but diplomatic. "She wanted something that would taint Jim's view of me and make him rethink his decision to marry me. She was unsuccessful in that mission."

Both detectives nodded while Jim smiled across at her. Bobby looked ready to intervene, but she had already decided that she had probably said as much as she was willing to and more than enough for the detectives in their search for background information.

"I think we are done, Miss Winters," began Masterson. "We have spoken to Michael Rose, the P.I. and he has confirmed his investigation in London and we are still looking for Miss Adams, but your father is quite clear that she paid him to stop you marrying Mr Maybury."

Tasha swallowed hard, still hoping her father's part in this might be proven untrue, but in reality she knew it couldn't be because he still saw her as nothing more than a payday.

The detective offered her a sympathetic smile before continuing. "He has confessed to following you around L.A. for a couple of days before he watched you on the night of the crash. He saw you leave here and park in the lot of a convenience store where he received a message from Miss Adams to say enough was enough and he should do something to stop your marriage. He decided the something was to cut your brakes, which he did before observing you watching some children playing with their families in a children's playground. He then followed you back to your car and pursued you as you headed up into the hills and we believe he ran you off the road, although, he has yet to admit that he did that deliberately. He admits his part in things, so I think his conviction is guaranteed…" he paused. "But with respect, your father was purely the gopher in this. Miss Adams is the brains behind it and manipulated your father so is far more dangerous than your father could ever be."

Tasha stared at the police officer's summing up and agreed with him because he had never threatened her life as she'd been his cash cow, but Mickie had no need for Tasha before and certainly would have none now.

"If you're interested, your father has been assigned a public defender, but he may need someone a little more, erm, expensive." It was Murphy's turn to offer her a sympathetic smile now before he glanced across towards Bobby.

"Then maybe he should have thought about that before he tried to kill my fiancée. In fact, I think you should lock him up and throw away the key. Now, if that's all?" asked Jim angrily.

"Yes, of course. Thank you for your time and co-operation." Masterson got to his feet and waited for his colleague.

Jim escorted them to the door and while they were alone Bobby said, "Tasha, I don't know whether you're considering representation for your dad, but if you are, promise me you'll square it with Jimbo before you act or you could be the shortest serving wife he's had."

"Really?" Tasha's nervousness was clear to them both.

"You know he doesn't like things keeping from him anyway, but he is all for the death penalty as far as your dad and Mickie are concerned so…"

"I get it. Thanks, Bobby." She smiled as Jim returned.

"Right, that's me off to court, catch you later, Jimbo. Tasha, give Abby a call, she misses you," he called as Jim followed him out of the room.

"Okay and thank you," replied Tasha as she heard the front door opening then closing.

Jim slumped down next to Tasha and pulled her close as he kissed the top of her head, "Are you okay?"

"I suppose so. This is all such a mess, isn't it?" she asked nervously.

"Hey, you're not to worry about it, any of it, baby," he told her seriously, tilting her chin so she had to look at him.

"I'll try," she replied. "Do they know about Mickie and the cancer thing?"

"The police?"

Tasha nodded.

"Yeah, they took a statement from me when you were in the hospital. You look tired, honey. Go and take a nap."

"Jim, I'm fine. I don't need a nap, or a lie down or anything else other than a normal life." Tasha attempted to leap to her feet but settled for more of a staggered hobble. "I want things to go back to normal. I want you to go to work, to stop standing over me and sending me to bed twenty times a day, alone," she told a wide-eyed Jim who was looking up at her.

"Baby, I want to take care of you and I am out of my depth here because I don't know what I would do if I ever lost you and I almost did, didn't I? I thought I had, I really did." Jim looked sad and desperate. "I don't do half measures, Tasha, you know that, so I can't just go back to normal and pretend like it never happened."

"I understand that, Jim, but you can't keep me locked up here, living in sweatpants or pyjamas. If you need to keep me safe by employing security staff I understand that, even if I don't like it, but we need, I need, to go out. I need to see people and if you need to come with me to do that fine, but you need to go to work at some point. Maybe after my family have gone home you could go back, for a couple of days at least. I promise not to go out alone and when I'm here Sandra and Mike are usually around and Juan and Philip are across the drive. Sara and Abby are both eager to visit and I need to start looking at my schedule and work."

She saw the look of total objection on his face and laughed.

"Not all of those things at once, but I'm going crazy here. I want something on my mind and swimming around in my head other than the idea of my own father taking money to kill me. Something that doesn't involve Mickie hating me enough to conspire to remove me from your life permanently. I don't even know how to process those thoughts. I know I'm not perfect, I have made mistakes in my life but I don't consider myself a bad or evil person and yet the fact that this has happened because of other people's deliberate actions forces me to question that."

Pulling her closer to gently hold her, Jim said nothing. He tried to absorb her words and the thoughts that were awash in her mind and then, with nothing to say to remove those thoughts, knowing she needed to work through those ideas over time, he returned to her original suggestion for him going back to work.

"I wish I could make things better for you, honey. Look, I'll think about work and we'll talk about it after your folks have gone home. But you do look tired." He got to his feet, seemingly unwilling to concede his final point.

"I am going to get bed sores if I spend much more time in bed, James," she cried as a final protest while Jim stood before her with grim determination on his face. "Fine. I will go for yet another lie down, but only if you come with me."

"Deal," he agreed victoriously and took her hand before he led her upstairs.

Chapter Five

It was a couple of weeks after her grandparents had returned to London before Tasha decided to broach the subject of Jim returning to work again. However, having had the day from hell she probably should have thought twice about broaching it at all.

If she was honest, her day from hell had been a week from hell. It had started with cross words between her and Jim. Tasha was becoming increasingly frustrated with his need to keep her close and to keep her at home, although she understood his reluctance, well, refusal to allow her out alone. However, when she'd suggested going down to the stables to ride he had vetoed that too. Even when she'd offered to take some security with her it had been a big fat no, unless Jim came too and the truth was that she wanted, needed a break from him. Just a small one. In the end she'd remained at the house or the pool and Jim had been within earshot if not sight at all times.

Tasha's week was made worse by the fact that Philip and Juan had gone away for a few days meaning she had no friends nearby and with her family already at home she was beginning to feel increasingly isolated. Lizzie had been to stay for a couple of days but the truth was that Tasha wasn't really in the mood to cope with a hormonal teenager who seemed particularly moody this week, nor did she have any desire to discuss whether she had heard things when unconscious, unlike Lizzie who seemed fascinated by it. Sandra was refusing to allow Tasha to so much as make a cup of tea, although she suspected that the other woman might be working under orders from Jim, and Mike was rarely around.

Physically, Tasha was healing and wasn't as tired as she had been but was still overly aware of the impact the most mundane of activities had on her energy levels and her body in general. Tasha had never considered herself beautiful but knew she was attractive with a nice body shape that was in good condition, or at least it had been before her crash. Now her body bore the scars that told the story of her battle for life. She'd been surprised at the amount of scarring on her body when she'd first looked at it, but was getting used to it, kind of. Her greater concern was that Jim would have a problem with them. That they would make her less attractive to him and be a constant reminder of what had happened to her, something he felt guilty about, not that he had any need to, not in her mind, but he did. They were yet to become intimate again, having done no more than kiss, cuddle and hold hands and even those actions were gentle and loving rather than passionate and that too concerned her.

Emotionally, she was struggling a little more. Tasha was still finding it difficult to understand her father's reasoning behind trying to kill her, although she was choosing to disbelieve that was the case. She instead chose to view his actions as being something that had gone wrong; yes he was trying to stop her from marrying Jim, but he couldn't really want her dead, could he? Every time she went over it in her mind that was the question she kept coming back to. Why would he want her dead? She was his child and surely somewhere in his heart and soul that meant something to him, she meant something to him, didn't she? When all was said and done she could serve no purpose dead, but then, currently, she was serving no purpose to him alive. Everything was jumbled in her head and a big mess. Then there was her mother who had sold story after story about her suffering following this incident and although legally there were topics she couldn't discuss she managed to get around them and was clearly still cashing in on Tasha.

There was still a huge blank void about the time between getting back in her car and waking up in the hospital. The doctors had said this was quite normal and often happened as the brain could and would shut down memories of traumatic instances.

Some days, when Tasha tried to talk to Jim about everything in her head, she stopped short of opening up entirely as she knew he was suffering too and had struggled to come to terms with everything that had happened, including the weeks she couldn't remember. That   made her feel guilty so that when she opened conversation she quickly allowed it to dry to avoid hurting him further or forcing either of them to face their own feelings of guilt.

Then there were the nightmares that had started once she'd returned home and been off all medication. They were like nothing she'd experienced before. She had one most nights, some worse than others and this last week there had been some really bad ones. They varied from simply reliving the experience of waking up choking, to others that involved her father and Mickie chasing her and finding her over and over again, chasing her, hurting her and taking her away so that she would never see Jim again.

Last night's was a new one, it still involved Mickie and her father capturing her and then rather than taking her away from Jim they took him from her. She'd experienced dreams where Jim had left her, chose Mickie over her, but this one was something different. They had done terrible things in her dream, hurt him and then eventually killed him, while she watched and then they'd laughed at her, Mickie had laughed at her and then her father had taken her home to Liam. The nightmare seemed to last for hours until she eventually woke up in a pool of her own sweat and tears, crying, sobbing and calling out to Jim who had simply pulled her to him. He'd held her as she cried, telling her that it was *okay*, that it was *all over* and that she was *safe*. Unfortunately, she couldn't stop thinking that it wasn't over, couldn't be until Mickie was found and judging by the state of her *it* wasn't safe, although she did at least feel safe.

So, her bad day had really been a bad week meaning her decision to open up a conversation about Jim going back to work and life going back to normal couldn't have been more badly timed than to it was over dinner at the vineyard, her first real trip out since being discharged from hospital.

"Are you planning on returning to work this week?" she asked bluntly, feeling brave in company.

"I have no plans one way or the other," Jim replied, already looking slightly irritated.

"I'll be fine." She knew he was concerned about leaving her still. "Sandra will be around and security." She was attempting to use their presence to her advantage but sighed, already tiring of their presence.

"And Abby has said she's happy to help out," said Bobby supportively.

"I don't need a sitter." Tasha pouted and rolled her eyes. "I'm not a child or an invalid," she added more calmly.

"We'll see." Jim dismissed the idea in two words.

"Will we? Or will you continue to keep me a prisoner?" She was ready to cry at the thought of being confined to the house and smothered by Jim for another week or more.

"A prisoner? That's a little dramatic, isn't it? Jim's house is as far removed from a prison as any place I've ever seen," said Bria, leaping to her brother's defence.

"Even a gilded cage is still a cage." Abby interjected, equally as defensive of her friend.

"I'm not discussing this further, Tasha, not here and not now." Jim spoke with anger and threw in a cold stare in her direction to fully convey his determination to end this particular conversation at this time and in this place.

"I don't suppose now would be a good time to plan another night out then." Philip laughed, genuinely hoping to lighten the mood and lift the tension, but failed miserably as Juan gave him a dig with his elbow.

Jim furiously muttered a single word to his son's attempt at humour, "Really?"

All of that hung over them, weighing heavy in the air before Tasha excused herself from the table and rushed to the bathroom where she ended up huddled on the floor, crying and shaking, leaving a hive of activity and mutterings behind her.

"You see what you've done now?" Jim turned on Philip ready to fire accusations at him.

"It was a joke," he protested.

"And yet nobody is laughing, Philip." Jim was furious but the truth was he wasn't entirely sure who his fury was with.

"I don't think I'm the one responsible for her running off to the bathroom," said Philip bravely, but the truth was that he wasn't going to be the scapegoat here. His words had been intended to break the ice and ease the tension you could cut through. It had been bad enough before he and Juan had taken a few days away, but it had intensified one hundred-fold by the time they'd returned. "You are killing her with kindness." Philip realised his choice of words may have been insensitive but attempted to continue speaking to Jim who looked as though he was ready to explode one way or another when an obviously scared Lizzie spoke.

"Is Tasha okay?" Lizzie's voice echoed with concern and worry.

"No, Lizzie, Tasha is far from okay." Jim got to his feet but was unsure where to go or what to do for the best.

"Son, you need to let her breathe," said Jack calmly as everyone else seemed to look at each other nervously.

"Breathe, Dad? That is precisely what I am ensuring she continues to do." Jim glared at his dad, shocking everyone around them.

"Jimbo…" started Bobby.

"Not you, too? I thought you got this," cried Jim before Abby intervened.

"Right, all of you sit down and shut up! Lizzie, Tasha is fine, or she would be if she could at least move from one room to another without an escort or an inquisition. She just needs to get her head around everything that has happened. It's a lot for any of us to understand so imagine how hard it is for Tasha. Philip, I don't think she's quite ready for your jokes yet, soon I'm sure." She smiled.

"I should see if she's okay," said Jim, getting up again.

"No." Abby stared up at him, a determined and dogged expression on her face. "You stay and I will go while you think about loosening the leash." Once the last word was out she immediately regretted it. "I know you care and I know you want to keep her safe, Jim, but get smart with it, you're not thinking straight. You will drive her away. She's young and terrified." Abby turned to follow in the same direction as Tasha, not stopping until she reached the bathroom door where she tapped it gently.

Tasha sat on the floor, crying still but called, "What?"

"Tasha, it's me, Abby. Can I come in?"

"Yes," she replied and as she saw Abby looking down at her she cried harder.

"Oh, Tasha, honey." Abby joined her friend on the floor and with her arms wrapped around her she rocked her gently.

Maisie began to clear the table while everyone else sat looking awkward and uncomfortable until Bria broke the silence, "I'm sure she's a lovely girl in her own way, Jim, but she may not be wife material."

A shocked silence replaced the earlier awkward one as everyone else stared across at her. Bria was undeterred and seemed almost oblivious to the shaky ground she was walking across.

"She's an actress and all of this drama is par for the course for her and she's foreign, but do you really think she will settle here? Look at her family, they're dysfunctional to say the least." She suddenly noticed the daggers she was being subjected to from just about everyone now, yet still she wasn't quite done. "She is emotionally unstable—I'm just saying," she said in her own defence.

"Then don't," snapped Jim. "She, Tasha, is perfect wife material as far as I am concerned, Bria, but the fact that she was almost murdered, you know, the drama, because of me has tipped her over the edge slightly. Actually, scratch that, me being totally absorbed by the fact that the person who wanted her dead is still at large has turned me into someone who will not allow Tasha to take a breath without me being there to oversee it and that is what has tipped her over the edge. And do you know what, Bria? I have no clue what to do or how to deal with the absolute fear that lies across my chest like a cancer that Mickie isn't done trying, and the overwhelming panic that if I leave her alone for a split second that is when Mickie will strike, to the extent that it is killing me to sit here with all of you knowing she is out of my sight. So please, just don't say anymore or I may say something we all regret." Jim was almost relieved to admit the extent of his own fears.

"Right," said Bobby, taking charge as he saw the looks of shock and concern on everyone's faces, especially the children. "Let's open up the garden. Lizzie, would you get some sodas sorted?" he asked as he ushered the kids out of the back of the house.

Lizzie nodded with a worried expression on her face that lifted slightly as Philip and Juan joined her.

Bobby continued, "Sophie and Bria you could help Mom clear away and Dad, could you get Tasha a very large brandy? You and I, little brother should go and find our women folk."

Jim got to his feet and gratefully followed Bobby through the house.

"Thank you," he said genuinely grateful for his brother's input.

"No problem." Bobby slapped Jim's back in that way that men seem to use as a show of love and support. "I figured you needed a hand and as my wife had started the job."

"Yeah, where the fuck did bad ass, shouty Abby spring from?" asked Jim making them both laugh.

"She likes Tasha and wants to help, and I think she decided that if you are going to keep turning her offers down..."

"She'd take matters into her own hands," said Jim.

"Something like that. Did you see Martin's face?" Bobby laughed with his brother again until they heard the sound of crying travelling down the corridor from the house bathroom.

"You okay?" Bobby knew his brother was as far from okay as he'd ever been.

"Yeah, I just feel so helpless and I hate it when she cries," admitted Jim.

"Well, you might just need to suck it up little brother," warned Bobby before they reached the bathroom door where the sad scene of Abby holding Tasha and rocking her as she cried took both men by surprise.

"Baby," said Jim hesitantly.

Both women looked up and with a flick of his head, Bobby

summoned Abby away. She unwrapped herself from Tasha's arms and legs and swapped places with Jim.

Bobby took his wife's hand and led her down the corridor where he kissed her gently. "You, Abigail Maybury, are a very nice lady."

Back in the bathroom Tasha somehow found herself sitting in Jim's lap and totally enveloped by his embrace that held her tightly as he took over the gentle rocking motion Abby had started while Tasha continued to cry, but more gently within the safety of Jim's embrace that she'd earlier felt she was being stifled by.

It was another half an hour before Tasha's tears stopped fully and she finally spoke. "I'm sorry for making a scene. I thought I might be safer discussing things in company," she admitted.

"We need to talk, honey, you and me, not with company, but not now. I just need you to know that I'm so scared of what could have happened and my part in it that I can't think straight, but I know we can't go on like this, so I promise, tomorrow we talk, properly, okay?"

"Thank you," she said with her voice breaking slightly. "I'm scared too, Jim, but I can't live like this, under constant scrutiny. I need you to treat me like you used to," she told him as he shifted her so she was facing him.

"What do you mean, like I used to?"

"I get that you want to protect me, but I feel like a child or something you're responsible for out of duty or obligation, even the way you look at me," she said nervously, not wanting him to misunderstand or for her words to make him even more protective.

"Baby, I do want to protect you and I see that as part of my job, the job of loving you. But what do you mean the way I look at you?" He was confused and actually had no idea what she meant.

"Do you remember when I used to worry that all we had was sex and when that faded we'd have nothing left?" She moved closer onto his lap.

He nodded.

"Well, now it kind of feels as though we have lost that and we have the love left but with that comes the duty and obligation."

Her words made him frown. He was still clueless as to where this was going and he did feel a duty and obligation to her, but he loved her more than anything and whatever he did or felt was out of love, always.

"Jim, you seem to go out of your way to avoid being with me, intimately. I know the doctor said four to six weeks but we shouldn't have made it beyond the third week. You have always been reluctant to add to any injuries I've had, but I need you to still want me, to desire me, not just to want to make me better and protect me out of duty and guilt." Her explanation gave some clarity for them both.

"You think I don't find you attractive anymore?" He shook his head. "Jeez, Tasha, you are way off the mark, honey. I would like nothing more than to be throwing you down and fucking you senseless at every opportunity, but your body has been through so much," he cried, wincing as he remembered, not that he ever really forgot just how much it had been through.

She looked at him sceptically making him laugh ironically.

"You don't believe me? Tasha, I swear, baby, I think of kissing you and touching you, of being inside you and making you come more than ever, it's like a hobby I have." He laughed, then arched a brow at her disbelieving expression. "I swear to you that my desire for you is as rampant as it ever was. I lie and watch you sleep then hate myself for being so turned on by you; I wake up every morning and forget how badly hurt you were and I want to wrap my arms around you, to kiss you and touch you and then I remember and hate myself a bit more as I leap out of bed. I avoid being anywhere near you when you get dressed or shower because I'm unsure if I can trust myself with you."

"Really?" Tasha asked, still not entirely sure that the reason he avoided being near when she showered or undressed was down to the change in her body and the scars it bore.

Jim nodded. "Really. What can I say to convince you? Tasha, I am more intimate with my right hand than I have been since my early teenage years and I only ever think of you, baby, of us being together, of times we've been together, in bed, in the car, at the stables, my office at home, at work, everywhere."

"Really?" she repeated. She desperately wanted to believe him, to believe that he loved her as he had previously, that his desire to be with her wasn't purely out of guilt and duty because if that was his motivation then their marriage really was doomed and he would soon be on the lookout for number eight.

"Really." He laughed. "That word, *really*, is becoming a mantra here. Tell me how I can convince you?" He studied her face for a few seconds.

She shrugged, but then flushed making him laugh.

"Ah, I see. You're horny and this is all an elaborate ploy to lure me into the sack." He grinned, holding her against him tightly.

"I wouldn't have put it quite that way, James," she protested, still embarrassed by his comment and the element of accuracy in it, at least the part about wanting him.

"Oh, baby, that is so the way to put it. James, really?" He laughed. "Come on, let's get off the bathroom floor and collect the brandy Bobby has insisted you need and then we'll go home and tomorrow we talk, okay?" He got up, lifting them both to a standing position and placed a delicate kiss to the tip of her nose.

Embarrassed, she walked back into the main room and was relieved to find only Bobby, Abby, Maisie and Jack there.

"Sorry," she began before a glass of brandy was thrust into her hand by Jack who gestured for her to sit down and say no more.

She reluctantly drank the liqueur that burned and stung her throat as she sipped it.

Maisie took a seat next to her, taking her hand in her own. "Tasha, I just want to say that if you feel you need to talk I am always available, unless you'd like someone professional, a counsellor, and then I know of some very good people," the older woman offered, sounding loving and maternal which made Tasha tearful again.

"Thank you," she managed to reply with a weak smile.

Gradually the others all reappeared and it was at that point that Jim decided they should go home. "Come on Lizzie, we're going, Tasha's tired."

"I was going to stay with Philip," she replied a little nervously.

"There's no need," said Tasha reassuringly, not wanting to drive Lizzie from her home.

"I know, but we're going out for the day with Mom and Lenny tomorrow so we thought it made sense," said Philip.

"If you're sure." Jim sounded slightly relieved.

The drive home was quiet and Tasha felt strangely relaxed after her meltdown and managed to fall asleep briefly. She awoke as the car stopped at the front of the house where Jim was opening the passenger door to help her out.

"Hey, baby, we're home." Jim led her up the steps to the front door, gently holding her hand in his.

Smiling, she felt nervous of what could or would happen once they entered the house and closed the world out behind them.

Chapter Six

Sensing Tasha's apprehension as she stood at the front door, Jim slipped a reassuring arm around her waist. "Honey, there is absolutely no pressure for anything."

"I know," she acknowledged, adding, "I might go and have a bath before bed."

Tasha was unsure whether she had fallen asleep in the bath or maybe she'd just drifted off into her own world, a world where this was just a normal night, a night that didn't feel quite so monumental. She knew sex wasn't everything in a relationship, but it was significant in her relationship with Jim. It had been, and although she didn't believe he would cheat on her, well, not the old Tasha anyway, a new Tasha that didn't satisfy him in the same way was a different matter.

She'd heard nothing beyond the confines of the bathroom so when she re-entered the bedroom to find Jim emerging from the walk-in wardrobe wearing just his boxers she jumped a little.

"Hey baby, are you okay?" He sounded almost nervous of her reply.

"Yeah, fine, thank you." She was unsure what else to say.

Passing her, he entered the bathroom where she heard the shower turn on and then shut off before she heard him brushing his teeth. In his absence she'd cast aside the towel she'd been wearing and replaced it with a short, white robe. Her hair was pulled free of the clip that she'd employed to keep her hair dry in the bath and brushed it quite forcefully with a paddle brush as she looked out through the open door to the balcony onto the gardens and pool below. Wondering why she suddenly felt so nervous the sound of the bathroom door caused her to take a very deep breath.

"Tasha," said Jim as he wrapped his arms around her waist. "There is no rush for anything, baby. We can get into bed and go to sleep." His words and the offer behind them were genuine and she believed them.

"I know, but I don't want to go to sleep." She turned to face him briefly before dropping her eyes.

"Hey." Jim tilted her head up so she looked at him again. "I'm not quite sure why either of us is as nervous as we appear to be. It's not like we haven't done this before, is it?"

"I know, it's weird, isn't it? I just want everything to be right, like it was before," Tasha explained honestly.

"There's no reason to think it won't be," he told her as he ran a hand through her hair. "Unless Stan has moved anything." He grinned making her laugh.

"I think everything is exactly where it was." Suddenly she began to question whether anything had moved or changed.

"Well, in that case." Jim lowered his mouth towards hers.

As soon as his tongue licked across the seam of her lips and made its way into her mouth, exploring her, reclaiming her, it felt completely right, as it always had done.

Tasha felt the tie of her robe being undone before the robe was pooling on the floor leaving her naked, literally as well as metaphorically exposed. She moaned into Jim's mouth as she felt the hardness of his arousal pressing against belly.

"I have missed you," groaned Jim as his lips left hers and a hand found first one and then a second erect nipple, pinched and tight, desperate for his attention.

"Oh yes," she moaned as he brushed them in turn while she lowered her hands behind the waistband of Jim's straining boxers and after circling his already glistening erection with her thumb, she gripped his shaft tightly and began to pump her fist slightly.

"Oh baby, this may not last long if you do that." His voice was hoarse as he placed his hand over hers to still her.

"Then take these off and take me to bed," she pleaded, tugging at the elastic waistband impatiently.

"With pleasure, honey."

A confident smirk spread across his face as he complied. Tasha looked at him, studied him and was in no doubt that her control freak fiancé had returned, or maybe he really hadn't ever left.

Lying in the middle of the bed Tasha briefly felt vulnerable until Jim appeared over her and returned his attention to her mouth, ears, neck, collar bone, chest, breasts and abdomen where he paused to kiss across the scars she now bore making her tense, remembering that she no longer had the relatively blemish free appearance she'd once had.

Jim was completely in tune with her breathing and movements and although he said nothing, he felt her anxiety that evaporated when he looked up and smiled. "Beautiful, baby, always beautiful to me."

With her earlier reservations forgotten, Jim lowered himself between her slightly spread legs where he appeared to pause to study her most intimate area intently.

"James," she started, unsure what, if anything she wanted or needed to say.

"Ssh." He deliberately blew across her skin until her clitoris stood proudly from beneath its hood. "That's better," he said, seemingly to himself. "Let me see you, Tasha," he told her.

Knowing exactly what he meant, she allowed her knees to drop further to the sides as she drew her feet up, closer to her body.

"You really are very beautiful, Tasha. You really need to see yourself like this baby, pink and swollen and so, so wet." He ran a finger along her sex, spreading out her own very obvious arousal making her moan and bite down into her lip simultaneously.

Smiling triumphantly, he slipped a finger inside her, causing her to arch her back, desperate for more.

"So greedy, honey," he crooned as he withdrew his finger and drew it into his mouth sucking long and hard. "I have missed you, Tasha. How you look and sound and how you taste."

Tasha moaned as he spoke to her and was almost beside herself as she waited for his next move which was to simply rest his hand against her. She pushed down the bed against it to try and gain some pressure, some relief, but as she moved down he moved his hand so that it now rested on her mons making her buck her hips against him. He laughed as he removed his hand again.

"James, please," she begged.

"What baby?" he asked with feigned innocence in his tone.

Tasha was in no way taken in and only heard the torment there. He was going to drag this out until she was one big, crazy ball of arousal, willing to do just about anything for release and in her current state of desperation she didn't doubt there wasn't much she wouldn't do. She was already almost frantic with need, but knowing he was going to deny her, tease and torment her gave her a near overwhelming sense of relief because it meant things could be as they were. She could still be the woman Jim wanted and the one James needed. God, how she'd missed him.

"Please, I need you."

"For what? What do you need me for, Tasha? What do you want?"

"You, I need you," replied Tasha desperately.

"For what though?" he repeated, smiling.

"Please touch me, make me come," she cried, thinking his plaguing of her and his dialogue might make her come even if he didn't touch her.

"How would you like me to do that for you?"

Any remaining nervousness Tasha had felt was gone and it really was like James had never been away.

"I don't care, I just need it," she replied honestly.

"Mmm, I could do it like this." First one, then a second finger impaled her and began to move in a circular motion making her moan and writhe. "Or," he said as he stopped. "I could do this." Slowly, he moved his face towards her then licked along her drenched length before gently flicking at her clit.

"Oh yes, please."

She reached for his hair to tug and feel the strands, but also to hold him close, maybe even prevent him from stopping. It didn't. He stopped again.

"Do you think you deserve it though, baby? You did make quite a scene tonight."

She froze with a start that there was a possibility that their first sex since her accident might be a frustrating experience for her. She hadn't even considered that option and God forbid he should backtrack further and hold her responsible for the row they'd had on the night of the actual accident or revisit her kiss with Gerry.

"You ran out on me, too, before your crash." That eerie mind reading thing really was an encumbrance at times. "But none of that matters, honey. You and me, that's all that's important here. I need you to come for me, Tasha. I need to see and feel you coming, squeezing all around my dick, baby, making me come until you have milked every last drop into your pussy, our pussy, my pussy," he said before driving into her firmly, in a single thrust, making her cry out something inaudible, a sound he caught between his lips that were on hers again. "Mine, baby, all mine, all of you," he told her, capturing her lips again, recapturing them from Gerry she thought, although that was unnecessary because like the rest of her, her lips and kisses belonged only to him.

Within about ten thrusts, Tasha could feel that Jim wouldn't take much longer if he continued at such a relentless pace, but she was so close herself it didn't matter.

"Come on, Tasha," he told her breathlessly. "How could you ever think that I didn't want you, baby? I could fuck you forever, in fact, that's my sole ambition in life," he groaned.

"Oh yes, God, I'm going to come," she told him between pants, making him move even faster.

"Yes, Tasha, for me," he grunted as his own climax crashed into him taking her with him in a sea of expletives, moans and sweat until they were both still, Jim lying along her length, breathlessly exhausted.

"Are you okay?" He was concerned for her physical welfare, but also realised he was allowing her to bear most of his weight, so holding her hips firmly he hooked a leg behind hers and rolled them both over until Tasha was straddling him, still coupled.

"Yes. I am very okay." She grinned, lowering her upper body to rest against his. "This is what I've missed." Smiled Tasha as she felt and heard the constant and reassuring beat of Jim's heart beneath her.

"You've missed being impaled on my dick, is that what you're saying here?"

Tasha laughed as she sat up and realised that he was hard again. "No. Well, yes, but I meant being close, but as you seem to have recovered." She gently began to rock against him, making him smile up at her.

"As do you," he replied as his hands found her still aching breasts.

****

Tasha woke alone, late and after a quick shower made her way downstairs wondering whether she should have been a little less energetic in last night's activities as every muscle in her body seemed to ache. She found Jim on the phone in front of his computer where he waved for her to join him. After kissing him gently on the lips she picked up his empty cup and gestured it towards her lips to offer more coffee.

Nodding, he continued his conversation with Marc, she believed. "Yes, Tasha is great, so I'm thinking I'll come into the office in the morning and take it from there."

With a smile, Tasha went to get more coffee for Jim and tea for herself.

Sandra was just about to leave the kitchen when Tasha arrived, making the other woman pause for a chat. "You look well rested this morning. It's good to see."

"Thanks. I slept really well. Proper sleep for the first time since I came home," Tasha explained, thinking she'd had less sleep the previous night than earlier nights, but better sleep, a more sound sleep with none of the nightmares she'd suffered since her accident.

"That's good. It must mean you're on the mend and Jim seems happier today so he must have noticed too." Sandra sounded genuinely pleased.

"Yeah, I think he must. How's Mike? I haven't seen him for a few days," said Tasha, eager to change the subject from Jim's chipper mood.

"No, he's gone home for a few days, to see his family."

Tasha finished making her tea and moved onto Jim's coffee.

"Didn't you want to go with him?" Tasha couldn't hide her curiosity.

Shaking her head, Sandra tried to clarify, "Mike was married when we met, with a daughter. She's your age now. I'd already planned to move out here and I was killing time until I came out. I thought Mike was a final English fling and then he suggested coming out with me, leaving behind his wife and daughter. I was horrified at the prospect." Sandra's disturbed expression suggested she was reliving the moment.

"And?" Tasha was interested to hear more of Sandra and Mike's get together.

"And, I bolted. The idea of him leaving them for me scared me so I upped and left, but he followed me and we've been together ever since. I'm still the bad lady that tempted him away as far as his mother is concerned and his ex-wife I suppose. His daughter, Gabby, has never known any different really and comes out a couple of times a year, but Jim has vetoed all visitors for the time being, so Mike has gone to her, but he'll rearrange her visit I'm sure."

"Why has Jim vetoed visitors?" Tasha knew the answer already and answered for herself, "Me. Sorry to have messed up your plans, and Gabby's."

"No problem, he has a point really. Anybody could have an ulterior motive to get close to you so he's doing the right thing, isn't he?"

"I suppose," agreed Tasha before excusing herself with the drinks in her hands.

Jim was just finishing a call when Tasha reappeared in his office and as she put the cups down, he pulled her onto his lap.

"Good morning." He nuzzled her ear.

"Morning." She leaned into his touch. "You're working."

"Yup, but I'm done for today. I thought I would go into the office tomorrow, just for the morning, if you don't mind." He turned her face to his.

"Not at all. I may see if Abby's free for a catch up."

"Whatever you want, baby, but do not go out alone."

"Jim," she started.

"No!" His voice carried a stern insistence. "I mean it, Tasha. If you can't guarantee you'll do that, then I'm going nowhere."

"I promise I won't go out alone," she agreed, holding her hand up like a scout.

"By alone I mean without security," he clarified.

"I figured that." She pouted.

"Maybe we should look at getting you a bodyguard," mumbled Jim to himself.

"What? No. I don't need a bodyguard." Tasha shuddered at the thought of it. She could think of nothing worse than having someone attached to her at all times, watching and monitoring her every move.

"We'll see," he mused momentarily.

"James," mewled Tasha gaining Jim's full attention.

"Baby, you have got to be kidding me. I know they say get back in the saddle, but again?" He laughed.

"What?" No." She laughed too, realising he thought she was using her James seductively. "That's not what I meant. I've been thinking, about us and our wedding," she explained.

"Ah, I see, and what have you come up with?" He reached for his coffee as she turned slightly to face him.

"I want to marry you and I know I still need to check out my work commitments so I don't know that we would have the amount of time we'd planned," she waffled.

"Right."

"But I don't want to wait if we don't have to, so—" She took a very deep breath and continued, "Let's go to Vegas."

"What?" cried an amazed Jim. "You want to go to Vegas to get married?" He placed his coffee cup down on the desk.

"Yes," she replied, nervous that he might hate the idea or want a longer engagement.

Jim stared at her and laughed again before clarifying further. "You want us to get married in Vegas, soon?"

"Yes," she replied in a near whisper now.

"What about the wedding you'd planned?" He'd regained his composure, her blurted out suggestion having knocked the wind out of his sails somewhat.

"I don't know. I just woke up this morning and knew I wanted to be married to you, as soon as possible. If that's what you still want."

Jim said nothing as he reached across Tasha to the computer keyboard and quickly typed something.

"Pick a flight baby." He grinned at her.

"Really?" she asked with a mixture of excitement and nervousness.

"You betcha. We're going to Vegas to get married just like I said we would." He was beyond smug.

"But this is my idea," she insisted.

"No way. Vegas was always my idea, even before I met you," he insisted. "When do you want to do this?"

Tasha looked at the dates of flights before them on the screen and shrugged. "Maybe Friday or Saturday. Do we need to do anything to arrange a wedding?"

"Dunno, but I know a wedding planner who will," replied Jim, grabbing his phone.

"No." Tasha took his phone from him.

"Change of heart, honey?" Jim stroked the nape of Tasha's neck, needing her to be sure of this.

"No, but can we talk it all through and then if we need to, we can call Kayla and if not, we can keep it to ourselves?"

"Sure, we can, over breakfast, come on." He got to his feet, put her down on hers then led her to the kitchen where he proceeded to cook some bacon and scrambled eggs.

Once sitting at the table in the privacy of the dining room, Jim opened up wedding conversation with a grin, "So, Natasha, talk me through our wedding."

"Initially, I was thinking just the two of us grabbing the next flight to Vegas, but I don't want anyone to be upset by not being there, like Pippa and Lizzie."

"So, what are you saying, that we bring them all out to elope with us?" asked Jim seriously.

"It seems to defeat the object if we do that and then we need everyone to be available. No, that's not what I want." She sighed.

"Hey, that's cool with me and I am sure everyone will understand our reasons."

"We could do the big thing at the vineyard as a reception for everyone. Lizzie and Pippa could wear their dresses at least," said Tasha thoughtfully.

"Okay. What about witnesses? There are plenty of people in Vegas who would oblige," Jim told her.

Shaking her head, she looked up from her plate. "Hear me out and if you think it's an awful idea we'll go with strangers off the street."

"Go on."

"What about taking Bobby and Abby with us to act as witnesses. Bobby and you are obviously close and Abby is probably the nearest thing I have to a friend out here, except for Juan."

"I'll call Bobby later and invite them over and we can check if they're free." Smiled Jim.

"You think that's okay?" she asked nervously.

"Tasha, I think it's a brilliant idea, baby, and if anyone objects then tough because it's our wedding and our life, isn't it?" He took her hand across the table.

"Yeah, but I would hate to upset any of our family members."

"Look, let's sort the logistics then meet with Kayla and discuss the vineyard idea. We can even tell everyone that it's our wedding, but have a blessing of some sort as you'll already be Mrs Maybury by then." He grinned, the grin increasing as he said Mrs Maybury.

"Okay, Mr Maybury," she replied, grinning back at him.

****

"That young black guy on the gate is very, very pretty," were the first words Abby spoke the following morning as she came rushing through the hall to the back of the house where Tasha was getting up to greet her. "Hey, sit down and tell me why Bobby is meeting me here this afternoon?" she asked bluntly making Tasha laugh as Alexi came into view with Sandra.

"Hi, are you better?" asked the little girl, understandably nervous having witnessed Tasha's meltdown at the vineyard.

"Yes, much better, thank you." She felt relieved when Alexi

relaxed as she hugged her.

Alexi sat between her mother and Tasha. "Travis said I could ride with him today."

"Yeah, Uncle Jim said you were going to put Travis through his paces." Laughed Tasha as Travis appeared at the back door.

"Morning, beautiful ladies, and you, Abby."

His smirk and Abby's sneer made Tasha laugh.

"Screw you little, cousin," spat Abby seriously, making Tasha laugh more.

"Back at you, Abs. Alexi, let's get saddled up," he said to the little girl before turning to Tasha. "How you doing, Tasha? Security are really intense, aren't they?"

"I'm fine thanks, and if by intense you mean they ask a million questions before they'll even check for your name on their very exclusive list, then yes, they are intense."

Watching Lexi head out with Travis, Tasha turned her attention to Abby. "What's the story with Travis? I've asked Jim but he's very vague."

"He is my cousin. My mom's sister married a Texan rancher and moved south, Travis is their youngest son. He's a good guy, but a little dumb, especially where love is concerned. He was seeing a local girl who cheated on him with his friend and when he found out, he went berserk. He loved and trusted her, both of them. Anyway, he kicked off big time and beat his friend to a pulp."

"Really?" Tasha struggled to picture Travis out of control like that.

"Hell yeah! He ended up in jail on assault charges and Bobby represented him in court and cut a deal; if he found a job and someone to vouch for him, he stayed out of jail."

"Jim?" Tasha wondered if he wanted to rescue or save every underdog he came across, like her.

"Yes, Jim. He'd met Trav a few times when he'd visited us and liked him well enough and felt sorry for him. Bobby explained the deal he thought he could make to keep Trav out of jail and he offered immediately. He did need someone to look after the stables when he bought the house I guess, but he only had about four horses at the time, for the kids. That was about four years ago and Trav has been here ever since and built the stables up."

"Jim does love a cause, doesn't he?" asked Tasha but not necessarily requiring a reply, although Abby gave her one.

"I think that's Maisie's influence, the innate need to overcome injustice. Bobby would have made a fabulous D.A. but he wants to defend not prosecute and Jim has always sided with victims rather than bullies, except for when he was cheating on his wives I guess." Abby regretted her final comment as she saw Tasha's face change. "God, Tasha, I didn't mean that to sound like it did, sorry."

"It's fine. I kind of get what you mean and I love that he wants people to be treated fairly, but I do sometimes worry that he fell in love with the idea of saving me," Tasha admitted warily.

"I don't know that he realised you were a victim when he fell in love with you. He called Bobby on the Sunday morning to discuss how overwhelmed he was by his feelings for you," Abby revealed, rendering Tasha almost speechless.

She paused and wondered how much Abby knew of that conversation and how much she'd reveal when the sound of the front door closing made Tasha jump nervously until she heard Lizzie's voice.

"Tash."

"In here," replied Tasha, still a little nervous and jumpy.

"Hey," cried Lizzie as she rushed over to Tasha where she hugged her firmly. "Could we hang out while Daddy's at work?"

"Who's we?" asked Tasha curiously.

"Me, Dylan, Danielle and Rory," replied Lizzie.

"Who's Rory?" interrupted Abby.

"He's the boy that Danielle likes," whispered Lizzie with a giggle that Tasha reciprocated, unlike Abby.

"And how did you get him past security?" asked Abby sternly.

"We told them he was Josh who is on their list and they know me and as I was with that Ray guy from security..." she said proudly.

Tasha didn't see a problem, unlike Abby who explained

Lizzie's mistake.

"You know that your dad is going to freak when he finds out you've invited a complete stranger to the house and done so by lying and deceiving the security that is in place to keep you all safe, especially Tasha, and by doing all of this you have now compromised her safety."

"It wasn't like that. He's just a guy from the year above us at school. Daddy probably knows him," protested Lizzie, thinking her aunt was being deliberately awkward.

"Just a guy who hasn't had his credentials or those of his family checked out. I don't fancy your chances of getting your dad onside with that argument, Lizzie." Abby sounded almost cross with Lizzie's naivety.

"We won't tell him." Lizzie still didn't understand Abby's obvious concerns and thought she was overstepping the mark on what did and didn't concern her now.

"You may not, but we, or at least I have to. What if something happens or if Rory tells a friend who tells a friend who tells a friend who tells someone who is a threat to Tasha how easy it was to compromise security here?" asked Abby, growing incredibly frustrated with Lizzie and Tasha, who so far had voiced no concerns about the deceit used to get this unknown boy into the house.

"Don't you think you're overreacting slightly?" asked Tasha now.

Abby shook her head. Okay, so she'd wanted Tasha to speak up but this was not the intervention she was hoping for so went straight for the jugular. "Maybe, but this is not my call, it's Jim's."

"Abby, no. This is the first time Jim has left me in weeks and he'll be back for lunch, so if he has to know we can tell him then, but for now we might be better keeping all the kids together where we can see them. If there's a problem this place is swarming with security." Tasha saw a steely quality in Abby she'd never seen before and knew she was going to be immoveable in her viewpoint.

"You need to call someone up here to the house, to be on hand."

"Abby—" Tasha hoped to find a compromise but her soon-to-be sister-in-law cut her off.

"That's my final offer or I call Jim and fill him in and he gets to deal with this now," retorted Abby who Tasha had no doubt was more than a match for a Maybury man.

"Fine." Tasha pouted while Lizzie nervously mouthed *thank you* to Tasha before fetching her friends through.

They all paraded through the lounge and headed out back towards the pool with muted, *hey* and *hi* to Tasha and Abby. The newest member of the crowd didn't look like he was a danger to Tasha or anyone else. He looked a typical teenager; tall, gangly and awkward. He stared at Tasha for a fraction too long making her feel as awkward as he looked. Sensing it, the blond haired, blue eyed boy blushed and then spoke.

"Sorry, Miss Winters—I—erm—remember seeing you in pantomime a couple of years ago in Bournemouth." He blushed deeper.

Tasha smiled. "You don't sound like you're from Bournemouth."

"No. I'm a true Angeleno but my mom is English so we sometimes spend holidays over there. You were an awesome Cinderella." His words seemed to confuse the others.

"We have a tradition in the U.K. of live shows retelling fairy tales at Christmas time, pantomime, and it appears Rory saw me in one a couple of years ago," Tasha explained to nods and frowns from the others.

"Come on," called Lizzie as Tasha's phone rang.

She saw it was Angie and after exchanging pleasantries she wandered down to Jim's office to discuss business with Angie who had chosen to call Tasha when it was four in the morning for her to ensure her sleep wasn't disturbed.

Tasha returned to find Sandra and Abby both in the kitchen preparing some lunch.

"You okay?" asked Abby concerned.

"Uh? Yeah, fine, thanks," replied Tasha, distracted suddenly.

Tasha joined the other two women in the kitchen and began to chop some salad leaves and as the food was ready to serve Lizzie appeared with her friends.

"We're heading off then, Tash." She barely paused and expected no objections.

"No chance," said Abby bluntly.

"What? Why?" Lizzie was already preparing to argue.

"Because your dad will be here soon and I'm sure he'll want to speak to you," replied Abby, standing toe to toe with Lizzie while Tasha watched on. Yeah, she was more than a match for a Maybury, any of them, all of them.

"Tash!" Lizzie cried but Tasha knew Abby was right and suddenly felt tired at the prospect of a fight, with Lizzie or Abby and definitely with Jim.

"Abby's right. You're all welcome to stay for lunch though." Tasha avoided Lizzie's glare.

"I could just walk out, you can't stop me," shouted Lizzie.

"You could try, but I would call security before you had descended the front steps and then your dad." Tasha spoke with firmness, deciding enough was enough. "You made a choice this morning Lizzie, a poor one, not to mention deceitful so now you need to face the consequences of that."

"Tash, I'm sorry, I didn't think." Lizzie hugged Tasha. "You know I love you."

Tasha hugged her back and smiled at Abby who was watching the exchange with a roll of her eyes. Feeling her resolve melting Tasha was tempted to send Lizzie and her friends on their way, but Abby seemed to sense this and intervened.

"Maybe you need to explain that to your dad then."

"Yes," agreed Tasha. "He'll be back soon and you know what your dad's like, he'll want to know."

"He'll want to know what?" asked Jim who had entered the house in silence and was now standing next to Tasha with an arm slipping around her waist as he kissed her gently on the head followed by Bobby who looked on confused by all the people standing around the kitchen.

Sandra said a quick hello before excusing herself and looked relieved to be leaving. Tasha watched her back getting farther away and envied her ability to slip out when things looked set to get awkward or fraught.

"Come on, what will I want to know?" repeated Jim.

Tasha felt sick at his possible reaction, but more at the embarrassment Lizzie might feel if he found out while her friends watched on.

"Lizzie and I will explain later, but lunch is ready, and I've invited Lizzie's friends to join us if they want to," Tasha said a little too lightly and high pitched judging by Jim's suspicious expression.

"Hmmm," was his only response.

Lizzie looked relieved and clearly had no intention of staying and spending any more time with them than she had to. "No offence, but could we eat outside and use the pool, rather than eating with you?"

"Sure," Tasha agreed immediately and was glad when Travis and Lexi appeared.

"Daddy," the little girl called as she propelled across the room and into Bobby's open arms.

Tasha suddenly felt sad and emotional that she had never had that reaction to her own father, ever. Noticing the change in her body language Jim pulled her tighter towards him and stroked her bare shoulders briefly.

"I'm going to get changed." He headed for the stairs and called to his brother, "Do you want to ditch the suit, Bobby?"

Bobby kissed his daughter then his wife before following Jim upstairs.

"You are too soft on Lizzie and if you don't tell Jim about this morning before I leave here today then I will. I have to," said Abby seriously.

"I don't want her to be in trouble in front of her friends, but we'll tell him," Tasha assured the other woman.

"Abs, can Lexi spend the afternoon with me too? I even have a picnic ready for lunch," said Travis from behind them.

"Please, Mommy, say yes," pleaded the little girl excitedly.

"Sure." Abby kissed her daughter and sent her back to the stables with Travis leaving just Abby, Bobby, Jim and Tasha to lunch together in the dining room.

Once Bobby closed the bedroom door behind him, he grinned at his younger twin brother who was already discarding his work wear and heading into the bathroom. Bobby stood out on the balcony and watched the kids poolside and wondered what all the whispering was about.

Jim returned to the bedroom wrapped in a towel. "Bathroom's all yours if you want to freshen up and I'll grab you some sweats and a t-shirt."

"Thanks. Is everything okay downstairs, with the kids and Tasha?"

"I think so, although something has obviously happened." Jim passed Bobby some clothes.

"Tasha looks well though, considering, after the other night." Bobby looked around the bedroom and laughed.

"What?" asked Jim confused.

"If you were showing me round your crib it would be about now that you'd say *this is where the magic happens*." Laughed Bobby, making Jim laugh too.

"You have too much time on your hands if that is what you've come up with." Jim pulled his track bottoms on.

"She's okay, though, Tasha? And you and Tasha, right?" Bobby sounded worried.

"Yeah, she's good, still a bit freaked out by everything that's happened, but we talked and we—well, I don't need to draw you a diagram. We're good, thanks."

"I'd really like to see a diagram if you have one though." Grinned Bobby.

"No chance," shouted Jim as he threw his wet towel in the direction of his brother's face.

Chapter Seven

Tasha had almost forgotten the reason for inviting Bobby and Abby over together until after lunch when Jim said, "Tasha and I have been talking about the wedding, our wedding."

"You haven't had a change of heart then?" Bobby laughed at his own joke, making Tasha laugh too as she shook her head.

"No, quite the opposite."

"We are going to Vegas, at the weekend or early next week and we were hoping you'd both be free," said Jim.

Abby let out a loud squeal making Tasha smile and Jim and Bobby wince.

"We haven't told anyone else," Jim said, thinking Abby holding this in for the next week was a big ask.

"And we're not going to, not until afterwards," explained Tasha, on the same wavelength as her fiancé.

"We thought we may get Kayla to organise what everyone would believe is our wedding at the vineyard, but it will be more of a reception." Jim smiled thinking he and Tasha were almost like a tag team sharing the details.

"We're in. I'm sure Maisie will happily take care of Alexi for a few days or my parents," cried Abby excitedly.

"If not, you could bring her, but we were hoping to keep it quiet," said Tasha, hoping her subtle reminders would ensure Abby kept a lid on the news.

"Let me check my schedule, but I think I can square it." Bobby smiled broadly, glad to see his brother and his wife-to-be looking genuinely happy.

Both women smiled across at each other, struggling to

contain their excitement while Bobby simply raised an eyebrow that his brother had indeed gone with the joke plan of ensnaring lucky seven quickly then taking her to Vegas before she changed her mind, although Bobby couldn't blame Jim. Why wouldn't he want to marry Tasha? She was bright, funny and off the scale gorgeous, plus she got his brother in ways his previous wives never had. She made him happy in ways none of the others even came close to. He then turned his attention to his own wife who was giggling like a schoolgirl with Tasha. Abby looked vibrant and sexy as hell with her throaty laugh and excited clapping. Remembering his own previous marriages, he frowned. He should have waited for Abby to come into his life, like Jim wished he'd waited for Tasha, but then neither of them knew that what they'd previously felt wasn't enough, wasn't the real deal. It certainly hadn't been for Bobby and he knew that with the exception of Sara nothing had ever come close for his brother either. It was his brother that interrupted his inner musings by changing the topic to the morning at home while he'd been at work.

"So, what have you two been up to all morning?" Jim looked across at Tasha.

"Nothing much, just chatting really, catching up."

"What's with the new horny teenage boy in my house?" asked Jim seriously.

"A friend of Lizzie's," replied Tasha calmly.

"Who? What's his name? Who ran him through security?"

"Ah." Tasha nervously looked across at Abby now. Abby who had been spot on about his reaction to anyone new entering the house.

"Tell him," encouraged Abby.

"Tell me what? Is this what I walked in on earlier, in the kitchen?"

"Yes." Tasha's confirmation came in a low whisper. "Promise me you'll stay calm and not say anything to Lizzie in front of her friends."

"Just tell me what has happened," ordered Jim impatiently.

"Not until you promise. Promise me, please. I don't want her to be embarrassed by you in front of her friends."

"Tasha!" Jim's impatience had turned into annoyance.

"Promise me. I'm begging you. I know how embarrassing it is to be in trouble with a parent in front of other people—"

He cut her off as he took her hand in his. "I promise. Just tell me, baby, I'm getting scared here."

Tasha explained how Rory happened to be in the house and the tactics Lizzie had used to gain his entry through security. Abby looked on and exchanged several glances with Bobby as Tasha not only recounted events, but defended Lizzie's actions at every opportunity to Jim's and Abby's annoyance.

"I think my daughter and I need to talk." Crossly, Jim got to his feet, preparing to pursue Lizzie, determined to get some answers and dish out some kind of chastisement for breaking his rules by breaching security.

"No!" Tasha leapt up too. "You promised."

"Fine," he huffed, clearly regretting his earlier promise. "But at least let's go and find out who the hell this boy is."

Sitting poolside, the four children were laughing as Tasha, Jim, Bobby and Abby joined them.

"Hey, Daddy," smiled Lizzie as she looked up into the shade that Jim standing over her had created.

"Hey, sweetie. Nice to see you again Danielle, Dylan," he said before turning to Rory. "And you are?"

"Rory, Mr Maybury, sir," he replied nervously.

"And do you have a surname, Rory?" Jim smiled, putting the boy at ease while Lizzie began to shift very nervously, understanding why her father had approached them. He knew what she'd done.

"Yes, sorry, sir, Rory Di Marco."

"Di Marco? Any relation to Gina?" asked Jim.

"She's my mom," smiled the boy broadly.

"The Gina Di Marco?" Tasha stood open mouthed.

"Yes, honey." Jim turned back to Rory briefly. "How is she? I can see you take after her. I think you were only about seven the last time I saw you. And your dad, how's he doing?"

"Good, thanks. Dad is overseas shooting," started Rory then laughed. "For your studio so I guess you knew that."

Jim grinned. "Say hi to your parents." With Tasha's hand

tucked in his, he led her back into the house followed by Bobby and Abby.

"Oh my God! Rory's parents are Gina and Paolo Di Marco," Tasha squealed making Jim laugh.

"Yes."

"I know but *the* Gina and Paolo Di Marco," reiterated Tasha, adding far too many e's on her *the*.

"Yes honey, *the* Gina and Paolo Di Marco, the same Paolo Di Marco who could have been shooting you in Morocco right now if you'd taken me up on my offer to fill in for my pregnant leading lady," Jim told her.

"No way. Fuck! Why didn't you tell me that?" she cried and found herself pulled into his grip and held firmly against him.

"Baby, we both know you would still have said no." He stared down at her darkly.

"I think I would probably have told you to go and screw yourself," she said defiantly, but more so making reference to their first night together. She shrieked as she realised Jim's hand had landed squarely across her behind.

"Jimbo, get a frickin room!" cried Bobby laughing.

"We have a room, a house full of them and people in each of them, so for now, Natasha, we will focus on flights to Vegas." He grinned before heading off to his office followed by Abby, then Tasha and finally Bobby.

Bobby pulled Tasha back and once he was sure they were alone he awkwardly began to speak. "Can I have a word, Tasha, in private?"

"Yes, of course." She pointed towards the dining room and wondered what he might want with her. What he was going to say that couldn't be said in front of Jim.

Once the door was shut behind them, Bobby turned to face her and although he was smiling he looked less than happy. "There's no easy was to say this Tasha, so…I've had a call from a public defender, the one who is representing your dad."

"What? Why?"

"He knows that your dad needs a good defence attorney if he stands any chance of getting a lenient sentence or even acquitted so when he figured that your Mr Maybury is my brother he made contact to see if you were in a position to assist or at least visit him." Bobby sighed. He knew one way or another this would mess with Tasha's head and cause something of a shit storm, especially as there was no way Jim would agree to her visiting the man responsible for almost killing her, never mind bank rolling his defence.

"He wants me to pay for a good attorney? No, correction, he wants Jim to pay for one."

Bobby nodded.

"And this public defender thinks that if I meet with him he can persuade me?" Tasha felt conflicted and confused.

"No, you misunderstand. He wants you to visit with your dad," clarified Bobby to a stunned Tasha.

"Shit!"

"Yup. I will come with you to visit him if you want me to but only if you speak to Jim first and he agrees," said Bobby firmly.

"Have you told him?" Before Bobby had a chance to respond she answered her own question, "As he isn't currently screaming and shouting with a scowl on his face, you obviously haven't. Will you stay while I tell him, please?" There was a note of pleading in her voice.

"Sure thing." He smiled before opening the dining room door to usher Tasha out whilst pulling his phone from his pocket.

By the time they reached Jim's office Bobby had cleared his schedule for Monday, Tuesday and Wednesday.

"We thought you two had got lost." Jim looked across at them suspiciously.

"I've cleared everything from Saturday until Thursday." Bobby ignored his brother's comment.

"Then we need to book some flights and plan a wedding." Jim smacked his hands together loudly. "Baby, get your ass over here and choose a flight," he called to Tasha who happily settled into Jim's lap in front of his computer where he wrapped his arms around her tightly.

"So when are we going to Vegas?" squealed an excited Abby, making Tasha laugh.

"Abby, you do remember that this is a secret you're in on, don't you?" Jim frowned and shot Bobby a *keep your wife in check* look.

"Honey, you need to calm down," said Bobby gently as he took the chair next to his wife. "So, Tasha, when are we going?" he asked, deflecting attention from Abby.

"Sunday morning and then we could get married on Monday and stay for a couple of days if you fancy?" Tasha grinned at the others around her.

"That is a plan, Natasha." Jim selected their tickets and booked their flights, having never felt happier than he did at that second. "Now we need to find a hotel and decide where we're getting married."

Loading possible venues and accommodation via a search engine Tasha frowned at all of the packages popping up on the screen.

"What?" asked Jim studying her expression.

"This all seems superfluous," she pouted. "Why would you want a limo to drive along the strip of whatever it's called, or chocolate dipped strawberries in your room? Look, there! They have a staircase for *that special romantic photo opportunity*," she read from the screen disparagingly.

"You don't want a special romantic photo opportunity?" Bobby scratched his head in confusion.

"But it's like something from Gone with the Wind," gushed Abby, making Tasha frown more.

"If I wanted a staircase, I would be getting married at home in some manor house or stately home, not in the most garish, tacky place on Earth," cried Tasha as the others stared at her, all of them confused now.

"Way to sell it, baby," said Jim with a wry smile.

Turning in his lap to face him, Tasha hoped he wasn't reconsidering running off to get married because she'd now spoiled it.

"It is what it is, Vegas, and I love the idea of us getting married there. It's fitting for us, this whole whirlwind thing we've been caught up in. Plus, we each have responsibilities meaning I like the idea of doing this for us with Kayla organising the reception for everyone else. I wasn't saying that our wedding or our marriage will be garish or tacky, just Vegas, so all we need is a hotel to stay in and a guy dressed as Elvis to marry us." Tasha wedged her knees each side of Jim's thighs, reached up and ran her fingers through his hair and pressed down into his groin forgetting that Abby and Bobby were still there. "Oh," she bit down into her lip. "Make sure the hotel room has a very big and comfy bed because I have no intention of leaving it unless I really have to."

"Honey, I may even tie you to the damned bed," he replied knowing she was desperate for that.

"Then make sure it is big, comfy and suitable to be tied down on."

She grinned at him, relishing the pinch of his hands that held her hips against him slightly too firmly. He was so handsome and as much as she desired him it was the sudden feeling of overwhelming love that made her lean in to kiss him. The sound of Abby's laughter surprised them both judging by how they both jumped.

"It's a good job we are so broad minded." She laughed, watching Tasha blush.

With a shake of her head as she glanced across at Bobby, Abby laughed again at her overexcited friend and her amused husband. Turning to her he gave her a grin, not a smile but a full on grin as he reached for her hand that he took in his causing her pulse to quicken. With a quirk of his eyebrow and a small wink she was melting. She knew exactly what that look meant making her wonder if she too could get away with leaping into his lap or finding a room.

"You need to take lots of cold showers, both of you, separately," smirked Bobby, his attention back on his brother and Tasha, although he still kept Abby's hand tucked in his. "But please tone this down when my daughter is in the vicinity," he said more seriously.

"Sorry," replied Tasha turning back on Jim's lap so she faced them and the computer screen but found herself distracted by the erection she'd aroused in him that was currently pressing into her behind.

"Right then." Jim deliberately flexed beneath her making her smile. "You really want to do the Elvis thing? Isn't this just how

I said it was going to be?" he asked rhetorically as he reached around Tasha and found Elvis weddings.

Scrolling down, Tasha stopped at one. "I like the look of him, book him if he's free."

"Just like that, based on a thumbnail?" asked Jim.

"Just like that. Hotel," she said, thinking that was all they needed to arrange.

"Leave that one with me, honey. We have flights and a wedding booked, baby, so as of just after three p.m. on Monday we will be married."

Abby and Tasha immediately began to clap and then laughed in stereo making them laugh more.

"Jimbo, we have a week of this ahead of us," smiled Bobby, shaking his head at his brother.

"I know." Wearing a smile, Jim lovingly held Tasha as Lizzie appeared in the doorway.

"Hey Daddy, we're heading off—"

He cut her off. "I don't think so, Lizzie. You and I need to talk before you go anywhere, sweetie." Jim spoke with a gentle but firm tone that told her it was non-negotiable.

Lizzie stared at him briefly and even opened her mouth as if she was considering speaking, offering an argument against it, but said nothing before turning on her heels, presumably re-planning her afternoon.

"Don't be mean to her, please," said Tasha with knots in her stomach that Lizzie may be in trouble for bringing a friend home.

"Tasha, I'm not discussing this with you, but if you would all excuse me for a while," he said standing, putting them both on their feet.

"Come on," called Abby as she grabbed Tasha's arm. "Let's go and see how Lexi is getting on with Travis."

"Okay," agreed Tasha, reluctantly. Suddenly she noticed Bobby giving her a visual nudge.

She mouthed a *later,* thinking Jim was going to flip out at the idea of her father making contact and that would not be conducive to him not being mean to Lizzie who had just reappeared with her friends who she was seeing out.

"Bobby, come on, Lexi will be stoked to see us both watching her." Abby took her husband's hand while her other one was still holding Tasha's arm.

"Lizzie, let's go outside," suggested Jim, leading his daughter out to the pool.

****

Having walked down to the stables they watched Lexi grooming a horse, chatting away to him while Travis guided her through each step of the process. Leaning against the fence alongside Abby and Bobby, Tasha found herself grinning as she watched the little girl smiling and laughing without a care in the world and tried to recall the nearest she'd ever got to that carefree, content feeling and was unsure if she ever had before meeting Jim. Even now, after her accident, when she still had so many thoughts and feelings rushing around her head, when she was at home with Jim, just the two of them, a contentment washed over her like it never had before they'd met. He centred her, acted as an anchor and allowed her to feel all of the positive feelings rather than only the negatives, although the negative ones were still there, just not as loud.

"I can't believe you could have had anything you'd wanted for your wedding and you chose, Elvis," interrupted Abby, nudging the other woman.

"What can I say? It doesn't matter where, it's who, plus I'm number seven on Jim's list of brides so..."

"So what?" asked Abby confused.

"Where did you get married?" asked Tasha.

"We went to The Bahamas and got married on the beach, it was very romantic." She grinned.

"Nice, and where did you marry the first twice?" Tasha turned to Bobby who was on the other side of her.

"Church first time and a hotel second time," he replied without missing a beat it seemed.

"So why didn't you get married in a church or a hotel, Abby?" Tasha was sure she heard the penny drop in her friend's head when she figured it.

"Ah."

"Exactly. I was limited on places if I didn't want to be forever compared to a predecessor or at least their wedding to my husband and that Vegas thing was there from the first day I met Jim. It just seems fitting."

"But you could have had Caesar's Palace, The Venetian or Donald Trump's place, anything you'd wanted, Jim would have gone with." Abby still wasn't quite getting the Elvis thing.

"I neither need nor want any of those places with limos and chocolate covered strawberries in my room. I want to marry Jim, as soon as is reasonably possible and whilst I feel bad for my family and Lizzie and Philip it's for me and Jim, unique to us. Oh, I don't know, it probably doesn't make sense to you, but it does to me, I think." Grinned Tasha as Bobby spoke.

"I get you, Tasha. It's about you and Jimbo, and you need it to be your wedding, how you want it, with no distractions or dramas and you deserve that. I'm not saying our folks and Lizzie and Phil won't be disappointed, but they'll get over it and be happy for you." He smiled then kissed Tasha's cheek. "You need to tell him what I told you though," he whispered discreetly.

Nodding, they were joined by Lexi and Travis, ending their conversation.

****

As they approached the house again, Tasha immediately noticed Lizzie who looked a little less exuberant, but still poolside, as was Jim.

"Hey, Lizzie." Tasha called softly as she put a hand on the girl's shoulder and leaning into her ear asked, "Are you okay?"

Looking up, Lizzie smiled weakly and shrugged as Tasha wedged herself next to her on the lounger where she lay.

"Daddy was very angry with me for lying to get Rory into the house."

"Oh dear," empathised Tasha as she became aware of Jim and Abby watching them.

"He threatened to ground me, for the rest of the summer and he said that if I ever sneak anybody into the house again he will ground me forever, cancel my phone and stop my allowance." She looked devastated at the thought of it, but totally convinced he'd follow through with all of the threats made, Tasha wasn't convinced he would, although...

"Oh dear," repeated Tasha, stifling a small smile.

"He loves you, Tasha." Lizzie sounded surprised at the realisation making Tasha laugh rather than smile.

"I know," she acknowledged.

"No, I don't think you do." Lizzie leaned in closer to explain, "I have always been Daddy's favourite person in the world, well, me and Philip, and his other wives, including Mom always came second to us, but you come first Tasha, above me and Philip." Her voice carried a mixture of shock and upset.

"I think the thing with my crash and being hurt has sent him into extra crazy where I'm concerned, but the security is for us all Lizzie; me, you and Philip, to keep us all safe," she said reassuringly as she took Lizzie's hand in hers. "I don't know what it was like with his other wives, but I do know that nothing and no one could ever be more important than you and Philip, ever. The way he loves you two is very different to how he loves me, so maybe he loves us the same amount, but different in the way he actually loves us. Does that make sense?" asked Tasha nervously, as she thought that running off to get married without her and Philip could make Lizzie question her father's feelings for her further.

"Thank you, Tasha. I do love you and I'm sorry for not thinking about bringing Rory here." She hugged Tasha tightly. "And thank you for not letting Daddy go off while my friends were here."

"No problem, Lizzie. I love you too, you know, you and Philip and I'm glad that I get to share your dad with you."

Tasha kissed Lizzie before she walked over to where Jim was talking to Bobby and Abby.

"The sight of you two conspiring chills me to the bone," said Jim with an arched brow.

"I resent the inference in that sentiment, Mr Maybury." Tasha pouted as she sat between Jim and Abby.

"I am not convinced, Natasha." He smirked before asking with concern, "Is Lizzie, okay?"

"Kind of. She seems genuinely sorry for compromising your security here and I really don't think she saw that she was doing any wrong," explained Tasha to a frowning Abby, a smiling

Bobby and a serious looking Jim.

"But that's the biggest issue, honey, she doesn't think, a bit like you," he added with a smile.

"Yes, well, she also thinks that you love me more than her and Philip." Sighed Tasha.

"I hope you told her to grow up and stop being so spoilt," snapped Abby, shocking the others.

Tasha noticed Jim glaring slightly at Abby before firing a warning glance at Bobby.

"No. I was a little more tactful and empathetic to her feelings than that," said Tasha to a doubtful looking Abby. Smiling at the other woman Tasha tried to explain, "Look, this can't be easy for her; she is a hormone filled teenager who lives across two houses with a stepfather who openly disapproves of most things she likes and a father who by his own admission allows her to have anything she wants so long as it's safe and appropriate. She has had five stepmothers who seem to have been very different from her own mother and each other but who all knew that she was beyond their remit and she manipulated them and their situation to her own advantage. Eventually she gets it all straight in her head and no stepmother to contend with and bang! I turn up and from day one everybody is saying I'm different, which I guess I am; I'm foreign, I'm close in age to her, I have a sibling her age and I am struggling to fit into my role here, but the one thing she had to hang onto was that she, she and Philip were still number one on Jim's list. Then she sees things that tell her she's not, I am, and whilst I know I'm not, she doesn't. So, what I actually told her was that I believed her father loved us all the same amount, me, her and Phil, but in different ways."

Bobby grinned across at her while Jim just stared at her, almost in awe, while Abby said nothing, her expression betraying nothing of her thoughts.

"Oh, and I told her we have seriously hot sex that clouds her father's judgement," Tasha added dryly.

"Tasha, please tell me you didn't." Jim looked horrified and a little afraid until Tasha laughed.

"No, of course not. You are so easy to wind up."

"That is gonna cost you, baby," he replied flatly making her smile until Bobby caught her attention by mouthing *tell him*.

"Lizzie," she called. "Abby and I are going shopping tomorrow, but she's clueless about where I need to go, so I was wondering if you fancied it?" Tasha knew Lizzie already had plans to go out with her friend Danielle for the day.

"I can't!" cried Lizzie disappointed. "Deanna is taking us out." She pouted and frowned.

"Don't worry, we can go next week, but would you find me the best places to go for some shoes and clothes? You know the kind of things I like. Maybe you could email me the details."

"Sure thing. Daddy can I use your computer, I've left my laptop and iPad at Mom's?"

"Sure, sweetie," he called to her.

"My iPad is on the bed if you prefer." Smiled Tasha.

"Okay," cried Lizzie running into the house.

"What are you up to?" asked Abby.

Ignoring her, Tasha turned to face Jim and took a very deep breath. "There's something you need to know, but I need you not to go completely ape."

"Go on." Jim bristled as he sat more upright.

"I've had a message, through Bobby from my dad's public defender—" was as far as she got before Jim leapt to his feet and replied in just one word.

"No!"

"Jim, please let me finish. He wants to know if I'll visit my dad, to what end I'm not sure, but the defender knows he needs a good defence attorney if he stands any chance of getting a lenient sentence or acquitted. He contacted Bobby with a message when he figured that you two were brothers to see if I was in a position to assist or at least visit him." She hoped she'd remembered correctly what Bobby had told her earlier.

"And you have told him to go fuck himself!" snapped Jim and although unsure whether it was a recommendation or a question Tasha shook her head.

"I haven't said anything. I wanted to talk to you first and as Bobby knows the legal stuff—"

"You thought you'd tackle me together," he accused angrily. "You know what I'm going to say, Tasha. There's nothing to discuss, and you—" he turned to Bobby "—I can't believe you would do this, bring this to my fiancée, in my home and not even mention it to me first." Anger, frustration and fear rolled off him as his face contorted through the rollercoaster of emotions he was trying to temper.

"Jimbo, I couldn't discuss it with you first because you would have said, *screw him and don't tell Tasha* and I'm obliged to tell her."

They all sat silently for several long minutes.

It was Bobby who eventually broke the silence. "You two need to discuss this together, but I've said I'll be at your disposal, legally, both of you. Abby, come on, we'll go down for Lexi and leave you guys to it. Call me later, yeah?" He looked at his younger twin.

"Yeah, whatever," replied Jim tightly as Lizzie appeared with sheets of paper.

"These are the best places Tash. I've emailed them too. I'm really bummed I can't come with you, but I can't cancel on Danielle now." Lizzie let out a long, loud sigh, feeling disappointed that she was missing out on what she perceived as spending time with Tasha and a shopping spree.

"It's fine and we'll go another time," reassured Tasha, knowing that the *shopping trip* had only ever been a means to get rid of Lizzie.

Bobby turned to his niece, "You going back to your mom's tonight, Lizzie?"

"Yeah, I should be going soon." She looked at her watch.

"We can drop you home, if that's okay with your dad?" asked Bobby looking across at a very annoyed looking Jim.

"Sure," he snapped and then looking at Lizzie, stood and smiled. "Tell Deanna to call me, about your trip out tomorrow." He pulled Lizzie to him and embraced her warmly. "Have fun, I love you," he said as he leaned down and kissed her, resulting in her grinning warmly at him.

"I love you too, Daddy, and you Tash. Okay, let's go Uncle Bobby." She grabbed her uncle's arm and headed down towards the stables.

"Jim," Tasha started as the others disappeared.

"Tasha, no. We'll talk later but I'm struggling to get my head around this right now. I need to go and book a hotel." He leapt to his feet and stalked towards the house.

"Jim," she called after him, unsure how to proceed or whether he was mad with her or her dad.

"Baby, please. Just give me some time," he said more gently, turning to face her.

"Please don't be mad at me for this," she pleaded making him frown and shake his head.

"I'm not mad at you. I'm really pissed that he thinks he has any right to ask for help from us after all he's done to you and the fact that you're even considering it confuses me, but I kind of love that you're thinking about it because it makes you you. The same you that stopped me speaking to Lizzie and embarrassing her in front of her friends." He walked back towards her. "And you that also reassured my little girl that no matter how pissed I am at her and how much I love you that she is still important to me, her and her brother." He pulled her to her feet and wrapped her in his arms. She slipped her arms around his waist, her hands beneath his clothes and inhaled deeply as the warmth of his skin warmed her whole body, inside and out.

"I really need to go and find us a hotel room to consummate our marriage, baby," he moaned as her fingers kneaded the flesh across his back down to his waistband.

"Now?" she moaned, looking up to find him staring down at her and smiling.

"It is quite urgent, honey, especially as we need a room for Bobby and Abby too, unless you want us all to share, but then I don't think my brother will want to witness me tying you to the bed and making you come over and over until you are begging to be fucked, although," he added, thinking back to Bobby's request for a diagram.

Tasha heard the sound that left her lips but was unsure whether it was a moan, a gasp, a sigh or a combination of all three, but whatever it was it made Jim smile.

"You have no idea how urgent this hotel room is, Tasha. I am going to make you do things you've never dreamt of and you will never forget," he pledged, darkly and mysteriously. "So, I am going to go and book our hotel and at some point we need to think of a honeymoon." He grinned before freeing himself from her grip and wandered back to the house a little lighter and more relaxed than he had been when he'd first begun his trip back indoors.

Thinking back to what Bobby had said about cold showers she wasn't actually sure there was a shower in the world cold enough to cool her ardour right now, so she needed a distraction and Lizzie's list of shops could provide her with that.

Chapter Eight

Tasha sat on the bed with her iPad when Jim appeared in the doorway.

"Busy?" he asked wryly, making her laugh.

"Shopping, so yes, very. I'm like a real housewife of Beverley Hills."

"Hardly, baby." He climbed onto the bed next to her. "What are you shopping for?" he asked curiously.

"I'm getting married next Monday so I may just need some odds and ends, maybe even a wedding ring." She grinned, making him grin too. "Oh, and my soon-to-be husband is a bit crazy, but richer than anyone I know and insists on paying for everything so I'm looking at very small, but expensive odds and ends."

"He sounds like a really great guy, this soon-to-be husband, but if you cast your mind back he already bought you a wedding ring." Jim closed her iPad case and put it on the floor.

"I meant a wedding ring for him. He's okay, though," replied Tasha. "If you like that sort of thing."

"And do you like that sort of thing, your soon-to-be husband in need of a wedding ring?" Jim lay on his side facing her.

"I guess he'll do until something better comes along." She flicked through the sheets of paper Lizzie had provided her with meaning she didn't see him move until he was over her and pulling the paper from her grasp, throwing them behind him.

"Hey, my shopping," she squealed and then began to shriek as he lowered over her, holding her head steady between his hands.

"I said, do you like that sort of thing?" he repeated, staring down at her darkly, making her remember just how much she wanted him.

"I love that sort of thing." She was desperate to feel his lips against hers.

"Good, because nothing and nobody else is ever going to come along for you, Tasha. You. Are. Mine. Forever," he told her, punctuating each word with nothing but sincerity in his voice as his hand made its way beneath the skirt of the strapless maxi dress she was wearing. Instinctively, she lowered herself down the bed and spread her thighs further making him smile. "You see, baby, mine."

"Yours." She moaned as his fingers bypassed the wet barrier of her black, lace thong and entered her with a gentle stroking motion.

"I really don't need a wedding ring, honey," he told her as he rotated his fingers inside her, stimulating her G-spot, making her buck beneath him.

"So greedy, Tasha," he chastised, but allowed his thumb to find her clitoris that he rubbed gently making her mewl and moan.

"Please, James, oh yes," she cried making him smile down at her.

"This is us forever, baby, just you and me. You know that, don't you?" he asked seriously.

After considering his question she answered, knowing that this was absolutely the right decision, like a moment of total clarity, possibly for the first time ever with total certainty she said, "Yes, forever."

Spurred on by her words and the conviction in her voice Jim brought her to a glorious climax involving her calling out to him as if he was lost and she was desperately searching for him. He proceeded to strip her off, then himself before lying down again between Tasha's open thighs. No further words were exchanged as something deeper, more meaningful passed between them with gentle love making rather than their more usual frantic sex.

Lying together naked and damp from perspiration, Jim considered her reference to him wearing a ring. "Do you want me to wear a wedding ring?"

Tasha shrugged, but said nothing.

"Come on, Tasha, you need to say what you want and you did raise the subject, so..."

"Yes, yes I would. Maybe I need you marked as mine as much as you need me branded," Tasha admitted. "And the fact that you have never worn one before..."

"Makes it a little more appealing, uh?"

"Yes. That makes me sound a little bit pathetic and very insecure, doesn't it?" She felt confused by the implication of that.

"No, baby, and I get that it must be tough to be viewed as the latest in a long line, well a line of seven. It looks like we're both going to be marked as you put it."

"Do I get to choose your ring as you have already chosen mine?" Her thoughts were suddenly filled with ideas about the ring he'd chosen for her and she hoped it wasn't too ostentatious.

Laughing, he rolled her over until she was straddling him and gazing down with a definite glint in her eyes.

"How could I possibly say no?" He grinned up at her. "You want to go shopping tomorrow?"

"I think I need to. I'll call Abby later to arrange the details."

"I can't do the morning," he told her matter of fact, making her frown down at him. "Is that a frown, baby? You know where they usually get you, don't ya?" He flipped her onto her back again so that he was over her and once more nestled between her thighs.

"That was not a frown, well, just a confused one. You are not coming shopping with us. It's just me and Abby for wedding kind of stuff, wedding night kind of stuff." She grinned as she reached up and ran a hand through his hair.

"And you know what size fingers I have?"

His question was innocent, but thinking about just how intimate she was with his fingers Tasha laughed.

"I know exactly what size your fingers are, James. Although I'm unsure if they could convert that to a ring measurement suitable for a shop assistant, so I may need to measure your ring finger in a more conventional way before I get there."

"I'm not sure about this, honey," he said with obvious concern for her safety.

"Please, James. I can't be with you all the time. I told you before, I need some degree of freedom. Even Lizzie gets more freedom than me at the moment."

"Not anymore she doesn't," he muttered to himself and then sighed. "You take security, at least two of them and at no point are you left alone."

"What about changing rooms? I can't imagine you want Ray, Joshua, Billy or any of the others seeing me in bridal lingerie." Her intention had been to tease him slightly but she also wanted some clarification on what he meant by not being left alone.

"Baby, your ass is going to be really sorry if you start playing with me on this one," he told her with a dark edge to his voice that told her he was deadly serious.

"I wasn't," she protested and found Jim raising disbelieving eyebrows. "Well, maybe a little, although my point was genuine, but I'll take them with me if that's what you want. What if I go to the toilet or to try things on?"

"I understand your point. You take Abby with you so if there's anything or anyone that poses a threat to you she can raise the alarm." Jim immediately regretted letting his guard down and revealing the fact that he still felt there was a threat posed when he saw the alarmed expression on her face. "Baby, I'm just being overcautious and super control freak, you know that, right?"

"I don't know, I guess so, but what if they never find Mickie, or stop looking, the police? They might do that. They won't look forever, will they? And then what? I have an armed guard permanently at my side?" Her questions were laced with fear that saw her beginning to panic as she tried to imagine working and living her life with Mickie or whoever else she may have paid still at large.

"Hey," soothed Jim, turning her face back so she was looking up at him again. "That's not how this turns out, baby, but we need to think it through, and I will, okay?" He leaned in to kiss her gently on the lips.

"I know you'll do what you can—"

He interrupted her with a kiss. He kissed her into silence

before he spoke again. "Trust me, okay?" he asked seriously.

"Yes," she whispered nervously as she realised they were both still naked and he was aroused again.

"I will do everything that can be done to keep you safe and to see Mickie behind bars alongside your father, okay?"

She nodded.

"You're my lucky seven, baby. Forever." His words were heartfelt and his tone grew husky with desire.

"Forever." She repeated his own word recalling that until she'd met Jim she hadn't truly imagined an actual *forever*, especially not one that was wrapped up in one person, but now it couldn't be wrapped up in anyone else.

She could feel him nudging against her sex and as scared as she was thinking of Mickie, her dad and her own safety, she wanted to forget about it for a while and get lost in Jim, again.

"James," she moaned as she wrapped her legs around him and encouraged him closer, urged him in.

"We still need to look at your work schedule, Tasha. We need not to be on opposite sides of the Atlantic for extended periods," he told her as he gently entered her and began to rock against her slowly.

"Oh yes," she said answering his question and encouraging him at the same time.

"You like that?" he asked, teasing her with his movements rather than his words.

"Yes. Touch me," she almost begged and was rewarded with a wicked grin.

"Where baby, tell me," he encouraged her.

"Kiss me," she moaned as he rocked against her more firmly before rotating his hips against her.

Leaning in and capturing her mouth was his response. His tongue slid between her open lips and overpowered her own tongue until she was whimpering into his mouth. His kisses deepened until she was breathless and his lips moved across her mouth, jaw, neck and throat.

"Please, James," she called to him.

"What, Tasha? Tell me what you want." It was his words doing the teasing now.

"Lower, move lower." A flush crept up her cheeks. She still had no idea how he made her do this.

Pushing his head down until his mouth was over her left breast, she rolled her eyes in response to him smiling at her.

"Ah, I see, you only had to ask, honey." He grinned. "Ask me, Tasha, ask for what you want," he tormented as he loitered over her breast, poised and paused waiting for her instruction.

"Kiss me, lick me, please," she cried desperate for his co-operation.

"Where baby?" He brushed his nose across her hard, aching, puckered nipple.

"My nipples, please." She almost sobbed and then as his lips closed around the hard nugget while his hand cupped the full, milky coloured flesh around it she shuddered violently.

Pulling back to admire the results of his work he turned his attention to the other one until she was bucking beneath and against him as every nerve end in her body went onto high alert waiting for her release to wash over her and as it crested closer she could barely think straight until Jim returned his mouth to her face where he nuzzled against her ear while her arms wrapped around his back that her nails were scraping against his skin.

"Not yet, Tasha, wait," he whispered huskily.

"I don't think I can," she replied, suddenly hoarse.

"Wait for me, baby." He reached behind him and pulled her hands free of him.

With her hands now at the side of her head and his fingers entwined with hers Jim glanced over her, propped up on his elbows that were at the side of her chest.

"I'll never let anybody hurt you again, Tasha, never. I love you so much," he told her as his own climax thundered towards its conclusion with a final thrust and a deep cry that was more than she could take, her own release steamrollering over her making her toes curl, her hair prickle and her sex burn.

Collapsing against her, his fingers still wrapped around hers, his face in her neck, Jim said, "So, we're agreed then, baby, I'm going to take care of you and keep you safe any way I can, we're both going to wear wedding bands and we will never be apart.

God, I love negotiating with you."

Laughing beneath him, Tasha realised she still hadn't told him about her call from Angie and they had yet to discuss the message from her father, but suddenly Jim's phone sprang into life, startling them both.

Releasing her and sitting up, Jim grabbed his phone while Tasha gathered her shopping lists and iPad.

"Hello," answered Jim. "Oh hi, Deanna."

Tasha rolled her eyes then grimaced at the other woman's name.

Jim shook his head as he continued the conversation he was having. "Tasha? She's good, thanks." He grinned across at her. "No, now's a great time for me, I just needed to discuss Lizzie's day out with you tomorrow."_

Tasha grabbed her dress and found her pants then redressed while Jim finished his call before checking messages or emails. She gestured to say she was going downstairs where she found Philip entering through the front door.

"Yo step-mommy dearest," he shrieked, hugging Tasha as she reached the bottom of the stairs.

"What are you up to?" she asked suspiciously.

"OMG, you are good. You're suspicious of me after just one sentence."

Laughing, Tasha took his arm and entered the kitchen. "Maybe it was the step-mommy thing. So, what are you up to?"

"Auntie Abby has been in touch and we are throwing you and the old man a party," he shrilled, confusing Tasha.

"Why?"

"Dunno, but Auntie Abby reckons we need a gathering on Friday, just close friends and family. She thinks we need to celebrate all things Jim and Tasha," he said as if he was announcing a new show.

"No," replied Tasha.

"Why?"

"It's like Fort Knox here, in case you hadn't noticed, so the chances of your dad agreeing to this are zero," Tasha explained.

"We could ask him," suggested Philip, hugging Tasha. "You are the best step-mommy ever, say yes, Tash, please and then ask the old man, pretty please," he pleaded.

"Ask the old man what?" came Jim's voice from behind them.

Spinning together and giggling as they did so caused Jim to frown at them, but in an amused way rather than with irritation.

"Ask away," he told them.

Nudging each other to ask neither of them spoke for a few seconds before giggling again.

"Or not." Jim prepared to walk past them to the kitchen.

"Philip comes with plans and ideas via Auntie Abby," started Tasha, deflecting Jim's attention to his son.

"What plans and ideas would they be?" Jim sounded suspicious.

"Party!" cried Philip sounding camper than anyone Tasha had ever heard.

"Do you practice that degree of gayness?" Her question made Philip pout meaning he looked as camp as he'd sounded before. Tasha laughed loudly.

"Yes, Natasha, I practise every night before bed. Now, Daddy," he started, making Jim even more suspicious.

"Daddy? This sounds expensive son, go on."

"Auntie Abby thinks we should throw a party to celebrate your engagement, rearranged wedding and the fact that Tasha is well. Friday night, what do you say?" Philip almost spat out.

"I assume you've been put in charge of planning?"

Jim's response surprised Tasha in as much as he appeared to be considering this idea when she would have expected a simple and straightforward no. Not only was she expecting it, she was hoping for it.

"Yes, I am planning from here and Auntie Abby is at the end of the phone." Philip grinned, holding his mobile phone aloft as if to demonstrate Abby's location.

"Jim, it's short notice and with everything else that's going on." Tasha hoped to encourage and support the *no* she thought would be a foregone conclusion. The truth was she was nervous. Scared at the prospect of a houseful of people, most of them she was sure would be strangers and with everything that had happened in recent weeks people scared her, strangers. Although, her life had taught her that whilst you should have a healthy distrust of strangers, those closest to you couldn't always be trusted.

"I want to see the guest list before any invitations are extended," replied Jim seemingly ignoring Tasha's input.

"Jim," she cried.

"What? Baby, it will be fun and a nice way to start our little vacation," he said seriously, ending any discussion she thought there may be.

"Oh, Daddy, you will not regret this," squealed Philip.

"I beg to differ," snapped Tasha petulantly as she stormed off towards the front door.

"Where are you going?" called Jim, concerned suddenly.

"To see Juan. You know, the one person around here that actually listens to me and hears what I say," she snapped back before slamming the door behind her.

Turning back to his son, Jim smiled warmly.

"Did I do good, Daddy?" he asked as if in a conspiracy.

"You did good, son. Now text Juan and make sure Tasha has arrived safely and then do whatever you need to do while I make some calls to make the end game." Jim ruffled his son's hair before heading into his office.

Philip followed his father once Juan returned his call and stood in the doorway as Jim prepared to end his call.

"Yes, thank you Sargent and I appreciate you coming to me in the morning. See you then," he said hanging up.

"Tasha is with Juan and he's got her to agree to dinner with him at ours while she bitches about you, which may mean Juan is bitching about me, so you've got a couple of hours at least and he'll let us know when they're done before he walks her back," said Philip.

"Good, thank you. Now scoot while I call Uncle Bobby and Katy Myers," he told the young man watching him intently. "What?"

"She's the one, isn't she? Tasha?" asked Philip seriously.

"She sure is. Come in." He suddenly wanted to reassure his son as Tasha had reassured his daughter. "I loved your mom when we married and the day you and then Lizzie were born really were the happiest of my life. I'd never felt love like I did, still do for the two of you. You both gave me a purpose I'd never felt before or since, until Tasha, but I should never have married any of the others. I'm not entirely sure why I did except for the fact that I did love them in my own way and I really believe in marriage. I want to be married, like my parents are, but had kind of settled for never marrying again when I met Tasha. I figured that whilst I believed in marriage, I seemed to be very bad at it. When I met Tasha I thought she was the most beautiful girl I'd ever met and within an hour of that meeting I liked her too, so much so that I talked to her about being wife number seven, albeit a little tongue in cheek but by the time she flew out here it was a done deal for me, Philip. I was completely hooked."

"A yes would have done," teased Philip, smiling at his father's obvious happiness.

Jim laughed at his son's slightly uncomfortable expression. "Sorry, but she will definitely be your final stepmother because if I can't make a marriage with Tasha work then I can't make it work with anyone," he said candidly.

"I'm no expert in these things but do not write that into your vows, *I am marrying Tasha because if I can't make it work with her I can't make it work with anyone.* Even I as a gay man know that chicks do not dig that sentiment."

"Duly noted." Jim smiled. "Now, I really need to get on so if you're okay with what you're doing."

"Yeah, I'm good." He smiled back. "Oh, and I'm glad you found Tasha, she's good for you, for us all and she not only puts up with Lizzie but she cares that she's okay with everything including feeling pushed out this afternoon." Philip left his father alone smiling, thinking that in a matter of days Tasha would be his wife and Mickie should no longer be a concern.

Chapter Nine

"You don't want a party?" Juan was about to make some coffee until Tasha brushed past him to open a bottle of wine.

With a nervous frown, Juan put the coffee back in the cupboard and grabbed two glasses instead. "You're not on meds, are you?" He held the bottle of wine in the air.

"Nope, so just pour," Tasha snapped, then realising she was getting annoyed with the wrong person she softened. "Sorry. I'm off meds and able to consume wine."

"Okay." Juan smiled as he half-filled the wine glasses. "So, the party?"

"I have no objection to a party as such, but it was kind of sprung on me. Philip appears with a plan he and Abby have cooked up and I want to say no because it's too soon—I like a party but I'm not at my partying best and to be honest the idea of a crowded room makes me nervous. I don't know why, but it does. So, I tell Philip it will be a no, that Jim won't have any of it and what does he do? He says yes."

"Maybe Jim just wants to celebrate you being well and your engagement. He does love you and he thought he was going to lose you, several times, we all did."

With a nod, Tasha reached across the table to take Juan's hand in hers giving it a reassuring squeeze that said she knew and understood how worried Jim had been, how worried everyone had been, but honestly, she was still worried. Every time she was alone in the house, no matter how fleeting, she was worried. Every time she was escorted by security, she was worried, worried that they either knew of a threat or on more than one occasion she had worried that they were the threat because if Mickie could pay her way to hiring Tasha's own father then any unscrupulous muscle for hire would be easy to bank roll. Her dreams were becoming a little less intense and frequent, but her sleep was still disturbed by thoughts and worries, and she woke up in terror at least once a week, dripping in sweat, crying incoherently being cradled by Jim. So, like she'd just told Juan, she wasn't really party fit yet. What she hadn't admitted to Juan or even herself until that very second was that she feared she might never recover sufficiently to be party fit again. Maybe the old Tasha had gone for good.

"Tash," Juan interrupted her thoughts and musing.

"What? Sorry."

"Do you need me to call for Jim?" Juan looked worried, more than that though, he looked scared and anxious.

Tasha smiled across at him and cast her mind back to his earlier words about Jim's possible motives in agreeing to a party right now.

"I understand him wanting to celebrate, I really do, but this is so unlike Jim. I would put money on the fact that when I leave here there will be a member of the security team overseeing my trip across the drive where my boyfriend will be waiting for me on the doorstep after you call or text him to say I'm leaving here, so why is he going to throw a party?"

"I don't know, I really don't," Juan replied, and Tasha believed him.

Maybe she was overthinking it and it was as simple as him wanting to celebrate their engagement, her recovery and their impending wedding, not that anyone else aside from Bobby and Abby were aware of that.

"Let me sort some dinner." He smiled, getting to his feet while she refilled their glasses to the brim.

****

It was at breakfast the following morning before Jim brought up the subject of Tasha's workload.

"Can you email Amanda your revised work dates today, baby?" he said to a slightly subdued Tasha courtesy of a little too much to drink with Juan the previous night and her reluctance to go ahead with this party that was all planned.

"No need," she replied shortly.

"Tasha, there is every need. I need to know exactly what you have committed to, when and where," replied Jim with a hard stare.

"Jim, I am going to be nowhere other than here until the New Year when Jon starts shooting his movie, assuming that isn't recast." Tasha sounded tearful.

"What? What do you mean?" Jim put his cup down, giving Tasha his undivided attention.

"Angie called to say that due to my inability to fulfil my contractual obligations, my part for the legal thing was reluctantly being recast which is understandable I suppose. Time is money and I wouldn't be able to fly to London for another couple of weeks. So, no work dates to email, revised or otherwise."

"That is bull," snapped Jim. "Time is money, but most of the money in question is mine, so if I'm okay with the cost they should be too. Baby, you are so not fired, either that or I will pull the plug on the whole damn thing." He pulled his phone out of his pocket before looking across at Tasha to confirm, "Did this come from Niall Taylor?"

Tasha nodded but as Jim began to select somebody's number from his phone she reached across the table and took it from him.

"Honey, I know your feelings on phones at the table, but this can't wait."

"No. Leave it, Jim, please. I never wanted to be bankrolled by you. I never wanted you to arrange work for me and although I got this part myself and your involvement was unknown at that point, I can't have you running to my rescue, so let them recast and make it without me."

"Baby, this is not me rescuing you. This is me throwing my weight around and fighting for unfair treatment of..." He struggled for the right word.

"Of your girlfriend, fiancée, wife?" Tasha still held onto Jim's phone.

"I like the sound of that, my wife." He grinned.

"Me too, so you make the most of the fact that you are going to get your wish of having me at home, waiting and wanton, wearing your ring and bearing your name, and I have to admit that the idea of that appeals to me. Let's have a honeymoon at home that takes us all the way to Christmas," said Tasha, getting to her feet and sitting across Jim's lap as she gave him his phone back.

"Are you sure? You know I would happily have you wanton and waiting at home for me forever, but you have always maintained your need and desire to work. Most of our fights have started with conversations about your work."

"I know." Tasha ran her fingers through Jim's hair. "But I'm okay with it, especially as it would have meant me being London based for what, a month, six weeks? I can't have my husband of a few weeks in L.A. while I'm in London for six weeks, needing to be kissed by him, touched, licked, tasted, fucked," she told him breathlessly as she rotated her hips and behind into his lap that showed definite signs of arousal.

"Say it again," said Jim hoarsely.

Smiling, Tasha repeated herself, "I can't have my husband of a few weeks in L.A. while I'm in London for six weeks, needing to be kissed by him, touched, licked, tasted, and fucked."

"I actually just meant the *my husband* but the rest was a bonus." Jim laughed while Tasha smacked his shoulder. "I really need to go to work soon, but I think I may need to kiss you, touch you, lick you, taste you and definitely fuck you, so I need you pantyless and wanton, waiting wherever you want baby, now."

Leaping to her feet with a smile and a gentle flush to her skin Tasha flashed a grin at Jim. "I'm already pantyless and wanton, so you will find me waiting across your desk."

"Baby, you may never work again with offers like that," called Jim as Tasha opened the office door smiling.
****
Standing in her dress waiting to make her way downstairs for the party she still didn't want, Tasha smiled at the new dress she'd bought that was hugging her figure. She really was a vision of swirling beads, sequins and chiffon in her curvaceous

silhouette. Twirling, she could fully appreciate the floor length, dark pewter, lined gown with its boat neckline and rounded v back leading to the hidden zip concealed by a hook and eye fastener before the fitted bodice and hips led to inverted pleats at the skirt. The overall shape was an A line silhouette with satin trims at the neckline and cap sleeved cuffs. With matching satin covered, peep toe shoes the dress was lifted so that it no longer scraped the floor. Tasha added the finishing touches of long drop diamond earrings to the only other item of jewellery she wore, her engagement ring. Her hair was down and straightened while her make-up was almost invisible by its natural tones, only the odd hint of peachy pinks, lip gloss and mascara betrayed the fact that she was even wearing make-up.

After a deep breath, Tasha headed for the door. Maybe a party wasn't such a bad idea or at least the reason behind it; she was recovering and was glad about that. She was engaged and planning to marry the most wonderful man in the world and for that she was beyond happy, so happy that she had to metaphorically pinch herself each and every day. This was almost like the first day of the rest of her life, and what a life it was going to be.

She was almost at the bottom of the stairs when everyone who was already there turned to look at her and she swore she heard actual gasps. Jim appeared from the back of the house and for a second seemed concerned by the silence around him until he looked up and saw a blushing Tasha descending the last couple of steps.

"You are a very lucky man," said Bobby, back slapping his brother as he passed him to greet Tasha at the bottom of the stairs where Jim took her hand and kissed her gently.

"You look a million dollars, baby." He let out a low whistle that made her smile.

"Or at least fifteen thousand," she replied thinking about the cost of the dress and shoes.

"Worth every cent. You really do look amazing. I can't even begin to think how beautiful a bride you're going to be." He grinned as she took his arm and with a deep breath to stable her nerves allowed him to lead her out back where quite a few people were already assembled.

"You don't have very long to wait before you see exactly how I'll look as a bride," she told him with a grin.

"I am counting the minutes, baby and they can't pass quickly enough for me."

Her grin broadened until she felt an ache in her jaw, happy as she was that she could only detect sincerity in Jim's words. "You're not the only one who can't wait, especially with you looking so handsome." Tasha looked Jim up and down dressed in a pair of black suit trousers and a casual shirt with a couple of buttons undone and felt her heart flutter as her stomach flipped. She had never loved anyone more than this man, her fiancé, her husband as of the following week and she had certainly never found anyone more attractive.

"I'm beginning to wish this was a private party for just the two of us," said Jim as he guided Tasha towards the bar that was now set up in the lounge.

"You wanted the party. You, Philip and Abby," she retorted, bristling a little as she remembered how he'd agreed to throw the party she didn't want. "I don't think we should have sex," she seemed to suddenly announce.

"What? Ever? Because that is not working for me and I know it won't work for you," cried Jim, making her laugh.

"No, not ever, a few days is a struggle for us," she conceded thinking they were currently a couple of days sex free. "I was thinking until we're married. It's something we can look forward to, something to make our wedding night special."

"If you're sure that's what you want," said Jim seriously.

"Yes, I'm sure and I promise it will be worth the wait."

"Then I look forward to the next time I have sex, with my wife." Jim grinned at a laughing Tasha. "You are up to something, Natasha." He was suddenly suspicious of her with her laughter and a naughty glint in her eyes.

"Maybe," she teased.

"You are definitely up to something," he told her as his hand rested on her behind.

"I bought your wedding present," she told him.

"What is it?"

"I can't tell you until Monday. In fact, it will be better for you to find it yourself, on Monday."

"I could ask Abby." He smiled and threw in a waggle of his eyebrows for added effect.

"I gave her the slip, so nobody knows, just me and one other who you don't know," Tasha revealed.

"Security?" asked Jim with a smug smirk but as Tasha lowered her glance he lost any sign of amusement along with his previous playfulness. "Tell me that you weren't stupid enough to *give them the slip* because if you did," he almost threatened.

"Not like you mean. I arranged to meet someone about your present somewhere I wouldn't normally have done it, got it, so they were there but unaware." Even she felt a little confused by her own words and phrasing and she knew exactly what she had and hadn't done. "I can't explain without ruining the surprise, but I promise I was with security all day."

"Okay," agreed Jim reluctantly. "But if on Monday it transpires that you didn't do as instructed, your ass along with the rest of you will be mine and I would hate for our wedding night to prove a frustrating one for you, honey."

"So would I," agreed Tasha, confident that Jim would be equally happy with her gift and her use of security.
****

It was about an hour later, the party was in full swing and almost all of the guests had arrived when a panic struck Philip pulled Tasha to one side.

"Tash, I'm running back home to find Juan," he told her sadly.

"You okay?"

"We had a fight, me and Juan. I was a bit of a jackass so sent Lizzie to make him come over, but that was before you came down and neither of them are back, unless..." he said with a half-smile.

"Unless?" Tasha knew exactly what he was likely to say.

"Unless you'd go over and make Juan come back with you, and Lizzie who is probably now on his side since I was a major jerk," Philip admitted making Tasha smile.

"I'll go and talk them both round and get them over here to

suffer the party I didn't want with me."

"Tash, you are the best," grinned Philip as he hugged her warmly.

Tasha rushed to the front door where she passed a concerned looking Amanda and a very attractive dark haired and skinned thirty something man who Tasha assumed was Dom.

"Hi Amanda, give me two minutes and I will be back with Juan and Lizzie," Tasha called as she rushed past them and headed over to Philip's home where she tapped on the door as she tried the door knob and found it turned easily. Amanda's voice calling her name continued, but Tasha figured whatever she wanted to say could wait for the few minutes it would take her to return home, so ignored her.

Once in the hallway, Tasha called to Juan and Lizzie, "Hello, come on you two, Philip is getting jittery. Juan, where are you? Lizzie, your dad's waiting for you."

Making her way through the lounge and into the light and airy kitchen she stopped dead in her tracks at the sight that greeted her.

"Juan, Lizzie, what's going on?" Tasha asked with confusion and fear in her voice.

A loud, cold, maniacal laugh came from behind her and immediately she knew exactly what was going on. Turning slowly, Tasha took a deep breath as she came face to face with first a gun, a handgun and then the frozen blue pools of Mickie's eyes.

"I couldn't have planned this any better." She smiled but with no amusement. "I have the son's boyfriend that has been in need of payback for some time, the whiny daddy's girl that really needed a damned good spanking years ago, both of whom always ran back to Jim with all the bad things about nasty Mickie, and now, the cherry on the top of the cake, the English whore who took him away from me."

Tasha was unsure what to say or do as she stared down the barrel of the gun.

"Sit," snapped Mickie, laughing as Tasha jumped.

Mickie gestured towards the other two who were sitting against kitchen cabinets huddled together. They automatically made a space for her between them and as she sat in it, Tasha instinctively threw a protective arm around each of them.

"This really could not be any more perfect, could it?" asked Mickie rhetorically. "But what to do with you all next?" She took her phone out and snapped a picture of the three of them, scared and huddled together on the floor.

"Mickie," said Tasha calmly. "I'm sure you don't want to harm Lizzie or Juan, not really, so please let them go. Your problem is with me, not them." She hoped she could at least get the other two out of this ridiculously dangerous situation.

Mickie stared at her with no expression at all on her face and seemed to think about what Tasha had said for a matter of only seconds before shaking her head firmly. "I don't think so, Tasha. If Juan had kept his nose out of things between me and Jim then maybe I could have let him go and as for sweet, little Lizzie, well, she is the little bitch that always thought she should be the only woman in Daddy's life. You would never have liked me as a stepmother, would you?" She waved the gun at Lizzie now.

With tears running down her face Lizzie tried to reply, "I—don't—know—what—you—mean. I knew you liked my dad—I never did anything."

"So, you never went running back to Daddy with all the stories of what Mickie did and said? You really should have had a stepmother like me, Lizzie. I would have knocked you into shape, either that or you would have run back to Mommy and Lenny forever." She laughed and then more seriously turned to Tasha, the accusation in her voice clear. "But you came along and took him away from me. We were happy until you came along and messed things up."

"This is not Lizzie's doing," said Tasha and then corrected Mickie's incorrect statement. "I know you love Jim and you're upset, but you and Jim weren't happy before me. You may have been happy, but Jim? He considered you to be mutually convenient no more, so please don't make this Lizzie and Juan's fault."

Suddenly, without warning, Mickie stood over Tasha. She pulled her arm back before landing the gun across her cheek. Tasha let out a small cry as the pain registered and as scared and worried as she felt, she knew she had to get Lizzie and Juan safely out of the house before things got completely out of hand.

"Please, Mickie," Tasha pleaded. "They're scared, you've made your point, can't you let them go?" she asked, convinced that her thoughts that night at the charity auction when she'd considered Mickie deranged were spot on, more accurate than even she'd really believed.

"And what about you?" Mickie stared down at Tasha.

"What about me? I think we both know you're unlikely to let me go willingly, so I'm asking you to let Lizzie and Juan go, they don't need to be here, do they?"

Looking thoughtful, Mickie backed up against the island in the middle of the kitchen and pulled herself up. Sitting now, she cocked her head at Tasha. "Are you really that nice? So nice that you want the two of them to go at your own expense?" She stopped to take another picture on her phone.

Tasha was unsure if what she was asking made her nice because as far as she was concerned she was simply behaving in the way any normal and decent person would when faced with the possibility of being able to save innocent bystanders. She shrugged then tried to explain, "I don't think they should be here. Lizzie is a child and Juan is only involved because of his relationship with Philip."

"Fucking hell! You really are so nice, aren't you?" She laughed erratically then suddenly stopped. "He'll destroy you, Jim. There is no way you will keep up with him. He isn't soft and fluffy like you, he is hard and relentless," she spat.

Tasha said nothing but did think Mickie really hadn't been anything to Jim other than convenient if she believed he was hard and relentless. She had absolutely no first-hand knowledge of the gentle, caring, loving man Tasha knew and loved.

"Maybe we should all get better acquainted while I consider your suggestion." Mickie grinned. "I know, why don't I ask you a question, you answer and then I tell you something about myself. Right, I'll start. When did you first have sex with Jim?"

"Mickie—" began Tasha preparing to protest.

"No!" Mickie interrupted angrily. "These are my rules, you answer or I keep them both with you and involve them in our getting to know you game. I might do that anyway, but I'll be a little more invasive in my questioning if you don't follow the rules. So, when did you first fuck my then boyfriend, Jim?"

"Mickie, please, they don't need to hear this," Tasha protested making Mickie leap down and crouch before her, eye to eye with the gun firmly pointing at Tasha.

"Tasha, please, just tell her. Answer her questions, I don't care what you and Daddy have done. I kind of already guessed by how you are together that the two of you are you know, passionate," pleaded Lizzie with an embarrassed flush colouring her cheeks. She inhaled deeply, desperate to keep Tasha safe even if it meant hearing details of her father's private life.

"So, come on Tasha, don't be coy, we're all ears. When did you and Jim fuck for the first time?" Mickie reinstated herself to her former position on the island, grabbing a bottle of scotch as she went. "Spill!" she snapped before taking a large gulp from the bottle.

"I was in New York on the Friday, that's when I met Jim and when we got together," admitted Tasha, blushing furiously, hoping Lizzie wouldn't judge her harshly, not because she was ashamed, she wasn't, not about anything she and Jim had done or shared. She did however, believe that there really was no need for Lizzie to know these things about her father.

"You were far more of a whore than I'd given you credit for. I knew it was a whirlwind but on the first day, even before a date," commented Mickie as she took another mouthful of liquor. "My turn to share then; erm, I only ever dated Bobby to get to Jim."

"Poor Uncle Bobby," remarked Lizzie whose words alone gained Tasha's attention so that she wrapped her arm a little more tightly around her.

"Oh, Lizzie, I fucked your Uncle Bobby a hundred and one different ways during our time together, so I think I earned the right to get closer to your dad. Maybe you could call Uncle Bobby and see just how good I was."

The three of them sitting on the floor winced at the coldness of Mickie's summary and suggestion, but if she noticed she passed no comment.

"Maybe not. Next question for Tasha. How old were you when you lost your virginity?"

"Fifteen," replied Tasha immediately, refusing to be made to feel ashamed for the loss of innocence to someone she loved in order to somehow made it a good memory, untarnished by the reality of her life and situation at the time.

Laughing, Mickie shook her head.

"What to share next? Oh, I know, Jim's second wife, she didn't miscarry," cackled Mickie, the other's confusion was apparent. "She was pregnant when Jim married her, fuck, that's why he married her. But soon after they married, I found out she'd had some substance abuse issues in the past. Jim was unaware and he'd never have allowed a former junkie near his precious Lizzie and Philip let alone a new addition, so I gave her a choice, hang onto your new husband and lose the baby or vice versa." Mickie laughed again before another slug of whiskey and then whispered to them, "I even paid for her abortion. She was real stupid because she thought I would allow her to carry on like it never happened, but every time I needed something I reminded her of our secret until she became bitter and twisted and Jim divorced her. Next question Tasha, have you ever fucked someone for money, you know prostituted yourself?"

Tasha knew what Mickie wanted and was now sure that the whole purpose of this little getting to know you session was purely to distort and discredit Tasha as a friend, wife and stepmother.

"Not like you mean," said Tasha flatly.

"Huh-huh!" snapped Mickie as if Tasha had just answered a question incorrectly on a TV quiz show. "Let's try that one again, Tasha, but before you answer you just think about what a real chatty man Daddy is when he has a drink in his hand and cash in his pocket, not to mention Mommy dearest. So, have you ever fucked someone for money, you know prostituted yourself?"

"I'm not doing this," snapped Tasha defiantly.

"Fine." Mickie's smile disconcerted Tasha slightly before she turned to Lizzie. "Little, sweet innocent Lizzie. You have a boyfriend now, Dylan. Tell us about him. Have you kissed him?"

Lizzie nodded.

"Ah, what about him, has he managed to get his hands on your very pert and adolescent tits?" she asked Lizzie a little more darkly now.

Again, Lizzie nodded making Mickie laugh.

"Daddy is going to love this," she cackled and then pursued Lizzie some more. "Have you touched him Lizzie? Held his boner in your pretty, innocent, little hands?"

Another nod from Lizzie as a tear ran down her face forced Tasha to decide that Lizzie needed to get out of there quickly.

"I do love first love. What about his hands, has he got them into your panties, Lizzie? Has he put his fingers into your pussy yet?"

"That's enough!" Tasha got to her feet. "Have I prostituted myself? Yes, yes, I have and it's not something I'm proud of but I'm no longer ashamed of it, because of Jim. There is nothing you can reveal here that will put a divide between me and Jim. He knows everything about me and my family, everything I have done and why. Let Lizzie go, and Juan, they can't give you what you want or need," said Tasha confidently.

Mickie eyed her warily before pointing at a video camera nearby. "This is all going down in history. This is for Jim. He will know exactly what went on in here and all the revelations so even if you all get out of here he will never, ever look at you the same way again."

The sound of a sob from Lizzie was enough for Tasha to move even closer to Mickie where she repeated, "They can't give you what you want or need."

"What I want is Jim, but you took him from me, so how do you plan on giving me what I want or need?" Mickie asked with cold certainty.

"You know that no matter what goes down here you will never have Jim again, so I am guessing you plan on playing the *if I can't have him, you can't* game." Tasha knew that was the exact plan here.

"You bet. I may have underestimated you, you know, your bulldog spirit," Mickie sneered with an exaggerated English accent. "I thought if Jim saw your immaturity he would tire sooner, but even after your ridiculous starvation plan, he worried rather than getting tired and pissed off with you. The ex-boyfriend, needy siblings, he just kept coming back for more. He told me when you were in the hospital how special you were, and how afraid you were of me being in your lives. He even told me how you refused to add me back to the wedding list even though I was potentially dying of cancer."

"You weren't though, that was a lie," Tasha retorted.

"Shame really, not that I want cancer or to die, but he would have come to me, cared for me."

"He wouldn't," Tasha disagreed. "He told you at the hospital that he wasn't the person to help you through your non-existent disease."

"Yes, he did, and he told me you thought he was going to say I was pregnant with his baby when he told you I had cancer. That you were devastated and felt you'd be unable to compete with a child we shared."

Tasha was slightly startled at the details of what Jim had told Mickie regarding her feelings about her, but she reasoned that when the revelations were made Jim was in a dark and bad place, plus she knew Mickie was probably taking his words out of context, twisting them to make her doubt him so simply dealt with the facts.

"I wouldn't have been able to compete because you would have used a child to gain advantage."

"Damned right. Shame I didn't think of that though. He's a sucker for a baby, not that I want a child, never have, hate the whiny little bastards almost as much as I hate you!" Mickie shouted at Tasha, breathing her alcohol filled breath in her face. "I can't believe I didn't think of it. I got pregnant before, twice, accidently, once with Bobby's bastard and then with the now ex-husband of your new friend, Katy Myers. I knew I couldn't keep either; Bobby's because that would have put me off limits for Jim forever and the other, well, once I'd seduced him away from his wife, he bored me. At least you didn't play that one or I would have had to have killed you both, you and your bastard child. Now, what shall we do next?" Mickie asked with a smile that was too wide and too bright.

"Let them go, both of them, and then we can continue to the end," said Tasha.

"The end? You know what the end is, right? I am not going to prison so one way or another this is my last night on earth and yours too." She grinned at Tasha, oblivious to the increasingly noisy sobs and cries from Lizzie and now Juan.

"Please, Mickie, just let them go."

"One of them. You choose, which one?" Mickie looked surprised at her own plan. She grinned a wide and satisfied grin that suggested this choice wasn't going to be as easy as it should be for Tasha.

Tasha turned to face them both glancing from one to the other before settling her gaze on Juan. "Sorry, Juan. I need Lizzie out of here. I need to keep her safe."

Juan nodded. "Of course, I would have been mad if you'd chosen me over Lizzie."

"So, Lizzie is your choice?" Mickie didn't wait for an answer. She stepped forward towards Tasha who never saw the blow to her temple coming, only sensing she was falling, then she heard cries around her before nothing.

Chapter Ten

Coming to, Tasha winced, wondering where she was and what was happening and all too soon she realised and remembered. She was lying on the kitchen floor, cold with the feeling of another body against hers, Juan's?

"Juan," she called groggily before seeing Mickie staring down at her. "Juan," she repeated.

"Surprise," called Mickie as the body leaning against Tasha's moved and let out a little cry.

"No," cried Tasha as she sat up, turned and came face to face with Lizzie. "No. No. I said to send Lizzie out. She's a child. I needed to keep her safe. I made the appropriate choice," sobbed Tasha thinking of all the times Jim had accused her of making an inappropriate choice, not thinking before she acted and yet, this time when she had it had still ended badly. One look at Mickie's smug and sinister smirk of satisfaction confirmed that Tasha could never have made the right choice. The right choice would never have been permitted.

"Tasha, are you okay?" asked a concerned Lizzie, reaching up towards Tasha's temple that was bruised and coming up in a lump.

"Fine." She hugged Lizzie while Mickie watched them as she began to drink what was possibly a second bottle of scotch.

****

"How do you expect me to calm the fuck down while my fiancée and daughter are being held hostage along with my son's boyfriend by the woman that has already tried and failed to murder my fiancée?" Jim shouted across his office which had

123

now become a makeshift police incident room.

Sargent Masterson nodded his understanding at Jim while Detective Murphy tried to offer some comfort.

"Mr Maybury, we have negotiators on the way and SWAT are positioning themselves now and most people who take hostages mean them no real harm."

Jim glared at him. "Did you hear a word I said? This particular hostage taker has already tried to murder one of her hostages so I think your point is moot and if you had been doing your job correctly you would have apprehended Mickie when she turned up here. That was the whole point of this elaborate ploy, to draw Mickie out of hiding, to entice her with the opportunity to get to Tasha, but safely, under your supervision and at no risk to anyone, least of all Tasha."

He slumped into the nearest chair and roughly ran a hand through his hair wondering how this could be happening. He began to rock back and forth, bouncing on his feet slightly as he considered every outcome of this hideous situation. Jim was desperate for a positive outcome, one where both Lizzie and Tasha came back to him, safe and unharmed, but there was a gut churning fear that the outcome would be anything but that. Shaking his head, as if by doing so the dark thoughts would be dislodged, Jim returned his attention to Detective Murphy and their current plight.

"And yet here we are with Mickie gaining access to my home and family under your noses and it was Amanda, a guest here that recognised Mickie was on the grounds and raised the alarm, so please stop trying to offer me cold comfort and placate me or I will not be responsible for my actions. Oh, and if one hair on any of their heads is harmed, I will hold you, your colleagues and their incompetency personally responsible. Now what is the plan for getting them out of there?" asked Jim as Bobby sat next to him, ready to speak when another policeman appeared in the doorway.

"There's some movement over there," he said breathlessly, prompting movement from the Sargent and detective.

"Counsellor, can I leave your brother in your care?" asked Masterson as he headed towards the hall.

"Sure. Abby, go and take care of Philip with Mom please," Bobby told his wife, concerned that movement may be a bad thing in this case.

By the time Jim got to the front door, behind the police cordon with Bobby at his side, the front door of Philip's house was open. A white cloth of some kind waved from it. The sound of guns being cocked around them seemed almost deafening and the sight of red dots grouped together on the front door had Jim holding his breath. It was like one of those 3D images that your eyes need to adjust to and then bang the image is crystal clear. That is exactly how Jim recognised and announced, "Juan," who was walking slowly towards Jim's home under Masterson's instructions.

Juan was received by the detectives and everyone else who was there, but it was Jim he turned to first.

"I'm sorry, Jim. Tasha wanted Mickie to send Lizzie out but she sent me." He cried as Philip charged through the crowd to get to him.

"Are you okay? I thought she'd hurt you. I'm so sorry I was a jerk before, I love you," Philip told him in broken cries as he hugged his boyfriend.

Philip began to pull Juan through to the back of the house when Murphy intervened.

"Juan? We can get you checked out by the paramedics but we really need to speak to you."

"Yeah, fine. We need to get Tasha out of there, and Lizzie. I think she'll let Lizzie go but not Tasha, not alive," he said and began to sob as he was led into the formal lounge that had been commandeered as some kind of debriefing room where the medics were waiting.

Having had Juan checked over and happy he was unharmed beyond the shock of everything that had happened, the detectives began to question him about what he had witnessed in the house; how Mickie seemed, what she'd said, what weapon she had and where they were all situated. He answered every question that was put to him while maintaining eye contact with Jim who said nothing but listened intently to the information.

"Did Mickie actually say she was planning on killing Tasha?"

asked Masterson calmly, but eyed Jim with caution.

Juan's shoulders began to shake as he tearfully confirmed the detective's question. "Yes. She said she wasn't going to prison, that it was her last night on earth and Tasha's too."

"Why didn't she just try and get close enough to Miss Winters to take her out?" asked Murphy thinking aloud.

"She seems to want to make Tasha suffer," began Juan. "She keeps making her answer questions, embarrassing ones, about sex, her past and Jim and stuff to humiliate her I think and then she tells Tasha stuff about herself if she answers."

"What happens if Tasha doesn't answer, do you know?" asked Murphy.

"She's hit Tash a couple of times with the gun, but she's also turned on Lizzie when Tash wouldn't answer, asking her horrible questions, real personal stuff which then forces Tasha to answer because she wants to protect Lizzie," explained Juan tearfully.

"Has she said what she intends to do with Lizzie?" Masterson nervously watched a furious and heartbroken looking Jim as he waiting for Juan's response, then flicked another cautionary glance towards Bobby.

"No, but she seemed to agree with Tasha's summing up that it was between the two of them rather than me and Lizzie. We were just due some payback for crossing her in the past."

"Okay," smiled Masterson empathetically, turning as someone appeared at the door.

"Negotiator's here," the newcomer announced.

"I need to go and bring my colleague up to speed. May we continue to use your office?" Masterson asked Jim.

"Of course. Sargent, I need them both back safely, both of them," said Jim, sounding frail and helpless suddenly, unable to imagine surviving the pain of losing either Tasha or Lizzie and he knew if he did he would never forgive himself, not ever.

"We'll do everything we can, sir."

"Jimbo, do you want a drink?" asked Bobby.

"No. I'm just going to wait here a while. I'm not much in the party mood anymore."

"I'll wait with you. I wasn't suggesting re-joining the party," sighed Bobby, dropping down next to him once more.

"Juan, are you sure you're okay?" Jim watched the other man with paternal concern.

"I guess. Can we talk? I didn't want to say anything to the police about it," replied Juan.

"Come on." Jim leapt to his feet. "Let's go upstairs. Bobby?" He led the two others upstairs and into the bedroom he shared with Tasha.

"Tasha was weird, Jim. I mean I get the shock and fear, but she was kind of resigned to her fate over there. She didn't care about anything beyond keeping me and Lizzie alive and securing our release. I think she might do something if the police don't end it soon." Juan sat on the edge of the bed as Jim leapt up.

"She is far too fucking careless with her own wellbeing and that is entirely my fault. I have absolved her of all worry; all the things that motivated her to remain safe and well are no longer motivators because I have made them safe, namely Pippa and Dan so if she keeps you and Lizzie safe now then she has nothing to lose. She won't have let anyone down," Jim said, confusing Juan but somehow Bobby seemed to understand.

"Jimbo, she has you to live for and just because her siblings are safe from the dumb fuck daddy, she wouldn't want to leave them and never forget that for some reason she is desperate to be shackled to you til death..." Bobby immediately regretted his final comment.

"She will be shackled to me, twenty-four-fucking-seven if she gets out of this in one piece," shouted Jim.

"There's a video camera over there. I don't know if it's relevant but Mickie is filming it all to torture you with, after the event..." Juan allowed his voice to trail off.

"Come on. Bobby, go and find out what the fuck this negotiator has planned before I go over myself."

Bobby nodded and although he knew some people would think his brother's words about going over himself weren't serious or genuine, he knew they were. Part of him did wonder if that might be a better solution to this fiasco. Maybe Mickie would follow Jim's orders and directions when faced with him rather than being left to her own devices as she currently was, although she had clearly lost the plot big style, so maybe not.

****

"Now what are we going to do as it's just us three girls together?" slurred Mickie.

"Please, let Lizzie go home," Tasha pleaded.

"Soon," replied Mickie. "Now where we? Yes, you fucked Jim on the first night, have prostituted yourself and lost your virginity at fifteen. I never loved Bobby but fucked him often and well in order to get to Jim and orchestrated the abortion of Jim's baby with that stupid fucking woman he married after Sara instead of me," snapped Mickie angrily. "Tasha, tell me and Lizzie, what's it like for you in the sack with Jim? Does the earth move when he fucks you?" She laughed at Tasha's and Lizzie's expressions. "Oh, come on, we're all women of the world, or maybe I should ask Lizzie some more questions about her boyfriend," she threatened.

"No. Leave Lizzie, please. Yes, the earth moves as you put it. I have never known sex with anyone like it is with Jim." Tasha really hoped this would placate Mickie.

"See that wasn't so hard, was it? Unlike Jim. Your father really is an amazingly gifted lover."

Lizzie looked close to tears as her glance flitted between Mickie and Tasha.

"Mickie, please, will you let Lizzie go?" Tasha was fraught, desperate to get Lizzie out of this situation, so much so that she unashamedly begged the other woman to show some kind of compassion.

Mickie laughed, loudly and cruelly. "Later. A couple more questions and then you can stop worrying about Lizzie. Tasha, why don't you tell Lizzie and I how Jim keeps you in line in the bedroom."

"Let her go and I'll tell you anything you want to know," said Tasha feeling determined.

"Not the way it works, now tell us, or maybe you could explain to Lizzie just how talented Daddy is in the sack; what he can do with his fingers, his lips, his tongue, his dick, maybe you could even show her, although you are minus a dick, but I do like that idea." She cackled, jumped down from the island and leaned over, precariously wobbling as she did so to retrieve a courgette from the fridge and held in front of herself suggestively. "I toyed with the idea of having a couple of friends get to you first, Tasha. Big, strong, male friends who would have been only too willing to teach you a few new tricks, by force."

Tasha winced at the inference of her words and the images those words conjured. She stared at Mickie, unable to fathom why any woman, regardless of their anger, hurt, whatever their feelings, would even consider the option of arranging for another woman to be attacked, assaulted, raped. The sound of a wooden spoon being rapped against the counter top of the island regained Tasha's attention while Mickie continued to explain the reasons behind her previous plans.

"I thought that would be fair, to see Jim unable to look at you or touch you, knowing exactly what they'd done to you, but there was always a risk he would try to fix you again…so, here we are, me and you and little Lizzie."

Tasha held Mickie's gaze and knew exactly what she was suggesting with her *you and little Lizzie*. This really had gone far enough and Lizzie was going to leave, one way or another. Turning to face Lizzie, Tasha reached out towards the young woman and pulled her close, using the position to allow her to whisper to her. "You have to do exactly as I say, okay?"

Lizzie looked up at Tasha, tears overflowing and running down her face but nodded at the woman looking to take care of her and keep her safe.

"You two look pretty cosy as it is but I think a little kiss to start with." Mickie grinned.

Lizzie looked mortified as Tasha gave a slight nod in her direction. She gently cupped her face to turn her position so she was closer to the door into the hall and gently placed a kiss against Lizzie's closed lips.

"A little tame, but we'll get you there. I think some tongue action now," she cackled, slapping the courgette in her hand.

Tasha looked down at Lizzie, smiled and then winked as she gently kissed her again at the edge of her mouth before tracing a path to Lizzie's ear where she whispered, "When I say run, you run."

With a barely detectable movement, Lizzie offered the tiniest of nods, confirming that she understood what was being said to her, but also that she would comply. Tears were freely running down her face at the realisation that this was coming to an end, although she had no idea what that end would look like. Would Mickie flip out completely once Lizzie made her move? Would that run for freedom be successful and if it wasn't what would the consequence to that be? Would Mickie punish her? Hurt her? Kill her? She had zero answers for herself, but knew that she had to do what Tasha was telling her to if she stood any chance of really getting out of there.

She looked up at Tasha, another, small smile of love and gratitude for her stepmother in all but name and suddenly became concerned for her at Mickie's hands, especially once she herself had made her break for freedom. Lizzie had no doubt in her mind that Mickie would hurt Tasha, badly and her part in orchestrating Lizzie's departure may well be the final straw for her father's former lover.

Pulling away now, Tasha smiled down at the sobbing girl whose face she still cradled before turning to face Mickie putting herself directly in front of Lizzie, effectively shielding her from the crazed, gun waving woman before her.

"Still a bit tame, Tasha. A little tender for Jim I think," she sneered.

"Really?" asked Tasha. "Not in my experience; Jim is the best lover I have ever had, but he is so gentle and tender that it takes my breath away at times, but maybe that's because—" Tasha stepped closer to Mickie who was wavering courtesy of the scotch, "—he doesn't just fuck me, he loves me, and he makes love to me because I'm the woman he's going to marry."

Tasha's instincts were spot on about how Mickie, whose movements weren't as steady or as fluid as they would have been without the alcohol she'd consumed, would react were spot on. As she wobbled and flailed Tasha seized the opportunity to grab for the gun, but that was the one thing Mickie was still in control of, battling to hold onto it.

"Lizzie, run and do not stop until you find your dad and tell him I love him. Run!" she screamed in case there was any confusion as to what she was telling her to do.

Immediately, without hesitation she ran as fast as she could but felt as though she was a cartoon character running and running, but getting nowhere.

Tasha continued to struggle with Mickie, who despite the volume of liquor in her system still had greater strength than Tasha possessed, although Tasha was still recuperating from Mickie's previous attempt on her life. With Mickie seeming to gain greater control with every second that passed, Tasha dearly hoped that she might find some kind of superhuman power or at least an inner strength that would see her come out on top here.

****

Bobby had just finished listening to the negotiator's summary that he didn't believe negotiation would work and before he'd be willing to open talks with Mickie he wanted SWAT fully in place, briefed and ready to go in.

"Let's do it then," agreed Masterson. "And let's bring your brother up to speed," he said to Bobby.

They found Jim back in the formal lounge with Sara, Lenny, Philip and Juan.

"Why did she take Lizzie and Juan? I don't understand," mused Sara as Bobby appeared with the detectives.

"Ma'am, I don't think Miss Adams planned this out in such detail. We set the trap for her to turn up here, knowing there would be the party and reasonably this was her best shot at getting to Tasha, maybe her only real chance. I think beyond deciding to come here she wouldn't have planned anything else. The other lady, Amanda? She barely recognised her as she was tonight, in disguise, but said there was something in the walk that was familiar. Her ending up over the road, first with Juan, and then your daughter was unfortunate for them and probably fortuitous for her. I doubt she could have planned on Tasha turning up there as she only went over as a favour to your son. Mr Maybury, the negotiator," started Masterson, addressing Jim before noise from outside alerted them all to something happening.

Rushing out towards the front door they all saw the image of Lizzie running across the drive from Philip's home to Jim's crying inconsolably as she screamed, "Daddy, Daddy, Daddy!"

Jim barged past the police and picked Lizzie up as if she was a little girl, pulling her tightly against him as her cries got louder and louder.

"Daddy, Tasha said to run. She made me promise to do as she said and she said run, so I ran."

"Good girl." Jim kissed her head gently. "Lizzie, where's Tasha, is she okay?" he asked, scared of the answer.

"She was standing between me and Mickie, she said to run and not stop until I found you, they were fighting with the gun, Daddy," sobbed Lizzie as Jim set her down on the threshold of his home where her mother was ready to receive her tearfully. "Daddy, Tasha said to tell you that she loves you."

"This has gone on long enough and has certainly gone far enough!" roared Jim. "If you can't end this, I will."

Jim barged past the police assembled, preparing to enter the house where Tasha was when a single shot sounded from Philip's home resulting in a series of screams and cries around them.

Jim paused for a split second before resuming his plan and ran towards the house but was intercepted by the police who had appeared from nowhere, presumably these particular officers had been secreted around the properties. There were countless voices, all talking at once, to each other and via police radios before the SWAT team invaded the house simultaneously. Confusion ensued and Jim used it as a sufficient distraction to make the remainder of the short trip across the drive and entered the house. He heard Sargent Masterson say something about, *the fucking boyfriend is entering the property, do not shoot* but he hadn't considered his own safety. He just needed to find Tasha and see her, hopefully alive and if not, he would kill Mickie, actually kill her, murder her because without Tasha he had no reason to live anymore. Tonight really had proven that to him.

Charging through the house, calling Tasha's name, Jim headed straight for the kitchen where he knew Mickie had kept her and as he reached the doorway stood rooted to the spot at the sight of Tasha lying on the kitchen floor, slumped against the cabinet covered in blood; in her hair, across her face and neck, her beautiful dress that had looked so phenomenal earlier that evening, stunning everyone at the image of her wearing it was now drenched in blood.

"No, she's dead," said someone in the room prompting pain like Jim had never known, lancing through every muscle in his body right to his core. His soul and very being were being crippled as he absorbed the words he'd heard and the scene before him.

Masterson appeared beside him now and although it felt as though everything was moving in slow motion, he realised that only a few seconds had passed as paramedics rushed through and settled at Tasha's side.

Jim allowed his vision to shift to where a very large and intimidating looking SWAT marksman stood over a lifeless body, almost unrecognisable, Mickie.

"She's dead. Appears to be one bullet to the head. It ain't pretty."

Movement from the paramedics caught his eye again now— or was it—it couldn't be.

"Eh, there's my handsome fiancé. We sure know how to throw a party, don't we?" came Tasha's voice startling and stunning Jim.

Rushing down to her side, he reached for her and pulled her to him, unconcerned by the blood transferring onto him.

"Fucking hell, Tasha! You really scared me there. Are you okay? The blood, you're covered and there's so much of it."

"Not mine, I don't think, well, not much," cried Tasha, trying to get to her feet.

"Whoa, ma'am, let us check you over first," cried a paramedic.

"Mickie, she shot herself, right in front of me, it covered me, she said I had done this as much as if I'd pulled the trigger." Tasha cried as she looked up at Jim as more people appeared with a trolley and a body bag like she'd only ever seen in movies. "She said the guilt of her death would eat away at me and you'd end up hating me, always wondering just what I was capable of," Tasha sobbed uncontrollably as the reality of what those words might mean began to sink in and the shock of the night hit her.

"Baby, let's get you out of here." Jim scooped Tasha up in his arms before striding towards the doorway. "There's a video camera over there somewhere," called Jim as he signalled towards the location Juan had described before heading out of the house across to their own home, away from the scene of bloodshed, a dead body and a body bag.

Chapter Eleven

Five Days Later

"Tash, you look beautiful." Lucy grinned, looking at Tasha and her reflection in the mirror of the suite Jim had booked her into until they were married, when she would be Natasha Maybury. Her grin widened at the site of her friend looking relaxed, beautiful and happier than she had ever been, as happy as she should always have been and deserved to be. "You are looking really, really soppy though," teased Lucy, making them both laugh.

"Sorry. I can't believe I'm doing this and after the stuff with Mickie it seems even more unbelievable," explained Tasha, smiling thoughtfully as she stared at her bruises that Lucy had expertly covered for her with make-up.

"I know and that is also why we are all here with you. After calls from Jim with flights and hotels to check into rather than just the two of you running off without us."

"Sorry. I just wanted to marry him and after my crash nobody else mattered, and until you all turned up here last night, I really thought it was just Bobby, Abby, me and him on this trip."

"No. He decided after your crazy party that you should do this with your nearest and dearest, hence The Winters clan along with the Mayburys, and Marc and Marcia who I find a bit scary, and your super-duper bestest friend in the world and wedding dress designer extraordinaire. That's me, oh and Ryan."

"He really is very industrious when he sets his mind to it and he's managed with minimal delays. Now, come on, finish zipping me in or he may not hang around if I'm late," joked Tasha.

"Oh, Tash, he would wait forever for you, it's quite sickening," said Lucy seriously, then suddenly began to sniff tearfully.

"What are you doing? You're crying. You are the least crying person I know." Tasha was actually shocked at her friend's out of character emotional display.

"It's kind of my thing now, hormones," revealed Lucy.

"No," whispered a shocked Tasha.

"Yes. In about six months my baby will be saying hello to Auntie Tasha, and I may have been offered a job out here as a costume advisor come designer for a new TV series set in Victorian England."

"Congratulations, on the baby and the job," cried Tasha. Suddenly, suspiciously she asked, "Whose studio? It's Jim's, isn't it? Of course it is." She shook her head wondering if he had any more surprises in store for her.

"Yeah, but he just sent me an email with who to contact, that was all and Ryan fancies himself as some kind of personal trainer out here, so it's all good. Now, Natasha Winters, let's get you ready to become Mrs Maybury the last before Gramps arrives to escort us to the chapel."

The gentle tap on the door had Tasha taking deep breaths as Lucy opened it to reveal Paul and Celia followed by Dan, Pippa, Lizzie, Abby and Lexi, the three girls dressed in identical vintage style, calf length dresses in a very deep shade of purple that suited all of their complexions and colourings while Lucy, as maid of honour wore the same dress but in a softer shade of lilac. It was actually an idea of Kayla's to make the senior female attendant identifiable and Tasha was glad that she had, but it had been Lucy's idea to have the dark dresses with sashes in the same shade of lilac as her dress while her sash was the same dark purple of the other girl's gowns.

"Wow!" Dan pushed to the front to kiss his sister. "You are really, really beautiful, Tash, more than beautiful." He floundered suddenly.

"Thank you." Tasha gazed up at her brother and smiled, not at the sweet boy he'd always be to her but the young man he was becoming to the rest of the world.

"Jim is a very lucky man indeed, and not just because of how bloody gorgeous you look." There was a strange hitch to Paul's voice and along with his glazed eyes it suggested he might cry.

"Gramps, please don't or I will have mascara streaks down my face before we leave the hotel."

Her grandmother hugged her but said nothing before moving over so her husband could give their eldest granddaughter a huge cuddle that may have been more for his benefit than hers.

"We should probably go and let you two sort yourselves out. We will see you at the chapel," Celia said, letting everyone else know they needed to get going.

Tasha got lost in a sea of hugs, kisses and compliments before Lizzie finally stepped forward and with tears welling in her eyes hugged Tasha tightly. "I'm so glad you're marrying Daddy and that everything has worked out, you know..." She grimaced referring to their joint time with Mickie. "You really do look beautiful and Daddy will be blown away, like he always is when he sees you," she added, making Tasha smile at the genuine sweetness of her comment.

"Come on." Celia ushered then shooed Lucy, Lizzie, Lexi, Pippa and Dan out.

Abby hung back to exchange an air kiss with Tasha, protecting their make-up but was close enough to whisper, "Jim is going to want to consummate this marriage in the chapel and you and I will be sharing a name real soon."

"Come on," called Celia for a second time, coming back to herd Abby out. "Ten minutes you two and then you need to be in the car."

Tasha looked across at her grandfather who was standing opposite her in the lounge area of the hotel room they were in.

"Have you got everything?" he asked nervously.

"I think so; Grandma has my bag, Jim has my engagement ring and I hope my wedding ring, oh, Jim's ring," Tasha squealed, rushing through to the bedroom where she'd packed it along with her clothes that Jim had assured her would be collected and transferred to the hotel they'd be occupying together, as a married couple. Pulling it from her case she looked across at Paul and held the box aloft, "Would you keep it for me, until we get there?"

"Of course Nat, anything you want," he replied hesitantly.

"Gramps?" Tasha nervously wondered what was on his mind.

"Sorry, but I have to ask. I didn't do this for your mother and I do wonder if I could have changed things if I had, if we'd maintained full contact. Are you sure, Nat? About this marriage and Jim?"

"Oh, Gramps." She sighed sadly, wondering how she had managed to miss the guilt and heartbreak her grandparents must have felt at abandoning their daughter and in doing that not saving their grandchildren. "My mother is a law unto herself and I think she probably always was, meaning you couldn't save her, even if she needed saving. I used to tell myself she was as much a victim as us, but now I think she was always party to it, but me? I don't need saving, Gramps. Not from Jim. Before I met him I wasn't even sure if I believed in marriage, that it was relevant or necessary for me, but it is, completely and utterly. I can't wait to get to the chapel and to be married. I want to memorise every second of it so that I will always have the memories of the day I became Mrs James Maybury. This is the first day of my forever, my happily ever after. I know he can be intense, a pain in the arse, but I like that, I love it, I love him."

"Right, let's get you finished off then." Paul smiled, accepted the ring box and placed it in the inside pocket of his tux'.

Tasha smiled at her grandfather's reflection in the mirror she stood before wearing her white lace, fitted dress that clung to her whole figure, but seemed to emphasise the softness of her breasts, down to the beautiful curve of her hips and behind that Jim loved to touch and hold so much and the dip of her waist. The skirt filled out slightly as it passed her thighs and legs before turning into the chapel length train. She glanced up once more to her chest and shoulders that were virtually bare, aside from the thin straps of the dress and the pendant necklace she wore. She looked like a princess and she felt one too, complete with a crown, well, a tiara that sat in the up-do Lucy had put her hair into.

"Flowers for the bride." Smiled Paul. He picked up the hand tied bouquet comprising of a selection of white, purple and lilac flowers.

Brides in Vegas were ten a penny Tasha assumed, and still she and her grandfather gained lots of attention as they made their way from the hotel room down to the car. It was only as they got into the limo that Tasha realised they probably looked like a couple and giggled to herself, but said nothing as she knew her grandfather would be mortified at the idea of people viewing them in that way and would probably try to explain to them all that they were anything but a couple.

The journey to the chapel was short and speedy. Once there they were greeted by all of the Maybury women, Marcia, Ryan and the bridal party that had left the hotel before them.

"Where's Jim?" asked Tasha panicking.

"He's inside, with Bobby, Jack and Philip," Maisie explained, reassuring Tasha with a stroke of her hand.

"Hey there, girlfriend," called Juan as he exited the chapel with the lady who was overseeing the ceremony. "This is Lola and she has the power to make you say I do," he told her laughing.

"Is Jim okay?" Tasha asked Lola who smiled kindly.

"He is fine, excitable and desperate to see his bride," she replied in a deep southern drawl. "Let's get your guests in place and I'll show you in."

"Thanks," Tasha said on a deep exhale then took her grandfather's arm to follow the African American woman who was possibly only thirty-years-old with a confident and infectious smile that was immediately reassuring.

Standing in a foyer on her grandfather's arm, Tasha jumped when Lola reappeared with Elvis.

"You're my thumbnail." The grin on Tasha's face confused the man before her who had more than a passing resemblance to The King himself, but his voice sounded a little forced.

"Nat?" Paul looked puzzled. Tasha realised that she hadn't actually mentioned the Elvis thing.

"Ah, I may have forgotten to mention it. Elvis got the gig and is marrying us."

"Bloody hell, Nat. Just when I think you can't spring anything else on me." He sighed.

"Sorry." Tasha really hoped Paul wouldn't disapprove or think that the addition of an Elvis impersonator somehow undermined her love or commitment to Jim or vice versa.

"After getting yourself almost killed, again! Then finding out you'd planned to elope." He shook his head then offered her a half-smile. "It's going to be memorable at least." He laughed warmly allowing the tension to leave Tasha's body.

"If you'd follow me then ma'am, sir." Elvis grinned with a fake lopsided smile.

Tasha tightened her arm's link through Paul's and moved her flowers to her front before following Elvis through the vestibule and stopped at a set of double doors where the four bridesmaids all waited for them.

"See you at the other end of the aisle," said The King, leaving the bride and her grandfather with Lola who was positioning everyone to enter and running through final details.

"I'm going to open the doors," she said, "and then you three girls will make your way to the front." She addressed Lexi, Pippa and Lizzie. "Then you, honey," she told Lucy. "And finally, the blushing bride. Let's do it people." She giggled before opening the door and ducking inside.

Tasha watched the other girls enter and could see that the ends of the pews had been adorned in ribbons of white, purple and lilac and there were vases of fresh flowers in the same colours everywhere making her realise that Jim and Kayla had been very busy since Friday night making all of this happen. She could see that the aisle was an 'L' shape which would allow her to walk in without being seen before turning into the straight stretch of the aisle that Jim was standing at the end of. Seeing Lucy turn and wink as she turned onto the straight stretch Tasha grinned and led Paul through the doors. Pausing before they turned to where she would see her soon-to-be husband, she had to gather herself, slow her strides because she was at risk of dragging her grandfather down the aisle if her pace up to now was anything to go by.

"Steady Nat," he warned as they turned to see the

congregation gathered.

Tasha had to stop herself from running when her eyes found her fiancé standing in front of Elvis with Bobby, Marc and Philip at his side.

They all turned to look at the bride walking down the aisle and all four men wore blinding smiles, but Tasha was only aware of Jim's. She was halfway down the aisle when she saw him take a step towards her. His brother's hand rested on his shoulder, stopping him from striding up to collect his bride but that just made Tasha's smile broaden into a grin as she glanced at each side of the congregation.

On the groom's side were Jack and Maisie, Bria and Sophie with Martin and Derek, Sophie's husband. Then there was Abby and Marcia with Bria and Sophie's children while on the bride's side was Celia, Dan, the bridesmaids and Ryan. Everyone who mattered was there. She was only about eight strides from reaching her groom when her gaze fixed back on him, but apparently he had waited long enough because even with his brother's hand resting on his shoulder Jim headed for her and before she fully absorbed his movements he was there, standing before her, briefly halting her journey.

"Hey baby, sorry. I have waited too long for this to wait any longer," he told her loud enough for everyone else to hear and laugh with mutterings of *aww*. "You look beautiful, more than beautiful, too beautiful for me to describe," he whispered now and gently leaned in to kiss her lips gently. "Shall we?" He offered her his arm, an arm she accepted after moving her flowers to the hand that was still through her grandfather's arm. She slipped her right arm through Jim's left meaning she finished the journey down the aisle between Jim and Paul, holding onto them both and it felt like the most natural thing in the world.

The ceremony was fairly short, but quite traditional until it came to the vows that they'd written themselves; Tasha made references to the love, care and devotion she'd come to know since meeting Jim and her ability to reciprocate those things too. The extended family she now viewed as her own and how she couldn't wait to carry Jim's name and wear his ring. Jim smiled

141

down at her with every word and although they were surrounded by their nearest and dearest, they may as well have been alone. Jim began his vows talking about knowing that Tasha was his future, the only future he would ever need or want from the day he'd met her which made her throat burn with the threat of tears. He continued to talk about the privilege that would be his alone when he called her his wife making her smile but it was when he described her as the bravest, most courageous, generous and loving woman he had ever met that she thought she may lose the battle with her tears, but clung on, just, until finally, he added that she had completed his life. He explained that she had done that as his partner, the perfect stepmother to his children and the mother to his future children, but more than that she had completed him. That before meeting Tasha there had been a huge void in his life, a void he hadn't always been aware was there, but since meeting her the gaping hole had been obvious to him, as obvious as the fact that the chasm in his life was Tasha shaped and no longer present.

It was at that point that Tasha lost the battle with her emotions, allowing several tears to escape down her face.

"And still I make you cry, Natasha." He grinned with an arch of his eyebrows referring to the times he'd made her cry during sex which caused a flush of embarrassment and arousal to creep across her face but did stem her tears.

Tasha was trying to savour every second of her wedding, from the second she'd seen Jim, to Elvis asking who gave this woman to which her grandfather had replied, *we do, her grandparents*, the way her grandfather had metaphorically and literally relinquished his hold on her as he handed her over to Jim, the soft sniff of tears, happy tears all around and then the vows, like she would ever be able to forget them even if she wanted to.

"Do we have rings to cement your honka, honka burning love?" Elvis asked, making Tasha laugh.

"Yes," Tasha and Jim replied.

Bobby, who had been given the role of best man for this wedding, as he had been for Jim's first marriage, while the others had been Marc's, reached into his inside pocket and retrieved Tasha's ring. While he reached forward to place it in front of Elvis, Tasha turned to her grandfather who was already offering her the closed box containing Jim's ring. Pulling it free, she turned back and placed it next to her own ring and grinned up at Jim who looked down at the rings and back at her with a grin to match her own.

"Perfect, baby."

They reached the part of proceedings where they exchanged rings and before they knew it Mr and Mrs James Maybury were walking back up the aisle to applause after their first kiss as a married couple.

Once outside there were lots of photos, congratulations and hugs before the wedding party were packed into different cars to head off for a wedding lunch. Jim and Tasha got into their limo first and were finally alone, well, alone with a chauffeur.

"I can't even begin to tell you how happy I am right now, honey," Jim said. "You look amazing and I really wish we were giving lunch a miss because my appetite is not for food. In fact, I wish they'd had a room at the chapel," he said seriously, making Tasha laugh as she recalled Abby's words at the hotel and then her laughter was stemmed by Jim's lips covering hers as the sound of the privacy screen went up, albeit briefly due to the short journey to their lunchtime destination.

****

"What are you doing?" squealed Tasha excitedly as Jim lifted her up into his arms.

"I'm going to carry you across the threshold, Mrs Maybury." He grinned at her before planting a single kiss on her lips.

"You could have warned me." She giggled. Nestled against Jim's chest her arms snaked around his neck allowing her to hold him tightly as he opened the door to the honeymoon suite he'd booked them into in what appeared to be the swankiest hotel Vegas had to offer. "I have only just eaten, you can't go throwing me around," she warned.

"Yeah, well, it was a very small and quick lunch so you should be good." He stepped over the threshold.

As the door clicked shut behind them Tasha expected him to set her down on her feet, but he strode along the entrance to the suite still carrying her.

"I think we're over the threshold now," she pointed out while teasing the ends of his hair between her fingers.

"Yes, but you need to save your energy, baby."

"My energy?" She wondered whether he was keeping her wrapped in cotton wool forever after everything she'd been on the receiving end of via Mickie.

"Yes, your energy, honey. You're going to need every last ounce for our three-day Vegas honeymoon."

"Surely if I'm going to be in bed for three days energy shouldn't be a problem," replied Tasha mischievously.

"Oh, baby, this is going to be the best three days of my life."

Jim carried Tasha across the suite through a huge lounge area with a cinema size screen occupying one wall but before she could take any more of the room in, they were entering another room, the bedroom, which seemed a serious understatement for the luxurious setting they were in. Jim placed her down on her feet.

"Jim, it's beautiful. I never even imagined there were really places like this." She gasped, a little tearfully.

"Only the best for my wife," he replied as he wrapped his arms around her from behind watching the reflection of them both is the huge mirror they stood in front of. "When I imagined you as my bride I have to admit I could never have dreamt just how beautiful you'd look."

"Thanks, I think." Tasha frowned but also wore a small smile.

He laughed. "A frown, Natasha?"

"Only because I'm unsure if you just gave me a backhanded compliment," replied Tasha, defending herself.

"It was unintentionally backhanded, baby, but to clarify, I meant I'd imagined you looking beautiful, very beautiful. However, the way you look today surpasses just how beautiful I imagined you being." Jim dropped a kiss to her shoulder, still looking at their reflections in the mirror.

Tasha flushed slightly at the sincerity of his compliment, but had been shocked herself at the image that had greeted her when Lucy had revealed it to her earlier that day in a similar mirror in the suite of a neighbouring hotel she'd been holed up in over the previous day and a half with her friends and family. Jim had surprised her by flying everyone out to Vegas to join them after their original plan to do this low key seemed no longer appropriate after their unconventional family unit had come so close to being torn apart again by Mickie, but they had come out the other end, survived it. Jim had decided they should witness and celebrate their marriage together, as Lucy had explained earlier to her and Tasha had to agree that it was definitely what she'd needed and Jim, yet again, had known what she required better than she had herself.

She felt Jim's grip on her tighten slightly and smiled again at the image of them both; the glittering of her diamond solitaire earrings and matching pendant along with a small tiara minus a veil were her only accessories as she'd left her engagement ring in Jim's care to allow for the addition of her wedding band. Her make-up was understated but sufficient to mask the bruises and cuts she still bore from her evening with Mickie, but they were barely noticeable at the moment. She was dressed in the fitted white lace dress Lucy had made. The overall plainness of it was lifted with intricate detailed lace. The train was now gathered at her side while the lace covered buttons hiding the zip were currently covered by Jim standing behind her in his black tuxedo that appeared slightly longer in length but with narrower lapels than previous tuxedos she'd see him wearing. The colour of the jacket was in stark contrast to the almost blinding white of the shirt beneath it.

She'd almost hoped that Jim would opt for a more traditional suit with a coloured waistcoat and tie or cravat originally, but looking at him now she didn't believe he could have looked any better or that she could have found him any more attractive than she did right now. Maybe it was a more English look she'd originally imagined for her groom, but she needed to remember that her groom, her husband was not English and the black suit with matching bow tie reminded her of that. Jim adjusted his position so one hand rested on her right hip as his other linked with her left hand to perfectly display their wedding rings making her grin.

"Nice choice of ring, Mr Maybury." She looked down at their

hands.

"Right back at ya, Mrs Maybury," he replied with a grin as big as hers making them both laugh at their identical bands that they'd each chosen for the other independently.

"Who knew my penny-pinching fiancée would choose a twenty-four carat, platinum wedding band from Tiffany no less."

"Mmm," agreed Tasha. "Indeed. And who knew that my cash splashing fiancé would choose such an understated twenty-four carat, platinum wedding band from the afore mentioned Tiffany."

"I kind of thought that a diamond band wouldn't be you, unlike an understated, plain band," said Jim, explaining his choice of ring.

"And I thought that you would be more comfortable wearing something simple and plain too," replied Tasha. "Especially as this is your first wedding ring."

"First, last, only wedding ring, Tasha." Jim's voice was a low growl against her neck and shoulders that were accessible courtesy of her hair being pinned into a loosely styled up do with only odd strands of curled hair softening the look around her face, ears and neck.

Tasha replied in a single low moan.

"Baby, we really are the perfect couple, aren't we?" Jim asked without requiring an answer as he continued to kiss across from one of Tasha's shoulders to the other. "You know, as beautiful as you look, I am desperate to get you out of this dress and see what's underneath it," whispered Jim against Tasha's ear as he made his way back across to her first shoulder.

"I thought we might take a look around first," Tasha responded honestly, but was as desperate to undress as Jim seemed to be.

He groaned against her back, disappointed that his need and desire for his wife was going to have to wait, briefly. Very briefly if he had his way. "Let's investigate this place together then. You can see everywhere you're going to be fucked before the event, and then I'm going to remove your clothes, slowly and we'll start our three-day Vegas honeymoon." Jim spoke with a husky rasp before releasing Tasha briefly. He retook her left hand in his right one to lead her around the suite. "This is our bedroom complete with huge bed that lends itself quite nicely to tying you down and up, baby." Jim spanked Tasha's behind firmly but playfully.

She looked around at the huge windows that almost surrounded the whole room offering breath-taking views of Las Vegas that could be shut out judging by the touch-screen control panel for the curtains amongst other things she imagined as they passed the wall mounted flat screen TV before finding herself standing in a bathroom that was bigger than any she'd ever seen.

"Oh, James," she gasped.

"You wanna skip the rest of the tour?" asked Jim, looking down at her making her look up at him confused. "James?"

"Ah, I see." Tasha considered delaying the guided tour, but didn't, she simply smiled.

"Come on, Tasha, quickest tour possible. Huge bathroom; two sinks and closets, separate shower and gigantic whirlpool deep-soak tub, oh and the toilet is next door," he said pulling her to the next room. "Toilet." He gestured to the door next to the bathroom.

The whirlwind tour continued including; private massage room and gym, bar and dining area for meals including the daily in-room breakfast for two and the coffee service he was championing. Daily maid service, touch-screen curtains, lighting and privacy controls, flat screen TVs.

He stopped at an iPhone dock. "For all your songs about marrying me and loving me forever," he announced with a grin.

The tour continued into the lounge area she'd seen as she was carried through and another smaller bathroom with a toilet and wash basin that completed the suite.

"We have access to clubs, casinos, restaurants and several shows that we won't bother with." They stood in the lounge again where Jim picked Tasha back up and before she could offer any objection or comment he added, "And now, Mrs Maybury I am going to carry you back to the bedroom and undress you."

"Just undress me?" she asked with a wide grin.

"Maybe, or maybe I'm going to undress you and then fuck

you like you have never been fucked before," Jim replied quite seriously making Tasha laugh at his less than romantic words as he carried her back to the bedroom where he stood her near the bed.

"So?" Tasha suddenly felt a little over scrutinised by her husband's eyes gazing down at her intensely.

A smile curved Jim's lips as he considered what to say but his hand lifted and rested against Tasha's face where he stroked across her cheekbone gently. She began to curl into his touch, almost cat like.

"I can't believe we're here, at last." She smiled up at him.

"Vegas?" he asked with an arched brow.

"Not really, I guess that was written in the stars." Tasha laughed, making Jim shake his head.

"It was always going to happen for my lucky seven," he replied.

"Mmm, but what I meant was this, being married, to each other. It seems to have been a very long and difficult journey to get here," she said but it was almost to herself.

"And then some, honey. So?"

"That was my question," Tasha told him stretching up and cupping her husband's face then grinned at her ring glittering. "I love wearing your ring."

"Good, because it's never coming off. Now, I need to get back to undressing you and fucking you like you've never been fucked before," Jim repeated, dragging his hands down her face, neck and across her collar bone until his hands rested on her shoulders.

"I really wish I never had been." Tasha wondered where those words had come from.

"Never been what?" Jim frowned as he prepared to move his lips to his wife's ear.

"Fucked," she replied bluntly causing Jim to stand up straight and study her face. "I mean, I wish tonight was the first night we —no—the first night I'd ever had sex, that you were the first man, only man to see me like this, to make love to me, James."

"Oh baby, I remember saying something similar to you and my ego still thinks that would be pretty awesome, but the most important thing here is that I'm going to be the only man that will see you like this, touch you, kiss you, make love to you from this day on and for me that is better than simply being the first," Jim told her as his arms seemed stronger, more purposeful in their pursuit to hold her, pull her close, remove the clothes that were nothing more than a barrier to getting even closer and getting his skin on and in hers.

Having already cast aside his own jacket, Jim made quick work of the zip beneath the buttons on her dress. He slid the gown down her body, slowly revealing her lingerie and body beneath it. Standing before her, Tasha heard a definite gasp leave her husband's lips as he drank in her appearance minus the dress that was pooled at her feet.

"I should probably pick the dress up," she told him. "I need to wear that again at the vineyard." She smiled, watching Jim's appreciative gaze fixed on her body.

"You stay there, I'll do it." He helped his wife to step out of the fabric around her feet that were still encased in white, glittery, heeled court shoes.

The dress was hung up in quick time allowing Jim to transfer his full attention back to Tasha standing nervously in the white silk, strapless, longline bra she'd opted for beneath her dress. The boned panelling through the longer line fabric and beneath the cups gave her even more of an hourglass figure than usual while the lace that was overlaid on the centre front panel and the push up cups added a hint of subtle femininity. The matching suspender belt she wore held up the sheer, lace topped stockings and the barely there thong that revealed her rounded globes entirely as she turned to show her new husband exactly what he was getting, was a perfect match for the rest of her lingerie with the same silk fabric overlaid with lace and tiny tanga style straps at the side attached with a gold coloured ring. The tiny white bow at the centre was enhanced with a pink bud as was the fabric between the cups and at her waist.

"Oh, baby, you are fucking perfect, beautifully perfect," he told her, stepping closer to pull her close and kiss her.

"James," she whispered as she came up for breath after he had kissed her, deeply, but gently, caressing her lips, tongue and mouth until she was dizzy with desire and breathlessness. "You seem awfully overdressed," she told him.

"Well, that will be resolved real soon, baby." He immediately began to pull off his clothes; tie, shirt, shoes, socks and finally his trousers while Tasha pulled the clips, grips and tiara from her hair allowing it to cascade onto her shoulders and back. "Better?" He moved closer again. "I have enough money to buy a new tux' if that one is creased, now where were we?" he asked, knowing exactly where they'd been.

Chapter Twelve

"I got you something, a present, a wedding present," Tasha explained, halting Jim's movements further.

"A present, for me? You've given me so much already, baby."

"I am quite nervous that you'll hate it," she admitted, but continued, "it's not really a gift I can physically give you, or take back—oh bugger." She suddenly realised for the first time that it was something she was stuck with forever. "You just need to find it, discover it, on me while I hope and pray you like it," Tasha rambled.

"Discover it?" Jim sounded and looked confused.

"Maybe if you finish undressing me," she suggested with a blush again.

"With pleasure." He grinned, spun her around and began unhooking the hooks and eyes of her bra. Pausing at the halfway point Jim ran his hands down the length of her body until he found the clips holding her stockings up and with a deft movement flicked them free of the fabric and returned his attention to the bra. Kissing across her shoulders he triumphantly cast the bra aside before spinning his wife back to face him then sat her down on the edge of the bed where he settled at her feet to pull off her shoes. That preceded the rolling off of the stockings from her legs then leaned in again to kiss her lips, jaw, neck, chest, abdomen, hips, inner thighs, all the way down her body to her toes and back up again.

"I haven't found my present yet," he said from beneath hooded eyes.

"Look harder," she replied with a squeal as she found herself flipped over onto her front allowing Jim to stroke and caress her behind until he undid the hooks of the suspender belt, allowing it to fall away. Finally, he hooked his thumbs into the tiny string sides of her thong and with a gentle lift of her hips he was stripping her completely bare.

"I really do not deserve you, Mrs Maybury," Jim groaned, returning to lie along the length of her legs and back, obviously naked and aroused as he carefully held his own weight on one arm while the hand of his other arm stroked down to her hip before sliding between Tasha and the bed. "Ah," he whispered with confusion as his fingers stroked across her mound that seemed to be covered with something still. "What do we have here?" Rolling from her, allowing Tasha the space and freedom to move onto her back, Jim's eyes were immediately drawn to the covering he had felt making him smile.

"I think I may have discovered my present, baby." He stared at what could only be described as a square of gauze taped to her mound, gauze decorated with a bow, as if gift wrapped. "You've gift wrapped your pussy for me?" he asked with a grin and a shake of his head.

"Not really, remove the gift wrap," she encouraged, although she felt sick with nervous excitement in case Jim hated it or even in case he didn't.

He was clearly still confused as he reached forward while Tasha sat herself up, resting her elbows and forearms against the bed.

Jim's finger and thumb found the edge of the tape and pulled it back along with the dressing to reveal his wedding present. With eyes as big as saucers he stared for long, tense seconds before the biggest of smiles spread across his face and then he was back on the bed between his wife's thighs covering her, preparing to make love to her for the first time.

****

The sound of Jim's phone ringing woke Tasha from the brief nap she'd been enjoying. Jim was already scrambling in his trousers that were on the far side of the bedroom where they'd been tossed when he'd undressed. Sitting up she looked across at him crouching over the phone that had now stopped. She stared at him shamelessly, wondering how she'd got this lucky, to find herself a loving, caring man who absolutely adored her, of that she had no doubt and he really was beautiful with a physique that at forty would be more than a match for any man, even twenty years younger, especially his well-toned, rounded, muscular behind that her eyes were glued to.

"You're staring," he said without turning around making her frown in confusion. "And a frown, Natasha." He pointed towards their reflections in the windows that were still free of drapes.

"Ah, I see, literally." She laughed. "Who was calling?" she asked as he turned to face her before striding back towards her in all his firm, muscular, handsome glory.

"Lizzie," he exclaimed climbing back up the bed towards her.

Lying against the mattress she giggled and then thought of Lizzie and all she'd been through making her wonder what she'd wanted.

"You should call her back." Tasha worried there could be something wrong.

"I should have left her in L.A." Jim frowned, leaning in to kiss her lips gently.

"Ah, poor Lizzie," cried Tasha as she reached up to pull Jim's face towards her own.

"You are too nice, honey," he told her as he allowed her to bring his lips to hers.

"And you are—my husband, my handsome husband," she told him, making him smile. Briefly she thought of Mickie saying something similar about her being *that nice* and whilst Mickie had meant it in the most negative of contexts Tasha chose to see her niceness and consideration for others as a positive. "But the last few weeks have been hard on Lizzie, on us all, but she is so young and the stuff with Mickie," Tasha began but drew a sharp breath in, feeling a little overwhelmed as she remembered her time in Philip's kitchen with Juan and Lizzie.

"Hey, it's over," Jim reassured her as he pulled her closer.

"I know, but it's still in our heads, all of our heads." She knew the *all* extended to Jim who had been resolute in his desire to avoid discussing how he'd felt, how he still felt on the back of it.

"I am sorry, baby, for allowing it to happen, for endangering you—" He got no further before Tasha interrupted.

"You were trying to protect me. I wish you'd told me but I in no way hold you responsible. What happened was not your fault, not even the fault of the police, not really. It was all down to Mickie, just Mickie."

"I should never have exposed you to her," Jim said with a sad and guilty expression.

"James, she was unhinged, she was mad about you," she replied with a short laugh as she tried to lighten the moment. "She hated every woman you ever met, loved and married but never tried to kill any of them so how were you to know? You couldn't."

"I don't deserve you." Jim repeated his earlier words.

"Nor I you, and yet here we both are." Tasha smiled before she felt Jim's lips moving against hers, only to be interrupted by the phone ringing again.

Jim frowned and growled at the same time.

"Be nice, please. She's been through a lot," Tasha repeated, placing an encouraging hand on Jim's arm.

"Okay, baby, but you hold all thoughts of our honeymoon," he told her as he answered the call. "Hey, Lizzie, are you okay, sweetie?" he asked gently, making Tasha smile at the gentle man she'd married then felt sad at the guilt he'd begun to express at what had happened to her, Lizzie and Juan at Mickie's hands. The truth was he'd been a victim of Mickie for years without realising it. "Not tonight, no. Lizzie. Where is everyone else? Uh-uh, okay. We're all meeting for lunch tomorrow before you go back to L.A. with Philip. Yes, Tasha is fine. I love you too."

With a long sigh Jim sat on the edge of the bed, worrying Tasha.

"Is she alright?"

"Yeah, she's had a fight with Alexi which then means she's had a fight with Abby. Juan and Philip are out so she just wanted to hear a friendly voice."

"You're worried about her." Tasha loved the father her

husband was. "We could meet her at their hotel and have dinner if you want or bring her back here," offered Tasha genuinely as she got on her knees to crawl across the bed until she had her front pressed firmly against Jim's back, her arms draped around his neck with her hands resting on his chest.

"Not a chance in hell, baby. This is our honeymoon and this is why we should have come here alone, just the two of us, but we didn't, but thank you. I love how you love my kids. We'll do lunch though, tomorrow, like we arranged." With the subject closed for him, Jim lifted one of Tasha's hands to his lips then kissed the finger with her wedding ring on it.

She nodded, accepting his decision not to alter their plans but then had an idea. "Could you pass my phone, please?"

His response was a shake of his head and a frown.

"Please, just two calls and two minutes."

Conceding, Jim freed himself from his wife's embrace and passed Tasha her phone. With a smile, he watched as she first called her grandparents and asked them if Lizzie could hang out with them, maybe sleep over and then she called Abby and told her that Lizzie had been invited to spend some time with Pippa in the suite her family were occupying. Abby huffed and groaned but put Lizzie on the phone to Tasha who sounded close to tears as she agreed to the plans Tasha had made for her. Hanging up, Tasha returned to her place beneath the bed covers and realised Jim was on his feet and rummaging in a bag. As he turned, he held up a selection of handcuffs, rope and ties.

"You are the best wife and stepmom my children or I could ever wish for, so I think you should be rewarded and you have waited for this since New York. Happy wedding day, Mrs Maybury." He grinned as he pulled the sheet off her and momentarily joined her on the bed where he stopped at the juncture of her thighs and leaned down to kiss his gift, her wedding present to him. "You really have taken that whole branding idea quite literally, but I fucking love this, baby." He grinned.

"I thought you might, well, hoped." She glanced down at the sight of her new husband kissing her bare sex emblazoned with her fresh tattoo declaring her as:

Owned by
James Maybury

"Did it hurt?" He slowly traced the letters with his finger.

"Like a bitch." She laughed when his touch began to tickle. "Were you surprised?" His expression when he'd first discovered it when stripping her suggested he had been shocked and surprised by the tattoo.

"Mmm, but I understand why you ditched security to get my gift and I now know why you decided on no sex until we were married."

"I wanted it to be a surprise and it was a little sore because of the earlier waxing and the tattoo."

"The bareness was as much of a shock as the tattoo, honey, but I kind of like that too." He grinned before sitting back and holding the handcuffs aloft. "Time to get your reward, baby."

****

Tasha and Jim were the last to arrive for lunch, but as Jim held out the chair next to Lizzie for his wife everyone smiled.

"Did you all have fun last night?" Jim glanced around the huge table they all occupied.

A variety of yes, muttering and smiles were heard in reply to his question.

"We went to the casinos, how about you two, what did you get up to?" Philip asked, almost instinctively.

Everyone stared at him disbelievingly.

Tasha broke the silence with her retort. "You so don't want to know the answer to that question, Philip. You really don't."

"Enough you two." Smiling, Jim took Tasha's hand in his beneath the table.

The truth was that they had enjoyed their first night as man and wife but in between bouts of love making and hot and steamy sex including Tasha's wish of being tied to the bed there had been sleep, sadly, not sound sleep for either of them.

Tasha had woken in a panic, calling out for Jim, coated in a sheen of sweat after waking from her new recurring dream of Mickie shooting herself. Jim had held her close, cuddled her and calmed her until she was able to doze back off. Unfortunately, her sleep had been fleeting when she'd stirred about forty minutes later feeling cold and alone. Waking, she'd discovered she was alone in bed. Throwing on Jim's shirt as her cases were still packed, Tasha went in search of him and didn't need to go far before she'd found him sitting on the sofa in the lounge area nursing a generous measure of something that looked like scotch.

Squeezing Jim's hand back beneath the table a little more firmly, Tasha recalled how sad and forlorn he'd looked as she'd studied him before making her way to stand before him.

"Hey there, gorgeous husband," she'd said with a half-smile.

"Hey yourself, beautiful wife," he'd replied with a smile that never quite reached his eyes.

"James," she whispered sadly as she placed herself in a straddle across his lap.

"Baby—"

"No, this is not your fault, what happened. It breaks my heart to see you looking so sad."

"Tasha, honey." He'd sighed as if unsure what else to say. "I know Mickie was responsible for her own actions, but I played a part in how it worked out. I can't believe that a woman I knew for over twenty years was that unhinged and dangerous and I never once suspected the depths she was capable of sinking to. How the fuck did I miss it? We spent time together, jeez I had a relationship with her, and I missed it all. Surely there must have been signs I should have noticed?"

Gently cradling Jim's head, Tasha tilted it so that he could no longer look down at his glass but had to look at her.

"I don't know if she was always that way, maybe time and life, a lonely and unfulfilled life made her that way. But whatever it was it wasn't your fault, not any part of it. Our home was more secure than government buildings but somehow she bypassed the security and was lucky enough to chance upon me, Juan and Lizzie. Nobody could have predicted any of that. She didn't hurt any of us, not really, not badly and I have never wished another person dead in my life, nobody, and yet I am glad she's dead. What you did, the set-up, was the right thing, the best thing because I'm unsure I would have remained cooped up in the house for much longer. I would have given security the slip or managed to find a way to have some freedom, we both know that and then she would have struck and without security and the police on hand she could have done anything she wanted."

Jim nodded but still didn't seem entirely convinced by her words meaning Tasha needed to do or say something more. Something that would make Jim see and believe that this was not down to him and that Mickie's behaviour was out of control and the depths she would consider sinking to were beyond anything he might have imagined she was capable of.

"We agreed not to discuss everything all at once, but maybe you need to know this—something I thought it was best not to tell you."

Jim looked up with a hint of concern reflected in his eyes. He knew there was so much more that he didn't know about what had happened in Philip's house but everything he had discovered had been bad and he had a horrible feeling this was going to be no different.

"Without your little sting with the police she would have got to me. We can probably both agree on that. She told me she'd thought of doing things differently, but I don't think the trap was conducive to that."

With the burn of tears and the feeling of fear at what Mickie could and would have done without Jim providing her with a chance to make a *safe* move, Tasha prepared to continue.

"Baby, I don't understand." Jim rested his hands on her hips and gently rubbed the skin there.

"She'd considered having some friends get to me. Big, male friends who wouldn't have been gentle. She wanted to ruin me for you, to make it so you couldn't look at me without seeing what they'd done and although she didn't succeed in the way she'd planned, her actions are impacting on us right now."

"Fucking hell, Tasha. I would have killed her, all of them..."

"Yeah, well you don't have to. Mickie did it for us and as I say I'm glad, but not if it hurts you and I know you have Jon and Helen on your mind too, but I'm still glad she's gone."

Jim nodded and reached up to pull Tasha's left hand to his lips. He kissed each of her fingers before tenderly placing his lips to her palm then pulled it over his heart.

"Me and you, baby."

"Me and you," Tasha had repeated.

"So, my very wise wife, what do we do now?"

"When things are tough, we help each other through it; I will tell you 'til the day I die that this is not your fault and when I wake up crying there are nobody else's arms I want to be held in. But right now, I think you need to ditch the whiskey and come back to bed with your wife."

Jim released Tasha's hand to pour her a drink while Lizzie leaned in and kissed Tasha on the cheek whispering, "Thank you."

"Could you pass the salt please, Lizzie?" asked Abby tersely, making Tasha frown.

Lizzie passed her aunt the salt and attempted to make conversation but Abby seemed to cut her dead, earning herself a glare from Bobby.

Jim said nothing but Tasha knew he'd seen the exchange.

"Hey Tash, has Jim told you we're staying over at yours for a few days when you get back?" asked Pippa.

"No, he hasn't," replied Tasha honestly. "But that will be nice, for us to spend some more time together." She grinned.

"Maybe Lizzie could stay and see if she can't find someone a little older to pick fights with," snapped Abby, interrupting Tasha's conversation with her sister.

Bobby muttered a token, *Abby* but she was unapologetic judging by her expression.

Tasha didn't even wait for Jim to intervene as she turned to Abby who was opposite her. "Back off, Abby. I don't know what went down with you guys last night, but you're supposed to be the adult here, so act it. If Lizzie did something awful then maybe you should have the decency to tell Jim in private and if it wasn't that awful then get over yourself and stop bitching at a child.

Abby stared at Tasha briefly before saying, "I am protecting my child."

"No, Abby, you're holding a grudge, so like I say, if what Lizzie did was so bad speak to Jim, if not, then act your age. Oh, and I admire you protecting your child, but make no mistake if you attack Lizzie then I too will protect my child."

Tasha could feel all eyes on her and didn't like it. She was in the middle of a potentially public scene so excused herself, leaving everyone else staring at her back.

"Nice one, Abby," said an angry Bobby with a shake of his head.

"How is this my fault?" she protested.

"Because last night was blown out of proportion and Tasha's right, you're holding a grudge, against a child."

She seemed to take stock for a few seconds before turning to look at her niece. "Sorry Lizzie, but when you fight with Alexi and she feels hurt, it hurts me too."

Lizzie looked tearful and scared by Tasha's disappearance but nodded at her aunt.

Jim stretched across and took Lizzie's hand and after kissing it he got to his feet. "I'm going to find my wife."

"Jimbo," called Bobby, causing his twin brother to turn and face him. "I think Momma Bear has claws."

"So it would seem," agreed Jim with a huge grin as he recalled how Tasha had stopped Abby's attack on his daughter and referred to her as her own child.

"Hey, there's my wife," he said spotting her as she left the bathroom.

"Sorry, I just needed a minute, away from the table. Is Lizzie okay?" She immediately found herself wrapped in Jim's arms where he kissed her gently and tenderly.

"You are something else, honey," he whispered against her ear before releasing her and taking her hand in his. "Let's go and play nicely, eat lunch and then we'll lock ourselves away for the next two days, and I may have a little honeymoon surprise up my sleeve, deal?"

"Deal." She grinned.

Chapter Thirteen

A month later, with a short, but very satisfying honeymoon in Vegas followed by a few days in Bora Bora along with their *formal* wedding reception at the vineyard, Tasha was feeling unwell. After several days of feeling *under the weather*, mood swings and frequent trips to pee, so frequent she knew she needed to see a doctor for antibiotics, she made an appointment with her ob/gyn doctor, Mitch Marshall.

Jim left for work in the knowledge she had a *serious* case of cystitis that was all his fault, an accusation he'd willingly accepted with a smile. Knowing that not only was Tasha's cystitis otherwise known as honeymoon disease because frequent, vigorous sex was attributed to its cause, but also because he had never been happier in his entire life.

The sound of Jim's car pulling up outside caused Tasha's stomach to churn and her tears to threaten to overflow, again. She'd cried for most of the afternoon after returning from Mitch's office and had sent Sandra home as soon as she'd returned so she could have the house to herself to fall apart at Mitch's diagnosis.

"Hey baby," called Jim as soon as he entered the house.

In a slight panic, Tasha rushed for the kitchen and began to potter, but actually did nothing.

"Hi," Tasha called overly optimistically, stifling a sob as Jim leaned in and kissed the back of her neck.

"Do you want to go out for dinner tonight?" he placed a hand on her behind thinking he was happy to stay in, but also liked a date night with his new wife too. A huge grin spread across his face as it always did when he thought of Tasha full stop, but especially when he thought of her or called her his wife.

"Erm, no, not really," stammered Tasha, still avoiding facing her husband.

"What's wrong? Jeez, Tasha I forgot you were at the doctor's office this morning. I was going to call you, but got caught up with work." He spun her around to face him and immediately looked panic struck as he saw her emotion filled face. "Honey, what's wrong?"

"Nothing." Tasha neither looked nor sounded convinced.

"Tasha, there is clearly something not right, so tell me what it is. You're scaring me."

Dipping her fingers into the back pocket of her jeans, Tasha retrieved the cause of her distress and held it out to show her husband whose expression was one of confusion now. Lying in the palm of her right hand was a lightly squashed and compressed plastic tube of some four centimetres.

"What's that?" Jim was still confused.

"That," began Tasha taking a deep breath, "is my contraceptive implant."

"Why is it in your hand and not implanted in your arm?" Jim was struggling to understand what was unfolding.

"It appears that it's broken, ineffective," faltered Tasha as she battled the emotions and tears she was struggling to control. "It was implanted deeply, too deeply. Possibly during my crash it got moved, damaged and was moved. Mitch isn't entirely sure how or what happened, but it's fucked!" She sounded angry rather than upset as she slammed the plastic down and then held her severely bruised arm out to show just how deeply it had been implanted.

"Ouch, that looks sore." Jim grimaced and reached across to gently kiss her bruised flesh before thinking through fully the implications of what Tasha was saying, almost scared to allow his mind to process all the possibilities. "You're okay though? Have you had another one put in, chosen something else or are we going to discuss that?"

Tasha shook her head. Her brain refused to order or utter words but allowed tears to fall. When she saw Jim's confused face she realised she had to tell him about her day, all of it.

"Nothing to discuss. Not right away. Good news is, I do not have cystitis or a urinary tract infection. In fact, I am in tip top condition," she revealed with a wry smile and tears on her face.

"Baby, you've got me real scared now, not to mention damn well confused. Just tell me what the hell happened with Mitch."

"I'm pregnant." Once the words were out, said aloud, unable to be ignored or taken back she allowed her tears to flow freely and for her sobs to join them.

Jim stared across at her looking a little shell shocked then smiled a half-smile at her.

"Oh baby," he soothed as he pulled her into his embrace where he held her, rocked her and when the tears had subsided sat her down on the sofa where he joined her. "How are you feeling now?" He gently kissed her forehead.

"Shit. Really, really shit." She sounded melodramatic to her own ears, but continued, "I'm so scared, Jim. I can't be pregnant, I just can't, and I don't want to do this. I can't do this." She held her head in her hands. "It might be wrong I suppose. Maybe we should get a second opinion."

"Tasha, you're pregnant and you can't wish this away, honey," he told her seriously. "No number of opinions will make you less pregnant."

"But we hadn't planned on having a baby yet, maybe never. I can't do this, James. I'm not ready."

"I think you will find that decision has been taken out of our hands."

"It doesn't have to be out of our hands, does it?" Tasha knew that it was, even before she looked at Jim's face and saw his horrified expression at her suggestion.

Thinking about Mickie's revelations about Jim's second wife having had an abortion behind his back she felt doubly guilty and began to cry again. "Sorry," she said sincerely. "I just need to get my head around this. It's a shock. A huge fucking shock. I was just thinking aloud and there are other options, generally. I just don't know if I can do this. You're pleased, aren't you?" she knew she was beginning to ramble as she scrutinised her husband's face.

"I could lie, but I won't. Yes, I'm pleased, thrilled, but I'm trying to contain it as you're struggling with it, but the idea of you carrying my baby makes me very, very happy."

"I'm going to lie down." Tasha got to her feet with a desperate need to put some distance between her and her husband while they were in such different places.

"I'll sort dinner in a while," he told her, but stopped short of declarations of love or offers to join her as he figured she needed some space and so did he because his heart was fit to burst with pride, love and excitement.

Once upstairs and after yet another trip to the bathroom, Tasha looked at her naked body in the mirror and tried to find some signs of pregnancy, but found very few, if any. Her breasts looked heavier, slightly, and her nipples were darker than she'd remembered but beyond that she looked exactly the same as she had when she'd gotten married, although by Mitch's estimation she was already pregnant when they'd married, just. Thank fuck Mickie hadn't realised that. She allowed her mind to briefly visit possible outcomes of that night in Philip's kitchen if her pregnancy had been known; having already done away with one of Jim's babies, Tasha was sure another one would have been easy, Mickie had told her as much. A cold shiver ran over her body as she realised that neither of them would have been allowed to leave alive, her nor Mickie. None of them; her, Mickie or Baby Maybury. Throwing a loose fitting t-shirt on, Tasha wondered how the hell this was going to be resolved, so crawled into bed and decided to forget about it, to sleep and dream about anything other than cherubic looking babies with gummy smiles and chunky thighs which was how she imagined her own child of the future.

****

It was dark when Tasha stirred and realised it was two in the morning, meaning she had missed dinner and slept through from early evening. Rolling onto her side, Tasha shuffled back until her back was nestled against Jim's front. His breathing and light snoring made her smile and relax again so sleep could wash over her once more, although when she thought of Jim's pleasure at her pregnancy she found her anxiety levels rising. The feel of his arm looping over her exposed middle made her momentarily soften again until his hand settled on her belly where he gently cupped her lovingly and protectively stroked her. He was already in that place, the one for expectant parents who smiled constantly and *couldn't wait* for their *precious bundles* to arrive healthy, with ten little fingers and ten little toes. God, she felt sick and was unsure whether it was pregnancy related due to hormones or pregnancy related because she was actually pregnant.

Trying to shift her position was impossible. Every time Tasha moved away, or tried to, Jim pulled her back and held her tighter. She was unsure whether he was awake or asleep and didn't want to wake him if he was still sleeping and risk the prospect of a discussion. After the sixth or seventh attempt to move failed, Tasha resigned herself to lying still despite her desire to get up, to grab a cup of tea, maybe even a slice of cake or chocolate, but her husband seemed determined to keep her exactly where she was, lying in bed next to him.

It was six o'clock before she was freed from Jim's embrace and her head was virtually lodged in the toilet with near certainty that the vomiting she was experiencing was the start of morning sickness. Jim tried to support and comfort her, but was obviously wary of her reaction to him, after all, he had admitted his pleasure at the situation while she was still talking about options. Options she didn't have as far as Jim was concerned, but he wasn't going to push that discussion yet. Hopefully, Tasha would reach that conclusion herself.

"Is the offer of breakfast going to trigger more vomiting?" asked Jim as a freshly showered Tasha sat on the edge of the bed wearing yoga pants and a t-shirt.

"Depends on whether you'll accept that I can't eat it." Even the idea of food made her feel ill.

"I'll get you some crackers and tea, or water." He smiled at her, with kindness and sympathy before leaning down to gently kiss her lips. "I love you, baby, and this will be okay."

Getting to her feet slowly, Tasha wondered how this was ever going to be *okay*. She went through the options in her mind again as she milled around the room, making the bed and straightening things up. She could put the baby up for adoption. Not a hope in hell of her going through the whole pregnancy and being able to give the baby away, her baby and that was without taking the *Jim factor* into account. She could terminate her pregnancy, that was possible from all perspectives, medical and emotional, but it would be at the cost of her marriage. She knew Jim would never forgive her if she killed their baby, his baby, like number two had. Remembering her own termination aged sixteen, the horror of it and the difference in how each of her unborn babies had been conceived, she decided not. She was not Mickie, she didn't hate kids and couldn't just get rid of them without a second thought. Or, she thought as she stared at her reflection she could have the baby and judging by the fact that she had subconsciously shoved Jim's rolled up hoody up her front to emulate a larger baby bump she may have made her decision already. Not that there was ever really a decision to be made.

A plate with some crackers and plain biscuits on it sat opposite Jim on the table next to a bottle of water, an empty glass and a freshly brewed cup of tea.

"Did you make the tea?" asked Tasha. She would be less capable of drinking a cup of tea made by Jim while her stomach was flipping than she normally would.

"Fortunately for you, no. Sandra did, and she has made herself scarce as I am in a weird mood and you dismissed her yesterday."

"She's pissed off with us then?" Tasha felt guilty for making the other woman uncomfortable the previous day.

"Yeah, but she'll be cool when she understands." He reached across to take her hand in his.

"Bacon makes me want to throw up it seems, and coffee, oh and eggs." Tasha leapt up and ran for the downstairs bathroom.

Looking down at his unfinished breakfast, Jim shook his head and muttered to himself. "It's gonna be a long eight months, Jimbo."

When Tasha returned she found him with a bowl of cereal and a glass of juice while her crackers and biscuits remained untouched.

"And tea," she added, tipping the contents of her cup away and swallowing hard. "I really don't know if I can do this, Jim," she admitted honestly.

"We'll do it together." Jim's smile was tentative, scared of saying the wrong thing. He was suddenly reminded of an injured animal as he watched his wife's expression. He was scared too, scared half to death that a move that was too quick or a wrong word would startle her, spook her into doing something that would cause her greater harm.

"Except we won't, will we? I will do this while you continue with your life like a normal person," she said sadly.

"Natasha, what are you thinking? What do you want to do?" He sounded more scared than she did.

"I'm thinking that the contraceptive implant was my worst idea to date. That I should have gone with the pill or the jab in the arse and avoided being here, in this position, and what I want is to go back at least six weeks and check my contraception, but they are no longer options, so..."

"So? So what? I still want you to be happy, Tasha. That's still my main mission in life," he told her sincerely making her smile.

"As far as I see it, we, I have two options. Have a baby or terminate it." She flinched at his expression at the word terminate. "We had kind of agreed to have a baby, some babies in the future and I'm seriously freaking out, I can't deny that. I am scared, scared like I have never been scared before and we both know I have a huge amount of experience with fear, but this is different. I'm scared of failure, of being the biggest fuck up there has ever been in the history of fuck up parents. I have no such fears for you. You are a brilliant father with a proven track record and you come from good parenting stock, but me —"

He cut her off. He needed this not to turn into a self-loathing tirade from her based on the fact that her own parents had been less than useless and that somehow that was her fault and in turn it would make her the same kind of parent they had been. She wouldn't. She would be amazing, of that he had no doubt. "Tasha, baby—"

She cut him off now, needing to finish speaking. "No, please, let me get this out. I need you to understand. Look at where we've both come from and how far we've come in such a short time. So much has happened; I fell in love with you and ended up here as a wife, a stepmother, an out of work actress who keeps managing to force producers to recast every part I get, with all of my family on the other side of the Atlantic, even the fucked up ones. Except for my father who is awaiting sentencing for my attempted murder. Someone has held me hostage and tried to murder me, twice, after deciding against having me gang raped. It's a lot to take in. We are both still carrying the baggage from all of that, but our wedding was like the first day of the rest of my life and now, a month later, I'm pregnant and it's a shock. A huge, knocked me on my arse, fucking shock. You told me I can't wish it away and I do know that. I don't know if that's what I want to do, not really, but maybe I just want to postpone it, but I can't do that either, so I am left with have it or terminate it."

"And?" asked a nervous looking Jim.

"I don't know what having a baby will mean, not really, I can imagine, but I don't know. I do know what a termination means and although I would never have saddled myself with Liam's baby. I could never have had his baby. But the termination?" She puffed out a huge sigh as she attempted to contain her emotions. "Well, it was horrendous, before, during and afterwards. I still feel guilty about what happened. This, however, is completely different. Our baby couldn't be more different." She sipped her water that she held in one hand whilst placing the other on her belly. "It was conceived in love. There is nothing dirty or wrong about our baby and that scares me even more, but I know I can't get rid of it. It's ours, yours and mine together. It will be perfect. It couldn't be anything else." There was a distinct quiver to her voice that quickly turned into a break as Jim looked across at her with a heartfelt expression on his face.

"You mean?" He needed greater clarification.

"I mean, you have knocked me up and we are going to have a baby, but it's going to cost you."

"Cost?" asked Jim tersely making her smile.

"Oh yeah, but maybe not in cash or via your little, black, plastic card. Anything I want or need, you are going to have to provide for me; weird food cravings, back rubs, foot massages, clothes with an elasticated waist and sex whenever I say, however I want it," she told him and was surprised to find that she was already becoming aroused at the idea of sex.

"Now that I can commit to, so long as you remember that this will be a time sensitive agreement, for say eight months," he said with an expression of uncertainty at the idea of Tasha calling the shots.

"Mitch reckons I am around six weeks so about seven and a half months."

"Am I allowed to be excited now? Can I come over there and hold you, kiss you and be very, very happy that we're having a baby?" A huge grin spread across his face and he did nothing to hide it.

"On one condition, well, actually two conditions."

"Go on," encouraged Jim.

"One, we keep this to ourselves for a while and two you don't freak out at me when I freak out at this whole thing which I imagine I am going to do often because this is out of my control, oh and there's a third condition," she suddenly blurted out.

"Okay, number three?" Laughed Jim.

"I need a trip to your office before you go to work," she confessed, causing an arched brow and a smirk from Jim.

"Do you? Now?"

"Yes, now, because I am seriously horny."

"Oh, baby, you will never convince me that this horniness is anything to do with pregnancy, but as I agreed to fulfill your wants and needs you should get your sexy, pregnant ass in there."

Chapter Fourteen

Seven months later

"What do you plan on doing today, baby?" Jim drained the coffee from his cup.

"I thought I might call Lucy and see if she fancies coming over with Skye. I can't believe Lucy and Ryan are parents."

"Banking some last minute revision hours, honey?" he asked with an amused face until Tasha got to her feet and was obviously suffering some discomfort as she held her hand against the huge baby bump she was carrying. "Hey, you okay?"

"Mmm, just fat and uncomfortable." She sighed at her own attempts to pull a carton of orange juice from the refrigerator, attempts that failed.

"Let me get that, Tasha." Jim had already retrieved the juice as Sandra appeared.

"You okay?" she asked Tasha who was still shuffling around uncomfortably.

"Yes," she snapped, becoming irritated with everybody. "I am fat, uncomfortable, and desperate for this child to vacate my womb, although I'm unsure if my body will ever recover," she told them both, sounding tearful suddenly.

"Hey, baby," soothed Jim, turning her to face him to hold her gently. "This child, our child will be here any day now and I know you're struggling, but you are beautiful, honey, and I love you."

"You know you're only saying that because this is all your fault," Tasha told him with a frown.

Laughing, Jim leaned down and placed a gentle, tender kiss on her nose. "Happy to oblige, Mrs Maybury. I have a meeting I can't really get out of, even on a Saturday as people have flown in from Europe and Australia, but I can be home this afternoon if you want me to be."

"Depends. Can you guarantee you'll get this baby moving if you come home early?"

Laughing again, Jim replied, "Honey, we have tried everything to evict him, or her, the last shot being about an hour ago in the shower, but I am at your disposal if you want to try again, but for now I have to go. See you later." He kissed Tasha gently on the lips while rubbing a hand across her bump that suddenly sprang into life at his father's touch. "Be good, both of you, and if you need anything call," he told her, heading for the door with a glance in Sandra's direction.

"Am I the most miserable expectant mother you've ever met?" Tasha asked despondently as she cleared the breakfast things away.

"No. I think you're a typical mother to be at around nine months pregnant; fed up, tired and ready to be un-pregnant."

"Mmm, I do want my baby, even it was a bit of a shock," she replied, making Sandra laugh.

"A bit of a shock? I seem to remember you being in total denial for the first three months and Jim walking round like a dog with two tails."

Tasha laughed and nodded as she reached into the fridge where she pulled out a large piece of cheese and a jar of chocolate spread. "Yes, well it was a shock. I thought I was sorted for three years with the contraceptive implant. How was I to know that my accident had broken it, damaged it, whatever the bloody hell it did? Add to that the fact I thought I had a bout of post honeymoon cystitis that turned out to be a six-week embryo, it was a shock."

"I imagine it would be," Sandra said with a nod.

"I don't know that I'm any more ready now. This wasn't in my immediate plans. We hadn't even agreed that we'd have children, although I think we both knew we'd have our own family one day, eventually."

"But maybe not quite so soon?" Sandra asked with a warm smile that suggested she already knew the answer to the question she'd asked.

"No. Everything is all out of sequence a little bit now. I was going to work for a while, get my face and my name out there whilst enjoying being married, a newly wed and here I am, unemployed, eight and a half months pregnant and happily married but not quite your average newly wed."

Sandra seemed to be looking at Tasha carefully, carefully and a little warily as if she wasn't sure whether to respond or not, but she did. "I can understand what you're saying, Tasha, but everything happens for a reason so maybe this is how it's meant to be."

"Maybe," Tasha agreed with a ready smile. Sandra was right, this was clearly how it was meant to be for her and Jim and their baby.

"Can I get you anything?" Sandra watched Tasha devouring a large finger of cheese coated in chocolate as she attempted to return the juice to the fridge.

"No thanks. I might just go back to bed for a while. Did you say you were grocery shopping today?" asked Tasha.

"I was, but you probably shouldn't be left alone," replied the older woman with a more concerned expression on her face now.

"Sandra, I will be fine. I feel bad enough thinking that you're working on a Saturday just because Jim is and I'm pregnant, but Jim is at the end of the phone if I need him. I also have Philip across the drive and Abby, Lucy, Sara and even Bria if I get desperate, and let's not forget Mike next door who I am sure has a list of instructions so please carry on with what you have planned."

"Okay, if you're sure."

"Absolutely," Tasha said before heading for the stairs where she stopped halfway up with a pain that had her doubling over before completing the journey and climbing into bed.

Lying on her side, Tasha curled into a ball, as close to a ball as she could with her very pregnant belly in the way and remembered her wedding to Jim and her life since that moment.

As she replayed her words to Sandra about the timing of her

pregnancy she realised the timing of everything with Jim had been off in her own mind. When she'd met him and they'd spent that first week together it had been a whirlwind and although it had been a week she'd never forget, part of her had wished it had been a few years later. Two or three years later would have found her better prepared, ready for the pig-headed freight train that her husband was. Those years would have enabled her to gain more work and professional experience and then she would have embraced everything the first year with Jim had thrown up rather than kicking back as she had so often. With a single chuckle, she acknowledged that she was always going to kick back against so many of Jim's ways and demands.

They really had endured so much together; the whirlwind romance, dealing with her parents and Liam, trying to blend their family to include her siblings, grandparents, Lizzie and Philip and now their own child, their marriage and that was without her even considering the impact of Mickie on their lives. Maybe this was exactly as it was supposed to be and meeting a year, two years later it wouldn't have worked. In that time Mickie might have managed to sink her claws in even further and manipulated her way into Jim's life and heart.

Mickie was still a blot on the landscape. Tasha still had the occasional nightmare that centred on her, but they were the exception rather than the rule now. It was Jim who was more affected by Mickie. He still felt guilty, maybe he always would, not that he should in Tasha's mind, but he did. He felt bad that he'd ever exposed Tasha to Mickie, but more than that it was that he'd underestimated Mickie's love and obsession for him as well the depths she'd sink to in order to remove Tasha from his life.

He had, in those first few weeks after Tasha's crash and then Mickie's death, tortured himself with all of the choices he'd made where Mickie was concerned, often asking himself if he'd missed signs that she'd been unbalanced all along, that there were no lengths she wouldn't go to in order to become Mrs Maybury.

Tasha's personal belief was that Mickie was unhinged and probably had been all along, even if it hadn't shown. However, once she'd seen an opening for herself in Jim's life as something other than a friend she'd seized it fully, but that is when Tasha had come along and gate-crashed the party. Tasha could almost feel some sympathy for Mickie as she imagined how it must have hurt her to hear everyone saying how different Tasha was, how different Jim was because of her. But then Mickie had tried to manipulate every situation that involved Jim in order to gain some ground, like she had with number two and her abortion.

A wave of tightness suddenly caught her off guard but Tasha felt it was a signal from her baby, a reminder that she needed to focus on happy thoughts, not dark thoughts of Mickie. It was also confirmation that a few more years of professional and personal independence would have meant she wouldn't be where she was and neither would he, or she, her baby that was safely tucked up in her womb and refusing to be shifted, no matter how she tried to move him and she'd tried relentlessly to do just that over the last week or so; she'd tried eating ridiculously spicy food, drinking raspberry leaf tea until she thought she might soon resemble a raspberry, exercise, she had done more exercise in the last couple of weeks than the previous couple of years, brisk walking and swimming were the ones Jim hadn't vetoed after finding her down at the stables and saddling up the chestnut stallion he'd always banned her from riding. And then there was sex, lots and lots of sex, including that morning in the shower. Although her hormones had gone into overdrive during early pregnancy, by the time she'd hit the third trimester she was too tired and felt far too fat to be as passionate as she had been pre-pregnancy and early on. However, as she'd read that sex could trigger labour she had forgotten about any issues of self-consciousness and body image and had literally been jumping on Jim at every opportunity and although he knew her main motivation wasn't him or even herself he happily obliged, but so far nothing had worked.

With her grandmother's words, *you can't rush a baby to be born, he will come when he's ready and not before*, ringing in her head Tasha decided she was probably right and despite her worries about not being attractive anymore, about being fat with stretch marks another try when Jim came home wouldn't hurt because he never made her feel anything less than beautiful, never had, not since the second he had set eyes on her.

With happy and emotional tears threatening to strike, Tasha closed her eyes and wrapped her arms around her belly, cuddling her baby as she fell asleep.

It was another couple of hours before Tasha woke, still feeling restless so took a long bath and after dressing in a floor length maxi dress made her way back downstairs to an empty house. There was a message from Jim waiting for her.

<Hey Baby Momma, have just spoken to Sandra, you shouldn't be alone. Call me when you wake up. Love you, baby, both of you. Baby Daddy x>

Smiling at his message and the handles he'd adopted for them after watching some TV show where a teenage mum had referred to her child's father as being the baby daddy she began to text back but was caught off guard by a pain that was spreading across her abdomen, like earlier, but this one was more of a wave than before. Blowing and panting, she was relieved when it passed quickly. She abandoned her text to Jim and instead text Philip.

<Hey Phil, are you home? Can you come over please? Tx>

Philip came bursting through the door a few minutes later dressed in sweats and a t-shirt looking as though he'd just rolled out of bed as another wave of pain crashed around Tasha causing him to panic.

"Shit Tash, are you okay? Oh God, of course you're not! Is it the baby? Are you having the baby, oh no, I can't do this," he cried.

"Philip, please calm down. I think I'm in labour, yes, but I won't need you to be my midwife anytime soon I don't think. Could you go upstairs, to the nursery, there are two bags in the closet, can you bring them down and then I'll call your dad."

"Sure. That I can do." He ran for the stairs, immediately falling up them making her laugh momentarily proving he might just be the distraction Tasha would need as she internally panicked at the reality of her situation.

Philip returned carrying the bags to find Tasha leaning across the kitchen counter and panting.

"Got 'em. Have you phoned the old man?" He looked scared suddenly.

"Philip, please don't look like that. I am shitting myself here without you looking more scared than I feel. You're not the only one doubting their ability to do this, but I have no choice anymore. Call Amanda and see if your dad's free, please." She began to pace while rubbing her belly and talking to her unborn baby, "I know I wanted you out, but you needed to wait for Daddy because I am clueless here."

"Hey, Tash, we'll do this together right, me, you and junior?" asked Philip in an attempt to reassure her and succeeding until another contraction hit as the call connected to Amanda's phone who herself was pregnant, but was about three months behind Tasha. "It's just ringing out."

"Of course, it's Saturday. Amanda doesn't work weekends. Shit! Call your dad's mobile and if there's no answer call Marc, he's in the meeting too," Tasha told Philip before doing a strange combination of a pant and a blow.

Dialling his father's number he frowned as it rang out for what felt like forever before Jim acknowledged the call that he thought was from his wife.

"Hi baby, are you okay?"

"Dad it's me, Philip, on Tasha's phone," he said, clearly stressing again. "She thinks she's in labour, she keeps making strange noises and blowing and panting."

"Okay, son, I need you to stay calm and time the contractions, can you do that?" he asked while talking to Marc at the other end, "I have to go, Marc, Tasha's in labour." He then appeared to speak to the others present. "You'll have to finish up with Marc, my wife has just gone into labour so I have somewhere else I really need to be."

"Dad can you hurry, I really don't know what to do, she looks weird again, oh shit!" cried Philip sending panic through Jim. "Tasha's just pee'd herself."

"I have not!" she screeched at her stepson. "Give me the fucking phone," she cried with an outstretched hand snatching the phone. "I have not pee'd myself," she insisted once she had the phone. "I think my waters just broke," Tasha explained and was ready to cry.

"Honey, you need to get to the hospital and I will meet you there," he told her calmly, sounding as though he was running as he spoke.

"No, I'll wait for you here," she protested.

"Tasha, you need to get to the hospital if your waters have broken. If Philip is unable to drive you, then tell him to get Mike."

"Where are you? I can't do this without you?" She was actually crying real tears now.

"You won't have to do it without me. I am getting into my car right now."

She heard the closing of his car door, reassuring her that he was on his way. "Sara said you almost missed Philip's birth but I'm not like Sara. I can't do this on my own. I'm not a nurse and I'm scared," she explained as another contraction hit her causing her to muffle a cry.

"Natasha, you need to do exactly as I say, tell Philip to go and find Mike, now," he told her, knowing Mike would be calm and get Tasha to the hospital safely. He waited for her to repeat his instruction which she did to a relieved looking Philip who ran for the door calling for Mike.

It was at that second when Sandra reappeared with a call of, "Oh bugger me, Tasha."

"Baby, I need you to put Sandra on the phone and get your ass to the hospital and I will meet you there. You're gonna be a mommy and I love you," he said as she passed the phone to Sandra who nodded and offered a series of yes, okay and of course when Mike appeared.

"Mike's here, so Tasha is leaving now," Sandra said, listening intently to Jim before hugging Tasha as she led her out to the car that was waiting and handed her phone back. "Good luck and when I next see you your womb will have been vacated," she said with a smile, repeating Tasha's own words from breakfast.

Jim had already called the hospital from the car to advise them that Tasha was on her way and by the time he arrived she was already there, at the desk refusing to be admitted.

"No, I need to wait for my husband. We're doing this together," she protested as she doubled over in pain.

"Mrs Maybury, your baby may not be prepared to wait for Daddy to arrive and we really need to get you checked over," said the nurse who was trying to coax her into a wheelchair.

"I'll wait. Philip, phone him again," she snapped while an almost dumbstruck Philip dropped her bags and reached into his pocket for his own phone as the stern looking nurse eyed Tasha with a mixture of annoyance and disbelief at her refusal to comply with her request and her behaviour that the nurse was probably interpreting as Tasha being a bit of a princess about giving birth. "Look," started Tasha, returning the other woman's feeling of irritation. "You may have people coming in here every day and shelling out kids, but they are not me and I am not them. This is the first time I've done this and I am shit scared. The only person who I trust completely to get me through this is my husband so if he isn't here I am going nowhere."

The nurse threw her eyebrows towards the ceiling as another wave of pain passed across Tasha's body.

"If he doesn't get here soon, you'll have to come in with me," Tasha almost threatened Philip who looked positively green now.

"What? I..." he started as the nurse made a loud tut sound earning her Tasha's full attention again.

"Look, lady, you are really beginning to piss me off with the looks, the tutting and the bad fucking attitude."

A tightening Tasha had previously felt seemed to soften, allowing her to relax slightly before Jim interrupted, "You're off the hook, son." He hugged his oldest child before turning to Tasha. "And you, Mrs Maybury, are going to get your ass kicked if you don't sit in the chair and do as you're told and stop swearing at the staff who are trying to do their job. Sorry," he said with a smile in the nurse's direction before looking down at his wife again. "I told you I'd be here, didn't I?"

"Sorry," cried Tasha as she finally sat in the wheelchair and was rushed down a corridor followed by Jim and Philip who was being given a list of instructions as they went; who to call, in what order and what to tell them, although Tasha's grandparents and siblings were booked on a flight that evening so they would be unable to get to L.A. any sooner, but hopefully they'd have their first great-grandchild and niece or nephew waiting to greet them when they did arrive.

Chapter Fifteen

"Four centimetres," announced the doctor, Dr Marshall, Mitch, after examining a disappointed looking Tasha. "You're gonna be a while yet so we'll leave you two for a short time, but if you need anything hit the buzzer," he told her with a smile as he left taking a nurse with him.

"This is it, baby." Jim smiled, taking her hand in his.

"Mmm. I still find this shocking, a baby."

"I know that feeling, but it's kinda cool too, a baby, mine and yours."

"I guess so, although I thought I'd be further along than four centimetres. Is Philip okay?" she asked with genuine concern.

"Yeah, fine, and these things can't be rushed."

"I was a little too crazy for him I think," she admitted making Jim smile at her.

"I like the idea of being the only man who can deal with you and your craziness." He sounded smug at the idea of being the only one able to deal with her full stop.

"James?"

"Natasha?" His tone was playful.

"We didn't talk about number two, did we?"

"Did we need to?" His expression became tighter suddenly.

"Sorry. It's just being here, about to have a baby and being pregnant. I've thought about her lately and you must have some feelings about what Mickie said."

"It was a long time ago, Tasha." He sighed, leaning back in his chair, pushing a hand through his hair. "I was at the point of apathy about my marriage to Vanessa and then Mickie drops the bombshell she'd previously had an issue with drugs and blackmailed her into aborting my child. Honestly, I have no clue how to deal with that or how to feel. My marriage would never have lasted but she should have told me. I would have freaked out, no way that I wouldn't have with all the facts, but she would have kept the baby and not perpetuated the lies. And I would have cut Mickie loose at that point too. You would never have had to deal with her, honey."

"I'm sorry." Tasha adjusted her position until she was standing up, leaning over the bed and swaying, desperate to ease her husband's sadness and guilt.

"You have nothing to be sorry about. This is not of your doing, none of it. You were a child yourself when this was all happening, dealing with your own family shit. God, that sounds wrong, that you were a child when my wife was aborting my baby," he told her as he stood behind her, wrapping an arm around her, kissing her neck that was exposed courtesy of her hair being up in a ponytail.

"I'm sorry it's come back to confuse you and has made you sad. And Mickie, she was crazy enough to have refused to be cut loose and that is not and never will be your fault." Tasha reassured Jim with a stroke of his arm.

"You are too good for me in every way, baby," he replied with another kiss, to her cheek this time.

"Hardly, I'm the one who doesn't deserve you so we might have to agree to disagree. Have you considered contacting Vanessa and telling her that you know? Telling her what you've just told me?" Tasha asked, moving conversation away from who did or didn't deserve the other as another contraction landed, resulting in her gripping Jim's hand firmly.

"Why?" He sucked up her pain with her. "To make amends? Make friends? I don't think so, honey. She killed my child, that's not something I can forgive. Jeez, she didn't even discuss it with me."

"I know." Tasha turned so she faced him and with her arms linked around his neck continued. "We both know how manipulative Mickie could be, Jim. I just thought it might help you to contact her and say I know what you did, it was wrong, you should have told me, but now I know. Sorry, it's not my business, but I don't want you to be angry or sad about it and I think you are."

"You want me to forgive her, to say it's okay?" He was as confused by Tasha's words and suggestion as he was at the idea of finding it in his heart to forgive his ex-wife.

"No. I want you to be able to tell her she was wrong, but it's done and you understand how persuasive Mickie could be. That you and she were never going to work if she couldn't be honest with you."

"You are amazing, honey. Amazing and honest beyond belief and that is what all of my previous marriages lacked, the total honesty. All the shit you've been through and yet you told me it all, openly and concisely. You refused to be moulded and broken by it. When you found out you were pregnant I know you were shocked and scared, but at no point did you try and hide the fact that you were considering all options."

"I would never have got rid of our baby, James. I promise," she replied tearfully as she recalled her horror at being pregnant and her declaration that she couldn't have a baby. "But this baby was not the cystitis diagnosis I'd anticipated."

"I know." He laughed. "Although I got the blame for the cystitis too, didn't I?" More seriously he said, "I would never have allowed you to make a decision as a knee jerk reaction, but it's the fact that you immediately said it to me, not your friends or your ob/gyn. It was me you told that you didn't feel ready for a baby and now look at us," he said with a grin as a longer and stronger contraction arrived. "And this is like no cystitis I have ever known. I will think about finding Vanessa," he conceded, helping Tasha to sit on the edge of the bed.

"I know you must have had some doubts about my intentions when I first found out. I mean, I'd already had one termination." Nervous tears threatened to fall.

"No, no, honey. That was completely different," insisted Jim.

"I know, but first I react badly to being pregnant and now I am almost defending your former wife who did exactly as I did —"

"Natasha, you need to stop that now or we're going to have a problem because what you did and your reasons for doing so were completely different to Vanessa's so stop, okay?"

"Thank you and I'm really glad that we're here, together, having a baby. I do keep thinking if Mickie had even suspected I was pregnant things could have turned out differently. Very, very different."

"But she didn't, and they didn't. Now enough of these dark thoughts, you just focus on positive, happy baby thoughts."

"Okay. Will you go and check on Philip please? He can come in if he wants to." She smiled.

"I'll be two minutes. Don't go having this baby without me," he told her with a smirk as he left.

****

It was another six hours before the doctor assured Tasha they were *almost there*. Her contractions were coming thick and fast with almost no gap between them.

"I've changed my mind," she cried as she attempted to walk unaided from the birthing pool to the bed. "I don't want a baby any more. I'd rather have cystitis. I can't do this."

"Sure you can. You're the most brilliant woman I've ever met." Jim's words made Tasha frown and pout at him.

"You have to say that because this is all your fault. You did this to me. Oh God," she cried as the pain struck again. "You have to know that we are never having sex ever again," she announced.

"Oh, Tasha, I think we both know that won't be happening." Jim smirked, looking across at Mitch who was smiling between the two of them.

"Yes, and even that's your fault. You're just too good at sex. You've made me need it. Oh shit!" she cried as another contraction threatened to knock her off her feet.

"Tasha," called Mitch, standing opposite her. "I think it's time, so I need to examine you, but can we decide where you're having this baby? Do you want to deliver in the pool?" he asked making her refocus.

"No, not the pool, it's making me seasick."

With a laugh, the doctor looked across at Jim while Tasha climbed back onto the bed.

"Right then, you take care of your wife up that end and I will concentrate on delivering your baby."

Tasha nodded and for no reason at all suddenly asked the doctor, "Mitch, you know my, erm, tattoo?" She almost whispered the last word, making the doctor and her husband smile at her for very different reasons; Mitch knowing that Tasha had forgotten it was there the first time he'd seen her post honeymoon and Jim just loved the idea of her being branded as his. He never tired of seeing the ink she bore, so much so she was now permanently bare there as she had been the first time he'd seen her wedding present to him.

"Yes," frowned Mitch.

"Everything stretches during pregnancy and delivery, so will my tattoo? If it does, will it go back? It won't be distorted or saggy, will it?" she asked quite seriously.

"It should all be good, Tasha. In fact, I don't think it's changed during pregnancy so no reason for it to now." He smiled as another contraction had Tasha crying out from between gritted teeth.

Having discarded the gas and air for making her sick, Tasha was considering asking for an epidural when a quick examination revealed her to be fully dilated and ready to deliver the baby, but together with her exhaustion and an increasingly distressed baby things were becoming a little more frantic in the room.

"Tasha, we need to get this baby out quickly and safely so when I tell you to push, I need you to push for all you're worth. Jim is going to help you do this, okay?"

Nodding, Tasha was becoming concerned. "Is everything alright?"

"I won't lie, your baby is getting a little distressed so we need to get him out soon."

"What happens if we can't get him out?" she asked tearfully, fearful for her unborn baby, doubling up as the worst contraction yet arrived.

"We will, but you may need some assistance."

A nurse suddenly appeared carrying forceps. The sight of them was enough to throw Tasha into something of a panic.

"Not a fucking hope in hell," she cried, startling everyone. "You are not coming anywhere near me or my baby with those," she screamed.

Moving so he was almost nose to nose with his wife, Jim smiled at her. "Tasha, listen to me, baby. If you really want to do this on your own you need to listen to Mitch and for once, do exactly as you're told, okay?"

She nodded compliantly as Jim nodded at the doctor who was settled on a stool between Tasha's thighs.

"Right then, when I say push, you push," Mitch told her, "and push."

Squeezing Jim's hand for comfort, support and strength Tasha pushed for all she was worth until she was told to stop.

"Good girl. We're gonna need another one of those and when I tell you to stop, you stop and pant. We don't want you to tear," the doctor warned a horrified looking Tasha.

"Tear? I can tear? Why did nobody tell me that before?" She was horrified and a little scared as Mitch spoke again.

"And push again—push, push, push, push, push."

She followed his instructions and soon after, when he told her to pant she did exactly that with the fear of tearing fresh in her mind.

"Okay then, we have the head so we're nearly done, and push again now."

With what felt like her last ounce of strength, Tasha pushed with everything she had left. Bearing down she sprayed from between gritted teeth with her chin bedding down into her chest and really hoped she didn't poo herself. That would be mortifying, but before she could process that thought further, she heard a cry and suddenly a small, pink, bloody baby was being held aloft and thrust towards her.

"Momma say hello to your son." Grinned the doctor as Tasha looked down in awe.

"A son? He's a boy? We have a baby boy," she said between sobs. She looked between the baby curling into her embrace and her husband who was crying at them both.

"We sure do," Jim told her as he kissed first her and then the baby, wiping tears off his face. "And he is beautiful, perfect, like his mommy."

"Is he okay?" Tasha wondered why he'd cried so briefly and was now so quiet and still.

"He is absolutely fine. I think he's just happy and content lying with Mommy and Daddy," said the nurse standing over them. "We're going to get him weighed and cleaned up a little and then he'll be right back." She reached down for the baby. "Does he have a name?" she asked looking back towards Jim and Tasha.

Tasha looked up at Jim who replied to the nurse's question, "Connor."

"Really?" asked a shocked Tasha. "You said you hated the name Connor."

"I did, but it kind of grew on me, like you." He leaned in to kiss her on the lips, gently, lovingly.

"Hey, that's what got you two here in the first place," teased Mitch making Tasha blush and Jim shrug.

"Then book us in again for about ten month's time." Jim's huge grin made the other man laugh as the nurse reappeared with their baby, with Connor, Connor Maybury. He was wrapped in a blue blanket and wearing a blue woolly hat.

"Who wants this handsome young man then, all six pounds four ounces of him?" asked the nurse.

"You go first," Tasha said to Jim who beamed with pride as he held his son for the first time.

"Hey, baby boy, how you doing?" he asked the little boy who was gazing up into his eyes before beginning to cry. "Oh, I see. I get that I'm not as pretty as Mommy, but you'd better get used to this face because it's with you forever buddy."

"Let's get you all settled and then I believe you have lots of visitors." Smiled the nurse. "Are you going to nurse him?" she asked Tasha who looked confused until the other woman's glance lowered to her breasts.

"Oh, yes. I'd like to," she replied as Connor's cries began to get louder.

"He seems happy to know that, so maybe Daddy would like to go and share the news of his arrival while you two get yourselves sorted."

Passing the baby over, Jim seemed reluctant to leave, but once Tasha was settled and comfortable, with their son safely wrapped in her embrace and suckling on her breast, he smiled and knew that no matter what he'd felt before this moment, this was complete and utter happiness.

"I'll go and tell everyone." He kissed his wife then paused for a last look at them in the doorway. "Should I send everyone home, it's almost eleven o'clock at night?"

"If Philip and Lizzie are still here they should come and meet their new brother, before anyone else does," Tasha replied.

"And that is why I love you, Mrs Maybury, and why our son is the luckiest boy in the world, because you're his mommy."

The nurse grinned across at Tasha as Jim left. "Does he have a brother?"

With a smile Tasha nodded as she stroked her baby's dark hair down as he continued to feed. "He does, Uncle Bobby," she told Connor. "Married, happily, sorry," she said to the nurse now.

The nurse remained nearby and talked Tasha through feeding the baby, about timing him on each breast and changing sides, the importance of her own healthy eating and drinking to maintain a good supply of milk and just as she had moved Connor from the left side to the right and made herself look decent again the door burst open to reveal a still proudly grinning Jim, a subdued looking Philip and a squealing Lizzie. Lizzie's high-pitched squeal startled Connor briefly judging by his eyes shooting open, but only briefly and it didn't pause his feeding.

"Yes, you recognise that sound, don't you? That's Lizzie, she does that a lot." Grinned Tasha as Lizzie enveloped them both in her arms.

"Wow Tash, he's so tiny. Can I hold him?"

"He didn't feel that tiny about twenty minutes ago, but he does look really small. You might just want to give him a minute before holding him. He drinks milk like Philip drinks Tequila slammers," she joked making Philip smile at her.

"I'll have you know I am off Tequila. Well, Juan banned me after I was sick in his shoe last time."

Jim frowned while Tasha laughed. "You best get back on it

for our next night out. You might need to give me a few months though because I too am banned from drinking for a while longer, courtesy of Connor's drinking."

"That's slightly gross." Philip's deep frown and slightly nauseated expression made the others laugh.

Removing Connor from her breast and managing to cover herself at the same time, Tasha patted his back gently, offering him to an excited Lizzie who had already got her phone out and before she'd sat back down with the baby was uploading a shot to Snapchat, Facebook, Twitter and Instagram.

"Lizzie, he is not an accessory and I do not expect to see his photo appearing all over the internet on a regular basis," chided Jim.

"But for today and to avoid a press release, Connor can go viral," Tasha told her with a big grin that her baby was already adored by his big brother and sister who was desperate to share news of his safe arrival with the world

"Thank you. Dylan was here earlier, but he had to go, so I've text it to him," Lizzie explained before taking another shot of them all together.

Chapter Sixteen

Once everyone had gone home, Jim climbed up onto the bed and pulled Tasha towards him while glancing down at their sleeping son in his mother's arms.

"So, what do you think of motherhood so far?"

"It's wonderful, he's wonderful, and I know everyone must say this but he really is the most beautiful baby I have ever seen."

"He certainly is, honey," said Jim as Connor's face began to contort until he was wearing an expression resembling a pout. "And he has your mouth." Laughed Jim.

"Mmm, maybe, and your nose and eyes."

"Yup, he is gorgeous."

Laughing, Tasha asked, "Are you allowed to stay?"

Jim shrugged. "I'd like to see them throw me out on our anniversary."

"You remembered," Tasha's slightly excited words caused Connor to let out a restless moan. "I remembered earlier but then I forgot with everything that's gone on today."

"Of course I remembered, although when I first saw you I never imagined that a year later we'd be here, married, with a baby."

"No?" queried Tasha with an arched brow.

Jim shook his head. "It was the Saturday before I really knew you were going to be my lucky seven."

"Really?" Tasha couldn't hide her surprise. "People have passed comments about us and you being different with me, but did you really think of me in those terms so soon?"

"If by those terms you mean, did I know you were special and I would never ever meet anyone else like you and that I couldn't let you go, then yes."

Almost stunned into silence by his admission, Tasha leaned down and kissed the baby's forehead before looking at Jim and simply saying, "Wow."

"Have I rendered you speechless, Tasha?" Jim wore a wry smile that Tasha returned.

"Kind of. I knew I liked you and you made me feel different. I did wonder a couple of times whether being your lucky seven would be so bad and the next thing I knew I was flying to L.A. with you."

"That flight in that dress." He frowned.

"I like that dress, although I may never fit into it again." She sighed with a concerned look down at her still swollen and now wobbly belly.

"I'm sure you will, baby. With sensible eating and exercise, no starvation," he warned. "But even if you never wear it again you need to know that I prefer you without clothes anyway."

The sound of Connor crying pierced the silence between them, just a single cry as if he was startled.

"Oh, son, we really need to talk." Jim took the little boy from Tasha and paced towards the window where he rocked him as he began to speak. "You have to remember that you are the most important person in our lives and the beautiful English lady is Mommy and the milk machine, but she is my wife, so don't even try and cut in when we're discussing her inappropriate clothing or how we met or how hot she is, okay?" he asked before turning back to face Tasha as he rocked his son to sleep.

"Did I tell you about Howser?" Tasha asked, earning herself a frown, possibly just for mentioning the other man.

"Tasha, if you are about to tell me he has turned up and hit on you again I really can't promise that I won't do something unpleasant."

With a laugh, Tasha shook her head. "No. I spoke to Sara last night, or the night before and she was saying that when he and Rosa split a few months ago he'd said it didn't feel right and they weren't really going anywhere. They wanted very different things."

"I think they always did...he wanted you," muttered Jim before refocusing on his wife. "Is there a point to this, baby, because you are beginning to spoil my anniversary mood?"

"Sorry, yes. Well, it turns out that they did want different things because Rosa is like Lenny and wants respectability and to keep up appearances, but not Howser. He has moved to Boston and set up home with two nurses, one male and one female," Tasha explained with a huge grin and a suggestive wiggle of her eyebrows that did cause Jim's lips to curl.

"You mean—" was as far as he got before Tasha interrupted and completed his sentence.

"Yes, he and they are a couple, no, a couple's two, a group, a ménage, well, whatever it's called. They're all in a relationship together so I am guessing I wouldn't really have been his cup of tea as there's only one of me."

"Natasha," Jim warned and without any other words Tasha knew that her husband had tired of the conversation and inference that there was ever a Tasha and Howser.

"Sorry, but you know what I mean."

"Hmmm, I suppose. At least you didn't sandwich yourself with him and one of his friends." Jim frowned seriously.

"Hey, I am a one-man woman and that one man is you, well, I might be a two-man woman now that our son has arrived." She grinned suddenly as Jim moved closer, still rocking Connor.

"He might just be the only other man I will share you with. Now, our son appears to be asleep, so assuming he stays that way for a couple of hours we should get some sleep too, baby."

****

Tasha had stopped listening to the million instructions she'd received from the nurse, Maisie, Abby and her grandmother when Jim arrived and after kissing her turned his attention to Pippa who was holding the baby.

"Hey, Pippa. I told you he was handsome, didn't I?" He perched on the bed next to Tasha.

"He is so sweet," she agreed, smiling down at her nephew while Jim turned towards his wife.

"You okay?" He gently pushed her freshly washed hair back

off her face.

"Mmm, can we go home yet?" She suddenly looked sad.

"We'll have to ask the doctor."

The other women around him began chatting together about their own thoughts, ideas and experiences.

"They are driving me fucking crazy," Tasha whispered, making Jim frown.

"Baby, that mouth," he cried with a half-smile now. "Ten more minutes and then we throw them out and sleep."

"You think we can?" Her grateful smile suggested she liked the idea and was relieved Jim was there to take care of everything, to take care of her because there is no way she would ever have thought to ask everyone to leave when she knew they all loved her and Connor.

"You bet we can."

With everyone speaking at the same time Tasha could barely decipher who was saying what. She really was grateful that so many people cared and wanted to offer their thoughts and experiences, but she didn't want to hear it all because this was her baby, her body and it was her turn to do this her way.

Briefly, as her grandmother offered her a small smile, Tasha felt slightly guilty that she was being ungrateful for their love and care so chastened herself. She thought that under normal circumstances a new mother would have her own mother on hand to offer support, guidance and advice but she didn't have that, not that she wanted her own parents anywhere near her or Connor, but the strange and poignant realisation made her feel sad. Her grandmother seemed to understand her thoughts were taking her to a dark place and shook her head, as if to say negative thoughts had no place here, with her beautiful new baby and her future just waiting to be explored and experienced. With a quick sniff to hold back any tears that might be about to appear, Tasha refocused on her son who was making a strange squeaking sound as he was cradled by his auntie who was clearly smitten.

It was exactly ten minutes later when Jim looked at his watch. "Right Grandmas and Aunties, my son needs feeding and my wife needs to sleep so feel free to visit the hospital cafeteria or go shopping, but your time is up."

"James!" cried his mother. "You can't do that, we want to spend some time with Connor."

"And you have and you can visit again later, but Tasha is tired and too polite to say so, whereas I—"

"Sorry," interrupted Tasha awkwardly, knowing she could feed Connor in their presence and she wasn't tired enough to need a sleep so Jim was simply making excuses to give her some kind of breather from them all and their best intentions.

"No, darling, we should be apologising. Gramps and Dan want to visit later so I'll come back with them." Smiled her grandmother.

"Of course, and you're going to stay with us for a while, aren't you?"

"Tash, look at him, we may never go home," cried Pippa excitedly as Connor began to fidget in her arms.

Watching them leave Tasha felt more guilty, especially as Pippa stood and reluctantly prepared to leave with a kiss for her nephew and then one for her sister as she handed the baby back to his mother.

"Pippa, give it half an hour and you can come back, but not the motherly fonts of all knowledge," called Jim as she reached the door and was rewarded with a huge grin from both Bailey sisters.

It was Sunday afternoon before Tasha and Connor had been given the green light to go home and after an uncomfortable conversation about contraception with the nurse and an appointment for her post baby check-up six weeks' later Tasha was relieved to be going home. With just the three of them in the car she felt content and hoped Jim had ensured the house wasn't teaming with yet more visitors. She really just wanted to go home and settle in with her baby and to get on with the rest of her life.

The house was silent when they entered. Tasha was trying to carry something, a bag, flowers, balloons or her baby, but Jim was having none of it. He had Tasha's bags in one hand and Connor safely strapped into his car seat in the other.

"Jim, let me get the stuff out of the car."

"Not necessary, we'll get you and Connor settled in here and then I'll get the other stuff."

"If you insist." Tasha released a long, loud sigh on an exhale.

Jim ignored it. "I do. As our son is asleep we'll get you a cup of tea and then bring his bassinet down before I get the other things from the car."

"I'll make the tea, you get the basket and while I move Connor from his car seat you can get the things from the car."

Jim smiled as he pulled her close against him. "See, we can do this, baby. You and me together, we can take on the world."

Tasha looked up to gaze into her husband's eyes and felt overwhelmed all over again in the knowledge that he was hers. "God, I love you." She softened into his grip. Finding his lips with hers she wondered if it was normal for a new mother to be reacting so freely to her husband on such a basic level.

"And I love you too." He tilted her head back to gaze down at her longingly. "What is in your head?" He wore a sexy half-smile.

"Seriously? I am thinking that there is no way I am going to get to six weeks without needing to feel you inside me."

"Jeez, baby, you'll be lucky to get to six days if you keep talking that way, but I love that you're still so eager."

The sound of the front door opening and closing ended their conversation, but still holding each other they turned to find Philip and Juan walking towards them.

"Hi Tash, Jim, how're you all doing?" Juan was clearly embarrassed at walking in on them, Philip, not so much so.

"Yeah we're good. Where are my family? I'm not complaining, just curious."

"Dad said you might like some peace when you got home, so Mom has taken them out and then was taking them back to hers for dinner, so they could be some time, although I reckon Lizzie will hitch a ride back here with them. Just a warning," explained Philip.

"Thank you and Lizzie is welcome whenever, it's fine," replied Tasha, wanting Lizzie to feel as welcome as she had before Connor was born. She headed into the kitchen. "Does anybody want a drink?"

"Not for us, we're heading out too. We just wanted to say hi," replied Juan who was standing over Connor. "This is so weird because he looks like you, Tash, but also like Jim."

"Thank you for calling my baby weird." She smiled as she put the kettle on to boil while Jim headed back out to the car, laughing at his wife's quick retort to Juan's observation.

Philip followed his dad, leaving Juan with Tasha. "Are you okay? I know it was a shock to find yourself pregnant, but now he's here—"

"Yeah, I'm better than okay, thank you." Instinctively she hugged her friend, loving him for caring enough about her to check that she was *okay*.

"Everything's out of the car, so let's move the little guy as far as his bassinet, once I've brought it down." Jim smiled, heading for the stairs and returning a few minutes later with the baby basket that was placed in the corner, next to the far end of one of the sofas, but away from any draughts or direct sunlight, all points Jim talked through as he set it up.

Juan and Philip left and once they'd gone Tasha lifted Connor from his car seat making him wake briefly, but with a few whispered words and a kiss he was falling back to sleep in his mother's swaying arms. She gently placed him down in his basket, pulled a thin blanket over him and gazed down at him for a few seconds before taking a seat next to Jim.

"I'm not quite sure what we should do now," admitted Tasha. "Although I quite enjoy just sitting and watching our son."

Tasha moved again so she was looking over at Connor who was sleeping peacefully on his back. With one arm at his side and the other by his ear, she smiled at the image of him and then the little kitten like sound he seemed to make as he yawned. It was amazing to think that just a few days before he'd been safely tucked up inside her. It actually seemed infeasible that he'd ever fitted in there now that he was here. When Tasha had said she enjoyed watching him she hadn't been lying or exaggerating, in fact, that was all she'd been doing since his birth. She was in total awe and utterly amazed that she had in any way been responsible for making him. That he was hers and was perfect in every way. Perfect, untainted by life and totally innocent and she knew she would do everything in her power to ensure he remained that way for as long as possible.

"Tasha." It appeared Jim was repeating her name. "We can sleep, eat, take a bath, whatever you want, apart from sex." He grinned.

"I'll drink my tea and then I might send some emails and texts."

"Or you could sleep, eat or take a bath," he repeated.

"I thought they were suggestions." She frowned at him and thought emails and texts would allow her to watch over her son for a while longer.

"No, baby, they were your choices really. I'll fix something to eat for us both and then after Connor has been fed again we'll catch us some zzzz's, deal?"

"I should just say yes, right?"

Connor began to cry before his father could answer his mother's question but his smile confirmed Tasha's thoughts.

Chapter Seventeen

About a month later, after her family had gone home and Jim had returned to work full-time things were returning to normal for everyone except Tasha. She found that her nights consisted of going to bed early, waking to do night feeds, changing Connor and settling him again then trying to go back to sleep for a couple of hours before doing it all again and the sleep deprivation really was like nothing she had ever known. Jim was brilliant and took his turn, but as she was the milk machine she still needed to be involved, although she had woken a couple of times to find her husband placing Connor between them in their bed so she literally just had to offer him her breast which he always eagerly accepted.

Her days were similar in that they revolved around Connor's routine of feeding, changing and sleeping, but he was beginning to stay awake now and liked to be talked to, sung to and enjoyed looking around at his surroundings. She was enjoying being a mother, but she was struggling to adapt to the loss of independence.

Sandra was becoming the one person she saw the most of, and that was okay, she liked Sandra and the older woman was brilliant with Connor, often giving Tasha a break, if only to grab a shower in peace. That just made her realise that her role as a mother was overshadowing everything else, but she assumed that was normal.

She still hadn't got around to getting an agent in L.A. and hadn't needed one because once she discovered she was pregnant Jim had pretty much vetoed everything work wise including the movie project with Jon, which yet again had seen her role recast which ultimately meant she was still being solely represented by Angie in London. Angie had kept in touch as a friend but had been quiet professionally so when her phone rang and she saw it was her, Tasha assumed it was a friendly chat she was calling for.

Adjusting her position so Connor could contentedly feed, she answered her phone as Sandra appeared with a cup of tea and a snack which she always did around this post breakfast feed time. Tasha smiled up at her and thought this was probably similar to what other young mothers experienced in normal families with a normal mother of their own.

"Hey Angie, how you doing?"

"Bloody marvellous, you? How's your gorgeous husband and the sprog?" As always she made Tasha laugh.

"Good. We're all good, thanks."

"Well, it's about to get a whole lot better," Angie teased. "I had a call after you did that interview at home with Katy Myers last week where you were all mother earth crossed with yummy mummy."

"Right." Tasha's laughter made Connor gaze up at her causing her to smile down at him and blow him a kiss.

"Robbie Newman has been given a TV show; celeb, fashion, gossip, magazine type show and they want you to be their face from The States. The remit is that you will do some features on what's hot over there, but they want the mummy focus too, so as well as the weird and wacky beauty treatments side of things they want to see what it's like being a celebrity mum and a celebrity baby. Knowing Jim, he won't allow you to take off to film around the world with or without his baby so I thought this may suit you."

"I dunno Ange, you're right about Jim, but I'm unsure whether he'll agree to anything involving Connor."

"I'll send you the full details and the numbers for Robbie, who is executive producer with Mel Riley who remembers you from one of the pantos you did with her so speak to Jim and call them if you're still unsure. It might be the kind of thing you can slot in with being in L.A. and having a new baby." She made complete sense, but whilst considering Jim's reaction, Connor began to cry, while Angie laughed with a slight cackle thrown in. "And I think your son may have just agreed with Auntie Angie."

"Send me the details and I'll look at them because if I'm honest I think I may need more in my life than being a wife and mother, even if I do love Jim and Connor more than I knew was possible."

Connor's crying grew louder and after shaking her head at Sandra's offer to take him from her, Tasha ended her call with Angie. "Ange, I have to go, but I'll call you in the next couple of days with a yes or a no, but can you let Mel and Robbie know I have their offer and am seriously considering it and thanks. I love you."

"Hey, you soppy cow, it's my job, and I love you, too. Kiss Connor and tell him to shut the fuck up when Auntie Angie calls." She hung up while Tasha laughed, got to her feet and threw her son up onto her shoulder where she patted his back gently.

"Auntie Angie sends you a kiss, and, well, I can't actually tell you what she said." Tasha turned to face two big brown eyes staring at her, two dark brown eyes that were just like his daddy's and laughed as she imagined ever being able to tell him what Auntie Angie said. "Don't go accusing me with Daddy's eyes, Connor James Maybury," she told him as Sandra reappeared smiling.

"I still can't believe you got both of your names in there and none of Jim's."

With a short laugh, Tasha replied, "Apparently, Connor grew on him but the James took considerably more convincing and those two may have been my choices but my golden ticket seemed to be that as a boy he would always be a Maybury and would never have anything of mine, not that I would ever want him to be associated with my parents, but I think it suits him."

"It does." Sandra smiled, leaning in to look at the little boy with nothing but warmth and affection. "May I? Before I go and iron your clothes, little man." She stretched out her arms towards him.

"Sure, he likes you, which is fortunate as we're the two main women in his life," said Tasha handing him over.

"Glad to be in the top two because I think I fall a little more in love with him every day." Sandra smiled down at the baby warmly as she cradled him in her arms.

"Do you regret not having children of your own?" Tasha thought she was crossing into seriously personal information now.

"Sometimes, like when I watch you with Connor, but I'm not you. Mike isn't Jim and it would have been hard for us, for me and Mike to manage and I like my life, so occasionally, short regrets, but I have the best of both worlds now. I get to see this handsome boy every day, but when he cries I can hand him back, which I'm going to do now because I think he may need a clean nappy."

"Thank you so much," Tasha said with a grimace as she took her son back from the other woman. "And thank you for saying nappy and not diaper," she added using a very over-exaggerated American accent for the word *diaper*.

"Yeah, some words just don't work for me, but you'll have to get used to it because not only is your husband American, your child is too."

"He is, isn't he? I knew that but hadn't really thought about it. Which means, once again that my husband was right and I really am going to have to get fluent in American English."

Once upstairs, Tasha placed Connor in the huge white crib that almost filled one wall of his nursery that was the room next to her own. Closing the blinds, she leaned in and kissed her son whose yawning made her smile.

"You are so cute, baby, but Mommy needs an hour tops then we'll go out. Maybe we could visit Daddy after a trip to the park or something, okay?" she asked as Connor yawned again before closing his eyes and succumbing to sleep.

Two and a half hours later Tasha was entering the studios where she now had clearance to enter at will rather than having to wait while security phoned through to have her visit authorised. Most of the security people knew her as did the admin staff in the office block, but many hadn't yet seen Connor so it seemed to take forever to get as far as Amanda who immediately rushed to greet Tasha warmly before gushing over Connor who she'd seen several times since his birth.

"How are you finding it?" Tasha gestured towards the other woman's expanding baby bump.

"Tiring and I'm looking forward to starting my leave next week." She excitedly shook the rattling toy attached to Connor's stroller, ignoring the fact that the baby was still sleeping.

"The last few weeks seem to take an eternity to pass, don't they?" Tasha asked and smiled as Amanda nodded with a grimace. "We'll have to get together and do lunch with the babies when yours appears," suggested Tasha before considering the implication of Amanda not being in the office. "Who'll cover your job when you're away?"

"One of the girls from the pool has been appointed. She's in with Mr Maybury at the moment," replied Amanda but before she could say any more Tasha laughed.

"I thought you were over your Mr Maybury thing. Jim told me you'd resorted to a very stern Jim when I was in hospital." Tasha smirked, stopping just short of laughter, unlike the other woman who along with a laugh, blushed.

"Yes, well, I needed to get his attention, but here I will stick to Mr Maybury, as should everyone." Amanda suddenly looked very uncomfortable once her cryptic words were out. She scurried back to her desk making Tasha suspicious about her husband's new P.A. but before she could speak the sound of Marc's laughter and that of a woman screeching from behind her interrupted them. Tasha continued to gently rock Connor, soothing his startled response to the woman's ear-piercing laugh before turning to greet them where she found Marc smiling warmly. The woman, a tall, willowy blonde who was probably only in her late twenties with big blue eyes and pouty lips viewed her with a very unfriendly expression.

In that instant, Tasha was very aware of the short comings of her post baby body that still had about half a stone to shed and some serious toning up to do. Despite her outfit of black skinny jeans and bright yellow t-shirt that flattered her current shape she couldn't compete with the woman opposite. She studied her for a few seconds more and knew she was someone who could turn any man's head, including Jim's.

Despite having come very close during their heavy duty petting sessions, or making out as Jim called it, they still hadn't had sex, and she was still two weeks shy of her post-delivery check-up. All through their relationship sex was the one consistent thing they had and during much of her pregnancy she had been even more desperate and demanding of him courtesy of the raging hormones flooding her body.

Marc broke her thoughts as he reached across and kissed her cheek before turning back to the woman who was now joined by Jim who made some comment that caused this woman before her to shrill again, waking Connor abruptly, causing him to cry loudly. The woman, rather than apologise pulled a distasteful expression incensing Tasha further.

"Hey, baby." Smiled Jim, moving beyond the woman and Marc to kiss his wife and look down at his crying son. "Hey buddy, did Rachel wake you up?" He unfastened the little boy from his restraints to lift him out, soothing him immediately.

Rachel, as Tasha now knew her, pushed past Marc and steered herself between Tasha and Jim, turning her back on Tasha to reach across Jim's arms to stroke Connor's face, then ran her fingers across Jim's arm as she returned her own arm to her side.

"He's very handsome. He looks like you," she told Jim causing Tasha to stare between this woman, Amanda and Marc before rolling her eyes. "He'll be a real heart breaker, like you," she added now making Amanda stare as wildly as Tasha while Marc shifted uncomfortably from one foot to the other.

"Can I hold him? I'm really good with babies, love them. I can't wait to have my own," gushed Rachel, completely pissing Tasha off who knew there was only one reason for her to be telling Jim this.

It looked as though Jim was about to hand their son over to this woman when Tasha intervened by removing her son from her husband's arms.

"Sorry, he's fussy and more importantly, so am I," she told the other woman before turning to her husband with Connor in one arm and steering the pushchair with the other. "I'll wait in your office."

Marc called after her, "I love you, Tasha. You need to drop in more often."

"I may do that," she called over her shoulder but didn't look back, she just settled herself on the sofa and waited for Jim.

"What the hell was that?" he asked closing the door behind him.

"I was about to ask you the same thing," she retorted.

"Tasha, she works in the pool—"

"And she's your new Amanda," Tasha finished.

"You don't like her," he said flatly as he sat next to her and reached across to take Connor from her. "If I'm allowed, if you and he aren't too fussy." He lifted the baby onto his shoulder. "Have you been for a trip out with Mommy?"

"She fancies you," Tasha stated, ignoring Jim's question to Connor.

"I fancy you," he replied, making her smile a little.

"Mmm, but do you fancy her, too? Rachel." Tasha somehow managed to make the woman's name sound like she was mocking it.

"You have nothing to be jealous of, Tasha." Jim's tone was soothing, needing her to feel reassured, but the truth was he was deadly serious; he not only loved Tasha, but he absolutely and utterly found her to be the most attractive woman in the world. "Is this hormones, honey?" Even with his gentle tone he managed to inflame the situation.

"That depends. Will it be hormones that cause your mid-life crisis that results in you fucking the blonde bird out there and ending our marriage?"

Jim shook his head calmly, but Tasha could see that he was becoming irritated with her and her raised voice.

"Lose the mouth in front of Connor. I am not having a mid-life crisis and Rachel holds no interest for me, nobody does, nobody except you." He got to his feet and gently placed his son back into the stroller.

"I don't like her." Pouted Tasha. "She was rude and dismissive of my mere presence. She tried to hold my son."

"Our son," corrected Jim.

"She touched you, she looked at you like—oh my God!" she cried a very unwelcome penny suddenly dropped. "I thought she fancied you. That she wanted you, and she does, but it's more. She looks at you like she knows exactly what you bring to the table and she does, doesn't she? You've fucked her?" It was a statement as much as a question.

"Tasha," he began.

"Oh fuck, you have! And now you expect me to be perfectly okay with her being here, with you every day when it's quite obvious that she isn't done." Tasha had gone to a full-blown shout that startled the baby, the sound of raised voices, her raised voice that he was unused to hearing.

"Stop shouting," Jim told her firmly as he stroked a finger across Connor's cheek, immediately calming him. "When have I ever given you cause to doubt my love and fidelity to you?" He paused, clearly expecting an answer.

"You have six ex-wives and a track record." Her reply was tearful more than angry.

"Jeez, Tasha! Six ex-wives you knew about and a track record I told you about. I never lied to you about what I was and yes, I've fucked her, Rachel, once. One night and I had no clue she worked here. We met at a function, she was waiting staff at the function for her brother who was the caterer. I was there alone and we talked and when I was leaving she was outside trying to find a cab so I offered her a ride and it happened. I never even stayed the night or gave her my number. I didn't even remember her name and then about six months later I saw her here in the elevator, but that is it and she was sent along with six other possible assistants from the pool and Marc and Marcia selected her as the best candidate."

"Do Marc and Marcia know about you and her?" Tasha asked, unsure why that was relevant or had any bearing on anything.

"Marc does because he was with me in the elevator that day, but Marcia, no. If you want me to revoke the offer I will, or give her another sideways move, whatever you want because I can't have your head having crazy thoughts all day."

"If I say I want you to get rid of her you'll find a way to offset that won't you? Insist I do or don't do something with someone?"

"Maybe. I don't have anything in mind, baby, but you know I remember everything and I am Mr Control Freak," he acknowledged as he gave a quick glance in Connor's direction who was settled once more.

"You need to let her know that she is very old news. That I am the only woman you want even if I'm not quite the woman you signed up for, but—" was as far as she got before Jim's mouth was over hers, kissing her breathless.

Unsure just how it happened Tasha soon found her legs wrapped around Jim's middle while she lay flat out beneath him on the sofa.

"James," she moaned against his lips as her fingers laced through his hair.

"Right there with you, baby," he replied as she realised one of his hands had made its way under her t-shirt and was teasing her nipples through her bra.

"Please," she pleaded. "I need you," she panted making him smile.

"What about your doctor's appointment?" He continued his assault on her breasts she desperately hoped would not begin leaking milk.

"I don't care. I want you, now." She was rewarded with another kiss, a deep one that saw his tongue gently dipping into her mouth, exploring every corner. "Please say you have a condom."

He grinned down at her as if he knew some great secret. "Honey, I have been carrying one with me for the last week and half, since that night in the hot tub," he told her making her laugh as she recalled the night they'd come closest to breaking the six week rule which Tasha had now decided wasn't a rule as such.

"Have I mentioned how much I love you?"

Her question caused a high arch of his eyebrow. "Not since you arrived here and in case there was any doubt, I love you too and I don't even see women as attractive anymore unless they're you; you are my wife, my friend, my lover, the best mommy my son could ever have and you really are the most beautiful woman I have ever known, the way you look, the way you smell and the way you feel," he told her making her sniff back tears, happy tears, sentimental tears.

"Sorry, this is hormones. I can't cope with you saying such nice things." She sniffed again.

"Sorry, baby. Let me try a slightly different approach then; I love the way your skin reacts to my touch, the way your breath catches in your throat when I do this—" he teased her nipple again and as if on cue her breath caught in her throat making him smile triumphantly. "I especially love how wet I make you. How greedy you are, you and your pussy for my dick and I really, really, really love the funny little noises you make when I make you come, the fire of the passion in your eyes, just like they are now Tasha."

"James, please," she mewled.

"Hormones gone, honey?" he asked with a grin then frowned as his hands moved to her hips. "Jeans, Natasha?"

"So it seems, but I didn't come here to get fucked, well maybe," she admitted making him laugh.

With a single shake of his head he rubbed a hand over her denim clad behind. "You're going to have to pay for the jeans, you and your ass." He pulled his purple tie free of his collar and began to undo the buttons of his pristine white shirt. "Lose the jeans Tasha, and then you're going to get fucked and spanked baby."

Leaping to her feet Tasha quickly cast her jeans aside revealing a tiny, white, lacy brief.

"You definitely came here to get fucked, baby." Jim grinned, throwing his suit trousers across his desk before stepping out of his jersey boxers revealing a huge erection that made Tasha lick her lips. "Not today, baby. How long do we have before our son demands your attention?"

"He should be good for another hour before he needs feeding," replied Tasha, watching Jim's naked body sitting on the sofa where he watched her.

"In that case, Mrs Maybury, bring your mighty fine ass over

here and ride me," he told her holding the wrapped condom in the air like some kind of incentive and prize rolled into one.

Chapter Eighteen

It was exactly an hour later when Connor woke and Tasha was still sitting in Jim's office, on the sofa where earlier he had literally put her across his knee and spanked her for the first time since she'd discovered she was pregnant and that was after she had, in his own words *ridden him*, until they were both breathlessly sated. They had shared the bathroom to clean up, but somehow ended up getting a little dirtier first, including Tasha getting her earlier wish to taste Jim, a wish that had been delivered with her kneeling before him, his hands tightly wound in her hair and her breasts leaking milk everywhere, resulting in them showering together in the relatively small shower cubicle. But now, redressed and feeding her infant son she looked the picture of sweet innocence as she drank the tea Amanda had made for her.

"I need you to be okay with Rachel working for me, Tasha," he suddenly announced, startling her and Amanda who was just about to leave them alone.

"And if I'm not?" Tasha was unsure what else to say.

"Are you telling me you're not?"

"I don't know. First impressions weren't good and the additional information you've revealed makes me uncomfortable."

Reaching for the phone on his desk he spoke to Amanda. "Can you ask Rachel to come through please?"

"She's just popped to the bathroom."

"When she comes back then, and Amanda, did you fill her in on Tasha being my wife and how sickeningly in love with her I am?" He winked at Tasha, making her flush a little.

"Yes, Mr Maybury," replied Amanda flatly but Tasha suspected she was smiling.

"Good, so send her through when she gets back, thank you."

"What are you up to?" Tasha pulled a muslin cloth from Connor's bag whilst watching her husband with suspicion. She placed the cloth on her shoulder then put the baby up there for winding before covering herself. A couple of tiny burps later Tasha switched him to the other side and was still feeding the baby when Rachel appeared in the doorway, opening the door without knocking, confirming for Tasha that she really didn't like this woman.

"I normally like people to knock on my door and wait to be called in rather than just walking in."

Rachel blushed at Jim's word and looked suitably chastened. "Sorry, Ji, Mr Maybury," she said, presumably remembering her position.

"Come in, Rachel. I wanted to introduce you to my wife, formally, rather than standing in the middle of Amanda's office."

"Of course." She wore a tight smile before taking several steps closer.

"Please, take a seat," offered Jim, gesturing to the visitor's seat on the opposite side of his desk, the one he'd already moved so it faced Tasha. He moved so that he was sitting next to Tasha, smiling down at his contented son being fed. He stroked his head gently. "Tasha, this is Rachel, Rachel Perry, and Rachel, my wife, Natasha Maybury and my youngest son Connor."

"Hi, nice to meet you—erm—sorry about before—out there. I hadn't realised who you were." Rachel sounded and looked embarrassed.

"Well, now you know," said Jim. "I can't stress to you enough, Rachel, how important your relationship with Tasha is here. You will, at times be Tasha's link to me and you will also be responsible for managing her schedule, professionally, along with my own."

"Oh." There was no disguising Rachel's displeasure at the prospect of this judging by her sour expression. Her loud, disgruntled sigh confirmed it.

"Is that a problem for you?" asked Tasha. With a smile she continued, "I don't especially need my professional commitments scheduling, and they're few and far between at the moment, but Jim does. He likes to know where we'll both be at any given time. Amanda has done it since we first met and seems happy to do that for us, however, if you don't want to then you need to say now."

"Are you saying I need to become your wife's friend, like Amanda?" Rachel addressed Jim.

"No. In fact, I would actively discourage that. Amanda's friendship is all Tasha's doing. Me? I'd like my wife to be as distanced from my past as humanly possible. I would hate for her to be hurt or tarnished by anything I may have mistakenly become involved with," he told Rachel tactfully, but clearly making her understand that their one-night stand had been, for Jim, a mistake.

"May I speak frankly?" asked Rachel.

"Please do." Tasha was beginning to admire the other woman's ballsy streak.

"I was offered this job based on my professional qualities." She turned to Jim again. "I am up to the job, but if a condition of this role is to pander to your wife's whims then it may not be the right job for me."

Tasha watched the other woman's expression, strong and firm and definitely admired her directness. Glancing back towards her husband she was unsure if he felt the same.

"Nobody needs to pander to my wife's whims, no one except me. This job is a good opportunity for you, Rachel, and although it is temporary while Amanda is taking maternity leave it could lead to a similar role on a more permanent basis if things work well," Jim told her, dangling a rather obvious, *do as you're told, don't piss my wife off and you'll do well* carrot.

"Of course, Mr Maybury, thank you," Rachel replied with her gaze fixed on Jim.

"Thank you for your time." Jim was dismissing her.

Getting to her feet Rachel looked back at Tasha. "Mrs Maybury," and left.

"I still don't like her," said Tasha with a frown.

"Good." Jim leaned across to kiss her lips gently and grinned. "Because hell will freeze over before you'll be socialising with Rachel."

"Angie called me earlier, to discuss some work that might be on offer to me." She thought she should at least mention this now.

"Where? When? She does realise you've just had a baby, doesn't she?" He was as irritated as Tasha had anticipated.

"I haven't got exact dates but soon and it's a U.K. show—"

"Not happening, Tasha. No way," snapped Jim, leaping to his feet as Tasha returned the baby to her shoulder to wind him. "You have Connor so he has to go where you go and he is not going to the U.K. for weeks on end to be palmed off on a nanny on set while I am here."

"Have you quite finished?" Tasha got to her feet too.

"What do you think?" He stared at her with a determined expression.

"Connor." Tasha gently addressed her son. "Daddy really needs to calm down, doesn't he?" The little boy stared up at her, bobbing his tongue out and making her laugh. "Go and tell Daddy to chill his beans," she told him almost singing the words as she handed him to his father who accepted him with a smile.

"Hey, buddy, and maybe we should remind Mommy that she is playing with Daddy and that is going to come back and bite her in the ass," Jim told the little boy who stared at his father's expression transfixed.

"Don't discuss my ass with our son." Tasha sounded genuinely outraged.

"Didn't bother you earlier when it was getting spanked, baby." Jim pointed out making her blush and him laugh. "I mean it Tasha, about work. I can't have you two so far away from me for weeks and I want Connor to be at home with us for a few more months. I thought we'd discussed this before he was born."

"We did, but if I get all of the details, can we discuss it later? I didn't say it was in the U.K. I said it's for a U.K. show."

"So, it's being filmed over here?" clarified Jim.

"Yes, so can we talk later, at home?"

"Sure, but I really have to be getting on now, baby."

211

"We should be going anyway. Do we have condoms at home?"

Jim arched a brow at her inquisitively. "There are some, a few in our bathroom, why? What do you have in mind, Mrs Maybury?" he asked as he kissed his son and strapped him back into his stroller.

"I figure now that we've failed to reach the six week mark we might as well fuck at every opportunity." She bit down into her bottom lip, imagining the possibilities.

"Oh, honey, I have missed you and the smart mouth. You should go home via the store and buy more because I have every intention of making up for lost time, Tasha, starting tonight. You just remember that the rules haven't changed; you play with me and piss me off and I may have you begging and crying and still not coming."

"Yes, James," she replied in a breathy whisper, her eyes cast down.

"Tasha, you need to go before I am ripping your panties off again and fucking you across my desk minus a condom."

She could actually think of nothing she wanted more, but couldn't risk getting pregnant again, not so soon.

"Oh, baby." Laughed Jim. "We should have an early dinner and an even earlier night, now go, while you can."

Tasha was pulling up outside the house when she heard another car coming up the drive behind her. She smiled at Bobby and Abby as they came into view while she was taking a sleeping Connor from his car seat. She pressed the fob to lock the white, top of the range, Range Rover she drove, another gift from Jim, but this time chosen together, based on her safety, and Connor's as her main passenger.

"Hello, you two. Are you playing hooky?" She climbed the steps to the front door and let them in.

"That unfortunate boy looks seriously like my brother when he's sleeping." Bobby grimaced, possibly not realising that he was grimacing at his own appearance as well as his brother's as they looked very alike.

"Then he's a very lucky boy." Smiled Tasha making Bobby laugh and shake his head.

"You two are sickeningly happy, but I'm happy for you both."

Tasha lay Connor down in his bassinet and entered the kitchen where she made coffee.

"It's nice to see you both but I'm guessing there's a reason for you being here together instead of somewhere else, together." Grinned Tasha, making the other two laugh at her observation.

"Cut to the chase, Tasha." Abby looked at Bobby, silently urging him to speak.

"This is not to say it's our turn for the big family Fourth of July thing, is it? I don't even know what that entails," she told them as panic rose in her.

"No, no." Smiled Bobby. "It's us this year. I wanted to speak to you about your dad."

Carrying the coffee back to where they sat on the sofa next to Connor Tasha looked nervous. "My dad?"

"Yeah. I have a friend in the D.A.'s office and he thought we might like the heads up on this; there has been some communication from your government representatives to ours about having your father shipped back home to serve his sentence. Your mother has engaged the services and support of a charity that are suggesting that she, as an innocent in this, is being punished by him being imprisoned over here. She is actually now classed as disabled I believe."

"I don't know what to say, Bobby, and I don't think drunk, apathetic and alone makes her disabled." Tasha sat down on the coffee table opposite him with a perplexed expression. "Will they go for it over here?" She tried to untangle then order the multiple thoughts and questions queueing in her head.

"I would," he told her bluntly. "It may be viewed that he is not the U.S.'s problem and that England should foot the bill for his incarceration. His intended victim, you, isn't even an American citizen."

"I suppose you can see their point, and I think our prisons would be an easier ride than yours. Could they cut his sentence?" Tasha sounded genuinely scared.

"He could apply for an appeal or a review of his sentence I imagine."

"What about the injunction?"

"Injunction?" Bobby was confused and struggling to keep up with his sister-in-law's flitting thoughts.

"Jim took them out when I was in the U.K. and when he was first arrested over here. Would they still be valid and what about Connor, could he come near Connor?" Tasha was becoming tearful and genuinely distressed making Bobby regret doing this without Jim's knowledge or presence.

"Hey," soothed Abby, moving over to sit next to her friend and sister-in-law. "I think you may be getting yourself upset over nothing here, right Bobby?" Abby gave her husband the perfect cue to continue.

"Abby's right, Tasha. We're talking about the possibility of your dad being sent to a prison, a maximum security facility I would guess for someone convicted of attempted murder and conspiracy to commit murder. He's not being released. In the event he is ever paroled or released then you could apply for a restraining order under Californian law, although he'd struggle to legally gain entry to the U.S. with his criminal record. I just wanted you to know in advance because sometimes, when there is a public interest aspect to these things nobody knows until it hits the news-stands. Are you okay? Do you need me to call Jimbo?" Bobby was worried about his young and clearly shaken sister-in-law and knew his brother, although guaranteed to be pissed about this, might be the only one to calm her back down.

"I'm fine, it's just a bit of a shock. I wasn't expecting it. When he was sentenced I thought that was it, done, but now it may not be, but I'm okay. You don't need to call Jim. I'll tell him later so he may call you for specific details."

"That's not a problem," replied Bobby as Connor began to cry.

The baby sounded distressed, properly distressed as though frightened. Tasha turned, startled by his unusual cry and wondered if he'd had a bad dream, assuming babies had dreams. Tasha picked him up and comforted him, held him close to gently kiss him while whispering tender words to him.

Watching them, Abby smiled up at her. "I was really worried about you becoming a parent so soon and you being so young, but you're a natural."

"Thank you," replied Tasha. "It all came as a bit of a shock if I'm honest, but he's very easy to love." She rocked Connor gently until he drifted off to sleep again.

"Hey, don't keep him all to yourself, Auntie Abby would like some love too," the other woman cried, holding her arms up to receive the little boy.

By the time Jim arrived home Bobby and Abby had left and Tasha was calmer about the information her brother-in-law had delivered, not that she wasn't still struggling to know how she felt about things, she was. The idea that her father might be given the opportunity to return home, to the country of his birth didn't worry her, in fact, she thought she might prefer that to him remaining in the U.S. Although her nightmares had continued to decrease over the last few months, she still found herself waking from a dream where her father was standing over her with some frequency. She knew once she woke up that her dream was just that, but she still found it disconcerting and unnerving to think he could find her and break in if he were able to escape from prison. However, if his prison cell was in the U.K. he would be too far away to make her nightmares a reality. It was ridiculous, she knew it was, but she couldn't quite shake that fear.

She was bathing a yawning Connor in his own bath that contained a sponge cut out that allowed him to lie safely in the water, floating while she washed him and talked to him from her position kneeling on the floor.

"Hey, you two, my two babies," Jim said from the doorway behind Tasha making her jump slightly while Connor began to search the space around him for his daddy's voice. "Well, hello, baby." Jim leaned down to kiss Tasha's lips gently. "And hello, buddy. How you doing?" he asked and was rewarded with a gurgle from his son. "That good, huh? Although I like it when Mommy bathes me," he said with a wicked grin at his wife before rolling his shirt sleeves up. "How about Daddy finishes bath time while Mommy does whatever Mommy needs to do."

"You'll get no argument from me. I'll go and find some dinner and then I will be back up for when you are dry and dressed and ready for feeding before bed little man." Tasha planted a kiss on her son's nose before getting to her feet to kiss her husband on the lips.

It was only about fifteen minutes later when she returned to find a crying Connor rubbing his eyes while being fastened into a baby grow covered in dinosaurs.

"Here she is, the milk machine. Daddy just doesn't cut it when you're hungry, does he?" Jim looked across at Tasha who was already sitting in the nursing chair and undoing the buttons on the loose fitting shirt she was wearing, preparing to feed their son.

Within seconds of being handed over to her, Connor was suckling against his mother's breast, contentedly feeding while Tasha simply enjoyed the closeness and the opportunity to just look at him, study him.

"Are you okay? You're not still thinking about Rachel, are you?" asked Jim seriously, watching his wife stroking their son's forehead.

"No. Sorry. Bobby came round earlier, with Abby," she began.

"And?"

Tasha explained the purpose of their visit, yet surprisingly Jim said nothing until she had finished.

"How do you feel about that, honey?" He sat on the footstool in front of the chair she sat on.

"I don't know. So long as he can't turn up or cause disruption for Dan or Pippa. I just need us all to be safe from him, especially Connor," she admitted tearfully.

"Baby. I have learnt my lesson the hard way, allowing your father and Mickie the chance to get anywhere near you, twice. It won't happen again, ever. You believe that, right?" he asked and she couldn't deny that she did. He spoke with such conviction and she trusted Jim like she had never trusted anyone, ever.

She nodded and he smiled at her lovingly.

"Good, and we will make any legal arrangements required, okay?"

She nodded again.

"I'm going to take a quick shower while you settle Connor and then we can have dinner, talk about this work offer and then I am taking you to bed."

"Sounds like a perfect evening, Mr Maybury, especially as this is usually Connor's six-hour sleep."

"Glad you approve, Mrs Maybury." He smiled before leaving her alone with their son in the nursery while his own smile dropped once out of sight.

Chapter Nineteen

Once Connor was settled, Tasha went downstairs and after preparing dinner went back upstairs leaving Jim talking on the phone to Bobby. Taking a quick shower, she decided she should make more effort to look less *mumsy*, so, wrapped in a towel entered the wardrobe to find something to wear, something that was sexy rather than functional for breastfeeding. Skimming through the rails she laughed as she paused at the grey shift dress she'd worn for that first flight to LA.

Unsure whether it still fit, she pulled it from the hanger and selected a set of black lace underwear comprising a push up bra and a pair of lace top stockings. Dressing, Tasha hoped that having just fed Connor she was safe from her breasts leaking milk. The dress was slightly tighter across the chest and hips, but possibly looked better for it. Maybe her post-baby body had some perks after all. Slipping on a pair of black heels she knew how ridiculously overdressed for dinner at home she was, but she didn't care, for a few hours she just wanted to be herself; Tasha, Jim's wife, his lover and part of that was looking like she used to rather than only looking like a new mum.

Jim was still on the phone in his office when she got downstairs. Placing the baby monitor on the kitchen counter, Tasha smiled at the sound of her son's contented breathing as she threw together the stir fry vegetables she'd sliced earlier.

Jim's voice grew louder as it got closer and then came to an abrupt end momentarily,

"No, what? Sorry, Bobby. I got distracted." He stood behind Tasha, pressing the hard lines and curves of his body against hers. "Yeah and thanks again, bye." He ended his call and lowered his lips until they were pressed against Tasha's neck. "Dressed for seduction, baby?" he asked with amusement and arousal in his voice.

"Maybe," she replied as he pressed an erection into her hip making her gasp with anticipation.

"Well, it's certainly working, although you'd look highly fuckable in a sack."

She laughed.

"So, what have I done to deserve this then, honey? Our flight dress, stockings and shoes that I intend to inspect more closely when they're resting on my shoulders while I fuck you, would you like that?" A single moan left her lips, making Jim nip at her ear. "I'll take that as a yes." He snaked an arm around her waist before skimming up to cup the underside of her breast.

"James," she moaned as she tried to keep the stir fry moving.

"You bet, baby," he whispered, still mouthing her ear as his hand travelled down her body, over her belly that was almost back to its pre-baby flatness, across her hips and thighs until he reached the hem of her dress that he was now pulling up revealing her legs and stocking tops. His fingers traced patterns on the exposed skin above her stockings.

"Please," she moaned, desperate for him to touch her, to move closer to where she wanted his fingers, inside her. Broadening her stance she was rewarded with a thick finger sliding along her sex, first circling her clit then penetrating her.

"Oh Natasha, no panties, baby. You are so naughty, maybe I should have spanked you harder earlier or maybe I need to spank you again."

Tasha made no reply, her only response was her core leaking yet more moisture at the mere suggestion, coating Jim's fingers and hand.

"Jeez, honey. I don't need to even ask if you like my idea, I can feel it. You're so, so wet, you really need to be fucked, don't you?" His question required no real reply, a resounding yes was clearly evident and yet the darkness entering his voice meant Tasha did speak.

"Yes," she mewled and bit down into her lip as a second

finger joined the first and they were now rotating, brushing her sensitive spot, just how she like it.

"Stir," he reminded her, referring to the vegetables that were probably about to overcook but she didn't care. "This is why you can't ever work away from me, Tasha. You need this, don't you?" He waited, clearly expecting an answer.

"James." She was unsure what to say next because this was not the discussion she'd planned about work, yet she couldn't deny the truth of what he was saying.

"Answer me, Tasha, or I will take it as a no and just stop," he threatened.

"No, don't stop, please," she pleaded which she knew had made him smile. "I don't want to work away from you, not ever. I love you, I miss you, please, James," she cried, feeling a slowing of his movements, delaying her release.

"Yes, baby. Come for me, Tasha. Just for me," he told her as his fingers stroked faster and his thumb began to flick across her clit. "Spread your legs wider, baby. I want you wide open." His lips closed against her neck.

Her compliance was immediate as was the effect of it all resulting in her whole body quaking, inside and out until she was crying out, clutching the edge of the counter as sensation replaced previous sensation leaving her incoherent and struggling to remain standing as wave after wave of pleasure washed over her becoming more and more intense until the pleasure became almost painful.

"Fuck, Tasha. We will have to stop at one baby if this is what pregnancy does to your body. You're more responsive than ever," he told her, holding her tightly around the middle, holding her up, soothing her down from whichever higher plain her body was currently residing on.

"You want another baby?" They hadn't planned a first never mind further additions to the family, but she hadn't expected this discussion so soon.

"Maybe, but we can talk about that later. Right now I want to taste you, Tasha. I plan on licking you dry."

She turned in Jim's arms so that she faced him and giggled. "I am loving that plan but it may be seriously flawed."

He frowned, either at her amusement or the inferred suggestion that he wouldn't be tasting her. "How so?"

"In case you hadn't noticed, whenever you lick me I am many things, but never, ever dry."

"Ah, a challenge, honey." He grinned and lowered his lips to hers, then suddenly sniffing reached round her to turn the cooker off. "Dinner is burnt, Mrs Maybury, so let's adjust the original plan for the night."

"Go on." She reached up to stroke his face.

"I'm thinking I rise to your challenge and then I make slow, torturous love to you, Tasha. Then we eat, take out or whatever, I don't give a shit and then we talk about work and whether we want another baby or whatever you want. What do you say to that?"

"I say take me to bed, James." She wrapped her arms around his neck while snaking her legs around his hips.

"Should you be drinking?" asked Jim with a concerned frown when Tasha opened a bottle of beer for each of them as he lay the pizza box on the table in the lounge.

"Jim, it's one bottle of beer, lite beer at that. I'm not suggesting an all-night bender." She handed him his own bottle with absolutely no intention of giving up her own.

"Okay. You look very, very sexy, baby." She looked down at herself dressed in a pair of yoga pants and a vest top. "You do," he told her sensing her disbelief. "I told you, even in a sack." He grinned, but meant every word, even with his arched brow that made her laugh. "Not that I didn't appreciate you dressing for dinner and your just shagged face and hair help."

"You are outrageous, Mr Maybury." Her mouth gaped open.

"Baby, you need to close that mouth or I will be finding a use for it, again." They both knew she'd have no objection to that but before she could voice that Jim passed her a slice of pizza. "Eat. You're my son's milk machine and refrigerator and you need to eat more. So, eat and talk to me. What's this offer Angie has for you?"

"It's not an actual role, they want me to be myself as a kind of L.A. correspondent for a daytime magazine show."

"What are you going to correspond on?" he asked curiously,

having no objection to what she'd said so far.

"From what I understand it would be looking at whatever is going on out here. It might be showbiz if something is breaking, or whatever craze is the in thing from beauty treatments to fashion, to family stuff, family stuff like baby kind of stuff. It seems now I have a baby people want to talk parenting stuff with me."

"So where would that leave Connor?" Jim turned so he could study Tasha more closely. He wanted her to be happy and fulfilled but not at their son's expense.

"For the most part, wherever I am, which would still be here much of the time and some of the items may allow Connor to be involved."

"Involved how?" Jim looked less than thrilled now.

"Well, suppose there is a new craze for new mums to run three miles a day with their baby strapped to their chest, or baby massage or baby gym, anything involving being a baby, they might want me to look at that, with Connor."

The frown on Jim's face was deep and fixed making Tasha wince as she waited for his response.

"He is not an accessory or an extension of either of us. Angie does know that she only represents you and not our son too, doesn't she?" He sounded angrily.

"I thought you'd be pleased." Tasha spoke quietly, deliberately keeping her voice low, not wanting this to become an argument. If she was honest with herself she didn't really think Jim would be pleased as such, but she didn't think he'd be opposed either. "This keeps me here, at home, with you, me and Connor. You don't like the alternatives." She pouted unsure how she was ever going to be anything beyond a wife and mother if this was as unacceptable as it appeared to be.

"I'm not too thrilled about this, never mind the alternatives. It is our responsibility to shield him from press intrusion, to stop his face being plastered across tabloids in the supermarket, but how do we do that, legitimately, if we then use him to aid our own careers or exposure." Jim ran a hand through his hair. He knew Tasha wanted to work, accepted it, admired it, but he'd hoped having Connor would have occupied her for longer than it had. He didn't want to be the one putting obstacles in her way and he really did have no objection to her working and building her own career and yet the idea of her and Connor being away from him was abhorrent. "But you want to do it?" He knew she was becoming restless and also acknowledged that he needed to give a little here.

"Jim, before I met you, just over a year ago, I was a young and hopeful actress, one with some talent and endless potential opportunities, opportunities you might have been involved in facilitating and then we met; you became the man I love, my fiancé, my husband, the father of my unborn baby, and now you're Connor's daddy and we have this great life together, but in all that has happened the one thing that hasn't is work. I refused to have you gift me work from day one and every other job I've got I haven't been able to fulfil due to things out of my control." She suddenly sounded breathless, gasping slightly at the overwhelming changes to her life in such a short time. "I don't regret us, or Connor, really I don't. The thing is, I barely recognise Tasha Winters in Tasha Maybury and that's mainly okay because Tasha Winters was seriously screwed up and you've sort of straightened her out."

"But you want to keep some of her?" He reached across and took Tasha's hand in his, gently stroking it.

"Yes, the good bits. I love being your wife and Connor's mom, but I don't want to be *just* a wife and mother. I want, I need to be me too which is what dinner was about, the dress. I'm still me underneath the elasticated waists and the breastfeeding suitable tops. This probably sounds crazy and I know hormones are still raging through my body but this is not a hormonal new mommy ranting, I promise, but now I am questioning my own motives for considering the use of Connor in my work."

"Baby, I love you and I want you to be happy, I want to make you happy. I would love for you to stay home and for it to be enough for you, but I get that it isn't. I can't tell you that I want you to pursue the full potential of your career because I want you to be my wife and Connor's mommy more, but we have to find a compromise. I can see that you and Angie are trying to do that, so tell her you'll take it subject to specific conditions being included in the contract."

"What conditions?" Tasha's suspicions were immediately raised. Jim was shrewd in business and controlling in personal issues and these conditions were likely to be potentially influenced by both of these aspects. Add to that the fact that he could be very sneaky she felt her suspicion was well placed.

"First, Connor is not in the contract at all, that's not to say you won't feature him in reports if it is suitable and appropriate, but this way we, you and I, determine what he is exposed to because I am happy for you to take him to baby gym or for a massage, but there are other things I would not allow. This gives us the say so over him and nobody else. Second, it is stipulated that your role is L.A. based, not *Stateside*. This is a big country. Again, that's not to say you won't be amenable to reporting from outside of L.A. but this way you stay in control. Third, you sign up for no longer than twelve weeks with an option to extend. You don't want to be tied long term and you may hate it. Finally, any celebrity type reports are subject to them not potentially creating personal or professional embarrassment or distress to you and if they're likely to, you have the option to veto them."

Staring at him, Tasha wondered how Jim made a yes sound like such a no. She kind of understood what he was saying and why, except the final point.

"What does that mean, my embarrassment and distress?"

"Ah, I thought you looked confused." He smiled, somehow pleased that his wife was still innocent enough not to see and understand all of the potential pitfalls of Hollywood and contracts. "Imagine an actor, maybe one who is a friend or acquaintance of yours or mine fucks up, gets caught with his pants down, has an affair, gets divorced, is getting married, whatever, and they ask for your take on it or use you to try and get a scoop. You give 'em a scoop and you are history in this town professionally, baby. And if it involves my studio or one of my productions..."

"I'm fucked personally? Is that what you're saying?" Tasha sounded tearful, confused as to how she was ever going to work successfully if every job and role might compromise her marriage.

"Not like you mean, but it causes potential problems for us if you are seen to be discussing one of my actors in a negative light when I, as the studio, may be supporting him fully and being really positive. Those are my terms, Tasha. Sorry if it seems harsh, but there they are."

"I kind of get it," she conceded half-heartedly because she did, kind of. "I'll call Angie in a minute, before Connor wakes up."

"And tell her to send me a copy of the contract and I'll get legal to take a look before you sign. Call her once you've eaten some more and then we can talk about extending our family." Jim grinned as Tasha stretched forward to kiss his lips gently and grabbed another slice of pizza.

Jim was lounging on the sofa with another bottle of beer watching Tasha looking nervous as she waited for Angie to answer her call. He'd meant everything he'd said to her; he wanted her to be happy and fulfilled professionally and personally but he wouldn't allow their home life to suffer for her work and Connor needed to be the priority, although he had no doubts that she always had their son as her priority above all else. Angie had just answered when Connor's crying sounded around them through the baby monitor.

Tasha looked at it startled until Jim looked across and smiled. "I'll go."

He planted a kiss on Tasha's temple leaving her watching his back disappearing into the hall, a very attractive back wearing one of his favoured white linen shirts over a pair of khaki shorts.

She'd finished explaining Jim's stipulations and with a promise from Angie that she'd speak to them the following day and get back to her, Jim returned carrying Connor and frowning at a wrapped nappy.

"Angie will speak to them and let us know." She looked down at their son who was gurgling up at her. "Hey, you're making a liar of me, baby. I told Daddy you were good for six hours and it's only been four and a half," she told him, making him fidget as he became more animated in his reaction to her voice. Tasha and Jim laughed at him, exciting him further.

"I think his premature wake up may have been due to needing

his diaper changed."

Tasha laughed.

"What?" Jim looked down at the hygienically sealed nappy in his hand.

"Sandra and I were talking about them before, nappies."

"Diapers," Jim corrected. "Remember Natasha, my country, sorry, our country," he said gesturing between himself and Connor, "our labels."

"Whatever." Laughed Tasha moving into the kitchen to put the kettle on.

"I will get rid of this." Jim held the nappy up and handed Connor over to Tasha. "And then, we'll talk babies, baby."

Sitting between Jim's legs on the sofa with her back pressed against his front, her legs drawn up, making a perfect slope for Connor to lie in Tasha couldn't believe she'd ever got this lucky or ever felt as happy as she did right now. Jim had his arms around her so he could touch his son whilst holding his wife who was stroking their son's face gently.

"You really are the most wonderful mother, Tasha." He kissed her hair.

"And you say the nicest things."

"It's true. Anyway, you sounded startled earlier when you asked if I wanted another baby, so?"

"You said about my body post pregnancy and I wondered if it was your way of saying you wanted us to have more children," Tasha explained honestly. "Oh, and you told Mitch to book us in again in ten months when Connor was being born," she reminded him making him laugh.

"I am still enthralled at the effect on your body of carrying this child. I hadn't really thought about having more, although I did once tell you if I had a younger childless wife I would want her to be happy and if that involved children that would be fine by me, so the real question is, do you want more children?"

"Not yet. I don't want to dive in and have another immediately, but I've been thinking about Lexi and how lonely she seems within the family and I know when I was pregnant Bobby suggested that if he and Abby were going to have more children they should do it sooner rather than later and I think

Abby thought about it, but then rethought it, I think."

"Mmm. That's a lot of thinking you've been doing. Bobby had no children with his first or second wife. He had no desire to have children. He had his career and loved the life of a wealthy childless man. When he met Abby he really liked her and they fell in love and got married and he was still happy to be childless."

"But not Abby?" Tasha put Connor's dummy in his mouth as he began to cry, hoping to put off feeding him earlier than usual.

"No. Not that she was that open about it. They'd been married a few months and Abby suggested starting a family. Bobby was not keen and told her as much, insisting she should keep her ob/gyn appointment to get her shot, but she didn't and got pregnant. Bobby flipped when she told him and Abby was surprised and upset by his reaction. He left her for a few weeks, stayed with me and tried to get his head around it. Unfortunately, Abby lost the baby and was devastated and so was Bobby, so he begged for forgiveness, they reconciled and a year later Alexi was born and Bobby loved her like he'd never loved anyone before and he couldn't wait to have more."

"Not Abby though?" asked Tasha.

"She was not a natural mother and didn't enjoy having a young baby. She suffered a little with depression but had also gained about sixty pounds during pregnancy and struggled to lose it which I think made her decide that Alexi would be an only child."

"Poor Abby, poor Bobby. I don't want Connor to be an only child so maybe in a year or two we could have another baby, or two. I know he has Philip and Lizzie, but it's not the same with them being so much older than him. They won't all grow up together and I love having siblings and I know you do too so why would we deprive him of that?" She ran her fingers through Connor's hair, teasing it up into spikes making Jim laugh. "Has Bobby said much to you about Mickie having been pregnant with his baby?"

"Not really. He was shocked by it then I think he figured Mickie's reaction was typical of her and that although he would have done the right thing by her and the baby it was probably for the best that Mickie remained childless."

"I guess, and you? Was she right about what her being your niece or nephew's mother would have meant?" Tasha continued to tease Connor's hair into spikes to calm her nerves as much as anything because this conversation, like so many involving Mickie was overdue.

"Yes, although she should have remained uncharted waters anyway, but less of this." Clearly any more talk of Mickie and babies with Bobby was going to remain overdue. "Let me take a look at my boy," Jim said, quickly changing subject. "He looks like a little monkey." Jim leaned over Tasha's shoulder to make monkey noises at their son who stared up at his daddy with a bemused expression on his face that made Tasha laugh.

"Nobody deserves to be as happy as I am right now," she said with a broad and genuine smile.

Jim kissed her head and whispered against her hair, "Yes they do, Tasha. You do, always did, honey. I just need to make you believe that."

Sniffing back unexpected tears she nodded. "Thank you."

Chapter Twenty

"Jim," called Tasha from Connor's nursery through to their bedroom where Jim was getting ready for work. "James!" she cried more urgently before picking the baby up and striding through to their bedroom where she almost collided with her husband in the doorway.

"What's wrong?" asked Jim breathlessly, dressed in only a towel.

"Connor is making strange faces. Do you think he's okay?"

"What do you mean, strange faces?" he asked with an air of concern he was hoping to mask as his wife was clearly worried.

"Look." Tasha walked past her husband and placed their son on the bed where she stood over him and began to talk to him. "Look," she cried as Connor began to pull faces again and then his strange face turned into a huge smile. "Oh wow, he's smiling," shrieked Tasha, causing her son to smile again as tears began to run down her face, happy tears, ecstatic tears.

"Yes, he is, honey. Morning, buddy. How you doing?" Jim's words triggered another smile to broaden across the baby's little face making his daddy laugh at him. "That good, huh? Although, I guess your life is pretty perfect, son; you've got everybody running around fetching and carrying, milk on demand, parents that really love you and your momma is the most beautiful MILF in the world, a momma that's crying again because you can smile now," Jim told him as he pulled Tasha closer to hug her and wipe her tears away until they were both startled by the sound of laughter coming from the bed in front of them.

"He's laughing," squealed Tasha, making Connor laugh

again.

Jim reached down and picked him up while laughing at him. "You think you're clever, don't you? Smiling and laughing and making Mommy cry. If you were any other guy or a little older I would put you on your butt for making my wife cry."

Jim handed Connor to his mother's waiting arms before placing a gentle kiss on her lips.

"Now that I know the house isn't burning down and Mommy was just excited by your strange smiley face, Daddy really needs to get dressed and go to work." Jim smiled before bestowing another kiss on his son. "What time's your appointment?" he asked as Tasha held her son close.

"Eleven thirty."

"Baby, I'm sorry I can't come with you," started Jim.

"It's fine. I'm quite capable of having a smear, an internal exam and arranging birth control without you." She hoped to relieve some of Jim's apparent guilt at being forced to go into work rather than take her for her post baby check-up. "I'll let you make it up to me later if you really want." She grinned suggestively but was interrupted by the sound of Lizzie thundering up the stairs.

"Daddy, Tasha, Connor," she shouted.

Connor jumped while Tasha and Jim laughed.

"I'm coming," called Tasha. "Breakfast in ten minutes, Mr Maybury."

"Be there in seven, Mrs Maybury," replied Jim, heading into the wardrobe.

Sitting at the kitchen table, Lizzie revealed the reason for her unexpected visit. "Can I hang out with you today, Tash?"

"I have an appointment with my doctor this morning, but we could do something later."

"Are you sick?" Lizzie sounded worried.

"No, just a regular check-up after having a baby."

"I thought you were going to see Amanda today?" Jim was already getting to his feet.

"I can rearrange." Smiled Tasha. "So, I'll get showered and dressed after breakfast. We'll go to the doctor's office, then we can have lunch and maybe some shopping, I think Connor could do with some bigger sleep suits."

"Cool Tash, you're the best." Lizzie leapt to her feet and hugged Tasha before turning to her father. "Daddy I need some new jeans."

"Then get some new jeans, sweetie. I need to go, but you be good, and Tasha call me when you get done with doctor." Jim kissed them all in turn and left.

Tasha was parking the car near the doctor's office when Lizzie decided to start a serious conversation. "Tash, you know Dylan and I have been thinking about sleeping together for a while?"

"Yeah…" Tasha paused and waited for Lizzie to continue.

"But after the stuff with Mickie..." she trailed off.

Straightening after strapping Connor into his stroller, Tasha placed an arm around Lizzie's shoulders reassuringly.

"I get it, Lizzie. That whole craziness with Mickie scared us all and threw us all off balance for a while so I understand why you wouldn't feel able to make that decision immediately, although I remember how close the two of you were getting, you and Dylan."

"We're kind of ready now and I was wondering about birth control," admitted Lizzie nervously.

"I think technically it's illegal for you both, but knowing that, if you have decided, both of you together, I think you're being very sensible to take precautions. Have you spoken to Sara about it?"

"No! God, Mom would be really embarrassing about it, so no."

"So, are you asking me whether you should do it or which contraceptive would be best?" Tasha wished she wasn't being asked this by Lizzie, Lizzie as in her husband's daughter, but was also quite touched by it.

"We've already decided, Tash, so we don't need permission, but I know you can get a shot, and you had an implant."

"Jeez, Lizzie, if my luck with the implant is anything to go by." Laughed Tasha looking down at Connor who was being pushed along the street by Lizzie. They both laughed before returning to the importance of their conversation.

231

"I never used anything other than condoms before I met your dad," revealed Tasha to a surprised looking Lizzie. "They stop you getting pregnant and prevent diseases and I know you are about to tell me that you and Dylan are exclusive, which I don't doubt, but sometimes people do things and aren't as exclusive as you might think or want, so I would say go with condoms."

They reached the building that housed Dr Marshall's office.

"And as if by magic, Lizzie, we might just be in the best place for you to pick up some information," she said to a horrified looking Lizzie, making Tasha laugh. "I meant leaflets and stuff, unless you want to sit in with me and quiz Mitch."

"No! I'll read the leaflets while you're in there. I'm going to look like a teen mom with Connor in his stroller and reading up on birth control," she exclaimed excitedly.

"Thank goodness your father isn't here." Laughed Tasha, as they entered the elevator together. She laughed louder when she imagined her husband's actual horror at his daughter's words.

****

It was just over an hour later with a clean bill of health and a supply of the contraceptive pill that Tasha was being shown to a table in a nearby restaurant with Lizzie and Connor.

"Do you know how many hideous diseases can be sexually transmitted?" Lizzie sounded horrified.

"A few." Laughed Tasha.

"I think you're right and we should stick to condoms," announced Lizzie.

"I'm glad you've decided and have made your own mind up." The truth was Tasha felt relieved more than glad that Lizzie had made her own mind up.

"You won't tell Daddy, will you?" Lizzie asked nervously.

"I have no intention of telling your dad anything and hopefully he won't ask," Tasha reassured her.

"Thanks, Tash." Lizzie grinned until Tasha's phone sounded a message alert.

"Bugger, I forgot to call your dad." Tasha fished her phone from her bag as Connor began to cry and the waiter returned to take their order.

Lizzie leaned down and expertly released her brother from the security of his harness. She held him safely in her arms and began to chat to him, the familiarity of her voice immediately soothing him until he contentedly gazed up at her.

"Lizzie, I just need to reply to your dad's message." Tasha smiled as the younger woman pulled out her own phone to message Dylan.

<Hey baby, are you still with the doctor? Is everything ok? Jx>

Tasha looked across at her son and stepdaughter and smiled at the image of them together, both of them relaxed and apparently happy. After the initial shock of being pregnant at all, Tasha's next worry had been Lizzie and her reaction to a new baby, a sibling who would undoubtedly force her to share her father beyond Philip and Tasha.

The next worry had been whether the baby was going to be a boy or a girl and there was no doubt in Tasha's mind that a brother would be easier to deal with in Lizzie's mind. Another brother was semi-known territory, but a sister, a baby sister might have caused Lizzie to really question her role in Jim's life at that point. After all she'd endured with Mickie, Lizzie needed some sense of stability and security, so it was fortunate that Connor had been a boy. Watching Lizzie jigging her brother in her arms with varying degrees of success as he began to become unsettled, Tasha smiled that everything was falling into place in her life.

As Lizzie's attempts at pacifying her hungry brother failed, Tasha took him from her and discreetly began to feed him, still amazed that they made clothes with fake pockets that were essentially flaps for booby feeding, and replied to Jim.

<Sorry, forgot to call you. Everything is fine. Mitch assures me that we won't need to buy any more condoms. Am waiting for lunch to arrive whilst feeding Connor, hoping nobody objects to me breastfeeding him here. Tx>

<Oh honey, you are reverting to type and not doing what you assure me you will do. Will leave you to eat lunch and if anybody objects to my son eating they can go and screw themselves. What do you mean about condoms? Jx>

<I love it when you get all arsy! No more condoms, I have the pill and Mitch says if I start taking it today I am protected immediately. He also made me pee on a stick after confessing that we hadn't made it to today sex free. You love it when I revert to type and infuriate you. Tx>

<Oh baby, I have missed you and your smart mouth. I assume you're not announcing another pregnancy. We should plan an early night, bareback again baby. Jx>

<Lunch has arrived, early night sounds good to me. And no, no pregnancy to announce. Tx>

"Tash?" started Lizzie as they began to eat their lunch of chicken salad, Tasha one handed as she held Connor in the other arm. "You know when we were with Mickie, at Philip's?" Her nervousness gained Tasha's undivided attention.

"Yes." Tasha wondered where this was going and as much as she was trying to put all things Mickie behind her she wouldn't if Lizzie had things she needed to work through still.

"The things she asked me—the things I told her—erm—does Daddy know about them?"

Tasha gently placed her cutlery down, not wanting Lizzie to think she was in anyway upset or annoyed with her. "Not really, I don't think. He knows Mickie asked you, us both some really personal stuff and that we replied and she had installed a video camera. The film is still stored as police evidence or has been destroyed I assume and although I told your dad everything about me and her, I never gave him details about you, just that she asked you some unpleasant things to goad me. Why do you ask?"

"I've thought about it loads since it happened and I guess I just wondered if he knew and if he was mad with me for the things I'd done with Dylan," replied a sad and worried looking Lizzie. "You know how he gets about other people with us, boys kind of other people.

Moving her own chair closer to Lizzie's, Tasha took her hand and shook her head as she prepared to further reassure her stepdaughter. "Lizzie, what happened that night was awful and that was down to Mickie. Your dad was furious with her, but not you, or Juan or me, just her and himself a little. Even if he did know what had happened between you and Dylan he would not be mad with you, nor even Dylan, not really. He knows you're growing up and he doesn't like it," laughed Tasha. "He hates it, but because he has had lots of wives and girlfriends he knows exactly how boy's minds work when they think of girls and that drives him a little crazy, to think they might think that way about you, but he knows it's normal."

Lizzie smiled slightly then turned things back to Tasha. "And you. He hates guys thinking of you that way?"

"Yes, and me, but because he knows me in a different way to you and in his mind you are still his little girl he hates men thinking that way about you a little more than he hates it about me."

"What did you mean, Daddy was a little mad with himself over Mickie?"

Tasha adjusted her hold on Connor, partly to find a more comfortable position but more to buy herself a few extra seconds to think about what she was going to say to Lizzie.

"He knows she never saw him as a friend. She always wanted more and he feels a little guilty for having let her remain close and become the danger she did. He also feels bad for setting up the trap that Mickie entered undetected, although he also holds the police department responsible for that too. I believe he threatened all kinds of repercussions if anything happened to any of us," Tasha explained with a small smile.

"Philip did mention how angry he was. I am so glad my dad met you, and made you move out here and marry him." Lizzie hugged Tasha until Connor cried and she added, "I am really glad you had Connor too."

"So am I, to all of the things you said." Smiled Tasha,

knowing that glad didn't even come close to how she felt about the things Lizzie had referred to.

****

By the time Jim arrived home, Tasha had already bathed and fed Connor and was just lying the sleeping infant in his cot.

"Night, night baby," she whispered as she leaned over to kiss him before switching on the baby monitor and heading downstairs where Jim was just placing his phone on the kitchen counter.

"Are you okay?" Tasha looked concerned at her husband's expression.

"Mmm, a long day just got longer," he said, causing her to frown in confusion. "That was Bobby," he told her with a glance down at his phone. "He's coming over."

"Oh, is everything okay?" Tasha wondered why her brother-in-law was coming over tonight and couldn't hide her nervousness.

"I guess we'll find out soon enough. I missed bedtime then?" He looked sad.

"Yeah, just, but you should go up and see him while he's all clean, sleeping and squidgy," replied Tasha with a soppy smile.

"Squidgy, huh?" He smiled back.

"Yeah, squidgy. You got a problem with my squidgy baby?" She giggled.

"No, no problem, with *our* squidgy baby, now get your sexy, on birth control ass over here and kiss me," he said, already reaching for Tasha's arm with an arched brow.

"Yes, sir," she replied and soon found herself wrapping her arms around his neck.

"I've invited Bobby, Abby and Alexi to stay and have dinner with us," announced Jim making Tasha laugh.

"That's fine except I only got two pieces of fish out."

"That is what take out is for, so..." He picked his phone up and dialled a local Italian restaurant that also offered a delivery and collection service. "Dinner will be here in just under two hours, so that leaves enough time for me to go up and see our squidgy son and for you to share a bath with me."

"Was that an invitation, James?" She smiled up at him as she

236

fingered the hair in the nape of his neck.

"James? Ready so soon, Tasha, but I thought of it as being an order more than an invitation, honey."

"Then I guess that's a date, oh, and you may want to get a haircut, unless you're growing it." She smirked as she teased the strands curling into his neck.

"Whatever makes you happy, Natasha, and you should know that there is only one thing I'm growing right now." He placed her hand against his groin that was sporting a rather large erection he flexed before picking her up and throwing her over his shoulder.

Chapter Twenty-One

Tasha sat in the nursing chair in Connor's nursery at four o'clock the following morning watching her sleeping son, trying to order the muddle of confused thoughts in her head, all of which had only been there since Bobby and Abby's visit the previous evening. She thought when Bobby had warned her that her father may be sent back to the U.K. to serve his sentence it had been a shock, a shock she thought she was okay with it. She had been until Bobby told her and Jim the deal had been done and now her head was swimming with a million and one thoughts about her father and all the things he'd done which included attempting to kill her whilst on Mickie's payroll. That thought alone prevented her from doing anything other than stew about all things Mickie, from their first meeting to their final one. She was unsure just how long she'd been sitting in the chair watching her baby son sleeping contentedly without a single care in the world and for that Tasha was beyond grateful. She only wished she could manage to sleep herself, but was then relieved she couldn't sleep because she was petrified that sleep would permit her mind to create dreams, nightmares that would conjure images of Liam, Mickie, her parents and all the bad things that had ever befallen her.

"How long have you been sitting there?" Jim startled her from her increasingly dark thoughts.

"I dunno. How long ago did you go to sleep?" She replied in a whisper as Connor moved and made a low mewl in his sleep.

"Oh, baby, this is no good for you. You need your sleep," Jim told her, crouching at her side.

"I can't and I like to watch him sleep." She lowered her glance and offered a warm smile in her son's direction.

"Tasha, I get that watching Connor sleep is pretty cute, but if you don't sleep too then he won't get the best of you later when he's awake and you're exhausted."

"You really are very sensible at times." Tasha offered a weak smile.

"Is that a thank you?" he asked with a grin. "What time did you last feed Connor?"

"About half one. He slept through til then, so probably a good job Abby and Alexi didn't wait for him to wake up so they could hold him."

"Yeah, and it's debatable who was most disappointed. Come back to bed, baby, please." Jim hoped to gently coax her but had already pulled her to her feet and was leading her towards the door.

Once in bed, Tasha happily allowed her body to soften and mould into Jim's and was in no way surprised when he opened the topic of her father.

"What are you thinking about your dad being sent back to England? You didn't say much about it earlier."

"I don't even know how I feel. I was okay before, well, it was more that my pregnancy blindsided me and took over my life and my dad went to the back of my mind until tonight and again he is asking to see me, and this might be my last chance."

"Shit, Tasha. Every fibre of my being is screaming for you to steer clear and never to waste your time thinking of that man and all he has done to you, but I get it's easier for me to say that than for you to do. However, I am trying really, really hard to be calm here and not fucking flip out."

"Thank you," whispered Tasha before adding, her voice getting louder with every word uttered, "and I have no idea what seeing him would achieve. It's a fucking nightmare, James. I just want a normal life without my family screwing it up, again."

"Honey, I know you're stressing, but please stop swearing and shouting about it. Why don't you sleep on it and tomorrow call Bobby? Talk to him about exactly what happens next and how long it's likely to take. I can't believe I'm going to say this, but if you need to see him to put it behind you then see him. Jeez, I will even come with you, but Connor goes nowhere near him or a prison, agreed?"

"Yes, thank you."

"Now, sleep," ordered Jim making Tasha smile a very small smile in the early morning light.

****

Four days later, Tasha was pacing the lounge waiting for Abby to arrive. Abby who was watching Connor while she and Jim went to visit her father.

"Maybe we should just take Connor with us, in case he wakes and won't settle for Abby," she suggested to Jim.

"No way, baby. We agreed, our son is not prison visiting and your father is never seeing our boy, so Connor stays here with Abby and Sandra," he said firmly as Sandra appeared behind them.

"Tasha, I promise I will guard him with my life and help Abby any way I can, but I'm sure Connor will be fine, he's fed and clean and has just gone to sleep, but if he becomes properly distressed I will call you."

"Sorry, I'm sure I'm being a pain in the arse, but I've never left him before and he is only a couple of months old."

"Baby, we all get that, but Connor stays here today. So, do you want to do this?" Jim was deadly serious. He couldn't care less if Tasha opted out of doing this, in fact, he'd be rather relieved because he had a really bad feeling that nothing good was going to come from it. His wife, however, although confused, *wanted* to do this, so he was supporting her, despite his better judgement.

She nodded and looked towards Sandra, hoping her reluctance to leave Connor hadn't caused offence in any way. "I didn't mean to suggest I didn't trust you with him."

Sandra smiled and nodded, as if confirming that she was anything but offended.

"In fact, there's nobody I'd trust more."

Sandra leaned in and gave Tasha's shoulder a reassuring rub before moving away slightly.

"So, are we doing this? You want to do this?" Jim asked.

"I think I have to do this," she replied as Sandra announced Abby's arrival.

After repeating dozens of orders at the two women she was leaving them with the job of caring for her only child. Jim virtually frogmarched her from the house and into his car to make the trip he'd hoped neither of them would ever have to make.

****

Having never visited a prison before, Tasha found it both scary and fascinating at the same time. Security seemed to take forever to get through but after being processed and having all the rules explained to them Jim and Tasha were led into a room where a jaded, thinner and sad looking Sam Bailey sat waiting. He attempted to get to his feet as he saw her approaching him, but handcuffs, shackles as well as the prison guards instructing him to sit down prevented it.

"Are those really necessary?" Tasha came to a standstill about three feet from her father and gestured towards his binds.

"Yes, ma'am," replied one guard. "We have rules to follow and one has already been compromised by you being in an open room with no screen."

Jim shook his head. Had she actually just asked if his shackles were necessary? Yes, yes she had. This man who was currently bound had repeatedly allowed others to hurt her in the worst of ways. He himself had physically punished her all of her life, and then, with the offer of money he had tried to kill her and yet, his beautiful, kind and loving wife had questioned the need for him to be restrained in such close proximity to her. She really was something else. He recalled her saying that Mickie had asked if she was really *that nice* when she held her captive. Yes, yes she was. Mickie would undoubtedly have seen that as something negative, a weakness and whilst it did frustrate him at times, with it allowing others to take advantage and potentially hurt her, Jim loved that she was indeed, *that nice*.

"Sorry, thank you," she muttered to the guards, not sure which sentiment she really intended to express.

"Take a seat please," said the other guard who gestured to the seats for her and Jim with just a table separating them from her father.

With his hand in the small of her back Jim guided Tasha to take a seat before sitting next to her.

"You look well, Natasha."

The flatness of Sam Bailey's voice unnerved Jim slightly as he'd expected a more humble or angry man to greet them, but the man before them was nothing like anything he'd expected.

"Thank you." Tasha could have kicked herself for extending polite words of gratitude. She reminded herself that this man, father or not, had no concern for her health or wellbeing. If he had, he wouldn't have tried to kill her never mind all the things he'd subjected her to and facilitated others to. Even with the reminder of that she found herself twisting her wedding ring around her finger nervously and smoothing down the plain white blouse she wore over black Capri pants.

"I wasn't sure you'd come. It's been a while." He spoke as if they hadn't seen each other for just a few weeks and previously been on good terms.

Tasha stared across at him while Jim looked between his wife and this man, unsure if he should say or do something, but the truth was he was unsure what was happening and had no clue how Sam Bailey could sit calmly and speak to his daughter without some kind of—what—an apology for trying to kill her? This was beyond fucked up.

"I'm not really sure why I did, but if you're going home I suppose this is the last chance for us to talk."

"You could visit at home."

Her father's suggestion, if that's what it was, surprised Tasha. Jim tensed beside her leaving her in no doubt that the mere suggestion had irritated him at best.

"I live out here now." Tasha thought this experience was far more reasonable than she'd expected but surreal all the same.

"I know, and you're married, with a son I believe." Her father remained expressionless.

"Yes, sorry, this is my husband, Jim. Jim, my dad." Tasha formally introduced the two men, somehow oblivious to the ridiculousness of their surroundings and situation.

"I'd shake your hand, but I'm indisposed." Sam smirked

across at Jim, his mask slipping slightly as he shook his handcuffs making Tasha feel uncomfortable while Jim looked ready to punch him.

"Honestly? I wouldn't accept." Jim's tone remained cold, completely over any intention or desire to continue dancing to the tune of reasonableness that his wife and her father appeared to be moving to.

Sam laughed in a way that chilled Tasha to the bone. The same laugh she'd heard countless times just before he hit her, or when he was about to point out that her objections to his plans for her were worthless and futile.

"I don't think your American husband likes me, Natasha."

Unsure what to say in response Tasha was relieved when Jim replied, "Don't like you? I despise you for everything you did to your daughter, each and every disgusting liaison you facilitated and how you used and took advantage of her; but most of all I hate you for trying to take her away from me, for taking money from Mickie in exchange for trying to kill my wife. However, most of all, I pity you for losing the people you should have held most precious."

Tasha watched as the two men stared for long seconds and then with a blink of his eyes Sam turned back to his daughter. "So, my grandson, is he here with you?"

Tasha felt as though her lungs had just had all the air punched out of them with that question. Why would she have brought Connor here and why would she allow her father anywhere near him regardless of where they were? And why was he claiming her son as his grandson?

"He's at home," she managed to mutter.

"Your mother writes often. She'd like to see you at home, Natasha, your real home and she could do with some help and support. She'd love to see her first grandchild."

"I—erm—I don't—erm—" she stammered, feeling the all too familiar panic and bile rise in her body at being faced with her father's unreasonable demands and she was in no doubt it was a demand he was making.

"Never gonna happen," intervened Jim. "My son is at home, safe. He will not be visiting prisons, nor will he be meeting you or your wife and as for her needing help and support, well, what goes around comes around because there was a time when Tasha needed her help and support and she left her to rot. So, like I say, never gonna happen."

"I suppose you have a team of nannies and servants, you and the rich yank," sneered Sam. He stared across at Tasha, but still ignored Jim. "You have no idea what it's like bringing a baby up in the real world. Most people don't have a string of lackeys cleaning up after snotty, shitty, ungrateful kids that winge and cry."

"We don't have a nanny and he is at home with his auntie." Tasha wondered why she still felt obliged to explain herself, but chose to ignore his disparaging comments about children, presumably her and her siblings if not Connor.

"Pippa is out here too?" Suddenly his interest seemed genuinely piqued as he shifted forward in his seat slightly.

"No, Jim's sister-in-law."

"Ah. How are Dan and Pippa?"

"Good, really good." Tasha smiled, then remembering the life she and her siblings had been subjected to, the danger, threats and constant fear, she suddenly hardened. "What do you want? Why did you ask me to visit, really?"

"There she is, hard faced, blunt, argumentative, Natasha. Ready to start a row with the person she's supposed to respect most." It was debatable whether her father was goading or accusing.

"You're kidding me? Respect? You?" she asked with a heavy shake of her head. "Dad, just spit it out, whatever you want from me. Let's not piss about anymore."

"Watch your mouth. Still got a vile, poisonous, toxic and too fucking clever for its own good mouth on you I see!" Sam snapped angrily as his bound hands flew up making Tasha flinch at the memories that movement evoked. Seeing her recoiling, her father just laughed.

"Still think these things are unnecessary?" asked one of the guards, stepping closer to his prisoner.

"Mr Bailey," intervened Jim, unsure what to say to end this hideous charade. "My son is at home being looked after by someone other than Tasha for the first time and this is the last place I want me or my wife to be, but we agreed she would do this, for her, so if you are just yanking her chain and playing stupid mind fuck games then this meeting is over."

"Why do you do that?" Sam turned his attention to Jim. "That whole *my wife* thing. Your wife is my daughter. Mine!" he almost growled. "She was my daughter before she met you and will be my daughter after you tire of her petty, insolent, whorish ways and whilst you may be related legally, it's my blood running through her veins, her veins and your son's," he claimed victoriously as though he had just scored some major point. "My blood, my DNA and I doubt the apple will fall far from the tree, so you just think on when you look at *your wife* and *your son*," he told Jim triumphantly. "If you knew the things she'd done..." He smirked smarmily making Tasha's blood run cold through her whole body causing her to shudder.

"My wife ceased to be your daughter the moment you first called her an inexcusable name or raised a hand to her or sold her off for your own benefit. There is nothing you can tell me that I don't already know, and I wouldn't recommend you telling anyone else or you would certainly be incriminating yourself and this meeting just ended. Tasha, baby." Jim turned as he got to his feet to find a white and shaken looking Tasha looking up at him with the haunted expression he hadn't seen for a while.

Taking Jim's hand, Tasha stood and prepared to leave.

"Natasha." Her father's call caused her to turn and face him. "I asked you here nearly a year ago. To see me. To help me. And yet again you let me down, and now, well I thought we should draw a line beneath things, but you should see your mother. She doesn't deserve the treatment she has endured at your hands."

Tasha shook her head and tried to think of something, anything to say as her father smiled and spoke again.

"Oh, and I should congratulate you. You accused me of prostituting you, but never in my wildest dreams could I have imagined a coup like the one you've bagged for yourself; a rich, older man to provide you with everything money can buy, and in return all you have to do is what you've always done best, lie on your back and open your legs."

245

Tasha felt sick and repulsed by his accusations, and then scared that Jim may believe anything he was saying. Jim's grip tightened on his wife's hand and was glad when she turned away without even attempting to discuss or defend herself against this evil man's ridiculous accusations, however his parting shot gained Tasha's attention fully.

"But your piece de resistance has to be the genius stroke of getting him to knock you up."

Standing no more than six feet from him and pushing her shoulders back to stand at her full height, Tasha shook her head, tears brimming her eyes.

"Oh, come on, Natasha, it can't have been coincidence that you were knocked up before the ink on the marriage certificate had dried according to my maths and it's not a criticism, far from it. I wish I'd thought of it. Liam's child would have been like the goose that laid a golden egg for me."

"You are disgusting," she accused, beginning to lose the battle with her tears. "The twenty-five years they gave you are nowhere near enough for a bastard like you. I hope you die behind bars for everything you've done to me, Dan and Pippa and Liam's child?" she asked with a slightly maniacal laugh that shocked her father and her husband. "I had it flushed away." Her father's expression of disbelief as he stared at her made her laugh more erratically. "Yup. He got me pregnant and Gerry paid for me to get rid of it. I would have topped myself before I'd have allowed anything that belonged to him to grow inside me, and the idea of providing you with another pawn to fuck up, well it was never going to happen." Tears ran freely down her face as she stood shaking.

Suddenly, the table was flying across the room towards her and her father was following it, but before he could reach her Jim had covered her and turned her towards the door, out of harm's way. Sam Bailey was still powering towards his end goal, Tasha, but there was no way Jim was going to allow him to reach her. He had told her many times since the attempt on her life that he wouldn't allow this man to get close again and he wouldn't. Jim sensed the older man's presence behind him and instinctively thrust his elbow back and hearing the crunch of bone was happy he had made sufficient contact as the two prison guards wrestled Tasha's father to the ground, restraining him as a siren sounded. The door flew open and Jim pushed Tasha through it towards a member of prison staff who received them to lead them back the way they'd come, leaving her father far behind her.

Chapter Twenty-Two

Tasha was unsure whether she'd spoken a single word after the five-word sentence she'd managed to string together as they got out of the room where her father had been. The five words she knew Jim had misunderstood.

"I want to go home," she'd said.

"We're going home, baby." Jim assumed she meant her home with him, not her home where she was born and raised, not London.

Since that point she had said nothing and was relieved to be getting out of the car. She headed through the front door where she was greeted by the sound of Connor crying and Abby attempting to sing at him while Sandra was reeling off a list of *he likes it when Tasha* suggestions. Fighting the urge to run to him she quickened her pace, but stuck to a walk until she reached his side.

"Let me." She couldn't risk more words, scared that any more than those two would allow her to physically and emotionally fall apart and she wasn't prepared to do that yet, especially not with an audience.

Taking her son from Abby, she stroked his face, brushed away his tears then kissed him, first his fingers, his hands, followed by his face and head where she inhaled the unique scent of him. She filled her nose with his aroma and could feel her need to cry growing as her young baby's tears and distress subsided.

"Hey, magic momma's arms," said Bobby, who Tasha had failed to notice was even there.

"I think he's probably hungry and tired." Tasha paused a little too long between words, fighting against her own body's need to let go of everything inside. "Thank you, both." Tasha glanced between a concerned looking Abby and the equally worried face of Sandra. "I'll take Connor upstairs, thanks again," she said and left them all looking across at Jim questioningly.

"Don't even ask. I thought it was going to be some kind of request for help or cash and it turned into the mind fuck of all mind fucks before he lunged for Tasha and we left him with two real big prison guards pinning him to the floor. So, a bad day all in all, and on top of that I have no clue what Tasha was expecting from today, but it sure as hell wasn't what she got," Jim said in way of an explanation.

"Bloody hell, Jim," cried Sandra. "Just when you think she's been through enough something else happens. I'm done for today, and I got the impression that Tasha might need some space, so..."

"Yes, thanks Sandra. See you in the morning," Jim replied before turning to his brother and sister-in-law. "I think I may have broken my father-in-law's nose or something during the fracas."

"Yeah?" Bobby sounded impressed, then turned more serious. "Well, if he attempts to press charges I doubt he'll get far but I've got your back." He grinned at the idea of Mr Bailey getting a taste of his own medicine. "Look, we're gonna shoot too, Jimbo, but you know where we are," replied Bobby taking the hint Sandra had dropped before her departure.

"Thanks, and thanks for watching Connor." Jim offered Abby a smile.

"He was okay until about ten minutes before you got home, I swear," she replied with a grimace.

"Hey, it's cool, babies cry, especially when they're hungry and in Connor's case only Tasha has what he needs then and he really is a momma's boy, so thanks."

The sound of the front door closing gave way to the sound of Jim's heavy breathing as he contemplated what might be waiting for him. Quietly, he made his way upstairs and initially headed for Connor's nursery, which was empty, but Tasha had been in there because the clothes his son had been wearing were now on the top of the laundry hamper. Moving swiftly to his and his wife's room Jim took a short detour via Connor's empty bathroom before he found them both lying on their marital bed; Tasha almost in the middle of the huge bed facing the door with her eyes shut, while Connor was positioned between his mother, whose breast he was suckling and a couple of pillows that ran along the edge of the bed.

One hand held him close to her, protectively, while the other ran through his hair, doing that thing where she spiked it up with her fingers. They'd both gotten changed he noticed; Connor was in a short sleeved romper, as if ready for bed, while Tasha was wearing a mid-thigh length, navy and pink floral bandeau dress that lent itself perfectly to breastfeeding. Making his way across the room Jim circled the bed and got on it behind Tasha without saying a word. Positioning himself so that his front was pressed against her back, slightly higher up the bed than her, Jim placed one arm over the top of her head and the other was now draped across her hip and belly with his hand settling on their son's behind.

"Hey, baby," he whispered against her head knowing she was awake.

Tasha made no response but his two words filled with love, compassion and concern forced the release of her tears.

"Oh, Tasha." Jim wrapped himself around her to hold her as tight as was humanly possible, leaving nothing between them. "Talk to me, honey. I have no idea what you're feeling or thinking right now."

"I can't," cried Tasha, struggling to get the words out between sobs, sobs that increased when her son began to cry, sounding as distressed as she was, something he never did when she was feeding him. "Oh God! And now I've made Connor cry. This is all my fault, everything."

"No. Don't you dare do this, Natasha," he warned as he released her and stretched across her to retrieve their son who had tears running down his face and increasingly loud cries leaving his mouth. "Come on, buddy," Jim cooed as he pulled his son close, soothing him then placed him over his shoulder where he proceeded to burp him while Tasha continued to cry.

Jim gazed down at the image of his wife somehow attempting to bury herself in the mattress, barely muffling her cries. Feeling helpless and conflicted between settling his son and comforting his wife, he opted for the former and then he would deal with Tasha and the train wreck her day had become.

Standing over Connor who he had just placed in his cot, Jim offered him his soother and listened to him suckle on it greedily. He laughed gently at him making the little boy grin up from behind the plastic oval disc of the dummy causing his daddy to laugh at him again which triggered a soother ejecting laugh from Connor that completely melted his father's heart.

"Ah, a wise guy, huh?" Jim leaned down to kiss his son. "Look, I realise I interrupted feeding for you, but for now this will have to do, son," he told him as he placed the soother back in his mouth. "Mommy is sad and Daddy really needs to do something to make her better, so you chill a while and when Daddy's made things good, you get to finish eating, okay?" he asked and smiled as Connor rubbed at his eyes while loudly attempting to get some nourishment from the latex substitute for his mother's breast. "Good boy," praised Jim as Connor began to drift off to sleep.

Climbing back onto the bed where Tasha still lay Jim rolled her so that she faced him and half wished he hadn't when he saw her sad face, wet with tears and big red eyes looking back at him.

"Connor is taking a nap, so we need to talk. You need to talk, Tasha," he told her ensuring there was no hint of a question or suggestion in his words.

"James," she began as if about to protest.

"Not a chance, Tasha. Today was beyond fucking hideous and I can only imagine what you're feeling and what is going through your mind, so, you need to tell me and we need to put that vile, despicable excuse of a father back in the past and leave him there, so talk, baby."

He lowered his lips to hers and kissed her gently and briefly, maybe too briefly.

"I don't know what I expected today, but not what I got and now I feel like shit," she admitted honestly. "I allowed him to get to me and that made me angry and I said things I never intended him to know, things he can use against me now." She thought of him selling stories of her abortion or even of her visit to see him with Jim, the negative spin he'd put on Jim's insistence that he would never see Connor, him nor her mother.

"Baby, it's done and we can get Jerome Stewart working on legal routes to keep a lid on things."

"I hate feeling this way. The way he makes me feel. The way I always used to feel. Fuck!" she cried in frustration.

"Tasha, shouting and swearing do not help. Calm down, honey, and talk to me, please. Let me help you to feel better. The way you should feel now rather than how you used to."

"I want to go home." Tasha repeated her earlier, misunderstood words.

"What? You are home," replied a confused Jim.

"James, I want to go home, to London," she repeated and clarified.

"Okay, let me check my schedule and we can take a break, maybe in a few weeks or a month or so," agreed Jim.

"I want to go home now." Tasha was unsure why the urge to go back to London was so strong.

Patiently and calmly while pushing her hair back off her face, Jim nodded. "For how long?"

"I don't know." Her reply was honest and immediate as was Jim's expression that changed from empathy to annoyance.

"You are not leaving me. Not over this. Not because of him," he snapped firmly.

"No, I don't think that's what I mean," Tasha told him, unsure just what she did mean.

"But you want to go to London without me for an unknown period, maybe an extended period, am I getting this right?"

Tasha nodded her confirmation of his summary.

"Well, there may be some delay; you'll need to arrange a flight, and wean Connor from the breast and hire a nanny, although I can do that once you're gone I guess," Jim said with a flat tone and a blank face.

"What? He doesn't need weaning and we don't need a nanny." Tasha was confused by talk of a nanny and weaning and concerned by her husband's calm acceptance of what she was asking for.

"No, we don't, but he does." Jim gestured in the direction of their son's nursery and expanded, "While you're taking your London sabbatical or whatever the fuck it is you think you're doing, Connor will need looking after and unfortunately I work so can't do it myself and if your breasts are in London and his mouth is in L.A. then we have a problem if he's not weaned."

Tasha could feel she was staring at her husband as she realised what he was saying to her. "James—" she began, but he cut her off.

"No! Not a fucking chance in hell, Tasha. He is my son and apart from the fact that he doesn't have a passport I won't have him in London indefinitely with you while I am out here. Especially when, by your own admission, you don't even know whether you plan on leaving me, although I can assure you you're not, but Connor is going nowhere under those circumstances. You have to know this." He rose from the bed, jumping to his feet and staring down at her wide-eyed expression looking up at him.

Moving into a sitting position Tasha spoke. "I want to take *my* baby to *my* home to see where I am from and to meet *my* people." She overemphasised each and every *my*.

"But you don't know for how long, or why or whether you plan on coming back, so it's not gonna happen. What people? Which of your people haven't met him yet?" he suddenly asked.

"My grandparents, Dan and Pippa would love to see him again, for real, not remotely, and then there's Angie, some old friends, and Aiden, and Gerry."

"You want to ship him off to Blighty to meet your ex-boyfriends? That is hardly a winning argument, Natasha." Jim's tone had surpassed flat and was currently surly and determined.

"No! Fuck this bullshit, Jim. I am going to get Connor a passport and take him home," she snapped back jumping to her feet, knowing that with the emotive subject and the shouting they were both moving towards this was likely to be a major argument.

"No, you're fucking not! He stays here, you are staying here, this is home, for you and him, so unless you can give me a reason why this trip can't wait for me to come too, well, the bullshit that is this conversation is well and truly over."

"You are so fucking unreasonable," she cried, heading towards the door but somehow her path was blocked by Jim.

"No, if I was being unreasonable I would be quoting our pre-nup just about now, so it's you that's being unreasonable, Tasha, not me. Give me a fucking reason!" He stood before her, breathing heavy, barely keeping a lid on his emotions and remained unmoveable despite her attempts to move him.

"I don't know," she screamed. "I just do. I want to go somewhere and be safe from everything, somewhere familiar," she cried and allowed even more tears to flow as she dropped to the floor before her stunned looking husband. "James, I am so sorry. I should never have gone today and I should never have allowed you to meet him, to see me like that. To see the person I was. I just have an overpowering urge to run away, to my home town so that if, when, the shit hits the fan again I won't embarrass you, hurt you or worst of all I won't have to stand by while you realise how wrong you were to marry me. To decide that what we have isn't enough and you leave me, or make me leave because I have nowhere to go other than London and you'll never let me take Connor. I know that. Tonight has proved that and I can't ever leave him. He is my baby. The one good thing I am responsible for. The one thing in this world that makes my life worthwhile and of value," she sobbed with wracking cries that shook her whole body.

"What? You are one seriously fucking crazy lady, Natasha Maybury." He dropped to his knees, putting him directly before her. Pulling her towards him he tilted her head so she had no choice but to look at him. His heart lurched at the sight of her, hurt, sad and ever so slightly devastated by the day if not her whole life, but his heart swelled a little too at the idea that the level of dread and pain at losing him and their son had literally brought her to her knees, physically and emotionally. "Let your no good father do his worst, neither he nor any revelations he can make will embarrass or hurt me. You don't need to run anywhere, other than here, home, to me and as for one of us leaving because I should never have married you, well you couldn't be more wrong about that; marrying you is the one thing I got right, possibly the first thing, the one good thing that makes my life worthwhile and of value." He chose his words deliberately, throwing her own words back at her.

She blinked, several times, the absorption of his words beginning to calm her.

He continued, "And although unexpected, our son is the second. I love all of my children and yet Connor brings with him something extra. Maybe because I'm older, or because he was born from the greatest, purest love I have ever known, I don't know, but you won't ever have to leave him, baby, because you are never going anywhere. It's you and me forever, I thought we'd agreed that. Our family is forever and you do not get to leave me in order to protect me from your past. I know your past and it's shocking that you endured it, more shocking that you survived it, but it doesn't scare me. Oh, and as far as meeting your father with you today, he was even more disgusting than I'd anticipated. I so wish I could have punched him, punched him really hard, and you—I don't think I have ever been prouder of you than I was in that room with him, honey."

"Really?" asked Tasha disbelievingly.

"Abso-fucking-lutely. Now let's get off the floor and get you cleaned up and then you sleep a while. When you wake up we can talk about London, but together, all three of us and no matter where you are I'm going to keep you safe, Tasha. Nothing is going to hurt you anymore, baby, okay?"

"Yes," she whispered hoarsely as she allowed him to pick her up from the floor to lead her to the bathroom where he pulled a wash cloth from a drawer and proceeded to clean her tear stained face before stripping her and depositing her back in bed, but under the covers and alone this time.

Tasha was already falling into a deep, exhaustion fuelled sleep before Jim left the room. He checked on Connor before going downstairs where he turned on the baby monitor and smiled at the sound of his son's soft snoring as he poured himself a large glass of bourbon.

"Cheers," he said to himself as he drank half of it in one

mouthful and hissed as the liquor burned his throat. "And goodbye Mr Bailey," he said with the other half of his drink. "And welcome back damaged, Natasha Winters," he added as he slammed his glass down on the kitchen counter.

****

It was the following morning when Tasha opened her eyes to find Jim still sleeping next to her that she remembered her worries and concerns from the previous evening. She'd slept through until two that morning after Jim had put her to bed and it was only because Connor had woken to be fed that she'd stirred. Once fed and changed, she quickly settled him back in his cot and returned to bed where Jim was sleeping soundly, and now he was still fast asleep proving that the last twenty-four hours had taken its toll on them both. She could still hear Connor's gentle breathing through the baby monitor and seeing it was now six o'clock knew he should be good for another couple of hours after her minor meltdown had thrown his routine off schedule the previous night.

"Morning, baby," said Jim from behind her before his arms snaked around her and pulled her closer. "How's life looking this morning?" He landed a kiss against Tasha's bare shoulder.

"Better, thank you." She smiled to herself. "Sorry I was a bit crazy last night."

"Oh, honey, you're crazy every night, so I'm kind of used to it," he told her, making her laugh as she smacked the arm lying over her body that was tightening around her, pulling her against him and revealing his erection rubbing against the globes of her behind. "But you're okay, right?" he asked more seriously.

"Yes, I think so. Yesterday was just, kind of everything I should have expected from a meeting with my father, but I'm fine," she assured him.

"You certainly are." He nipped a path across her shoulder as he rubbed himself against her once more making her giggle again.

"I love you," she said sincerely and hoped her behaviour and suggestions about going home and potentially leaving him wouldn't detract from his belief of just how strong her feelings for him were.

"I know you do baby, and I love you too. So much, Tasha."

"James," she moaned, pushing back into his body, his erection pressing into her behind insistently.

"What, baby?"

Her token James, already hoarse with desire and need meant they both knew exactly what she was saying, her words only confirming it. "Make love to me, please."

"Is that what you want, for me to make love to you? Because I will, God knows I need you, honey, but I was thinking that I need to touch you, to make you wet and then to fuck you until you're going crazy with desire, begging to come."

"Then you should do your worst," she invited, rotating her behind into his groin and making him laugh against her ear that he was mouthing.

Chapter Twenty-Three

A month later, Tasha was sitting in her lounge with Abby, Lucy and Amanda who was cradling her new-born baby boy, Isaac, while Skye, Lucy's daughter, was sitting on the floor in a cocoon of cushions in case her new found skill of pulling herself up failed, as it often did. Connor was lying in the middle of a doughnut of brightly covered sponge looking up at the toys hanging above him and gurgling loudly. Tasha felt totally content with her life and was working one day a week, often with Connor for the show in the U.K. for Robbie Newman.

"This would be so much more interesting with alcohol rather than coffee," moaned Abby as she accepted the cup Tasha offered her.

"Yeah, well some of us are still breastfeeding," replied Tasha while Amanda nodded.

"And some of us aren't," countered Lucy, grinning across at Abby.

"Okay," Tasha acknowledged. "You get my husband to agree to us sipping cocktails before lunch while we're all in charge of babies, or children," she added, looking at Abby, "and I will hire topless cocktail waiters to mix them, serve them and possibly even use their washboard stomachs to serve them on."

The others all laughed which made both Skye and Connor laugh too. Leaning over Connor, his mother cooed down at him, "And you need to remember that you are a real momma's boy and Daddy won't ever need to know what was said here, you got that?" She smiled as she picked him up and kissed him.

"Not a chance," cried Abby. "Connor will be just like Lizzie and Philip and tell Daddy everything he sees and hears, just like Alexi does. Maybury men make wonderful fathers whose children love them and trust them so they just spill, without even realising it. So make the most of your son being young enough not to know what's going on and unable to repeat what he hears because when he does you are seriously screwed." Grinned Abby until Lexi appeared with Travis and chastened her mother.

"Mommy, don't say those words. You know Daddy says they're not ladylike," the little girl said seriously, making the others laugh at their friend.

"Oh dear." Tasha grinned smugly. "You joining us for lunch, Lexi, or are you and Travis eating with the horses?"

"I thought I might have lunch up here and play with the babies for a while and then Travis is taking me for a ride later," Lexi replied.

"Well if your mom will watch Connor later I might come out with you, if that's okay?" Tasha looked between Lexi and Travis.

"Yeah, cool," replied Travis as Abby nodded her compliance with the plan.

"Later then ladies," called Travis as he left the house and headed back down to the stables.

"If I wasn't very happy with Ryan I could go for that whole cowboy with the southern drawl," mused Lucy, making the others laugh at her. "What?" She was clearly confused by the other's inability to understand her point. "He is bloody gorgeous. I can't believe you don't get it."

"He's my younger cousin, so eww," said Abby with an expression of distaste.

"And I remember the angry and confused boy that first came out here and it wasn't pretty," replied Amanda with a shake of her head at the memory.

Tasha frowned, realising again that this other woman, her husband's ex-wife, one of them, knew things she didn't, had shared things with her husband that she hadn't and for the first time in a while felt jealous and insecure somehow.

"Tell me you get it, Tash. Other than the accent he reminds me of Aiden in many ways," Lucy said.

"Really?" Tasha mentally compared the two men. "I guess so

in some ways. Travis doesn't do it for me, although I can see the attraction."

"Who's Aiden?" Abby had a mischievous smile spreading across her face.

"An ex-boyfriend that we, Lucy and I, will not be discussing," Tasha replied.

"Oh my. Lucy, I have just figured out that we are now privy to all of Tasha's secrets and boyfriends." Giggled Abby.

"No way, no how," insisted Tasha. "Jim would flip." She was relieved when Isaac broke the silence with his crying, which in turn triggered tears from Connor and Skye halting all further questioning.

Once lunch was finished and all of the younger children were having a nap Abby looked a little distracted, although Lexi was firing questions at her, so that might be the reason for it or maybe Tasha was imagining it.

Lucy broke the tension when she suggested a girl's night out and while Abby jumped at it both Amanda and Tasha were less sure of it.

"Oh, come on, Tash," pleaded Lucy. "It's been ages, like before you got married ages. We could do any night in the week if you don't want to party at the weekend and if it's going to be a big fat no to a club we could go for dinner and on to a bar, maybe a late night rather than an all-nighter."

Tasha looked around at the others and Amanda still looked wary, but less horrified than at first.

"Jim is unlikely to be happy about it and I am off drink, so it will be a sober night," Tasha told them all as Amanda chipped in with, *me too*.

With a laugh as Abby and Lucy high fived, Tasha did wonder whether this was all part of some earlier plan the two of them had cooked up. Her suspicions were further raised when Abby appeared to send a message on her phone once Tasha's agreement was made.

After watching Amanda and Lucy drive away from the house in convoy, Tasha dashed upstairs to change into riding trousers and a plain cotton t-shirt. She briefed Abby on where everything for Connor was but seemed certain he wouldn't require feeding.

Pulling her boots on she repeated her instructions about calling if there were any problems and went so far as to explain that there was water and expressed milk in the fridge, *just in case*. With Lexi's hand in hers they headed down to the stables where Travis was saddling up their mounts.

"Hey, ladies," he called to them making them both smile. "Tash, have you spoke to Dan lately?" The question seemed loaded and yet quite random.

"About a week ago, you?" She knew her brother and Travis had kept in touch and become friends.

"He called last night, he erm, kinda sounds lost," Travis said seriously.

"Lost?" Tasha was confused as to what that actually meant. Her expression must have said as much.

"Yeah. He still hasn't quite found his place at home," Travis revealed. "He's struggling to find a job in a kitchen that's not fast food or using a microwave and Pippa is doing some modelling shoots which he's happy about, but it makes him question his life more."

"Shit." Tasha immediately wondered how to make things right, or at least better for Dan when Travis continued and made her whole body hurt as though she'd been run over.

"Your parents—Tash, I'm only telling you this because I consider Dan a friend and he can't deal with this alone. I'm scared for him, scared he'll do something stupid."

"Go on." Tasha was unsure whether she really wanted Travis to finish his sentence but knew she needed him to.

"He's in touch with your mother who keeps taking cash from him and your father has started writing to him and wants him to visit him in jail." Travis sounded nervous but Tasha was unsure if that was because he was unsure of her reaction or if it was simply fear for his friend.

For the first time since he was sent home to serve his sentence Tasha began to wonder if it would have been better for her father to have remained in America. She had been glad of the geographical distance between him and her home, her child, herself. She felt safer knowing he was thousands of miles away and even with a miracle escape he couldn't get to her or come back and finish what he'd started. Now she realised how selfish and naïve she'd been to think of only herself and Connor where the vile and disgusting man who had fathered her was concerned. He still posed a danger, but not to her, not really, but Dan and Pippa…maybe not Pippa but this conversation proved her parents, whether behind bars or not were already proving they still posed a risk.

"He said something about your mom trying to get him some extra work..." Travis trailed off.

"Thanks, Trav. Leave it with me. I'll sort it. Well, we'll sort it, me and Jim." Tasha accepted Travis' offer of a leg up onto her mount but was unsure what she could really do when Dan was so far away.

****

Walking through the front door, Jim frowned at the unusual sound of Connor crying. Even for a baby he wasn't really much of a crier.

"Hey, we can all stop crying, Daddy's home," he called as he entered the big family room at the back of the house. His favourite room. It always had been but even more so now that he was sharing it with Tasha and Connor, his family.

"Oh," he exclaimed coming to a stop when greeted with the sight of Abby cradling a crying Connor who she was bouncing around.

"I think he might be hungry, and Tasha has gone for a ride with Trav and Lexi." Abby gave a small grimace as she looked down at Connor.

"Hey, buddy." Jim threw his suit jacket onto the sofa and lifted the little boy from his aunt's arms. "You hungry and the milk machine has gone out? We need to remind your momma that she needs to leave something for you when she's out." He soothed Connor who was quietening now at the reassuring sound of his father's voice.

"She did," interrupted Abby, holding a bottle of expressed milk in the air. "He won't take the bottle properly. I think it's a poor substitute."

"I would have to agree with him there," replied Jim with an arched brow and a smile.

"Eww, you are both sickeningly happy and in love. Can I ask you something?" Abby sounded quite serious.

Jim took the bottle from her and sitting down began to tempt his son to give the bottle a chance to satisfy him. "Sure." Smiled Jim as Abby sat opposite him.

"Has Bobby said anything to you?"

"Bobby has said plenty to me Abby, so you may want to be a little more precise."

"Sorry. About me, us?"

Jim smiled at her sympathetically. "You've been spending too much time with my wife. That was Tasha like precision. What about you, both of you?" He really hoped Abby wasn't about to reveal marital problems.

"Has Bobby said anything about wanting another baby?" She looked completely aghast that the words were out.

"Shit, Abby." He sighed. "You should talk to Bobby about that. About what he wants from his marriage and family, not me."

"I'm scared Jim. I love Bobby and Alexi and if things had gone better with my first baby I'm sure we'd have had more, but they didn't, and I'm scared; scared that if I have another baby history will repeat itself and if I don't, then I may damage my marriage beyond repair."

"Fuck, Abby." Jim felt compromised to be having this conversation with his sister-in-law and when he looked down at his son realised he was hearing every word he was saying, good and bad. "Sorry buddy, don't tell Mommy that Daddy's cursing in front of you."

He turned his expression from his son who was grinning from behind the bottle he was now almost willingly accepting to his sister-in-law. "Talk to Bobby. You have both been making sounds about another child since Tasha found out she was pregnant with Connor, and I don't mean to be an ass about this, but you are older than Tasha so don't have as long to consider it."

"Thanks for that Jim," she said with a wry smile, but knew he wasn't being an ass, he was stating facts.

"This is a conversation for you and my brother, but I get your concerns and reservations, so maybe you should consider all options."

"What options? I can only see two, have a baby or don't."

"Yeah, but the journey you take to get there offers more possibilities."

"What do you mean? You're talking in damned riddles, Jim," she accused.

He laughed and shook his head. "If you and Bobby decide you'd like to increase your family, but you don't want to carry your own child, your natural child, then don't. There are millions of kids in this world that need loving families like yours."

"Adoption?" She asked as if she was mulling the idea over.

"Yeah, or speak to a doctor about the likelihood of you having a repeat performance of your experience with Lexi, but first, talk to Bobby."

"Thank you," Abby almost whispered. "I'll speak to him."

"Good. How long has Tasha been gone?" Jim was happy to revert conversation back to his own family.

"About an hour."

"Is she okay?" Jim asked, suddenly worried.

"She's fine, better than fine. I think she went for Lexi as much as herself and we had a nice morning and lunch with Lucy and Amanda," said a laughing Abby.

"What?"

"I joked that the morning would have been much better with alcohol instead of coffee," she revealed earning herself a frown. "Oh, don't be such a misery with a bug up your ass. Tasha said if we could convince you that alcohol in the day with a house full of babies was an option she'd pay for topless cocktail waiters to serve them, possibly on their naked bodies."

"Did she now? Well don't be expecting that anytime soon or ever." He frowned.

"There was something with Amanda but I think Tasha was fine," Abby revealed, almost realising it for the first time.

"What? What happened with Amanda?" Jim was suddenly concerned because as far as he was aware any initial jealousy Tasha had felt towards Amanda was long gone and they were now friends, good friends, despite his reservations.

"Lucy said something about Trav. Something you don't really need to know about." Abby smiled. "But I pointed out he was my cousin and Amanda mentioned how he was when he first came here, how angry he was and Tasha looked awkward, like she was thinking about you and Amanda. I'm probably way off, but she did look distracted for a little while."

"Thanks. I'll see how she is later. She used to be jealous about my ex-wives, some more than others, including Amanda, but not for a while until things remind her of a time before us, me and her together."

"It's understandable though. I hate it when anyone mentions things involving Bobby and one of his exes and you can't tell me that it doesn't drive you crazy when she sees or speaks to Gerry or Jake," Abby said bluntly.

"I get it Abby," Jim replied with irritation at the reminder of Tasha's past as well as the thought of his own hurting her. "Sorry, Abby. Thanks." Jim smiled down at the empty bottle his son had just propelled from his mouth. "So maybe the bottle's okay when Momma's not around, uh?"

The little boy, relaxing back into his father's embrace began to gurgle and laugh up at Jim making him laugh down at his son in return. Glancing up at Abby, Jim decided she looked happier, relieved almost. Then he wondered whether he should give Bobby a heads up, maybe not. His brother had spoken to him, several times about adding to their family and seemed fairly certain that if Abby was receptive and willing, Connor would have a new cousin very soon. A loud burp from the baby broke the silence making Jim and Abby laugh and any tension left between them dissipated.

When Tasha still hadn't returned half an hour later and with Connor sleeping in his bassinet Jim was becoming restless.

"I might go and meet Lexi and head home," announced Abby.

"If you should see my wife would you tell her to get her ass back up here, I miss her."

"Come with me, bring Connor," Abby suggested.

"No, he's just gone to sleep so I'd rather not disturb him."

"I can watch Connor," said Sandra from her position in the kitchen. "If you want me to."

"Would you mind?" Jim was already on his feet and desperate to see his wife.

Sandra grinned. "My pleasure, you and Tasha hog his company too much."

"We won't be long," Jim assured her, heading for the back door. "I have my phone if you need me."

"And Tasha took hers," said Abby, following Jim towards the stables.

****

Tasha figured they'd been riding for about an hour and as they returned to the stable block she saw Jim standing against a fence smiling.

He grinned as the image of his gorgeous wife smiling and laughing came into sight, but as she saw him something else clouded her eyes. Something he didn't like and hoped he'd never see on her face again. Sadness. Sadness and fear.

"I thought you said Tasha was fine," he accused.

"She was," Abby replied with a frown.

"She isn't now and that is not because of Amanda."

Jim stayed where he was, waiting for her to come to him. Abby headed over to where the three riders dismounted and tended to the horses. He recognised the horse Tasha was on; the very strong willed, potentially volatile chestnut stallion who had been known to throw riders before, including Jim and Travis. A frown creased Jim's brow at the thought that Tasha could have been thrown. He made a mental note to find out what she was doing on such an unpredictable animal. At least she wore a helmet, as did Lexi, whereas Travis was sporting a Stetson. Jim smiled as he considered he had indeed taken the cowboy out of Texas, but maybe you could never take the cowboy out of the Texan. Tasha was stroking her horse and seemed to be whispering to him as he became a little antsy. Almost immediately he calmed down and began nudging his head and nose at Tasha.

"I get that," he said to himself, although he rarely calmed down when Tasha was stroking him and whispering in his ear, quite the opposite. She was usually responsible for him getting excited and at risk of him throwing her too, throwing her down, flat out before fucking her. He adjusted his trousers as his thoughts registered with his dick. Handing the horses over to the couple of assistants Travis had, the group of riders and Abby headed over to where Jim still stood.

"Hey, Jim, how you doing?" Travis wore his almost customary smile.

"Good thanks, you?"

"Yeah, good. Your lady rides well, she has a seriously good technique," Travis' words were innocent and intended as a horse riding compliment.

"Ain't that the truth," replied Jim, earning himself a sharp smack to his shoulder from Tasha who immediately figured her husband was enjoying the double entendre of Travis' comment far too much.

Abby laughed, as did Travis before saying, "I have to shoot, but thank you. I've had a blast and Tash, let me know if I can help."

Tasha nodded and thanked him whereas Jim was just irritated to know that whatever was wrong with his wife Travis was aware of it when he wasn't.

"We should get going too, we have agreed to have dinner with Bria and Martin for no reason I fully understand, but we'll see you for yours and Bobby's birthday I guess." Smiled Abby, reminding Tasha that the last year had gone by in a flash.

"You bet," replied Jim as Tasha hugged Lexi and said something he didn't hear but it must have been something sweet judging by his niece's huge grin.

"Hey, baby." Jim pulled Tasha to him as they were left alone.

"Hey. You're home early." She smiled up at him, wrapped her arms around his neck and prepared to tease his lips with her own. "I would have forgone this ride had I known you were knocking off early. Maybe I could have swapped my ride for a ride." She grinned, making Jim grin back. "Is Connor okay?" She suddenly panicked as she reached for her phone that was securely tucked in her pocket, fearful that she may have missed a call.

"He's fine," reassured Jim, pulling her arms back around his neck. "When I left he was fast asleep having drained his milk from the bottle and Sandra was watching him."

"He took the bottle? He doesn't really like it." Her voice betrayed her feelings of guilt and concern.

"Tasha, baby, he will get used to it. He'll have to because he can't be attached to your breasts forever. That's my job."

A laugh left Tasha's lips but her eyes were still preoccupied.

"Oh, and he took the bottle okay from me once I'd coaxed him a little. I think he knows that when you're trying to give him a bottle you're holding out on him, but he was fine. So, did you have a good ride? On horseback?" he clarified teasingly.

"Yeah, it was nice, although I still can't walk past that stable without blushing." She grinned and flushed red as she referred to their first trip down to the stables.

"Oh, honey. I would really, really like to have that stable made into a national monument. You were so fucking hot that day, in every possible way," he said hoarsely.

"James." Her voice became a husky whisper as he pushed the loose tendrils of hair from her face.

"Yes, baby. What do you want?" Jim knew exactly what she wanted. What they both wanted.

"You. I need you, now." With her arms tightening around his neck she wound her legs around his hips.

"And we both know I'm incapable of denying you what you need, honey." Jim was already striding towards the back of the stable block with only one destination and goal in mind.

"Where are we going?" Tasha clung to her husband tightly, unsure what they would look like to any of the stable staff who might see them, although, the staff were used to seeing them together, clearly in love and incapable of getting enough of each other, so maybe they wouldn't give them a second glance.

"Here." He placed her on her feet directly in front of him and ushered her through a doorway to a wooden building, almost barn-like.

Nervously, Tasha walked through the door and immediately saw that this was a storage facility, horse feeds mainly. Jim took her hand again and led her through to the back of the building to a set of wooden steps.

"Up there, Mrs Maybury." A firm slap was delivered across

her behind as encouragement and confirmation that she should start climbing the ladder.

"What for?" she whispered nervously, making Jim laugh against her ear as he leaned in to tease her with a nuzzle.

"You need me and I always need you, baby, so I thought we should make some time for a roll in the hay as the stables seem a little busy today."

"When you put it like that." Tasha scooted up the steps, giggling, until she was in the roof that was a real-life hay loft complete with endless bales of hay. "Are we playing cowboys then, James? Rolling around in the barn?"

"You bet we are, Natasha. Assuming playing cowboys involves you losing the trousers and me being inside you in five minutes flat."

"Why have we never played this before?" Tasha had already kicked off her boots and was unfastening her trousers.

"We're playing it now."

Jim's tone was gruff and dominant, just the way she liked him, as he threw his shirt down next to Tasha's boots and trousers before adding his own. She could already feel hot dampness swelling between her thighs when he reached across for her arm and grabbed Tasha's wrist. He pulled her to him then kissed her, but without any gentleness. It was a passionate kiss, so ferocious it almost left Tasha gasping for breath. Unsure how it happened they were suddenly lying on the floor, on the hay and although it was hard, prickly and sticking in unbelievably sensitive places it somehow added to the experience, emphasising her desperation and she was now beyond desperate. Her legs were splayed as Jim settled over her and between them.

"God, I fucking love you, baby," he moaned as one hand reached behind her to release her breasts from the designer nursing bra in a bright pink lace fabric she was wearing. "These really need not to go off if we have any hope of getting back home without everyone knowing you've enticed me up here." Jim grinned as he lowered his mouth towards one nipple that he grazed with his teeth.

"Fuck," cried Tasha, desperate for more and less as she attempted to arch into Jim's touch.

"Soon, baby," he replied, having taken her comment literally. "If we had all the time in the world I would have you like this for hours until you can no longer see straight. I'd have you begging Tasha, on your knees willing to do just about anything."

"I'm pretty close already," she admitted, lacing her fingers through Jim's hair, trying to entice his mouth back to her breasts.

"Nowhere near close enough and we're on a schedule here." He rested back on his heels, between her thighs, gazing across her body, admiring her for a few seconds and then he was pulling her pink lacy brief from her and opening her up. He stroked across the tattoo that marked her as his before two fingers plunged into her, making her moan and cry out. His fingers were rotating inside her, enticing her g-spot to deliver shards of pleasure which it did as soon as he touched it.

"James, I'm going to come," she cried hoarsely.

"That's the idea, Tasha," Jim told her as his thumb began to brush over her clitoris.

"James, not yet, please. Make me wait," she pleaded.

Jim frowned at her with a perplexed expression. "Wait? You want to wait, even though we need to get back?" He continued to eye her with confusion.

"Yes." Her orgasm continued to gain momentum due to Jim's hand still stroking her inside and out.

"You really seem to have forgotten how this works, Tasha. How I call the shots and decide what you get and how. Maybe I won't let you come at all and when we get home I will set into motion the plan of fucking you all night, keeping you so close to coming that it will drive you crazy and then, well who knows, maybe I will still keep you frustrated."

"No, please. I want to come, with you, together, please. I need us to be together, just you and me," she told him tearfully and suddenly the sad, haunted expression of Natasha Winters put in an unexpected and unwelcome reappearance, knocking the wind out of Jim's sails completely.

"Okay, baby. If that's what my wife needs, then that is exactly what she'll get."

Jim moved his hand that had earlier been taunting her, relocating it so it stroked her cheek gently. He replaced it with a single thrust before he was buried deep inside her, causing Tasha to arch into his body. Her legs wrapped around him. She pulled him closer still while her arms were thrown above her head, stretching into the hay behind her.

"You like that, honey?" He pulled back until their bodies were almost uncoupled making her panic that he might be about to stop, but then he drove straight back inside her, pushing her along the hay covered ground.

"Yes, like that, James. Don't stop, please, don't stop."

"I'm not stopping, Tasha, not until we're both coming. Together. You and me," he told her, using her own words which was enough to push her to the precipice of her pleasure.

"Come on, Tasha. With me, baby, now." Somehow he managed to move against her so he was pressing against her clitoris whilst still stroking her insides until she was screaming his name and holding him against her, desperate again, but in a very different way to how she'd been just minutes before. She knew Jim had felt it too, but he said nothing, he just held her tenderly, kissed her gently before he pulled free of her and passed her clothes to her.

"Let's go home and check on Connor, and then we can talk, okay?"

Tasha knew from experience that he was offering her no choice in whether she'd talk or not. She would because he'd seen that she'd needed what they'd shared. How she'd needed it her way and they both knew there was a reason for that, although he didn't know what it was, but she knew he knew there was something.

Approaching the house from the back, Tasha and Jim walked hand in hand and both smiled at the sight and sounds that greeted them; Connor was lying on a play mat while Sandra, Philip and Lizzie all leaned over him, talking to him and shaking toys while he simply lay there laughing and gurgling.

"He is so cute," cooed Lizzie.

"Yeah, I gotta say, babies don't normally do it for me, but maybe it's because he's our brother that makes him the exception," added Philip.

Jim looked down at Tasha who could see her husband was

beaming with pride at his three children together, yet it was Sandra's words that touched Tasha the most.

"He is no blood relation to me whatsoever and he melts my heart a little more every time I look at him. He even makes me regret not having children of my own because if I had I would have grand-parenthood to look forward to next."

Tasha squeezed Jim's hand more firmly at the heartfelt, emotional outpouring from Sandra who would have made the perfect grandma and yet she had no grandchildren to look forward to and one set of Connor's were the worst example of parents and in turn grandparents. Grandparents her son would never know. Jim leaned down and planted a single kiss to the top of Tasha's head before heading through the open door.

"Hey, are you all partying without us?" Tasha called, causing everyone to turn and face her, including Connor who was desperately searching for her.

"Tash," cried Lizzie, an unexpected, but always welcome visitor who was rushing towards the space where Tasha and her dad stood. "Hi, Daddy, can I stay over tonight? Mom and Lenny are being, well, weird," she said with a frown.

"I'll call your mom and if she's good with it, of course you can stay." Jim warmly embraced his only daughter.

"Can I stay for dinner?" asked Philip suddenly. "Juan's visiting his folks and I really can't be bothered to cook for myself." His honesty and lack of pretence made Tasha laugh.

"Sure," she said as Sandra turned towards her having picked Connor up to show him the location of his mommy.

"There she is," Sandra told him as he spotted Tasha and began to gurgle and fidget excitedly in the other woman's arms.

"Hey, baby," cried Tasha. "How have you been? Mommy missed you." She took him from Sandra and held him close to her chest, exciting him further as he smelled her aroma and the promise of a meal.

"Looks like he missed you too." Grinned Lizzie.

"I think he missed my boobs most of all," Tasha replied, moving Connor so he was cradled in her arms but facing out to try and avoid him triggering a major milk leak with an audience.

"Eww!" Philip's voice held a hint of disgust. "I still find that real icky."

"Hey, you don't like the fact that I breastfeed my baby you may need to find somewhere else to have dinner tonight." Tasha bumped her hip against his as she passed by him.

"Oh, step-mommy, you wound me. And I said I find it icky, I didn't say it put me off dinner," he replied with a false expression of offence making Tasha laugh again before looking at Connor.

"I think your big brother is attention seeking again, but we love him so we'll feed him and forgive him for being so needy."

"Right," called Sandra, "I will see you all in the morning."

"Thank you for taking care of Connor," said Tasha, surprising herself and Sandra when she leaned in and kissed the other woman warmly.

"No problem." Sandra headed for the door leaving the Maybury family together.

Chapter Twenty-Four

The sound of laughter rang around the dining room as conversation flowed and banter ensued. Tasha was feeling happy and tearful at the same time and wondered how this must feel for Jim; to have all three of his children in his home, possibly for the first time without other people being there, without outsiders or extended family members. He looked happy, truly happy and content. Looking at Connor sitting next to her in his bouncing, cradle seat that was on the table Tasha wondered how much of his older children's lives Jim had missed out on. The older children who flanked him at the table, adoration clear in their expressions and right then she made a vow to herself that he would miss out on nothing of Connor's life if she had anything to do with it.

Watching her own child smile as the other children's voices became excited or when they laughed made Tasha smile around at them all. The simplicity of sharing a meal and good humour as a nuclear family was so fulfilling and yet still a relatively alien concept to her. She couldn't remember ever doing this with her own parents and siblings. Sometimes when they all went to her grandparent's house they shared meals like this, like the first time she'd taken Jim home with her, but never with her parents. Meal times, if you could call them that in the Bailey family home were usually fraught and anxious at best. Her dark, sad thoughts were taking over everything else and she was forgetting about the pleasant thoughts the evening had evoked in her, leading her to less pleasant memories including Travis' words about Dan and the *help* their mother was giving him.

"Tasha," called Jim, sounding as though it wasn't the first time he'd spoken to her.

Looking down the table at him he smiled, but looked concerned.

"Lizzie was asking if she could help to bath Connor."

"Yes, of course. In fact, I might just go and run his bath now, before he falls asleep which will throw his routine out completely." She got to her feet, lifting Connor up onto her shoulder. "Come up whenever you're ready Lizzie," she called back as she left the room.

Watching her leave, Jim was now convinced that something had happened between her going down to the stables for her ride and her returning from it. Something more than Amanda. Something involving Travis, and their biggest common denominator was Dan.

****

The bath was ready and Tasha was just undressing her son when Lizzie appeared behind her.

"You sure you don't mind me staying over?" Lizzie's silent arrival startled Tasha.

"No, course not, this is your home as much as ours, you know that." Tasha carried Connor into the bathroom and lay him in his floating sponge.

"Can I ask you something, personal?" Lizzie sounded hesitant making Tasha nervous.

"Course, but I may not answer if it's too personal, for your sanity as much as anything if it involves your dad," grimaced Tasha.

"Eww, you are really making this awkward," shuddered Lizzie before continuing. "Do you think you were too young to have Connor? I know you love him and I guess you wouldn't change it, but he wasn't planned, was he?"

Tasha was washing Connor's hair, causing him to complain as she considered Lizzie's question and the reason for it.

"I don't think twenty-two is too young to have a baby as such. If you're in a secure relationship with a home and some financial backing, which I had, but I guess it is still young and it does limit your choices. I've lost work because I was pregnant and now I'm struggling to find work that will fit in with having a young baby. You're right that I wouldn't change a thing about Connor, but maybe if I could have planned it in a year or two years' time it would have been, not better, just more convenient. Perhaps I could have established myself as an actress before becoming a mother, but I love him more than I thought possible and if it was a choice between having him now or never, I vote now."

"Even though he wasn't planned at all? I remember you refusing to admit you were pregnant for a long time," said a wide-eyed Lizzie. "I was really worried about you, and Daddy, he was flipping out because you refused to fully acknowledge what was happening."

"Oh Lizzie." Tasha sighed as she finished rinsing the suds from Connor's head. She sponged his whole body before sprinkling and splashing water over and around him making him kick his legs and wave his arms excitedly, creating more splashing. "Look at you," she cooed, "you are such a big boy splashing Mommy and Lizzie."

The little boy laughed as he looked up at two sets of adoring eyes and splashed even more.

"Have I upset you bringing that up?" Lizzie sounded concerned, and why wouldn't she? Tasha couldn't disagree with anything she'd said about her reaction to finding herself unexpectedly pregnant, however she was more concerned by her stepdaughter's questioning because she suspected there was far more to it than simple curiosity.

"No, not really. Let's get Connor, dried and ready for bed and I will see if I can explain, then maybe you will tell me whatever is on your mind instead of playing twenty questions, okay?"

"Jeez, Philip is right, you really are good at smelling a rat." Lizzie thought she'd been discreet and clever in her conversation up until that point, maybe not.

Lizzie had attempted to put a nappy on Connor, and failed dismally, but it had been amusing if nothing else. His sleepsuit had gone on much easier before Lizzie sat on the stool at Tasha's feet as she began to feed her son and prepared what she was going to say to Lizzie.

"Okay," began Tasha. "I had no clue I was pregnant. Didn't think I could be because as far as I was concerned, I was protected. I had the contraceptive implant put in before I moved out here and it had proven good up until Connor." She gently rocked her son. "It was a few weeks after I married your dad that I felt a little out of sorts and thought I had at worst a urine infection so went to see Dr Marshall thinking he would give me a course of antibiotics, if that. He ran a few checks and tested my urine, I thought for infection, but he confirmed I was pregnant. I was knocked off my feet with that news. I had no idea how it had happened or how I was going to tell your dad. I didn't know if I was ready to be a parent and even with a positive test result I kept telling myself that it could still be wrong and I may not be pregnant."

Lizzie looked up at her and laughed with a shake of her head.

"I know, pretty stupid, but it's where I was at. Denial isn't only a river in Egypt," she muttered with a wry smile. Lizzie offered a short laugh but waited for Tasha to continue. "I also had no idea how your dad would feel about us having a baby. We'd talked about it, in principal and he was kind of easy either way, allowing me to decide if we had children as he already had you and Philip, but I knew he'd have wanted to be involved with the decision making and with a positive pregnancy test there was no decision to make. I was also a little nervous that he might think I'd somehow done it on purpose. He knew something was wrong within minutes of coming home and I hysterically told him I was pregnant, that I didn't want to be and was unsure if I could do it."

"Really? You considered not having him?" Lizzie reached up to stroke her baby brother's back, clearly surprised and sad at the prospect of him not being there.

"No," cried Tasha. "Not really. I was shocked and scared, unsure what a baby would mean for me, my new marriage and my career, and all of that on top of my own skewed upbringing. Your dad was happy about it, once over the shock, which took him about seven seconds. I think it did something to boost his overinflated male ego, knocking me up without even trying." She laughed recalling the thrilled expression on Jim's face then laughed louder at Lizzie's expression of distaste. "He talked calmly and sensibly about how things would change and apart from my work none seemed to be too huge and none seemed to bother him. He had an answer or a solution to any question or concern I had."

"Daddy really does have an answer to everything. No problem is too big for him to solve, is it?" Lizzie beamed with pride and total belief in her father's ability as a problem solver, not that Tasha could deny it. Her nod confirmed what her stepdaughter was saying.

"I never considered not having Connor, not really, except I did once say I couldn't have a baby which is when your dad pointed out that the decision over that had been taken out of my hands. It still took a few months to really get my head around it, but once I saw him on the scan and he began to move I was pretty sold on having a baby." She laughed. "Although I was knocked off my feet at just how much love I felt for Connor once he was born. So, how about you tell me what this is all about?" She swapped sides with Connor, giving Lizzie a few seconds to prepare what she needed to say.

"It's not me. You know I'm using condoms and Dylan nor I want a baby, not for a long time. It's Danielle, she's pregnant."

"Bloody hell, Lizzie." Tasha couldn't hide her shock, surprise, whichever it was. The young girl who was the same age as Lizzie and a regular visitor to their home was pregnant. "Wasn't she seeing Rory?" Tasha was sure she'd been seeing the half-English boy who'd seen her in pantomime a few years before.

"Mmm, except he went to England a couple of months ago and hooked up with a girl out there so Danielle kind of had revenge sex with a boy over here."

"Shit!" cried Tasha, startling Connor for a second before getting chastised by Jim who was passing by.

"Baby, please lose the mouth." He stuck his head around the door briefly. "As usual I am chilled to the bone at the sight of you two colluding." He entered the room with a frown, looking between his wife and daughter then down to his son who was contentedly feeding and falling asleep. "Looks like Juan is staying over with his folks so Philip's joining us for the whole night."

"He doesn't like being home alone." Tasha looked at her husband with sad eyes as she recalled the night in Philip's kitchen with Mickie.

"Hey, it's over, honey." Having sensed or maybe pre-empted her thoughts he took the few strides until he was next to her. He bent down to kiss her, then his son and finally Lizzie. "I'll see you two downstairs in a little while."

The two women waited until Jim had gone then Tasha turned her attention back to Danielle. "Right, so Danielle had revenge sex with a boy, who? Do I know him?" Tasha asked and breathed a huge sigh of relief when Lizzie shook her head meaning it hadn't been Dan who had been rather taken with Lizzie's friend.

"A guy from school, we went to a party and he was there, but he's a bit of a deadbeat really, he was just—"

"Available? Willing?" prompted Tasha.

"Yeah. She's really scared, Tash, and doesn't know what to do or say, so I said I'd speak to you." Lizzie smiled proudly, seeming to expect Tasha to wave a magic wand of sorts.

A long, low breath of uncertainty escaped Tasha's lips. "What do you expect me to do, Lizzie? I can talk to her about what it's like having a baby, but it was different for me. I was married and your dad was there to take care of us both. Does her mother know?" Tasha asked thinking about Deanna whom she still disliked.

"Uh-ho." Lizzie threw in a serious shake of the head. "I wondered if Danielle could tell her here with me, and you," Lizzie announced in an almost singing voice.

"You did, did you? I dunno Lizzie." She was desperate to simply say no, to dismiss if not veto the idea completely but looking at Lizzie's concern for her friend she could feel her objections waning. "Deanna and I aren't exactly friends and I would need to check with your dad—"

"If Daddy agrees, will you, please?"

"How do I end up in the middle of these things?" Tasha asked herself as she burped her almost sleeping baby.

"Because you are the best. I'm sure Daddy will agree especially when he thinks how cool it is that I'm not saying I'm pregnant." Lizzie giggled the last two words as Philip joined them and looked mortified having only heard the final words his sister had uttered.

"What? Lizzie!" he screeched, startling Connor making him cry out. Frowning apologetically, Philip continued in a whisper, "Dad is going to go ape and he will kill Dylan, not even Tasha will stop him and Mom and oh my God, what about Lenny? He might throw you out—"

"And breathe." Tasha got to her feet to address Philip. "Lizzie is not pregnant, so crisis averted, it's Danielle."

"Tash! It was a secret," cried a horrified Lizzie.

"Lizzie, I will speak to your dad tonight and Philip would never have believed he was mistaken without an explanation, so he needed to know before he ran downstairs and spilled his incorrect information to your dad. I'm going to put Connor to bed and we'll talk again in the morning." Tasha suddenly felt very, very tired and weighed down with problems, her own and now Lizzie's, well, Danielle's.

****

After a quick shower, Tasha was climbing into bed and wondered what else could crop up; Dan, Lizzie, Danielle, and most recently added to the list, Philip, Philip and Juan. She'd been sitting poolside with him drinking beer, just one bottle for her when he suddenly blurted out that Juan's family were trying to convince him that he wasn't gay, couldn't be and that it was time for him to settle down and get married. To a girl, one of their choosing, a second cousin twice removed or something. Poor Philip was beside himself knowing how much his parent's approval meant to Juan and seemed seriously concerned that he may give in to their demands.

Tasha had reassured him how much Juan loved him, but could offer no guarantees that family pressure wouldn't win out. Jim had been to check on Philip before following Tasha into their room and had just emerged from the bathroom looking concerned.

"This is not the evening I'd planned for us, baby," he said as he slid into bed next to her.

"That's okay. I guess this is one of the pleasures of having children," she replied as he pulled her closer against him.

"Mmm, I guess it is." His reply was flat, giving nothing away. He dropped a kiss to her nose and allowed his fingers to run up and down her arm. "Has Juan said anything to you about him and Philip? I know you're close and I wouldn't normally ask you to break a confidence but I'm worried—he's my son." His earlier flat tone had been replaced with one of concern for Philip and an apology for asking Tasha to break her confidence, if there was one to Juan.

"I know. I'm worried too," she told him and if she knew anything about Juan's plans she would have shared them with her husband. She hated seeing him concerned and he rarely showed this side of himself unless it involved her or the children. "Nope. He's said about his parents disapproving and how they're always trying to fix him up with eligible women. They seem focused on babies and a *normal* future, but nothing about this cousin or whatever she is."

"Maybe I should speak to him when he gets back," Jim started making Tasha smile up at him.

"What? Like, what his intentions are?" Giggled Tasha even though she knew her husband was deadly serious.

"Yes, something like that and I wasn't joking." He frowned.

"I know, that's what made it funnier," giggled Tasha again.

"I think somebody needs to stop laughing at me or there will be tears before bedtime, honey," Jim teased, although he was serious about that too, but good serious now, control freak serious rather than worried and pre-occupied dad serious.

"Do your worst, James," she taunted in return, making him grin down at her devilishly.

"Maybe later. What's the story with Lizzie?"

"I'm supposed to be the one that can smell a rat, but you put me to shame."

"Spill, baby."

"Danielle is pregnant and hasn't told her mom." Tasha's reply was blunt and concise but she had no intention of keeping these details from Jim. She knew he would be shocked, she'd been shocked, but once Lizzie had told her and involved her, she was always going to tell Jim everything. "Lizzie was hoping she could tell her here, with me and her to offer support." She grimaced at the thought of sharing a room with Deanna never mind being part of this messy situation.

"Shit! She's a kid—seventeen. Lizzie isn't planning on following suit, is she? If she is she needs to forget it or Dylan will be missing some vital parts of his anatomy," said Jim menacingly which made Tasha laugh again.

"Stop laughing at me, Natasha," he warned quite seriously.

"Sorry." She managed to bite back another laugh. "Lizzie has no desire to be a parent for a very long time, but I don't know that this has anything to do with me. It's not as though Deanna and I are friends, is it?"

"No, but if Danielle has confided in Lizzie and she feels your presence would help..." his voice trailed off, allowing Tasha to take this in and decide what she was going to do, knowing Jim had no issue with her helping if that's what she wanted to do.

"Really, you think I should do this? Me and Deanna, here, with the girls to break it to her that her kid's knocked up?"

"Why not? Unless you don't want to, which is fine, but if you and Lizzie want to, I have no objection. But you should only do it if you want to. If you don't then that is absolutely your call and Lizzie will have to accept that and respect it."

"I'll think about it," Tasha agreed. "Can we go to sleep now? I'm knackered, must be the fresh air from my ride earlier."

"Or the trip to the hay loft, for my ride earlier, oh, and that horse you were riding. I'm not sure he isn't a little too strong and opinionated for you."

Tasha softened into his touch and grip that was lying them both down in preparation for sleep.

"That hay got everywhere," Tasha said with a wide expression.

"You won't want to go back up there then."

"No. Not tonight anyway, not when we have a big comfy bed, oh, and that horse was just my sort of guy, strong and opinionated." Tasha softened further against Jim and began to drift off into a deep sleep immediately.

Chapter Twenty-Five

Lying on the bed with his legs loosely crossed at the ankles Jim was watching Tasha carefully, maybe too carefully.

"You're staring," she accused, reaching forward for the dress on the bed.

"You're mine, I'm allowed to stare," he replied with a small frown as the lacy A-line skirt fell to where it finished just above her knees. "You look seriously sexy, baby."

"Thank you." Tasha smiled as she took in her reflection and thought that the high neckline that gathered with a string of fabric that circled her neck then tied at the back in a bow was the right mix between sexy and safe.

"It's not too late to cry off," Jim told her as he drank in his wife in navy blue lace that had a slim-fitting bodice that really did flatter her post baby shape, especially with its wide waistband and looser skirt that gave Tasha an enviable hourglass figure.

"I have no chance of crying off. Abby and Lucy wouldn't even accept death as a good enough excuse, and I think Philip might need looking after." Tasha sighed as she dropped down to sit on the bed and quickly found herself wrapped in Jim's arms and pulled up the bed to sit next to him.

"Tasha, I love that you want to take care of Philip, but I'm not convinced going to a bar drinking is what is best for him right now. He is all over the place. He and Juan seem to be in a strange place and when Philip is in a good place he doesn't make the best choices in bars and with drink so in his current weird place—"

Looking up at her husband's concerned expression Tasha began to regret her decision to invite Philip along, to cheer him up. Moving so that she was straddling Jim's hips, Tasha stroked away his furrowed brow before leaning in to kiss him, gently. With her forehead resting against his she released a long sigh.

"I'm off booze so I will keep his alcohol intake to a minimum and it won't be a late night. I promise if Philip is getting out of his depth that I'll come straight home, we both will."

The sound of Connor crying forced Jim to move and ultimately ended the conversation they were having about Philip. Tasha knew her husband was concerned for his oldest son and so was Tasha. Things were a little rocky between Philip and Juan and although Tasha didn't really know the details she knew Juan struggled to completely resist the mounting family pressure he was under. The pressure to conform. The fact that Philip was still staying in their house each night confirmed he was struggling.

"Hey, buddy, come and say hi and bye to Mommy. She looks really pretty," Jim told the little boy from the other side of the baby monitor before reappearing in the bedroom where Tasha had added her shoes and bag.

"Hey, baby," she cooed to a very vocal Connor who was babbling at her with a smile. "You be a good boy for Daddy, Mommy will see you later," she told him before leaning in to kiss him as Philip called to her that Abby had arrived.

"Yes, and you be a good girl, too," Jim told Tasha who was landing a chaste kiss to her husband's cheek before heading for the stairs.

"I'll try," she called back to a frowning Jim.

The bar Abby had chosen was a new place, but very expensive and exclusive which Tasha was grateful for because she knew the last place she wanted to be was in a packed and overpopulated bar, especially with Philip. Lucy and Amanda who lived in the same neighbourhood had met them there.

With the first round of drinks ordered and them all sitting at a table they began making small talk. Philip was quiet and a little subdued causing more concern than his usual slightly over the top persona.

They had been there for probably only half an hour when a young woman approached the table and it soon became apparent she was an old friend of Philip's. She asked about Jim, Sara and Lizzie before looking around the table and asking about Juan. Philip simply said he was out of town before introducing her to everyone as an ex-girlfriend of Ricky's, Juan's brother. Tasha invited her to join them, an invitation she declined but she did invite Philip to join her friends, an invitation he jumped at. Tasha was relieved that he at least looked happier now, but was a little concerned that he might end up on tequila slammers and she had vowed to take care of him.

With Philip gone the four women very quickly settled into easy and slightly lewd conversation, especially when Lucy began to rate the waiting staff, a game Abby quickly and enthusiastically joined in with.

It was after a slightly older and very attractive member of the waiting staff had delivered a round of drinks that conversation became more personal with Amanda comparing the waiter to Bobby. Tasha thought it was very sweet that Abby actually checked out the man again and then dismissed him as being nowhere near as attractive as her husband.

"So, how did you and Bobby meet?" Tasha asked.

"Through work. I was new to the company and I'd seen Bobby a couple of times around the place but had never been brave enough to speak to him." Abby smiled and added, "He can be quite scary."

The other women laughed.

"Yeah, we get that, Abby. He is a Maybury after all," said Tasha.

"I never spoke and then one day we were in the elevator together and Bobby just stared at me. Still no words were exchanged and by the time I got out on my floor I was ready to pass out, throw myself at his feet or throw up, maybe all three and he just laughed."

"So?" squealed Lucy who was on the edge of her seat now.

With a laugh Abby continued, "There was a corporate gym and that's where we met next. I was sweaty and red and Bobby, well he was glorious in his workout gear, not that he'd started his workout...and beyond that my lips are sealed."

Abby slumped back in her seat while the others all stared at her, Tasha and Lucy open mouthed.

"Since when? Since when have your lips ever been sealed?" Tasha asked. "How can you tell us that then leave us bloody hanging? That's just cruel."

Abby shrugged as she sipped on her cocktail while Amanda giggled.

Lucy pouted at the idea of the undoubtedly interesting details of Abby and Bobby not being forthcoming. "We need another night out, with far more alcohol before we ask her how she and Bobby got together."

Philip had been back to see Tasha a couple of times and although he still seemed sad he was a little more settled after spending some time with Ricky's ex. Maybe she could relate to him as she must have known Juan's family, known of them and their thoughts and beliefs.

Amanda and Lucy had gone to the bathroom together leaving Abby and Tasha alone.

"Tash, can I ask you something, about Connor?"

"Of course. I'm something of a baby bore so I do love to talk about him." Tasha grinned.

"Well, it's kind of not about Connor, but about babies, having babies, about me having a baby," Abby blurted out.

"Are you pregnant?" Tasha whispered then frowned in the direction of Abby's alcoholic drink.

"No, but I want a baby. Bobby and I have talked about it and we want another child. Seeing you and Jim with Connor gave me the push to make a decision and after I spoke to Jim about it —"

"Jim? You discussed your family planning with my husband?" Tasha asked, slightly taken aback.

"Not entirely. I just wanted to know if Bobby had said anything to him. I knew he probably had but Jim told me to talk to my husband."

"And?"

"And we both want another child, but Jim suggested we should look at all options, including adoption because I don't know if I could cope with another pregnancy or the depression I suffered after Lexi."

"Is that something you're considering?"

"Yeah. I have an appointment this week with my doctor to discuss if another pregnancy would be the same and Bobby is looking into adoption and there's always surrogacy too."

"It would be lovely to welcome another baby to the family and I would love Connor

to have someone else to play with. I mean it's not like Philip and Lizzie are suitable to be his peers." Tasha smiled as she pulled Abby in for a hug.

"I dunno about Philip," Abby replied. "In terms of maturity. He is currently dancing on a table in just his underwear."

Leaping to her feet, Tasha swung round and was greeted with the image of Philip in a pair of bright orange underpants knocking back a shot of something whilst dancing on the table as his friends applauded.

"Oh, for fuck's sake!" Tasha cried, already striding towards him. "Philip," she practically screeched as he appeared to be about to shed his last item of clothing as some of the bar staff honed in on him.

"But Tash, I'm so sad," Philip said for possibly to twelfth time.

"I get that." Tasha spoke a little more gently now having already pointed out how lucky Philip was not to have been thrown out of the bar of arrested for indecent exposure. She shuddered at the mere thought of having to call Jim and tell him his son had been arrested when she was supposedly looking after him. "But this is not the answer, getting arrested."

"I know, sorry. I didn't think. Dad would have freaked out, and Juan, assuming he ever speaks to me again. What do I do if he doesn't come back, Tash?" Philip was beginning to lose the battle with his tears.

Tasha pulled him in for a tight hug. "I don't know. I suppose you would have to accept that and after licking your wounds you'd have to pick yourself back up and move on. I'm not saying it would be easy. I know it wouldn't, but that's what we have to do in life. Look, you need to speak to him, to know what he wants. You deserve to be loved, completely and unconditionally," Tasha told Philip and meant it. He deserved to be loved like she was loved by his father and although she hadn't always believed that, she did now. Believed it more and more every day.

"Thanks, Tash. Can we not tell Dad about the table and my near nakedness?"

"Yeah. I don't think it's in anyone's best interest for him to know so unless he asks if you danced almost naked on a table top, we should be fine," Tasha said with a wink as the others re-joined them.

After a couple of cups of coffee Philip seemed a little more balanced if not happy and with Amanda talking about needing to go home because of night feeds and Lucy groaning at the thought of an early start Abby and Tasha agreed to leave too but all agreed that they should meet up again soon, although Tasha decided it might be best to do it, minus Philip, until he and Juan had resolved whatever differences they had.

Once they returned home Philip went straight to bed whereas Tasha went to check on Connor who was lying awake, seemingly content.

"Hey, baby," Tasha called causing him to smile and wave his arms around until she reached down and picked him up. "Shall we have some one on one with a little supper thrown in?" she asked him as Jim walked in behind them.

"The supper is optional for me," he told his wife as he came to a standstill behind her and kissed her neck. "Good night?"

"Hmmm, interesting. Abby wants a baby, but I know you know that."

"Yeah, she and Bobby have mentioned it. Was that the highlight of your night out?"

"Yes, it kind of was," Tasha replied with a slightly disappointed expression that made Jim laugh.

"So nobody tried hitting on you or touching you? No podium dancing or vomiting in shoes?" he asked with a throaty laugh.

"No. Horrifyingly boring night."

With another laugh Jim said, "Thank you for keeping it tame and for taking care of Philip. I was half expecting to get a call from the police station asking me to come and bail one or both of you out for some kind of naked dancing on tables."

Tasha turned to face Jim and looked at him with a disbelieving and alarmed expression at his choice of words.

"What?"

Tasha replayed her own words to Philip about not telling Jim unless he asked about near naked dancing.

"Nobody was naked, but there was a little table top dancing and a few clothes shed," she admitted but Jim's response clearly showed that her words had been misunderstood.

"What? You had better be joking here because if you are really telling me that you danced on tables after removing items of clothes you and your ass will be sorry and you will be grounded for life, Natasha."

"No, not me." She frowned. "Although I might do it next time if me and my ass have to pay for it," she teased, but Jim ignored that.

"Then who was on the table?"

"Philip. He met some people he knew, had a couple of drinks and let off some steam. No more. I got him coffee and we talked. He just wants Juan to love him, like you love me, completely and unconditionally and right now he doesn't know if he does."

"Promise me you weren't thrown out of anywhere or removed by the police?"

"I promise."

"I think Juan and I really do need a chat because Philip can't carry on like this. They both need to know what they want for themselves and from each other."

"Yes, they do," she agreed with a smile.

"It makes me so happy that you are beginning to understand just how I love you baby."

"You make it easy for me to believe it even if I don't always understand why me…"

"I intend to make sure you believe it and readily accept it because it's no more than you deserve, Tasha. I assume Philip didn't want me to know about his naked dancing?"

Tasha nodded at his assumption about his son, but chose to

ignore the words about what she deserved.

"Okay, our secret," he whispered as he landed a single kiss on Tasha's lips before looking down at Connor, who smelling the offer of a meal was becoming fraught.

"Can you undo my dress please?"

"Anytime, baby." Jim laughed as he undid the neck fastening that allowed the dress to fall down enough to enable feeding.

"You can carry on to bed if you want to. He's probably only going to have a top up so I won't be long," Tasha told her husband as she sat down and began to feed her son.

"I'll go and lock the house up and I will see you next door, Mrs Maybury. I need my one on one time too, honey," Jim told her with a grin and a wink that only served to make Tasha smile and flush.high neckline gathered with a string of fabric that circles your neck and ties at back with a feminine bow. The slim-fitting bodice of this lace party dress has princess seams for a flattering shape with a wide waistband leading to an A-line skirt.

Chapter Twenty-Six

The sound of raised voices caused Tasha to wake before Jim's alarm went off. Nudging him as he lay behind her she recognised one voice as Philip's.

"Jim," she muttered as she gave him another nudge but there was no response. "James," she said slightly louder as she rolled over to face him so she could shake his shoulder too.

"Hey, baby." A lazy smile and a sleepy expression lit up his face. "Did you miss your booty call last night, honey? You're the one that fell asleep," he told her with a grin as he reached up to push her hair off her face.

"No. Listen. I can hear raised voices, Philip's," she explained and immediately Jim leapt out of bed.

He pulled on a pair of shorts and after unlocking it reached into the drawer of his bedside table and pulled out a handgun, shocking Tasha into near silence.

"What the fuck?" she asked as he headed for the door.

"We'll talk."

"Too fucking right." Tasha felt angry as she considered the fact there was a gun in their home at all never mind that it was loaded and Jim was expertly removing some kind of safety catch from it.

"Ssh, I said we'll talk." He frowned and opened the bedroom door where the other voice could be heard clearly now. Juan.

Jim replaced the lock on the gun and returned it to the drawer. He added a pair of sweatpants while Tasha pulled on a pair of pyjamas before going downstairs where they found an obviously upset Philip shouting at Juan.

"I deserve better than this," he cried.

"Phil, I'm just suggesting a break." Juan sounded just as sad as the other man.

"Why? For what? So you can try fucking your cousin and see if you can't un-gay yourself?" sobbed Philip.

"No! I don't know," admitted Juan. "I'm confused. We've been through so much. I've been through so much. You stayed here last night and several nights before because of what happened in our home and yet it didn't happen to you. It happened to me and an interior designer can't wipe out the memories and images in my head. Images I see every time I step foot in that house. Every time I am here. Every time I see Lizzie or Tasha. Happy now?" He sounded tearful himself, but it was Tasha who had tears running down her face.

This was her fault. If she'd never met Jim—

Seeming to sense her thoughts, Jim took her hand and squeezed it, leaning down and brushing her tears away with a shake of his head before addressing the two young men in his house. "Would someone care to explain why my wife and I have woken to the sound of you two fighting?"

They both spun and looked slightly embarrassed to have been discovered.

"Sorry," they replied in unison.

"Not a suitable answer at half past five in the morning." Jim sounded angry suddenly.

"Maybe we should take this home," suggested Juan making Jim and Tasha frown, but it was the latter that spoke.

"What? To the home that an interior designer can't wipe out the memories of what happened there? And it happened to me too, Juan. In fact, not wanting to make this a competition but it happened to me more than anyone so maybe you should stay here. Think about what it is you want to say to each other and why. I'll make some tea and coffee and then we should talk, all of us and maybe you two do need to talk, but not shout until Lizzie and Connor are woken up too." Tasha strode into the kitchen leaving the three men in her wake.

"I don't mean to be rude, Tash," began Juan, gaining everyone's attention. "But, with respect, this has nothing to do with anyone else—"

Jim cut in, knowing what Juan was saying and to a point agreeing with him, but there was no way he could or would allow the back off that was coming his wife's way to go unchallenged. "I would strongly suggest you think before you continue to speak." He gave the other man a hard stare, almost daring him to continue.

Tasha, seemed to be completely unfazed by Juan or his words and whilst she knew her husband would defend her, the truth was she didn't need him to right now. "Yeah, then if you really felt this way you wouldn't have done this here, in my home at stupid fucking o'clock, so tough."

Juan stared, open mouthed while Philip watched on.

"Oh," she continued, "And if you wanted this to be totally private you wouldn't have started this in Philip's occupied family home after disappearing to fuck knows where with fuck knows who."

"Tasha, baby," Jim said, chastening her use of expletives.

"Sorry," said Juan, accepting every word Tasha had said.

"Baby," Jim interrupted the cold stare Tasha was currently directing at her friend. "I'll go and check on Connor." Jim moved towards the kitchen where she stood scooping coffee into the filter.

"You and I need to talk after they have," she told him, gesturing towards the two young men sitting quietly together.

"Sure thing."

They all sat together for a time and although Juan was quite open about his feelings for Philip, he also admitted that he couldn't imagine a life without his family in it and they had implied that this may not be possible if his relationship with Philip continued. They had also suggested that a marriage to this girl, who was technically a cousin could produce children and give an air of respectability to Juan's youthful mistake which is how they'd described his relationship with Philip.

"A youthful mistake?" Tasha shook her head, but refrained from unleashing the tirade of expletives queueing in her mind as she took in Philip's hurt expression that broke her heart a little. "Is that how they see you and Philip or you being gay?"

"Both, I guess. There was a vague suggestion that I could always continue any extramarital relationship so long as I was discreet and that Lucia would be cool with that."

"Bloody hell," cried Tasha. "That is all kinds of fucked up." Clearly, the expletives weren't going to remain unleashed.

"Tasha," chastened Jim, "Please."

"Well, it is," she said in her own defence. "Juan, I love you, you know that and if what you want or need is marriage, children and a gay relationship hidden then you've made your decision whether you realise it or not, but will that be enough? You and Philip have always been so open and what do you expect from him in this? To accept and be cool with stolen moments and nights when your wife is out of town. To be second best to your family, to be compliant and faithful when he knows you're not? To be left alone during holidays and family celebrations? I think if you want that then you're asking too much," Tasha said honestly before Jim intervened.

"Juan, Tasha is right. This is too much to ask. Philip deserves a family, a home, and to be your first priority, but so long as you do the right thing by him I'm good with that. I'll respect your decision. What do you want, Philip?" Jim reached across to gently rub his son's shoulder, hoping to offer support and love in the simple touch.

Philip turned to his dad and smiled. Clearly his touch had achieved its goal. "Juan," he replied tearfully. "I want Juan, but he has to want me too. I can't want enough for us both or it will all fall apart."

"Then you two have some decisions to make," said Jim sadly. "We'll give you some space," he added as Connor began to cry upstairs.

The short trip upstairs to their recently awoken son was silent and the silence continued until Tasha was sitting in the nursing chair in his nursery feeding him.

"Since when have you kept a gun in the house?" Tasha rocked Connor gently.

"It's my constitutional right, honey," Jim replied, immediately irritating Tasha.

"Is that what I asked? Is it? How long?" she repeated.

"You don't have to be so mad about it, baby. I kept a gun for a long time and learnt how to shoot, but hadn't had one for a couple of years, until your dad ran you off the road and Mickie's involvement became clear in that."

"And you didn't think to mention it?" Tasha was becoming more agitated.

"No, honey, because I didn't want to worry you and you Brits get uptight about guns. We can discuss where I keep it if you want to."

Tasha let out a long sigh before Jim leapt up, making her jump as he headed out of the room. "Wait there."

Returning almost immediately, Jim held an A5 sized envelope in his hand and sat on the footstool at the bottom of the nursing chair Tasha still occupied with their son who was greedily consuming his breakfast.

"I was going to show this to you when I got home the other day, but you were out riding and then it all got a little bent out of shape when we ended up with a houseful." Jim reached into the envelope to withdraw a booklet, or book of some sort. He turned it to show Tasha the cover.

She frowned as she realised he was holding an American passport. "Your passport?" she said as a half question.

"You think?" With a triumphant smile he opened the document to reveal a photo of Connor. "Connor's passport came back meaning he can travel outside of the U.S. with us, so if you still want to take a trip back to Blighty, then we'll all be going, together."

"Really?" Tasha was suddenly tearful, thoughts of Dan filling her mind once more. "Thank you," she stammered sounding as emotional as she looked.

"No problem. I need my wife to be happy and you did freak me out with declarations of trips to London without me and for unknown periods, but it made me remember that I need to be more thoughtful of your home and family. As thoughtful as you are of mine, baby, so why don't you tell me what made you look so worried after your ride."

"You read me so well, every time," she mused with a half-smile as she sat her son up on her lap and began to pat his back gently. "I was going to speak to you when we were alone, but we haven't really had any alone time, have we? Not with a house full of children." She smiled.

"I really do love you, Natasha, for that comment alone," he said making her frown while trying to figure out which comment he was referring to. "Oh, honey, the fact that you have no idea what I'm talking about makes me love you a little more. You said that we had a house full of children, not that we had a house full of my children, just children," he explained. "And one of those children is your own age, yet you still class him as a child we have in common, even when you're getting him down from tables he's dancing almost naked on."

"Ah. All of the children are yours biologically, but if ever we weren't together I would hate for another woman to distinguish between our children and hers with you," replied Tasha thoughtfully. "And Lizzie is like Pippa who I always think of as a child and Philip is probably the least mature of them all in some ways, so they're all children."

"I don't know if I could find you any more attractive than I do right now," said Jim seriously, making Tasha's skin flush with desire and embarrassment.

"You know that Connor is not likely to have a nap until after you're at work, don't you?" she asked, wondering if she could convince her son to go to sleep so soon after waking.

A shake of the head was Jim's initial response. "No work for me today, baby. I thought we might plan our trip to London, but as soon as our son's eyes close you and I will be getting some serious alone time."

A breathy and needy gasp left Tasha's mouth and she was unsure just who was most shocked by it, her or Jim. His words weren't exactly evocative or explicit but she was already beginning to imagine the implications of them.

"Oh yeah, honey, in fact, I may take a real leisurely pace today. Maybe during morning nap I could just eat you, baby, from head to toe and everywhere in between until you are so close to coming that you can't think or see straight and then after lunch, Connor's lunch when he settles down for a little more sleep I could tie you up and touch you and stroke you. Lots of that thing you like with my fingers, stroking you inside, finding those sweet spots that have you coming fast and hard, but I don't think I'd let you come. I think you'd have to wait for it until bedtime and then I would fuck you, Tasha." He laughed as he watched her swallowing hard then added, "But maybe I would still leave your pussy empty baby. I could fuck your ass, couldn't I? We both know you like that."

"James." She stared across at him, unsure whether there was anything else she should or could say, making him smile again.

"I think you like my plan. What about if we invite BOB along to play? He could fill your pussy while I come in your ass. Would you like that, Natasha?" he asked darkly.

Tasha stared, still wondering how a normal conversation had got her here; aching, panting and very, very wet with arousal while her infant son sat on her lap.

"Yes," she managed to whisper.

"Then let's hope these kids, whoever they belong to get out of the house today and we can relive a few of our honeymoon highlights," he said, his normal tone reinstated.

Connor suddenly began to moan, apparently bored, bringing Tasha back to earth with a bump.

"You really shouldn't speak to me that way when Connor is here." She was flustered and angsty now.

"You are probably right, so Daddy is sorry, but meant every word of it. Come on. buddy, let's have a little bonding session while Momma calms herself down." Jim grinned, reaching forward to pick his son up. "And then she can tell Daddy what she was going to before we got a little distracted, oh yes she can," called Jim at the baby who began to gurgle in response. "Wise move to side with Daddy, son, after all he is the boss around here."

"It's Dan," blurted out Tasha before she relayed the information Travis had shared with her. "I don't know what to do, Jim. I need to keep him away from them, both of them. They're poisonous and Dan will end up getting drawn into something bad, really bad and he won't cope," she said, tearful once more. "Pippa is more like me than I realised, but like me now, her attitude is fuck them."

"Tasha, baby, lose the mouth in front of Connor."

"After the things you said, really?" replied a frowning Tasha.

"Lose the frown as well or I will be rethinking my plan for a far more frustrating one," Jim threatened and remembering what they'd been discussing, the importance of it and possible implications as well as his wife's worries, he softened. "Go on, please."

"Pippa is less concerned by our parent's existence. She figures they don't care about us, never did and after my dad and Mickie and the revelations of some of what he did, made me do, she wants nothing to do with them. She has us and our grandparents, and a fledgling career with friends, but Dan doesn't have any of those things other than my grandparents so is further isolated which makes him vulnerable to them."

"I get it Tasha, but we need to establish exactly what Dan's involvement with them is and see what he wants to do. He has us too, although I get that so far away he may not feel that he does."

Tasha nodded and smiled as Connor began to vocalise loudly at his father who was ignoring him.

"Hey, I'm here. I still got your back buddy, but Momma is sad and we need to make her happy so two more minutes and then we'll go downstairs for some guy time, okay?" he asked the little boy who gazed up at him adoringly. "Tasha, I'm not saying this to make you feel worse or to be a hard ass but if Dan maintains those strong and direct links with your parents I don't know that he can still count on having us," said Jim sternly but warily.

"You mean he has to choose, them or us?" Despite Jim's words to their son about making his momma happy he knew his threat had done the direct opposite, her face and sad tone confirmed that.

"Yup."

"We can't do that. I won't," she protested, but ultimately knew she couldn't expose Connor to her parents and in the end Jim would follow through with his ultimatum.

"Well unfortunately for you and Dan, I can and I will."

"James," she cried.

"No way, Tasha. You speak to Dan if you need to and see

what's happening or we wait and we go to London at the weekend and see for ourselves, which is my preferred choice."

Tasha nodded, unsure which option would be best.

"Good. I'll book the flights and somewhere to stay as we didn't extend the lease on the apartment. We'll do everything we can to make things good for Dan." Jim got to his feet with Connor.

"Everything?"

"Yeah, and then some, baby. Whatever it takes short of him inadvertently involving us with your parents. I'll go and see how things are with Philip and Juan and maybe we can have a peaceful breakfast."

"I'll be down in just a minute." Tasha slumped back into the seat and closed her eyes as she attempted to gather her thoughts.

Chapter Twenty-Seven

A couple of days later Tasha nervously received Deanna and Danielle in the hall where Lizzie appeared behind her and led them all into the family room at the back of the house where Tasha headed for the kitchen to make drinks for everyone.

"I'll just pop and see if Jim wants anything?" Tasha muttered nervously before rushing off to see her husband in his office where he was *working* which translated to avoiding the shit that was about to hit the fan.

"Hey, baby." He looked up with a smile as she stood in the doorway. "Was that Deanna I heard?"

"Mmm, which is why I'm here. I don't know if this is such a good idea," she admitted.

Jim got up and closed the distance so he could close the door behind her affording them some privacy.

"Then don't do it, honey." He smiled as he leaned in to kiss her lips gently.

Immediately she began to soften and yield against him. "I think it may be a little late to back out now, unless you think I can go back in there and say, *well thanks for coming over and now you need to sod off home*, what do you reckon?"

"I see your point, baby. So, maybe you just need to get your ass out there and let Danielle do the talking."

"Maybe. Oh God, what a mess! I feel so sorry for Danielle and Deanna, and I can imagine how Danielle feels." Tasha sighed as Jim pulled back from her and studied her face.

"Your situation, our situation with Connor was nothing like this," he began making Tasha shake her head.

"That's not what I meant. I was thinking of being sixteen and pregnant..." she allowed her voice to trail off and her expression to betray her feelings of sadness, confusion and shame.

"Honey, I'm so sorry. Sometimes I kind of forget that stuff," he told her, brushing her hair back and kissing her face tenderly.

"It doesn't help that Lizzie keeps looking at me as if I'm some kind of fairy god mother who can wave a magic wand and make this alright."

"I get that, but you don't have a magic wand so maybe she just thinks you can make this easier for her friend. That by being there it will be less emotive, I don't know."

Tasha thought Jim's idea made sense, that by being on neutral ground with other people there Deanna was less likely to explode in anger, disappointment or sorrow and by the time they got home she would already be calming down and beginning to accept the reality of her daughter's situation. When she thought back to the fear and abject horror at finding herself pregnant at sixteen, Tasha felt sick. She remembered the realisation that she was pregnant with Liam's baby and the terror that had filled her, unable to tell anyone. The crippling fear that nobody would help her and ultimately that she'd be forever destined to live a life with Liam and her parents. A lifetime of being used and abused by them all, her and undoubtedly her child, that poor innocent baby who had never asked to be conceived, but it had been. As had Connor, but whereas her son had been conceived in nothing but love her first child had never known love, nothing about its existence had been touched by love, quite the opposite.

"Hey, come here." Jim spoke with such gentleness and affection as he pulled her in for a loving embrace that she could feel tears escaping down her face. "Jeez, baby, this is too much. Let me go out there and tell them you're not well because you certainly shouldn't have to put yourself through this, not if it's taking you to those old, dark places."

"I just feel bad for how she's feeling," Tasha replied with a long hard sniff. "And then I feel bad that I'm making her situation about me."

Before Jim could respond further Lizzie's voice sounded with a knock at the door. "Tasha, are you coming back?"

Pulling the door open, Tasha smiled weakly between her husband and her stepdaughter.

"Lizzie, just wait a minute, Tasha and I need to speak."

"I'll be fine," Tasha assured Jim before their son began crying from upstairs.

"I'll go," offered Jim, already climbing the stairs to where Connor had been sleeping.

"Come on, then." Tasha took Lizzie's hand to re-join Deanna and Danielle. "Sorry," she called as she grabbed the drinks Sandra had finished for her.

Sitting opposite Deanna and Danielle, Tasha waited for someone to speak, but after an awkward silence that seemed to last forever Lizzie looked across at her with pleading eyes.

It looked as though Tasha's role in this included facilitating the necessary conversation. "I'm sure you're wondering why we invited you over, Deanna," she said with a strained smile.

"Yeah, well kind of. It's not more security issues is it? That was a pain in the ass," she said making Tasha laugh at her honesty.

"No, nothing like that and as bad as it was for you it was a hundred times worse here." She laughed but decided that things needed moving on. "Maybe you'd like to start things, Danielle," suggested Tasha hoping the floodgates would now open.

"Okay—erm—Mom—this is tough for me and I didn't know how to say this at home which is why we're here." She began to flounder.

"Are you taking drugs?" cried Deanna dramatically.

"No, no. God, what do you take me for?" she asked and then seemed to think about those words, the question that she really didn't want her mother to answer and certainly not after she told her what she had to tell her.

Tasha took Lizzie's hand in hers and gave it a firm squeeze before encouraging Danielle to continue. "Maybe if you explained what happened."

"Erm, you remember when Rory went to England a while back and he started seeing that girl?" Danielle looked so nervous Tasha wanted to cry for her.

"Ye-es," replied her mother a little hesitantly. A change in expression seemed to suggest her mother suspected where this conversation was going or at least feared where her daughter was taking it.

"I was hurt and angry, so I started seeing this boy from school and I, we, got close..."

"How close?" asked a wide-eyed Deanna, surely knowing what was coming now.

"Real close," replied Danielle who was beginning to cry. "Mom, I am so sorry," she sobbed.

"Are you ill? Did he give you something, some kind of STD?" Deanna asked, edging ever closer to the truth.

With a simple shake of her head Danielle finally blurted out the truth, "I'm pregnant."

A stunned looking Deanna hugged her daughter who cried gently. Tasha felt awkward and embarrassed despite the fact she was sitting in her own home. The scene unfolding in front of her was, or should have been, a private moment and now she felt she was somehow intruding.

It was Lizzie who spoke next as she joined the mother and daughter hug, totally oblivious to any intrusion.

"Hey, it's going to be okay you know. Now your mom knows you can decide what you want to do, can't she, Tasha?"

"Mmm," said Tasha growing more uncomfortable by the second.

"Tasha, baby, sorry to interrupt," called Jim from the doorway.

Tasha was happy to be interrupted.

"I think Connor wants an early lunch," he told her bouncing their son in his arms.

Tasha was like a rabbit caught in headlights now, unsure whether to disappear upstairs with Connor or to just take him from his father.

"Do you mind?" Tasha asked Deanna who had turned to smile at Jim and Connor.

"Carry on, it's your house," the other woman replied and with the words barely out Jim was dropping Connor into his mother's lap.

"There you go, buddy. Momma's got you and I'll see you

when you're done." And with that he was gone again.

Tasha spoke softly to her son and kissed him until he was giggling before putting him to her breast to feed him, discreetly courtesy of the button down t-shirt she was wearing.

Deanna watched her closely as Danielle calmed down and then began to question her daughter.

"Why are we here for this, honey? Were you afraid to tell me? What did you think I was going to do? What do you plan on doing? I dread to think what your dad's going to say," she said and appeared to be ready to continue with more questions.

Tasha sat back, relaxing a little with her son in her arms feeding contently while she watched the exchange between mother and daughter. Deanna, understandably, tried to gain as much information as she could, all of the questions that any parent would want answering, who, where, when, why and how type of questions. Tasha didn't need to know all of that information and zoned in and out as she concentrated on feeding her son but came back into the conversation as Lizzie chipped in again.

"We thought because Tasha has had a baby recently maybe she could help Danielle decide what she wants to do."

Deanna glared across at Tasha and because of Lizzie's phrasing Tasha actually couldn't blame her making her stiffen with anxiety.

"That's not quite how it was." Smiled Tasha.

"Then how was it?" Deanna angrily accused Tasha somehow as she seemed to mimic her accent.

Ignoring the other woman's angst Tasha explained, "Lizzie was worried about Danielle who had confided in her, so came to me and when it became clear Danielle was confused and hadn't yet told you, Lizzie asked if they could bring you here. This is not my idea of fun and I feel awfully uncomfortable and out of place so if you want me to leave I will and if you want me to stay I will. I think Lizzie thought because I'd found myself unexpectedly pregnant and I am the most recently pregnant person she knows that I might be able to help. I did explain that my situation was entirely different, but Lizzie just wanted to help."

"Sorry. This is just one hell of a shock," said Deanna a little calmer now.

"I can imagine," agreed Tasha, and although she couldn't really imagine how Deanna felt she knew exactly how Danielle felt as she sat back again and the questions continued.

By the time Deanna had asked all of her immediate questions and received some answers she turned her attention to what her daughter was going to do next.

"Do you want to have the baby?" asked Deanna. "I'll support you if you do but this boy has to be responsible too. Him and his family, and you will have to accept that you are stuck with him as the father of your child forever," began Deanna with a shake of her head.

"He's rich but he's a deadbeat. They're not together now and he doesn't know about the baby," contributed Lizzie.

"This just gets better," cried Deanna loudly causing Connor to pout in shock as he prepared to cry.

Tasha sat him up and made faces at him before Danielle finally spoke. "Lizzie is right. His dad's an attorney and I think they would want to see the baby and stuff, but him, he probably won't be involved."

"Oh, Danielle," sighed her mother. "Have you thought about a termination?" she asked thoughtfully.

"Or adoption."

Lizzie's suggestion startled Tasha with the idea of carrying a baby to term and then just handing it over. She gripped Connor more tightly, maybe too tightly as he began to cry.

Comforting her son, Tasha stared disbelievingly as Lizzie continued talking and Connor continued crying.

"What about if my dad and Tasha adopted the baby?"

Everyone stared at Lizzie and suddenly Tasha understood why this had been orchestrated to include her and why the location chosen had been her home. Fortunately, Jim appeared at that exact moment and shot Lizzie down immediately,

"Elizabeth, this is not a litter of unwanted kittens you are rehoming and if Tasha and I were looking at increasing our family we would not need your assistance."

"But Daddy," protested Lizzie.

"No! This is not even a discussion we're going to have, although there is another one we need to have later," said Jim firmly before taking a seat next to Tasha where he reached over and took Connor. "Hey buddy. What's all the noise for?" He settled his son on his lap.

"I am sorry Deanna, so sorry for all of this," said Tasha, suddenly overwhelmed with a variety of feelings and emotions. "I think we've been played somewhat. That somehow the girls thought they'd found a perfect solution, but they really didn't think this through." She turned her attention to Danielle. "I am so sorry that you find yourself in this position but I can't make this right for you. You need to decide, with your mother, what happens next, whether you have the baby or not and if you do I will do anything I can to help and support you. We all will. But I can't adopt your baby. Imagine how hard that would be seeing him and knowing he's yours and yet he wouldn't be. How would you feel if you thought the way we parented was wrong to you? How would you not try to intervene? We don't do personal adoptions like this in the U.K. they're illegal I think and I can see why after today but if you want to do that then there must be lots and lots of prospective parents who would care for your baby if you have him and if you don't, well nobody here will think any less of you, but I don't think you can have it both ways, to give him up and yet keep him in your life."

"Thank you, all of you." Deanna turned to her daughter, "Come on, let's go home and we can talk some more."

"Can Lizzie come too?" asked Danielle.

"No, she can't," interrupted Tasha, her fury at her stepdaughter suddenly rising and threatening to burst free. "Lizzie and I need to have a conversation that won't wait."

Both Lizzie and Jim stared at Tasha but while Lizzie looked nervous Jim looked quite proud of his wife. She was obviously going to take his daughter to task for her insensitive and ill thought out plan and it was no more than she deserved.

"If there's anything we can do," Tasha offered as Deanna got to her feet and gestured for her daughter to do the same.

The door had barely shut behind them when Sandra appeared. The atmosphere was thick enough to cut so it was no surprise when Tasha turned to the other woman and gave her an escape. "Would you mind taking Connor for a little while? He's fed and clean, so if you want to pop back home or take a stroll."

Without a question or even an enquiring look, Sandra nodded. "Of course, we can go and see Mike."

With a slightly forced smile until she took the gurgling little boy from his father to strap him into his stroller Sandra could feel the tension and anxiety rising all around her and was relieved to be disappearing through the back of the house.

Turning, Tasha stared across at a slightly nervous looking Lizzie who attempted to speak, "I know you might be thinking that was a bit weird—"

"Weird?" asked Tasha in a high-pitched tone, then took several deep breaths before continuing. She was relieved that Lizzie didn't take her temporary silence as an opportunity to continue speaking because she was unsure what she might have done had Lizzie tried to speak and make excuses. "This is so much more than weird, Lizzie. I have never felt so embarrassed or uncomfortable in my whole life and you, you," she cried twice with a point of her finger to emphasise the point that this was Lizzie's doing. "You brought this into my home. If you'd been honest with me from the start I would probably have still facilitated today, but could have explained to you, in private why your well-intended idea was complete madness."

"Sorry." Lizzie looked suitably contrite, but for Tasha that simply wasn't enough, not this time because she was angry. Angrier than she could ever remember being and the apologies that were leaving Lizzie's lips were actually causing her annoyance to increase rather than reduce.

"No! That's not gonna cut it here, Lizzie. I have done everything since we first met to be something between a friend and a surrogate parent to you. To love, respect and support you and I thought that was reciprocal, but this just shows me how wrong I was. I am so angry with you that I can barely think straight and I'm more than a little hurt," Tasha said with a break in her voice now. "Danielle needs to find a solution she is happy with and whether that means adoption, a termination or keeping her baby it has to be her decision, not mine and certainly not yours. How dare you do this to her. To allow this stupid fucking plan to even register as a possibility," shouted Tasha becoming angrier as she continued.

"Tasha, baby, please don't swear," began Jim but he was soon cut off too.

"Swear! I am using every last ounce of self-control not to scream, shout and break things. You have no idea how dreadful I felt before I knew we'd been pencilled in as the new parents. I was embarrassed for both of them and myself, not to mention my own emotions at the predicament your friend finds herself in." She glanced at Jim whose eyes held understanding of what she was saying and the relevance of it regarding her past.

Briefly, it looked as though Jim was going to intervene, maybe even just pull Tasha in closer and comfort her, but that was the last thing she needed.

Tasha quickly turned back to Lizzie before she lost what little control she clung onto. "How do you think that would have panned out for Danielle, coming around here and seeing her baby growing up and every time wondering how it would have been if she'd kept it? Hating herself every time she missed out on a milestone. Resenting us all a little more every single time her baby called me Mommy or when she was excluded from family time or celebrations. Maybe in a moment of madness she could have blurted out the baby's true parentage and screwed up another life a little more. I have always made allowances for you, Lizzie; your age and innocence, your parent's overindulgence, but this goes beyond youthful naivety," Tasha told her with a sigh.

Jim stood, quite literally between the two of them and unsure who needed his support the most he reached out with both hands and grabbed a hand of each of them.

"I just wanted to make things okay for Danielle and her baby," Lizzie said, somehow still maintaining the fact she'd acted appropriately.

"And what about me, me and my baby, your brother?" Tasha almost screamed. "You know how tough I found being pregnant and dealing with motherhood and I love Connor, I wouldn't change anything now, we've talked about this, but that does not mean that I want another baby in eight months' time. Even if I did that would be down to me and your dad to decide when and how, not you. With the best will in the world my time with Connor would be compromised by the addition of another baby, especially one I hadn't carried, one I would feel the need to bond with so that he never ever felt second best. If we had decided to bring a new baby into our family we would prepare for that, but we didn't decide, you did." Tasha sounded calmer as tears began stinging the back of her eyes. "I am not the hired help, Lizzie. Here to make your life and the lives of *your people* easier and more convenient, to fit in with what you deem necessary. Or maybe I am, in your mind," she said with the first of her tears escaping now.

"Tash," began Lizzie before Jim pulled Tasha towards him and kissed the top of her head before she pulled away and stepped back.

"No! This is not okay and I am unsure if things will ever be okay again. Just when I think I am settled with people who love me for me, who respect and value me, I get shafted and used all over again and I have been used all of my life. I finally thought I'd found a place where I mattered, really mattered for me, for who I am not just what I can do or provide for someone else." Tears ran down her face quicker than her hands could wipe them away.

"Baby, I get that you're angry, so am I, but don't do this, not when you're hurt. Not like this," Jim pleaded, pulling her back to him, holding his wife a little tighter.

"Then you do it. You make this right if you think that's even a possibility," she snapped. "I'm going to check on *my* baby." Tasha pulled away from Jim's hold again as she overemphasised the word *my* and followed the route Sandra had taken with the slam of a door leaving Jim and Lizzie facing each other.

"Daddy, I didn't mean to make Tasha angry," Lizzie said, crying too as her father pulled her into the space his wife had just vacated.

"That may be so, sweetie, but Tasha's anger is not really the problem. The problem is how hurt she is. How you've hurt her by manipulating her the way you did," Jim explained. "She,

Tasha, has been manipulated all of her life for other people's gain and she thought she'd found a place, I thought she'd found a place too, here, with us where that wouldn't be the case, but now, you've kind of proven that's not the case. That's what she was saying."

"Oh, Daddy, I am so sorry. I never meant for it to be like this. I just thought because Danielle is too young to have a baby and a termination must be a horrible thing to go through. I get how scared Tasha was before Connor was born, but now she is the best mom I know, and I figured Danielle's baby would be lucky to have her like we all are. I love Tasha but she won't let me apologise, she won't let me speak even."

"Because she's angry and hurt. Let her calm down a while and then try again and if it makes you feel any better, she wouldn't be so angry or hurt if she didn't love you too." Jim pulled his daughter closer into his embrace to hug her tightly. "I love that you care enough about your friend to try and fix things, and you are right about Tasha and Connor, but if you ever pull a stunt like that again it won't be Tasha's anger you'll be dealing with, do we understand each other?"

"Yes, Daddy," she agreed.

Chapter Twenty-Eight

Waking up in London gave Tasha an unexpected thrill, even though it was only half past three in the morning and she was awake courtesy of jet lag. Making a cup of tea, Tasha didn't hear anyone follow her into her grandparent's kitchen.

"Tasha, I wondered who was down here," came her grandmother's voice.

"Sorry if I woke you. I can't sleep, jet lag, although, Jim and Connor are fast."

"Is Jim happy staying here? He looked a little uncomfortable." Celia smiled as Tasha added a second teabag to another cup.

"He's fine, Gran. He likes his own space and is used to staying in his own place or hotels of his choosing, but I think he understands that staying here with you makes more sense because it will allow us to see plenty of you. Dan is here and we can assess what's going on with him and Connor's needs will be met far easier in a home than a hotel room."

Tasha smiled across at her worried looking grandmother. What she'd said was true and once her grandparents had offered to put them up and Tasha had expressed her desire to stay with them Jim had cancelled the hotel booking he'd made.

"I can't believe how much he's changed in real life as opposed to via the internet," shrieked Celia, gesturing towards a photo of Connor on the fridge door.

"I know, it amazes me every day how much he's changed," smiled Tasha proudly.

"So, what happens with Dan? I can't deny how worried I am,

but I really can't forbid him from seeing your parents, can I?" asked a concerned Celia.

"No, of course not." Tasha sighed. "Jim would disagree though," she added, nervously toying with the ends of her hair before expanding. "He thinks Dan has to make a choice. That he can't have us, me, him and Connor, supporting him if he chooses to keep them in his life."

"How do you feel about that, Tasha?" asked her grandmother, clearly concerned for all of her grandchildren.

"Torn. I love Dan and I know just how manipulative Mum and Dad can be, but I don't understand what they have that could be used to manipulate him if he didn't want to build bridges with them. Jim is adamant that he can't have both of us, which I understand because he's my husband and loves me and has seen first-hand what lengths they'll go to in order to get cash. I'm struggling though, Gran. I don't know that I can cut Dan off and if he does cut them off at my say so, Jim's say so, whether that makes us as bad as them for manipulating him to do things we want."

"Oh, Tasha. I wish I could wave a magic wand for you, darling. When we cut ties with your mother it was the hardest thing we ever did, but it was for the best. Best for us and we hoped it would force her hand, but it just made her stubborn and more determined to prove us wrong. I think she still is, even now, after everything they've done. I wanted to save her. She is my only child. It was horrendous. You can't imagine cutting her off like that, but your grandfather was like Jim, straight choice, us or him. She chose him and we had to accept that, no matter how hard it was. That's not to say we didn't make mistakes. We failed you children, you especially and I will always regret that, we both will."

"It wasn't your fault, Grandma. Really it wasn't," reassured Tasha. "Travis says Dan is struggling to find a path, unlike Pippa and I know Mum would see that and use it to her advantage, especially with Dad guiding her from prison visits."

"I suppose."

"Dad asked me to let Mum see Connor when I visited him in prison," revealed Tasha to a stunned Celia.

"What? What did you say? What did Jim say?" Celia shook her head at the sheer nerve of such a request.

"I don't think I said anything. Jim, on the other hand, set him straight and told him it would never happen. Can we keep Jim's ideas about Dan to ourselves until I've spoken to Dan properly and got a handle on what's happening with him?"

"Of course, darling, but I should tell you that Jim may find an unlikely ally in your grandfather if he insists you cut Dan loose while he maintains a relationship with your parents."

"Great. The two of them barking orders," said Tasha with a stifled yawn.

"Tasha, are things okay, with you and Jim? I couldn't help but sense some tension last night."

"Things are fine between us, but not so much so with me and Lizzie." Tasha found it a relief tell her grandmother the details of her recent falling out with Lizzie.

"Oh dear, how awful. That poor girl, the pregnant one. Although it must be hard for Lizzie too."

"So, you think I was wrong to be angry with her? That I overreacted?" Tasha felt startled that her grandmother wouldn't be on her side.

"No, of course not. She hurt you. Her ill thought out actions hurt you and angered you, rightfully so. You shouldn't be taken for granted and used as a solution to other people's problems and mistakes, but I don't think that's entirely what she did."

"No?"

"No, darling. She can see how amazingly supportive you are of the people around you and if her friend had to be in this position I think Lizzie thought there was no better person to help her than you. More than that, she knows the mother you are to her and Philip and now to Connor and that was what she wanted for that poor unborn baby, but she got it all skewed in her mind and acted impulsively."

"But she never once thought of me in any of it."

"No. She didn't, and that was wrong. You were right in everything you said to her but there will come a point where you have to forgive if not forget. You know Jim will only allow you to punish his child for so long," her grandmother pointed out.

"Is that what I'm doing, punishing her?"

"Isn't it? The fact that she wanted to and could have come with you suggests you might be."

Tasha knew her grandmother had made several valid points as a long and loud yawn escaped her.

"Go back to bed, Tasha, before your son decides he's had enough sleep and makes the early hours his new breakfast time."

"Thanks, Grandma. Goodnight." Tasha offered her grandmother a kiss to the cheek and a warm and loving smile.

Once back upstairs, in the room she'd slept in on numerous occasions, although not on enough occasions if she was honest. Tasha smiled at the sight of Connor sleeping in a cot that her grandparents had bought especially for their great-grandson's visit. He was stretched out with his arms lying above his head. The dummy he'd previously had in his mouth was now cast aside leaving Connor's mouth open slightly, breathing gently. Suddenly, Connor began to make mutterings that in turn made Tasha smile. The mutterings were followed by a strange little growling sound that made Tasha let out a laugh that led to the baby stirring slightly.

"Ssh." She put the dummy back into her son's mouth, jiggling it slightly until he latched on and was sleeping soundly again.

Still smiling as she climbed into bed, Tasha jumped as Jim spoke, "Hey, baby, you okay?"

"Mmm, I couldn't sleep, jet lag, so I got up and had a cup of tea with my Grandma." She smiled at her husband's rested face.

"That's nice. What time is it?" Jim looked disorientated.

"Half-past four."

"Jeez, we need to pick better flights in future or we'll charter a plane and sleep all the way here."

"Sleep? You think if we chartered a plane we'd sleep, Mr Maybury?"

"Good point. Connor could sleep and we could fuck." Grinned Jim.

"You seem very lively this morning," Tasha told him, reaching up to stroke his hair.

"Do I indeed? What about you, honey?"

"Wide awake."

"In that case." Jim reached across and cupped one of Tasha's naked breasts. His thumb firmly stroked her nipple, bringing the nugget of flesh into a stiff peak.

Tasha let out a low moan of appreciation and arousal.

"And this is why we should have stayed in a hotel, Natasha. Your sister is sleeping in the room next door, your brother is opposite and your grandparent's are down the hall, oh, and our son is sleeping at the bottom of the bed, so you need to be quiet, baby or the next week is going to be very frustrating for you."

"And you," she retorted with a pout, making Jim laugh.

"Oh, honey, I can do quiet like you wouldn't believe, what about you?" He lowered his hand until it rested at the apex of her thighs.

Tasha spread her legs trying to tempt Jim to move closer.

"As eager as ever, Natasha," he teased as he began stroking her, gently and only on the outside to begin with and then after spreading her further, opening her up he found her already wet. "Oh, baby," he whispered against her ear.

"James," she moaned in response and was rewarded with two fingers entering her. "Yes, like that," she encouraged, making him laugh in her ear now.

As soon as his fingers began to rotate in the way she loved so much Tasha cried out loudly.

"Oh dear, baby," teased Jim. "That quiet plan isn't quite working is it?" He removed his hands.

"No." She whined the single word response. Her desperation only served to amuse a smirking Jim. "You are such a fucking arse," she seethed and immediately found herself flat on her back with Jim over her and poised between her legs.

"You really are forgetting how this works, Natasha. Do you need a reminder?" he asked her darkly then thrust into her roughly.

"James," she whispered, already feeling the tell-tale signs of arousal gathering low down in her belly as she moved against him, arching her back when he hit a particularly sensitive spot.

"Oh no, Tasha. This is for me, not you, do you understand?" he asked with a dominant and dark glint in his eye.

"James," she pleaded, only partially hoping to dissuade him

315

from his plan of frustration for her causing her to question why she wasn't solely focused on chasing the end game.

"No way, Tasha." He rotated his hips deliberately, so that her own body began to conspire against her. "I said, do you understand?"

"Yes," she replied, equally excited and frustrated as she tried to distract herself with thoughts of anything other than sex and orgasm.

"Good girl." Smiled Jim as he began to move inside her, gently rocking the bed that was fortunately quiet and creak free. "I told you we should have kept the hotel booking, didn't I?" he asked as a finger and thumb created a pincer grip on her nipple that eagerly crested, begging for further stimulation they both knew would only push her closer to release.

Biting down into her bottom lip, Tasha managed to stifle her groans before replying to Jim. "Yes, we should have kept the hotel booking," she admitted in broken pants but knew that once her grandmother had asked them to stay, for them to get the most from their visit she'd wanted to stay in their home and she'd wanted Jim and Connor to stay there with her.

Tasha used every technique she knew to prevent her climax from taking over and was relieved that Jim wasn't going to torture her in an extended fashion, forcing her to fail in her attempts to avoid coming around him. They hadn't done this for a while. Jim hadn't done this for a while, the whole, *this is for me not you* thing. He had actually focused on her needs and pleasure regardless of her behaviour while she'd been pregnant and had been one great big ball of sexual need for the majority of the nine months. Tasha realised she was sorely out of practice at restraint as the familiar burning sensation filled the whole of her pelvic area, but then Jim stilled as he emptied himself into her forcefully.

"And now I'm a fucking arse," he told her before leaning down to kiss her nose and was then pulling free of her to roll onto his back. "What are you thinking?" asked Jim turning slightly to study Tasha's expression.

"I'm wondering whether we should have another baby," she replied, startling Jim if his expression was anything to go by.

"Really? I thought you'd decided to wait a couple more years," he said seriously until she began to laugh at him. "What? What's funny? Tasha!" he said full of irritation. "I don't appreciate you springing family planning changes on me and then laughing at me."

"Sorry," she said genuinely, sensing his confusion and irritation. "I was thinking, before, when you were being a fucking arse that we, you hadn't done that for a while, and never when I was pregnant."

"Ah, I see your point but maybe next time I wouldn't be so considerate." His tone and expression were unnervingly flat, causing Tasha to feel concerned at the validity of Jim's threat. "Except we both know that I couldn't deny you anything when you were carrying our baby and as you pointed out on dozens, hundreds of occasions I had done it to you, so it was only right that I gave you what you needed."

"Mmm, that's true. Maybe we should have dozens of kids so you'll always pander to my every whim," she suggested rolling onto her front to face him.

"Oh, baby, you wouldn't know what to do if I was permanently pandering to your whims. After all, I think I'm a far better judge of what you need than you are."

"You're probably right, Mr Maybury. So, we'll hold fire on baby number two."

"Sounds like a plan. If you're a good girl we may even find a time and a place where you don't have to be quite so quiet. But we, you, me and Dan will talk this morning and see if we can't figure out what Dan needs and why he is giving your parents the time of day."

"I'm a little afraid of his answers." Tasha looked and sounded petrified never mind a little afraid.

"You and me both, baby, but let's see what we're up against first. Try and get some sleep and when it's a more reasonable hour I'll call home and check on Philip and Lizzie."

"I wish he'd come with us." Sighed Tasha. "I'm very worried about him, him and Juan."

"I know, honey, and I really do appreciate you inviting him to join us here, but he needs to see what his life might be like without Juan in it and that would have been distorted here, with us," said Jim.

"I know, but I still can't believe he and Juan are going for a temporary break to consider *all options*, especially Juan and that bloody ridiculous *cousin come wife* idea." Tasha rolled away so her back was facing Jim.

"No, nor me, but we need to let them make their own decisions." Jim pulled her close against him. Holding her gently, hoping to ease some of her tension and worries about and for everyone else.

"How? How do you do that? Let them make their own decisions? What if they make really stupid decisions that are obviously wrong? I won't ever manage to do that with Connor." She sighed with an overwhelming feeling of uncertainty as she thought of her baby wanting to make his own choices, especially the wrong ones.

"You will. We'll do it together, unless he makes you cry and then I will kick his ass." Jim smiled, kissing Tasha's bare shoulder. "I think Lizzie felt a little pushed out when you didn't extend the invitation to her." Jim sounded slightly nervous to be bringing the subject of Lizzie up as she was still a bone of contention after the fiasco of Danielle's pregnancy meeting.

"Jim." Tasha sighed, rolling over to face him again, "Philip is having a really tough time and that is why I invited him to come with us. Lizzie is not having a tough time, well, except one of her own making and I didn't exclude her for any other reason than that."

"Baby, I love you and I get your anger and hurt but you can't hold this against Lizzie forever and you are the adult." He avoided the temptation to point out that Lizzie was his child and he wouldn't have her punished for one mistake indefinitely. He also stopped short of reminding her of her altercation with Abby the day after they got married. Tasha had correctly accused his sister-in-law of holding a grudge against a child, although he couldn't deny his daughter's crime against Tasha was far greater than the one against Abby.

"Yes, I'm the adult, but maybe you need to tell Lizzie that, not me. You might want to remember that she's hardly a little girl though." She pouted immaturely.

Jim said nothing, he just stared at her until after replaying some of her grandmother's words she continued to speak.

"I just thought the people I had around me now loved me and respected me enough not to play me that way. I just feel, I dunno, used, like I'm not valued like I thought I was. Shit! I sound like a stupid kid myself now, but I am hurt, Jim. No thought or consideration was given to me in that whole thing. Like she was adding some extra duty to an employee's list of responsibilities. I know it would have involved you too, and Connor and Danielle's baby but I honestly think Lizzie thought if I said yes it was signed and sealed and then that would be my life, providing Danielle with a get out of jail card but at the expense of..."

"Your own freedom and liberty," finished Jim.

"Yes. I'm struggling to get past the fact that Lizzie thought of Danielle, the baby, even Deanna before me. She considered their needs and what was best for them, but me, I didn't even get the most fleeting of thoughts and that hurts but it pisses me off too," Tasha admitted then went further in her admission. "I have no idea how I remained as calm as I did. It took all of my strength not only not to say some awful and hurtful things to Lizzie, but I really did have a near overpowering urge to slap her really, really hard and I am not a violent person. I hate violence."

"I got it, everything you've said, really I do, and I don't think you wanting to slap Lizzie and say hurtful things is a real concern because you didn't act on it, but I won't let you make this a bigger issue than it needs to be and you're holding onto it a little too tightly. So, pushing Lizzie away has to end, you're going to have to forgive her."

"I know," Tasha admitted with a loud exhale as she realised that her grandmother had been spot on about her husband only allowing her to remain angry at Lizzie for so long. "I'll text her later, offer an olive branch, okay?"

"Good girl." Smiled Jim, leaning down to kiss Tasha gently on the nose again making her smile, too.

"Thank you for allowing me let off steam and being a spoilt brat about it."

"You weren't, honey, but Lizzie made a mistake, no more, a huge one I know, but we've all done that. Now, sleep."

Chapter Twenty-Nine

Breakfast was lively; Paul was trying, a little too hard, to be the host with the most and possibly building bridges with Jim who was trying as hard to be receptive to Paul's friendly behaviour. Connor was gurgling loudly as he had the undivided attention of both Celia and Pippa. Only Tasha and Dan remained quiet.

"Tash, did I tell you that I might be coming out to The States for a shoot? Susie reckons young Brits in the U.S. will make a fantastic feature for the store and gain valuable publicity," said Pippa excitedly.

"Susie always reckoned there was a gap in the market for U.K. style across the pond and I believe the store is looking to merge with a U.S. chain, so it makes sense. You can stay with us when you come over, if you get as far as L.A. if you want, can't she?" Tasha turned to Jim.

"Sure, you can. You can even get up at three in the morning when Connor decides it's time to get up and play." Laughed Jim.

"I'd hate to deprive you both of that," replied Pippa as Connor reached up and tugged a handful of his aunt's hair.

"I think you've offended my son." Grinned Jim before Dan began to make his excuses to leave.

"Dan, can we have a chat?" asked Tasha nervously.

"We? Which we and what about?" Dan sounded offhand and suspicious, but Tasha detected nerves too.

"Me and you, and Jim." There was no way Jim would be excluded from this conversation. "Just a chat about everything, stuff, life."

"Do I have a choice?" Dan's offhand tone went direct to terse, gaining Jim's full attention and his intervention.

"Of course you have a choice," snapped Jim, "I mean, it's not like you're a child, is it? You're an adult, a man, responsible for your own choices and actions." Jim's words had been chosen deliberately and as Tasha glanced at her grandparents she could see they'd picked up on their meaning, but had Dan? "Are you free for the three of us to talk, to catch up, or not? If you are let's do it and if you're not tell us when you will be and we'll do it then."

"Fine, what do you want?" Dan was going out of his way to be awkward and prickly, which was very un-Dan like, but that was before he'd become involved with their parents again.

"Want? I want my wife to be happy and not worried sick about you, so how about you lose the attitude and think about how you want this to go down and we will talk later, at dinner." Jim got to his feet as if he was dealing with a business issue then turned to Tasha. "Baby, let's go and get ready and we'll spend the day with Connor. Maybe we could go to the zoo."

"I thought we were talking to Dan now," replied Tasha confused.

"We were, but I think he needs some time to order his thoughts, so if you'll all excuse us." With a smile for Pippa and Celia, Jim lifted Connor up into his arms and strode from the room leaving Tasha staring at her family members looking at her.

"What the fuck is his problem?" snapped Dan venomously. "He is not my dad and I don't see why I have to put up with his shit when you're the one who married him, not us," Dan told his oldest sister before leaping over the mark she didn't think he'd ever overstep. "You go on about how manipulative our parents were, what awful people they are, how they used us, used you and took advantage and yet you appear to have married a man who knocks their controlling ways into oblivion."

Without a first thought, never mind a second one she raised her hand and struck Dan's face with her open palm, hard, loud and judging by the way he held his cheek, painfully so.

"How dare you! Don't you ever compare my husband to

them. He is controlling because he loves me, me and Connor. He wants to make me happy which means taking care of us all." She trembled with sadness and anger that doubled when she saw her brother throw his eyebrows to the heavens as if to dispute her claims. "He has made me a better person. He accepts me with all of the crap I come with courtesy of them and he saved all of us from our wonderful parents. He bankrolled a legal team, P.R. everything to allow us to be free of them. They prostituted me for their own ends, beat us all, me more than you and never ever loved us, so don't compare my husband to those people. There is nothing he won't do to keep us all safe which is why we're here, to find out what the fuck you're doing allowing them back into your life, after everything they've done. Potentially you'll let them in to all of our lives. So, we'll see you at dinner," Tasha told her brother and left the room where her grandmother said nothing as Pippa glared at Dan and muttered curses at him.

Paul was the only one who spoke calmly. "Dan, she loves you, we all do, but we're scared that you're going to get drawn into their web and swallowed up. I know Jim and I haven't always seen eye to eye, but I'm with him on this. You need to keep away from them, while you can. Look what they did to Nat, they took money for dirt on her, dirt they'd facilitated and then your father tried to murder her, for cash and your mother had to have known what was going on. It's no wonder she took exception to you comparing Jim to them. He's done nothing but love her and take care of her so you should apologise."

Dan said nothing and left with a slam of the front door.
****

They were just walking away from the meerkats that had been Tasha's favourites, especially the babies, although, smiling, Jim realised that every enclosure they'd visited so far had been Tasha's favourite, especially the babies making him realise that motherhood really had changed his wife.

They both turned to look for the source of a voice they could hear calling her name.

"You are kidding me." Sighed Jim disbelievingly as they both saw Gerry and Kara walking towards them. Gerry held the hand of the toddler at his side and Kara pushed her empty pushchair nearby.

"Sorry," said Tasha with an apologetic smile, not that she'd known they'd be visiting the same zoo on the same day.

"Tash, how the devil are you?" cried Gerry. "I didn't even know you were over here." He pulled her to him and hugged her warmly with his free arm. "Hi, Jim." Gerry turned to face the other man before looking down into the pushchair and smiling down at the little boy gurgling up at him. "Hiya, matey, how are you?"

Kara looked on uncomfortably until Tasha turned to face her and with a smile simply said, "Hi Kara, how are you?"

"Erm—good—fine, thanks," she stammered nervously. "How are you, you look really well, motherhood must agree with you."

"Thanks, I think so, unless it's three in the morning. We were just going to get a drink, would you like to join us?" Tasha surprised everyone else with the invitation she'd extended.

Sitting around a wooden picnic table outside the cafe Tasha wasted no time in using Gerry's possible knowledge to her advantage.

"How are your parents?" She liked them, always had and was genuinely interested in their wellbeing.

"They're fine, thanks. They ask about you all the time and were thrilled to hear about Connor," Gerry replied with a smile.

"Connor?" Kara sounded annoyed as she watched her daughter standing over a sleeping Connor repeating the words *baby, baby* over and over.

"Yes." Tasha frowned in confusion at her former friend's unusual interest in her son's name. "Connor."

"I knew you'd had a little boy, I just wasn't aware of his name. That's what Gerry wanted to call Lottie if she'd been a boy, Connor" announced Kara and without even risking a sideways glance towards her husband Tasha knew he was glaring with a dark and angry stare.

"Then he has very good taste," replied Tasha in a voice that was just a little too high pitched, betraying her nervousness. "Anyway, Gerry, back to your parents, do they still live next door?" She had fond memories of the house next to her family home, identical in construction, yet so, so different. It had been filled with love and goodness rather than hatred and evil.

"Yeah, for now anyway. It's up for sale. They're finally making a move out of town slightly. Why do you ask? Or shall I just talk all things Dan?"

"Sorry," said Tasha sincerely. "That's why we've come over, Dan."

"I did wonder. Look I don't know much, Tash. Just what my mum's said and seen and from the fleeting conversations I've had with Dan. He has been visiting your mum, a couple of times a week. He does some shopping, tidies the garden and spends time with her. I believe he went to visit your dad with her last week."

"Oh no." Tasha sighed as Jim intervened.

"You believe?" Jim hoped to gain all of the facts he could.

"Yeah, Tasha's mum told me. Dan was there and didn't dispute it, but he looked really uncomfortable."

"Have you seen much of him?" Tasha's worry was increasing with each new detail.

"Not really. After you got married and he came back home I saw him socially about once a month. I had a show at a museum and asked him to help with setting it up and introduced him to the chef who was catering it. The chef offered him some help and guidance and he worked with him for about six months and then he became unreliable and the chef *let him go* and that coincided with him always having an excuse or other plans when I asked him to come out. I was worried about him, I even wondered—"

"Gerry!" interrupted Kara with a warning tone.

"Kara!" he snapped back. "I told you I'd tell Tash when I saw her and to be honest I didn't want to do this over the phone, but I met up with Pip a few weeks ago and she was worried too. I was going round to see him next time he was at your mum's and then I was going to call you," he said to Jim. "I was worried that it might be drugs or something, Princess," said Gerry sadly.

"Fuck!" cried Tasha, ignoring Gerry's term of endearment.

"Tasha, there's no need for that in front of children," Jim chastened making Gerry smile.

Tasha continued, "He became friends with Travis, who works for Jim and is kind of extended family. Travis is worried about him and reckons he's disconnected from everything. That he doesn't feel as though he fits in anywhere right now."

"I'd say Travis is spot on from what I've seen and heard and you're really not going to like this, Liam is another regular visitor."

"Baby, I think our conversation with your brother is more necessary than we thought." With a rough push of his hand through his hair, Jim sighed.

"Sorry I can't say something you want to hear. He and Deb remained in touch, didn't they?" Gerry looked across at Kara.

"Yes, she was genuinely fond of him and they got along well, even after they decided to cool things before he came out to visit you," Kara said with a sincere smile. "Deb knew you disapproved of her because of me and Dan didn't want you to feel awkward or uncomfortable so suggested they had a break, but stayed friends which seemed to suit both of them. When he came back from America they reconciled briefly, but Dan had changed, grown up a little shall we say and Deb found it hard to juggle Dan, college and her part-time job, especially when Dan was intent on partying hard every weekend. He was still meeting with Jake until he moved away and he and Gerry met up every couple of weeks. Deb and Dan decided what they'd had was probably over but still maintained a friendship and at that stage Dan was essentially still the same Dan. He changed a little after you were hurt and was so angry with your parents and the world in general which made him become a bit more of a loner."

Gerry nodded and interjected, "We went out when he first came back and he was wound so tightly he was just waiting for an excuse to explode and that excuse came in the shape of a guy in a club who was rucking with his girlfriend. Dan intervened and pummelled this guy to shit, but it wasn't him he was punching it was your dad and Liam. The things he shouted at him weren't about him they were about you, your parents, Liam and Dan's own guilt and it was only Jerome Stewart that kept him from being charged."

"James," whimpered Tasha fighting her desperate urge to cry for the pain and suffering her brother had endured, endured alone and without her even knowing about it. "Did you know?"

"About the charges?" he asked with a confirming nod of his head. "But I wasn't going to worry you until I knew there was something to worry about and courtesy of Jerome Stewart and one of his colleagues there was nothing to worry about," he told her flatly.

"You still should have told me," Tasha insisted but one look at her husband's face suggested he disagreed. "What are we going to do with Dan?" The wobble had returned to her voice.

"Hey baby, we've got this, okay?" Jim knelt at his wife's side. He brushed the hair that had fallen from her ponytail behind her ears and kissed her gently before turning to Gerry and Kara. "I can't say I was thrilled to bump into you guys initially, but I'm very glad we did."

"Understandable." Kara smiled a little awkwardly. "We kind of share a pretty mixed up history," she added as she agreed with her daughter that Connor was indeed a *baby*.

"Then you went and got yourself held bloody hostage and I think that was the final straw for Dan." Gerry sighed. "He came back after your wedding and knew you were safe and happily married and then pregnant, but he couldn't get beyond all you'd endured from birth right up until that point."

"What do you mean, couldn't get beyond it?"

"Every time we spoke he would talk about you. Kara and I and Deb would ask how you were doing, how your pregnancy was, anything and everything, and even if you and I had been in touch I'd still ask Dan and Pippa. Pip would be all gushing about everything, but Dan would revert back to everything you'd been through. He was melancholy and volatile, but still the same Dan we all knew and then he went to see your mother. I think to get some answers..."

"And?" asked Jim taking a seat between Tasha and Gerry.

"It went downhill from there. Within days he changed and removed himself from us all, the people who cared and his contact with her increased before your dad was sent home and since then Liam has reappeared on the scene," Gerry said with dread in his voice. "I tried my damnedest to keep him safe, Tash, but somehow I let you down, again, sorry," he said with just sadness now.

"Hey," Tasha reassured him as she moved so she was kneeling on the hard floor at Gerry's feet with her hands holding his that rested in his lap. "You have nothing to be sorry about. You did everything you could, and it was never your responsibility. Dan was never your responsibility and neither was I but you got me out of there and contributed to them financially to ensure I stayed free of them. You loved me, even when I was pregnant with another man's baby. You paid for an abortion, and you held my hand, literally and metaphorically," she said, and then laughed quietly. "You even endured the disapproving looks and comments at the clinic when I just cried and they took that to mean I wanted your baby and you were forcing me to get rid of it. You did more for more than was reasonable to expect and I am grateful. I will remain so, eternally." There was a break in her voice and both her and Gerry seemed oblivious to the presence of Kara, Lottie, Connor and Jim.

Chapter Thirty

Returning home, Tasha was relieved to find that the house was empty.

"I think the zoo has worn our boy out." Jim smiled down at his son who was lying in his father's arms sleeping soundly.

"I think it has."

"I'll take him up." Jim headed straight for the stairs.

Tasha watched him leave and wondered whether she should bring up the topic of their son's name. Her choice of name. A name it turned out was one she shared with Gerry. A shared name she had no idea existed until earlier that day. With a deep breath and a shrug, Tasha followed Jim, stopping at the threshold to the bedroom where Jim was lying their son down gently as he spoke to him.

"Take it easy, son. Just have yourself a nice sleep full of happy dreams, okay?" He gently kissed his son's head.

The sight of big, scary, masculine Jim turning into sweet, gentle, loving Jim never failed to warm Tasha from the inside out but watching him today almost took her breath away.

"Hey baby, you eavesdropping again?" He turned with a smile at the sight of her watching him.

"No," she protested making her husband laugh at her denial.

"Are you okay?" Jim was a little more serious as he took in his wife's sad and slightly haunted expression.

"I really don't know. This is all such a mess, everything," she began, tears filling her eyes.

Jim was already closing the distance between them and pulling her closer until she was engulfed in his arms and his embrace. "You want to talk?"

"I hit Dan."

"What? When?" asked a startled Jim at his wife's revelation.

"This morning. He was being a bit of a dick about things. Us. You. I smacked him across the face. At the time I thought he deserved it but the truth is I can't hit people because they say things I don't like or I'm no better than my parents or Liam."

Tasha found herself pulled down into a sitting position on the bed so Jim could see her, to calm her down and to talk to her. To make her listen. She was right that she couldn't go around hitting people because the words they uttered offended her in some way, but then he knew whatever Dan had said, whatever had literally forced her hand would have been about him. The idea that she was still looking for clues and pointers confirming she was no better than her parents, that she had somehow inherited their worst characteristics really did piss him off, enough that it made him mad, but more with them than her.

"You are nothing like them, and whilst you shouldn't have hit Dan I am sure he must have provoked you, but I also know you'll apologise and always regret that you did it."

With no argument offered, just a nod of her head Jim breathed an almost silent sigh of relief.

"Was there a reason you came up here?" He hoped to lighten the atmosphere and his wife's mood.

"I just kind of followed you," she admitted making Jim smile with an arched brow.

"Mmm, I wonder why you'd do that, Mrs Maybury."

"What? No," Tasha cried innocently then admitted, "although, as we're home alone and you did say that we might find an opportunity..."

"Then me, you and your mighty fine ass should see exactly what opportunity we have and then we might just have time to discuss our son's name before everyone else gets back and we set about sorting everything out and making you smile again."

Tasha was lying on her side, her back pressed firmly into Jim's front. The feel of gentle kisses on her shoulder made goosebumps rise all over her body until she was tingling with sensation which she knew was ridiculous, even for her as her breathing was barely back to normal after a short but rather frantic round of afternoon sex. As an arm reached around her middle and a hand skimmed up her body, pausing before reaching her breasts the sound of a deep and shaky moan sounded around them, confirming that not only was sensation coursing through her body but arousal was rising to the occasion too.

"So greedy, baby," Jim whispered against Tasha's ear as his hand continued its journey north, only to pass between her breasts inciting a disgruntled groan to leave her lips.

Laughter was Jim's response to that, but he did at least skim her nipples as his hand travelled south again; past her ribs, naval, belly and then slowed as it headed for her sex that was quivering with expectation and moistening once more with anticipation. Once Jim's thumb stroked her tattoo Tasha instinctively spread her legs, hoping to entice him in.

"You need more, honey?"

"Yes, lots more," Tasha replied to her husband's amusement.

"I don't know whether I should feel insulted that I don't seem to keep you satisfied." He laughed but did allow his fingers to dip lower until they were coated in her arousal that he was spreading along her length.

"You always satisfy me," Tasha assured him as two fingers seemed to spear her, causing her body to quake and clench around the digits that were beginning to stroke and arouse her. "But I can't get enough of you," she whined as Jim hit a particularly sensitive spot inside her.

"Ssh," Jim whispered against her ear when another, louder cry left his wife's mouth as he allowed his thumb to skirt around her clitoris that was over sensitised courtesy of their earlier bout of love making. "You need not to wake our baby up or you'll be anything but satisfied."

As if siding with his father Connor chose that exact moment to release a single cry before suckling loudly on his dummy.

With fresh arousal coating his fingers with every movement he made, Jim could feel just how close Tasha was to her release.

"James," she muttered between gasps and seriously considered biting down into the pillow her head was resting on because there was no doubt in her mind that she wouldn't be able to remain quiet when she came and as Connor had already been asleep for over an hour there was every chance she'd wake him up.

"I know, baby," Jim replied as he removed his hand from Tasha's body to adjust their positions.

With a hand resting between her shoulders Jim pressed gently on Tasha's back until her behind moved closer into his body, into his groin and erection that was eagerly seeking out her heat. After a minor adjustment of her leg Jim was able to easily slide into Tasha and maintain their spooned position.

"I love holding you like this," Jim told her hoarsely as he began to gently move against her.

Reaching behind her, Tasha cupped a hand around Jim's own thigh, confirming her own love of this position. The way Jim held her, as he was now, one hand laced through her hair, gently tugging and teasing her flowing strands while the other was draped across her hip, still dipping between her thighs to further stimulate and arouse her, but it was more than that. She thought of this position as being intimate, not just sexually intimate, but emotionally too. As he held her, Jim kissed her shoulder, neck and ear that he was also to whisper in, coaxing and encouraging her to find her release that really was speeding towards her. With every stroke, kiss and thrust he delivered she was edging ever closer to the point of no return until suddenly, with almost no warning the world around her stilled as a fierce burn radiated out through her whole body until it felt as though her toes were curling, her hair was standing on end while her cries were muffled by the pillow she was chewing on and that she imagined currently resembled the world's largest marshmallow.

A muted giggle left her lips at the image she must have presented with a face full of pillow as Jim rolled away and waited for her to turn to face him.

"So, Connor?" Jim asked.

"What about him? I think he's still fast," Tasha replied, confused slightly by her husband's question.

"Now may not be the best time for the smart mouth, honey," he warned but continued. "Connor, his name. Maybe you could explain to me how our son ended up with a name chosen by your ex-boyfriend."

"It really wasn't chosen by him. Not for us, for our son," Tasha began. "I swear to you that until today I had no idea Gerry had any feelings about the name Connor. You know we'd discussed children's names and had agreed on Lottie in principal, but Connor was never mentioned, not by either of us. You know when I was pregnant it took months to even come up with Connor as an option."

Jim made no reply for long, long seconds, maybe minutes before he nodded his head. "I want to believe that, Tasha, but it's a huge coincidence that he wanted to call his son Connor and we have. You called our son by the same name and although you and he discussed names you never came up with Connor together."

"I understand that but I had never considered that name until I saw that old film about that immortal guy who was called Connor."

Jim nodded again, but even if he'd planned on saying anything else it was at that second Connor himself decided to add his own thoughts, or at least his own cries to proceedings.

****

Tasha was in the kitchen helping Celia prepare dinner while Jim and Pippa watched some home video show on TV and laughed far too much leaving Paul to play with Connor, which he did proudly if it was possible to play pee-po with pride. Tasha's message alert vibrated in her pocket and retrieving it she frowned at a message from Dan.

<Can we talk, alone? Just you and me, no Jim. I won't be home for dinner so meet me somewhere. The park, the bandstand? Please x>

With a sigh Tasha replied immediately.

<Of course, half an hour x>

Now all she needed to do was to find an excuse to get out,

alone.

"Oh no," cried Celia looking into the cupboard. "I've run out of stock cubes. I knew there was something."

"I can fetch you some," offered Tasha eagerly.

"What's up?" called Paul from his position behind his hands before crying, "Boo," to Connor who was laughing heartily.

"Stock cubes," replied Celia as if it was some kind of unmitigated disaster.

"I can fetch you some," repeated Tasha but was somehow ignored again.

"Can't you manage without them?" asked Paul between his next pee-po.

"I suppose, but it's not the same," Celia insisted.

"For the third bloody time, I can fetch some," an irate and nervous Tasha shouted loudly.

Jim and Pippa both looked up with concerned expressions at Tasha's overreaction to the stock cube situation. Paul frowned between his wife and granddaughter before returning his attention to his great-grandson who was becoming irritated at waiting so long for the next round of pee-po.

"Well, if you're sure, Tasha," said Celia nervously, unsure how her granddaughter might react.

"Of course. Can I take your car?" she asked her grandmother who immediately nodded. "Thanks. I'll be as quick as I can." Tasha grabbed the car keys and her bag then attempted to get to the door avoiding Jim.

"Hey, baby." Jim followed her to the door. "You forgot my kiss, and Connor's."

Stretching up she kissed her husband gently and then added a second chaste kiss. "Pass that one on to Connor, please." She attempted to leave again.

"What's going on, honey?" Jim held Tasha's arm.

"Nothing, except the world is going to end without stock cubes, so I need to go."

"You're lying to me, Tasha," he said flatly causing her to sigh at the realisation she'd been caught out, but she didn't have the time or energy to explain herself.

"I will explain when I get back, I promise. This is just

something that I need to do, me and Dan, alone. He text me."

"Tasha," he began and she knew he'd be relentless now and insist on accompanying her so was relieved when Paul called to her husband.

"Jim, where are Connor's clean clothes, he's been sick."

That distracted Jim enough that he loosened his hold on Tasha giving her the opportunity to run to Celia's car, hopefully before he could catch up with her.

****

It took about twenty minutes to get to the park where Dan had asked to meet and as she sat in the car park with a perfect view of the band stand, Tasha text Lizzie, ignoring the messages from Jim and Pippa.

<Hey Lizzie, just a quick hello. I know things have been strained between us, but I need you to know that I do love you. I am still angry and hurt by what you did to me with Danielle, but I love you and you should never forget that. Hope you're ok and we'll see you next week x>

Looking up, Tasha saw a figure, slightly obscured by the piece of modern art that had been erected in front of the band stand but assuming it was Dan she got out of the car and headed over.

Chapter Thirty-One

Back at her grandparents' house Jim had just finished washing and changing Connor who had been sick, although he thought that was a serious understatement when he considered just how much vomit could come from such a small person. He wondered whether it was due to the heat at the zoo, but then reasoned that the heat in London on a good summer's day was several degrees cooler than in LA and Connor had been protected from the sun so maybe it was just a bug or the travelling.

"There you go, buddy," Jim told his son, leaning down to kiss him as he lay on the bed he and Tasha were sharing. Connor was still a little whiny and restless but Jim figured he'd probably got a tummy ache.

Carrying him back downstairs Jim was surprised to find Dan walking through the front door, alone.

"Where's Tash?" the younger man asked.

"I was about to ask the same thing," Jim replied concerned.

"What? We're talking tonight, right?" Dan stood confused as Celia appeared in the hall.

"Oh, it's you, Dan. I thought it was Tasha back, although you're late," she noted as the clock in the hall struck the half hour. "Are you feeling better, my darling?" she asked turning her attention to Connor, taking him from Jim.

"What?" asked Dan, agitation clear in his voice as the two men were left alone.

"Where's my wife?" asked Jim suspiciously. "If you have done anything to endanger her..." his voice trailed off.

"What? What are you on about?" Dan turned to hang his coat up.

"You text her and she's gone to meet you, just the two of you, ringing any bells?" Jim felt a near overpowering urge to punch the young man he'd pulled to face him and now stood toe to toe with, never mind slap him like Tasha had. The slap she'd felt so guilty about.

"I have no clue what you're talking about. I haven't text Tash today and made no plans to meet. I missed my bus and that's why I'm late but was expecting you and her as the welcoming committee."

Jim frowned and although the other man's words seemed genuine, they couldn't be unless Tasha was outright lying, which he didn't think she was.

"You don't believe me? Fine, check my phone." Dan reached into his coat pocket, then his jeans and finally emptied his bag. "Shit!"

"What?" Every nerve in Jim's body screamed that this was bad news.

"My phone's not here. I had it earlier when I saw..."

"Who?" asked Jim angrily. "Who did you see?"

"Mum, I saw our mum."

"And have you used or seen the phone since?" Jim sounded much calmer than he felt as panic and dread began to settle in the pit of his stomach.

"No. Shit!"

"What?" Jim's guts churned again.

"When I left her, Mum was waiting for Liam."

"This just gets fucking better," shouted Jim before storming back into the house. "Sorry folks, Dan has lost his phone, but we think his mother has it. She was waiting for Liam when Tasha received a text from who she thought was Dan. Nobody knows what the message said, just that Dan wanted to meet Tasha alone, so if you wouldn't mind watching Connor, Dan and I are going to find my wife and while we're gone, we'll be having a chat, just the two of us." Jim stared the younger man down and found little contentment in him looking away first.

"They won't hurt her, will they?" asked Celia. "There'd be no point..." she trailed off knowing there had often been no point in people hurting Tasha but they'd done it anyway.

"Go," called Paul urgently as Connor was sick again, over Pippa this time. "We'll deal with Connor, you just go and bring my girl home," said Paul to Jim.

****

Half an hour later Jim was pulling up in front of Tasha's childhood home in his hire car and thought that from the outside the house looked a dark and intimidating place even though it looked just like the other houses. Dan knocked on the door, but there was no answer. He knocked again, louder this time then next door's front door opened. Jim knew the man standing there was Gerry's dad as they were almost identical.

"Dan, you okay there?"

"No. We're looking for Tash. Long story but she thought she was meeting me but we think it may be Mum or Liam she's meeting. Sorry, this is Jim, Tasha's husband. This is Keith, Gerry's dad."

"Hi," said Jim impatiently.

"Pleasure. Your mum went out about forty minutes ago, I only know because I heard her laughing. I think she'd been drinking and I don't know if she was with Liam, but she was with someone."

"Thanks, Keith, any idea which way she went?" asked Jim.

"Yeah, left out of the gate, so I assume she was cutting through the park because there's nothing else down that way," replied Keith.

"Thanks again. Dan?" Jim called. "Do we walk or drive?"

"Walk, there's no vehicular access from this end," said Keith answering for Dan. "Let us know Tasha's safe."

"Will do," replied Jim, already exiting through the gate followed by Dan.

"Why don't you tell me exactly what's been going on with you," said Jim as an order more than a request.

As they swiftly moved towards the park, Dan began to fill in all of the gaps for Jim. He explained that once Tasha was safe and well, married to Jim and found out she was pregnant with Connor he'd been unable to get past all of the things Tasha had endured at other people's hands and all to keep other people safe; him, Pippa, Lizzie, Juan. He had, as Gerry had revealed, become a bit of a fighter and always threw punches intended for the likes of his father and Liam. Eventually, Dan had decided he needed answers so went to see his mother who'd played the role of manipulated victim to perfection until she'd sucked Dan in. She had asked for cash from Dan but he hadn't had any to give her as all of his funds beyond any wages he earned went through his grandparents meaning he couldn't syphon money off to give to her. With his mother making noises about selling stories about Tasha, in gaining some representation to get a better deal from the press, Dan had panicked, not wanting Tasha's past to be revealed to the world at large because it would only distress and hurt her and she'd already suffered enough, too much.

In order to gain some cash for his mother he'd delivered some parcels for Liam and although he'd suspected them to be drugs, he'd asked no questions and just done it, to help his mum out. To protect Tasha. By that time, Dan didn't know which way to turn to escape and ended up visiting his father in prison who'd welcomed him back to the fold, a fold where he'd ended up again and sinking deeper and deeper into it but had no real clue how he'd got there.

After his row with Tasha that morning he'd been able to see more clearly that he'd been stupid but had also been played and manipulated because of where his head had been at. Knowing Jim wouldn't take any crap or make allowances where Tasha and Connor were concerned, he'd decided he wanted no further part of it so had been to see his mum to tell her that. She'd been far more interested in Tasha's visit and her filthy rich husband than what her son did or didn't want to be involved with. Dan hadn't been entirely shocked by that but he'd been stunned when his mother had asked if he could bring Connor to visit her. Just Connor. Without Tasha knowing. Just once as he was her only grandchild. He'd been unsure why but now words like kidnap and ransom were spinning around in Dan's mind and that had given him the final clarity he'd needed to see straight. To see his mother for what she was again and to see himself and all the mistakes he'd made and been encouraged to make.

He assured Jim he would never have taken his son anywhere near anyone without permission and was apologetic for becoming involved again but after listening to Tasha that morning he had cut all ties once more, for good. Not that his mother was accepting that, but Dan was determined.

"Dan, I can't tell you that I'm not pissed to find myself in this hideous situation, one where my wife is in danger, again, but I kind of get what happened. Let's find Tasha and then we can sort out what happens next."

"I'd understand if you forced Tash to cut me off," he said sadly, resigned almost.

"Despite what you seem to think of me, I don't force your sister to do anything, not against her will, anyway. Tasha loves you, you and Pippa and I would never want her to lose touch with either of you and there's no reason for her to do so, unless remaining in touch endangers her. However, as I said, once we've found Tasha we can sort out what happens next."

They stood at the entrance to the park and looked around.

"Needle in a fucking haystack springs to mind here." With those words ringing in his head, Jim briefly allowed his mind to wander back to the stables, the hay loft. His lips curled into the smallest of smiles at the memory. He quickly shook it away because right now he needed to focus on finding Tasha.

"Bandstand," replied Dan.

"What?"

"When we were kids we would come down here. Tash would bring me and Pip down here, with Gerry, usually to get us out of the house if our parents were fighting, or worse still, not fighting. Tash would always end up on the bandstand, singing and dancing, putting on a show. It carried on for years." Dan smiled and as Jim smiled back at the thought of Tasha having a happy place his guts knotted at the expression Dan wore. It was the Natasha Winters haunted expression.

"What happened? What did he do?" Jim knew their father had to be involved in this.

"He hurt her, with his belt." Dan, unable to keep a lid on his feeling cried tears of guilt for his sister being unsafe again but also at the memory of the beating Tasha had endured. Her cries had echoed around the house as she'd suffered a beating he'd done nothing to stop because while Tasha was punished he was huddled in a corner with Pippa, his hands over his ears hoping to block out the sounds of her cries that still haunted his nightmares. "She hadn't done anything bad. He was just pissed off and when Tasha wasn't home he went out and found her in the street with Gerry and a couple of other kids; she'd already cleaned the house and cooked dinner for me and Pip."

"How old was she?" asked Jim nervously.

"About twelve, maybe thirteen, no more. He found her outside and dragged her home for everyone to see and when he got her inside he really pasted her with his belt so when he went out she decided she'd had enough and armed with a bottle of vodka and some pills she'd found she came here. To the park. To the bandstand and tried—she erm—fuck, I'm sure she wouldn't want you to know this."

"Fucking hell," cried Jim sadly, filling in the gaps for himself before hugging Dan as sobs wracked his body. "What happened to her?"

"Gerry. He was walking the dog and I think he knew Tash would be here. His family would have heard the noise from our house. She was very drunk but hadn't taken the pills because she was scared that if she was dead then that would make me dad's main target, and as for Pippa...Gerry took her home and gave her lots of coffee, but with a bottle of vodka missing and a hung-over Tash the next day she got another good hiding for nicking the booze. Nobody knows that story except Gerry and now you. He told me when I was first getting involved again at home. I think to show me how much Tash loved me and how low they'd sink, how far down they'd tried to drag her and still she had risen above it, but it suddenly made sense why she never ever came back to the bandstand. He even ruined that for her, her one happy place."

"Take me to the bandstand," ordered Jim, thinking that his initial mistrust and jealousy of Gerry was being wiped out by gratitude and indebtedness with every revelation.

Walking in step with Dan, Jim could just see the bandstand coming into view and was relieved to see three figures on it, one of them being Tasha. She stood before the other two, presumably her mother and Liam.

He pulled his phone out and called Jerome Stewart to check that the injunction against Liam was still valid. It was. He also checked what historical charges could be brought in relation to Liam and Tasha's father. Jerome was reeling off crime after crime and then explained that Mrs Bailey could be viewed as something of a facilitator and an accomplice. Jim gave Jerome an overview of what had gone on that night and he'd offered further advice on ways to proceed but explained that if the police were involved now there were no guarantees Dan wouldn't end up being charged for drug offences assuming the other two would sing like canaries and it would be impossible to keep the *details* off the newsstands. Jim decided that as he could see Tasha and she looked safe he would hold fire on the police, for now.

There were a number of bushes in place around the bandstand allowing Dan and Jim to get closer without being too obvious.

"Where is Dan?" Tasha sounded tearful.

"Safe. That's all you need to know," sneered her mother. "For now, so shut the fuck up and listen."

Tasha stared wildly between Liam and her mother wondering what the point of this was.

"I need cash and I need your father."

"And this involves me how?" Tasha sounded hard and antagonistic which concerned Jim and yet it also made him rather proud of her ballsy nature and gave him an insight into how his wife had survived to this point.

"You can give me both," her mother replied.

"No can do," Tasha told her. "Well, I could give you cash, but I won't, and you might need to try shagging the governor of the scrubs for Daddy dearest, or is she a woman. I'm sure one of the prisons over here has a female governor," said Tasha as if she was giving it serious thought.

A sharp slap echoed around the quietness of the park as Joanna Bailey stood in front of her daughter having delivered a single, stinging slap to Tasha's face.

"Shit," whispered Jim. Ballsy was going to get his wife into more trouble if she didn't temper it a little, but at least for now Liam's hands were being kept to himself.

"You can confess that your father was not the driver who forced you off the road, that Mickie told you that when she held you hostage. You can divorce that husband of yours and move back home to take care of your family. You can bring the baby too. There was a pop star on the TV the other day who had written a book about her disastrous marriage to an older man who had brainwashed her, like that Stockholm syndrome. You could do that because for some reason people like you."

Tasha stared at her mother while Jim wondered how anyone could be surprised by other people's ability to like Tasha. Even at her most infuriating she was highly likeable.

Tasha laughed at her mother as Jim and Dan exchanged a concerned glance.

"I love my husband and I would never consider divorcing him. Along with my son, he is my reason for getting up in the morning. I am nothing without him. Where do you fit into this?" Tasha turned to Liam.

"Your dad said we'd been having a baby." He sounded sad and overwhelmed.

"He had no right, but I was angry with him when I told him."

"So, it's true?" asked Liam.

"Yes. I was sixteen and you were my abuser, so I got rid," Tasha said coldly, although Jim was all too aware of the feelings of guilt and sorrow his wife carried with her at the termination she'd had.

"How can you be so cold?" Liam's question made Tasha laugh wryly.

"You, all of you, my whole fucking life until I went to New York made me cold and bitter. My husband makes me better. He makes me real which is why I had his baby and not yours and I have never regretted that beyond being responsible for having killed an innocent baby, my baby."

Dan was stunned by what he was hearing and Jim could understand better the earlier exchange between her and Gerry.

"You, you, you," screeched her mother. "You selfish little bitch! You think your father had the brains to sell you off to

Liam and hatch that plot with Mickie? I liked her, she knew exactly what she wanted and stopped at nothing to get it, like me. Now, you are going to do as you are told, otherwise I will be writing a book about my out of control famous daughter who fucked her way through London as a prostitute and even got knocked up and had an abortion before fucking Gerry who was head over heels. Then when he could no longer feather your nest sufficiently you moved on; footballers, photographers until you found your ultimate pay day in Mr Hollywood who you did allow to knock you up. I assume he pays well for fucking you and siring an offspring. Even if he divorces you I bet you are quids in. I always wondered who you were like, but we are two peas from a pod aren't we, you and I? Maybe that's why that Mickie despised you so much. She could see the similarities between us all, she even faked cancer! I bet they weren't cheap." Her mother gestured towards Tasha's wedding and engagement rings.

Tasha stared, stunned and sickened by her mother's words but knew she would never give up her husband nor the rings that represented their marriage. However, the most hurtful words were the ones that compared her to her mother and Mickie. She would die before she'd allow herself to become like either of them; bitter, twisted and cruel.

Liam still stared at her and had something clouding his eyes, something she didn't think she'd ever seen before, sadness.

"What?" Tasha asked him, hating being under his scrutiny.

"I can't believe you'd do that, to my baby."

"I did it," she confirmed, hoping she sounded hard and without regret because there was no way she was doing this. Dissecting everything to analyse it and allow either of them to make her the guilty, partly because neither she nor the child she'd aborted bore any guilt in this hideous situation.

"A baby would have changed things, Tasha. Changed me," he replied, startling her slightly. "I would have been a good dad."

Tasha could feel her eyes drying as she stared long and hard at Liam's words and the sentiment of them.

"Why? Why would you want a child in this?" she asked with a wave of her hand around them. "Who would want a baby to be born and brought up surrounded by violence and abuse? Nobody, Liam, that's who. Nobody normal anyway." Her voice was raised now as annoyance soared through her at the idea that any of them thought a baby was ever a good idea here; her father saw it as a golden goose, a cash cow and whilst her mother saw it as potential currency too, the insight into the depths her mother would and had sunk to meant she posed a greater danger to them all than her father had and then there was Liam. "Look at you, Liam. You would have been an awful dad; you procured a girl of what? Fourteen? Fifteen? You sexually, physically and emotionally abused that girl and you paid for it. You are involved in countless illegal activities including burglary, money laundering, loan sharking, protection rackets not to mention the drugs, although I thought you only dealt but your skin, eyes and shaking seem to suggest you might be using too. So, like I say, you would have been an awful dad."

Silence hung between them for slowly passing seconds until Liam spoke, stunning Tasha with his words, delusions and complete stupidity. "I loved you."

Suddenly, she was further stunned as she heard two words from the voice she loved most in the world.

"Hey, baby," said Jim as he climbed the steps of the bandstand.

Chapter Thirty-Two

Two words, that's all he'd uttered. *Hey, baby,* and immediately Tasha felt calmer and safe.

"Introduce me, honey," Jim continued as he wrapped an arm around her waist and pulled her closer. "Dan's safe," he whispered against her ear making it look like a gentle kiss.

"My mother, or at least the woman who gave birth to me, Joanna Bailey, and Liam Pickering my former..." she trailed off.

"Abuser, baby. I think you were right, although that would apply to my mother-in-law too. In case there was any doubt, I'm Mr Hollywood, Tasha's husband and no price would ever cover the privilege of siring children with my wife," he said pointedly as he stared at Tasha's mother. He could see some shared similarities between mother and daughter, although they were only fleeting and not something he was going to dwell on or ever mention to his wife.

"Well, nice to meet you I'm sure, but we really need to be going." Jim prepared to leave.

"We have video of Dan trafficking drugs," taunted Joanna, clearly knowing Tasha's Achilles heel.

Dan appeared from the shadows and shook his head at Tasha. "You don't get to rescue me this time, Tash. I did this so I need to clean up my own crap."

Tasha was confused by the notion of Dan with drugs but didn't question it at that point.

"Dan's right, Natasha. You don't get to play the hero this time," Jim told her as he watched her face crumble. "I do," he added. "Right, you all need to listen real good. We're all going to meet with Tasha's legal representative and you will both be signing documents guaranteeing your silence on all things relating to her, me, her siblings, our son and future children. In exchange, neither of you will face criminal charges for the historical abuse, neglect nor assaults on Tasha which I have already established will be viable and almost guarantee the conviction of you both. In addition, no further charges will be brought against her father for the same crimes. You will also hand over any and all copies of evidence against Dan."

"Maybe we'll take Dan down with us," goaded Joanna.

"That's your choice, but if you do I have it on good authority that you will further incriminate yourselves as dealers and distributors of illegal drugs and with evidence of the systematic abuse of your children he is unlikely to be convicted. In fact, he could claim a type of Stockholm syndrome." Jim smirked. "This ends, once and for all."

"I would need a financial incentive." Joanna Bailey's word seemed to shock Jim, briefly, but not Tasha.

Shaking his head, Jim took a step closer, "You do this my way first and then I will ensure you are appropriately compensated for everything you've done for my wife."

"James," cried Tasha, finally finding her voice.

"My way, Natasha. You ran out of chances tonight," he told her seriously.

"Deal," agreed Joanna smugly.

Liam looked across at Jim and appeared to be preparing to speak.

"You think yourself lucky that you are not sharing cell space with her no good father for the rest of your days and rest assured that if I ever find you in breach of the restraining order again I will fucking kill you. Do we understand each other?"

Liam nodded sheepishly as Jim pulled his phone out and called Jerome Stewart again, who with some reservations about the legalities of Jim's proposal agreed that they could draw up confidentiality agreements as big companies did with employees.

"You make sure you're there the day after tomorrow at two and I will ensure your payment is made, Mrs Bailey," he told Joanna formally.

"You should call me mum." She smiled.

Tasha looked across at Dan who looked as freaked out as Tasha felt but only Jim spoke.

"Not even if hell freezes over. Now, get the hell off my wife's happy place," he told the two people opposite him who readily complied.

****

Jim drove back in the hire car with Dan. They followed Tasha back in Celia's car, but very little had been said by any of them after Joanna and Liam left the bandstand. Tasha was gathering her thoughts behind the wheel of the car that was now parked at the front of the house when Jim opened the door startling her.

"Come on. I am guessing we may have missed dinner and Connor may need feeding. He was sick a couple of times." Jim took her hand to pull her out. "And then we are going to have a very serious conversation about keeping yourself safe."

"James," she offered in her own defence and as a protest.

"Later," he replied with determination as he tightened the grip on her hand to lead her indoors.

Entering the house Tasha heard her son crying and immediately followed the sound of it until she found him being carried around the living room on his great-grandfather's shoulder.

"Hi Gramps," she called as she was swamped briefly by Pippa and Celia.

"Thank goodness you're back," cried Paul. "You are going to be the bloody death of me." He lowered the little boy into his arms and offered him to his mother. "Physical violence is never the answer, but there are times when I am sorely tempted to put you across my knee, young lady."

"You and me both," muttered Jim while Tasha silently stared between her husband and grandfather.

"Sorry." Smiled Tasha as she lifted her baby into her arms and viewed him with concern. "Oh baby, you look poorly. He's very hot." She pushed his sweaty hair back off his face.

"He's been sick another couple of times," Pippa said seriously.

"Should we call a doctor?" Tasha's question seemed to show

348

her confusion and inexperience as a first-time mother.

"Babies sometimes get sick, Nat," said Paul reassuringly. "Maybe see if he'll take some water," he suggested.

Tasha looked across at Jim who was closing the distance between them.

"He is hot and he looks sick, baby, but Paul's right. We'll keep an eye on him and if he's no better in the morning we'll call a doctor, okay?"

Tasha nodded as she sat down with the bottle containing some previously boiled water her grandmother offered her.

"Sorry, I forgot the stock cubes," Tasha suddenly realised.

"Don't be silly," she chastened in response. "I have kept you all some dinner." Smiled Celia as Connor reluctantly accepted some water before becoming restless and tearful again.

Tasha patiently nursed her son for the next forty minutes as he dozed. At her husband and grandfather's insistence she even ate most of her dinner, albeit one handed. Jim explained what had happened and Dan promised everyone that he knew he'd made a huge mistake in getting involved with Joanna and Liam, regardless of his original reason or emotional confusion.

Paul voiced the words everyone else was avoiding when he said, "Dan, we love you, we all do, but drugs! You got off lightly and ignorance is no defence in law or morally so I really hope you have learnt from that mistake. What are you going to do now? With your life and your future?"

"I know Gramps and I'm so sorry, for all of it. I would never have forgiven myself if anything had happened to Tash tonight. I was thinking about moving away, making a fresh start with college and work."

"Oh Dan," cried Celia sadly.

"Celia, maybe it would be good for Dan," interrupted Paul seriously.

"Where will you go?" asked Jim, "Where do you fancy?"

"I dunno. My only real ties in life are Tasha, Pip and Grandma and Gramps and you all live on opposite sides of the Atlantic so I could go anywhere I suppose. Maybe Europe or Australia for a while. I know I need visas and I wouldn't be able to work right off but I have some savings and Jim offered me some money a while back so I could see where I fancy trying out and take it from there."

"What about L.A.?" Jim startled Tasha so much with his question, suggestion that she physically jumped, waking Connor abruptly, distressing him once more.

"What about it?" asked Dan, nervous that he might be misunderstanding the offer he perceived was being made.

Laughing, Jim expanded, "I'm offering you a chance in LA. Come and stay with us for a while. I know a few people I can introduce you to, chefs. See if it's what you want and if it is there are schools in L.A. you could go to, or New York. I can have my legal people look at residency issues."

Everyone was staring at Jim now as Tasha got to her feet in an attempt to soothe her son.

"It's just an offer, Dan, and if you don't want to accept it, that's fine. I won't be offended, oh, and if the idea of living with me and Tasha doesn't appeal then there's plenty of room over at the stables where Trav' lives."

"Thank you." Dan felt truly humbled that his brother-in-law would make such an offer, especially after his actions had endangered Tasha. Before he could say anymore Connor projectile vomited across the room.

It was three o'clock the following morning before Tasha managed to close her eyes, having changed Connor countless times and nursed him until he was asleep, but this was the first time he'd allowed her to put him down in his cot.

"We'll find a doctor when it's daytime," said Jim as she finally lay down next to him. "I think it's a nasty bug he's picked up. If he gets any worse we'll take him to the hospital."

"I hadn't realised that a body so small could actually produce that much waste." Tasha's disbelieving shake of her head made Jim laugh.

"Oh yeah. From both ends too."

They curled into each other and as sleep washed over them both Connor began to cry, but it was a different cry, one Tasha didn't even recognise as belonging to her baby with its high pitch and pained tone. Leaping up, she switched on the light and ran to where her baby lay before unnecessarily calling, "James," as he was already standing next to her.

Picking her son up, Tasha began to cry at how limp he appeared to be and it was as she cradled him that she noticed the swelling to the top of his head where his fontanel was swollen and dome like.

"Tasha, I need you to stay calm, but I'm going to call nine, one, one."

"Nine, nine, nine," Tasha corrected between sobs as Jim called for an ambulance and explained to the operator what was wrong.

He was unsure what the address was so with Tasha beginning to panic he found himself knocking on Paul and Celia's bedroom door where Paul took the phone from Jim and sent him back to his wife and son.

"Tasha, the ambulance is on the way, but you need to put some clothes on," he said looking down at her wearing one of his t-shirts, "Now!" he said firmly, startling her into action as he took their son, as frightened as she was when he gazed down at the little boy who meant everything to them and was clearly unwell.

****

Less than half an hour later, Connor had been admitted to hospital and a frightened Tasha had answered what felt like a million and one questions about her son while the medical staff worked on him. They took bloods, inserted drips and talked in a language Tasha didn't understand in a place where seconds lasted minutes and minutes lasted hours.

Eventually, a doctor came to speak to Jim and Tasha. "Connor's stable, but he is dehydrated and we think he has some kind of infection. We're running tests to establish what the infection might be. We've sedated him and he has a drip to keep him hydrated and he has a couple of other lines in for medication and as a precaution."

"What sort of precaution?" asked Jim.

"In the event that we need to operate or if his condition worsens." The doctor's explanation was interrupted by Tasha's crying.

"He'll be okay though, he won't die, will he?" she asked in

broken sobs as Jim pulled her closer.

"Mrs Maybury, we will do everything we can to make sure Connor makes a recovery but I can't give you guarantees and your son is a very poorly little boy. We'll get him up on ICU as soon as we can, but you can both stay with him."

Connor was quickly moved to ICU and although she was exhausted, Tasha found it impossible to sleep. A different doctor was responsible for her son's care and while she had no objection to the new doctor, Jim found it frustrating. He left his wife and son alone to phone Lenny to get his opinion and was reassured that the doctors were following the same protocol as Lenny was suggesting.

Tasha was sitting at her son's bedside when a message came through on her phone and with a sigh she looked down to see a reply to her earlier message to Lizzie

<Hey Tash, I really am sorry about the stuff with Danielle and I truly never meant it to hurt you. I miss you, Daddy and Connor but am ok. Danielle has her termination booked for today. She's sad and scared and I don't really know what to say to her. I love you too. Xx>

Tasha stared down at the message and wondered whether she should reply, but to say what? Other than Lenny and presumably Sara, nobody knew Connor was sick. She and Jim had decided to keep it to themselves until they knew properly what was wrong and they'd been given a prognosis so she couldn't say anything about Connor. She had no clue what she could say to reassure either of the girls about the upcoming termination. Suddenly, she wondered whether Connor being ill was some kind of punishment for her. For not being more understanding about what Lizzie had done, for not offering more help and support to her and Danielle when they'd needed it. Danielle was going to lose her baby that day and Tasha suddenly wondered if she was too.

Chapter Thirty-Three

Tasha sat in silence with Jim beside her. She watched her son lying in the huge hospital cot, scrutinising the rise and fall of his chest, holding her breath every time a rise didn't follow immediately from the fall. The only sounds she could hear were the beeps and pings of the machines that were trying to make her baby better, recording his wellbeing and with each one she heard the more desperate she became for them to be replaced with one of his snores, snorts or funny little breathing noises he so often made. The ones that made her laugh, although, so long as he continued to breathe Tasha reasoned it was a win. Staff came and went, doctors and nurses. All of them wore empathetic and reassuring expressions, not that anyone uttered actual words that made her feel anything resembling hope that her baby was going to be okay, but then the doctor had told them they had to wait and see how Connor responded to the drugs.

Another hour, maybe two passed before anyone spoke and then it was Jim.

"Let me get you something to eat, or at least a drink."

"I'm not hungry."

"Then a drink. Something. I'll get us both something to drink."

"Whatever. If it will stop you going on," Tasha snapped and although she knew Jim was as lost as she was and in no way held him responsible for Connor's illness she offered no apology. She watched him leave the room then returned her gaze to her baby whose face she began to stroke and fought the tears that wanted to escape but she knew if she allowed the first one to fall, she might never stop.

"Any news?" came Paul's voice as Jim battled with the overcomplicated drinks machine.

"No," he replied with a long, loud sigh and a run of his fingers through his hair. "I hate this, this feeling of powerlessness. Tasha is in with Connor and she just stares at him. She isn't speaking, moving or crying, nothing."

"It's a shock." Paul reassured him with a pat of his shoulder.

"I know, but I don't know how to make this right. What if something happens, to Connor?" Jim asked with a quiver to his voice. "She has been through so much and she survived it all, even the most horrific things, but this—losing Connor might be the one thing she never gets over and I can't help thinking if we'd sought help sooner…"

"Bloody hell, Jim. This is not your fault and if it is then it's mine too. Look, babies get poorly and they usually get better without all of this so it was bad luck but it's nobody's fault. I know we've had our differences but you love my Nat like no-one ever has before and although I tried to bring her home and hold you responsible when she was hurt, I was wrong. When I'm wrong I admit it, so sorry." He extended an outstretched hand of friendship or at least peace.

Taking the older man's hand Jim offered him a weak smile. "I know how Tasha feels in there," he said with a point down the corridor to where she remained with their son. "She feels helpless, lost and scared shitless, just like I did when she was in hospital. I spent hours, days wondering how I was going to take my next breath without her and now I am doing it again with my son, but this is worse. Not that I thought anything could be worse, but it is because I'm watching Connor fighting to survive and if he doesn't I know I'll lose Tasha."

Looking at the other man's shocked expression Jim reminded himself that this was Tasha's grandfather he was addressing and he didn't know everything Tasha had been through. Didn't need to and Tasha wouldn't want him too. Although, Tasha was unaware that he knew about her suicide decision that turned into a drunken stupor on the bandstand when the thing that had stopped her had been worry for her siblings, but if they lost

Connor would there be anything left for her to stay around for?

"You need to stop these dark thoughts," Paul chastened. "My girl, my Nat, she loves you and kids are resilient. They bounce back as quick as they drop and that boy is his mother's son so if he knows how to do one thing, it's fight. Now, you get back in there and take care of my girl, like you promised to."

Jim nodded and with two cups of something brown and relatively warm he returned to his wife and son with Paul's reminder of just how strong they both were fresh in his mind.

****

Another six hours passed and looking out into the darkness of the night sky Jim smiled a half-smile as he remembered holding his son on the night he was born and gazing out of the hospital window as he was now.

"What are you thinking?" asked Tasha who hadn't spoken since a token thank you for the coffee she hadn't drunk.

"About the night Connor was born," Jim replied with a quiver invading his voice followed by a tear running down his face that his hand was too slow to wipe away before Tasha saw it.

In the blink of an eye she was on her feet and standing before her husband, reaching up to wipe his tears away while her own flowed freely down her face. She was unsure how long they remained in the window but as they huddled together, her head resting against his chest with her arms wrapped tightly around his waist while he squeezed her to him and stroked her hair tenderly she was relieved that both of their tears had dried and there was a calmness settling between them.

"I didn't mean to shut down earlier, with the silent treatment," Tasha finally said, knowing Jim had found it hard to deal with her like that.

"That's okay. If that's the way you handle things, but it did throw me in case you held me responsible."

"Fuck! No, of course not. I'm shitting myself that he is so poorly, Jim, but never did I blame you. Why would I?"

"If I had said to come here sooner…"

"And if I hadn't gone to meet Dan or kept us both away from Connor…"

"Then it's not either of our faults," Jim said flatly before landing a gentle kiss to Tasha's head.

"We will discuss you going to meet Dan later, honey."

"I bet we will," she muttered knowing that conversation wouldn't be put off forever. "I just need my baby to be better," Tasha whispered, as if saying it any louder might jinx it.

"Me too, both of them," he replied, and he really did mean it. "But you forget, our boy is a fighter, like his momma."

"And a Maybury," Tasha added, thinking that might make him an even tougher cookie.

"He certainly is, baby, so why don't we go and hold his hand and tell him to get kicking this infection's ass."

Although still unwell by the time they were entering the early hours of the morning the antibiotics and other medicines were obviously doing something positive as Connor's colour and body condition began to improve. His sedation was being reduced so that he was gradually becoming more lively and aware and while he was still having loose bowel movements it was less frequent and severe.

It was after lunch when the doctor came by with some news on Connor's diagnosis and confirmed his earlier suspicion of gastroenteritis and whilst severe, he was happy that the drugs were having the desired effect. The doctor could see no reason why he wouldn't make a full recovery, but suggested Connor may be hospitalised for several days more. Knowing his son was improving and in turn that his wife was less stressed, Jim took Dan to meet with Jerome Stewart before Joanna and Liam were due to sign their paperwork leaving Paul with Tasha.

Connor's crying, his normal baby cry, demanding her attention was music to Tasha's ears and picking him up she could hold her tears and emotions she'd fought to keep in check back no longer.

"Hey, Nat, that'll do. He's on the mend. He's a tough cookie, like his mum, and his dad." Paul hugged his granddaughter reassuringly.

Tasha was unsure if her tears were only of relief and gratitude that her baby was improving, but the unleashing of her emotions was cathartic. With her breathing returning to normal she tried to explain her deepest seated fears. "Babies die from gastroenteritis. I know I said I didn't want a baby but I don't think I could carry on if anything happened to him."

"I know, my darling girl. He was just a bit of a shock for you wasn't he? But you're a wonderful mother. Now, no more tears and gloomy thoughts. Let's think happy thoughts and concentrate on getting you all back to normal, if any of you kids were ever normal," he teased, hoping to keep Tasha's mood and emotions even. He reached across and stroked his great-grandson's forehead. "I know Jim and I have had our differences, but I am very grateful you found him and that he is helping to sort Dan out. It's more than generous of him to offer his home, a job and an education."

"He really is one of the good guys." Smiled Tasha, gently rocking her son who looked up at her with a weak half-smile.

"I know he is." Paul smiled as he thought Jim's worries for Tasha without Connor might have been well founded, but fortunately the little man had pulled through.

By late afternoon Jim appeared and swapped places with Paul. Tasha brought him up to date with the information on their son before she left them alone together and found Dan sitting in the corridor.

"Hi." Smiled Tasha taking an uncomfortable seat next to him. "You okay?"

"I am so sorry for getting you involved again, Tash."

Her response was to wave off his guilty apology.

"Did Jim fill you in on our afternoon?" he asked.

"No. We just spoke about Connor."

"Of course, sorry, how is the little fella doing? Gramps said he's on the mend."

"Yeah, they think he'll be in here for a few days more, but he seems to be bouncing back." Tasha attempted a smile.

"You look tired, maybe you should go home..."

"I'll be fine. I can't leave him, not yet. I only came out to use the bathroom," Tasha explained making her brother laugh.

"How very American, *the bathroom*," he teased with a heavy accent.

"Oh God, don't let me become all Americanised," she cried.

"So, how did things go this afternoon?"

"Good. Jim is a complete arse, isn't he?"

Tasha laughed but couldn't deny her brother's description. "Thanks for the character assassination of my husband," she teased.

Dan shrugged. "Tash, he never cracked his face once and every time either of them tried to gain a little ground he shot them down. He's seriously scary. It was like being with the head of some Mafia family."

"Yeah, he can be hard-nosed about stuff, and at work he's used to being in charge, but this is about us. About keeping us all safe and he takes that really seriously."

"Everything is sorted now. Liam and Mum signed everything and Jerome Stewart left them in no doubt that they were both criminals and all it would take to see them behind bars would be one call."

"Good. Do you know if Jim gave Mum money?" Tasha remembered his offer from the bandstand.

"Yeah." Laughed Dan confusing his sister. "He started with a billion dollars."

"You are fucking kidding? I'll kill him. He has a family to support. Do we even have that kind of money? I don't even know how much money he has," cried Tasha as Dan continued.

"He wrote it down, Tash, and then he began making deductions from your worth. He did tell her he couldn't really put a price on you because you were priceless. That made me a bit sick in my mouth," teased Dan before continuing. "So, from the billion he made deductions for every bad thing she had ever allowed, facilitated or just not prevented and by the time he finished there was a cent or a dime or whatever."

Really?" She was shocked, not that Jim had made her mother accountable but that he'd got away with not paying her mother off.

"Oh yeah. He reached into his pocket and said, *but whilst in Rome* and he handed her a penny, one pence, Tash." He laughed. "Then told her he may have overestimated exactly what she was due and got up and walked out."

"No way." Tasha shook her head but admired her husband's

dealing of the situation.

"Oh yeah. I actually clapped, Tash. It was like the best movie scene ever. Oh, and I hope you don't mind but I'm coming to L.A. for a while; Jim said he'll book me a flight and I've spoken to Trav who is cool with me staying over at the stables with him. I'm coming out for a month and Jim has said he'll get people to look at visas, college, work and everything."

"That's great, so long as it's what you want. Please put yourself and your wishes first." She got to her feet and kissed her brother's head. "I really need a wee, and then I want to get back to Connor, but we'll talk again before we go home."

****

It was another week before Tasha was fastening herself into the seat of a privately chartered plane, heading home to L.A. with Jim and Connor. As the plane took off with her hand safely wrapped in the larger, protective hand of her husband she honestly felt as though all of the bad stuff in her life was over. Not every hiccup or obstacle that everybody experienced in the course of their normal lives, but murder attempts, being held hostage, crazy fucked up parents pimping her out, *just normal*, mundane hassles remained.

"You okay, baby?" Jim asked, sensing her mood.

She smiled up at him. "Mmm, good, really good. It actually feels as though things may be settling into some kind of normality."

"Yes, they do. Even Connor is relaxed enough to sleep," Jim said with a smile as he looked over at his son who was safely strapped into his own seat.

"Connor is always relaxed enough to sleep," Tasha replied with a laugh.

"Only when his momma's around."

"I love when you say things like that," she admitted while Jim was unbuckling both of their seat belts.

"What are you doing, Mr Maybury?"

"I thought we had an agreement on exactly what would happen on a private charter, Mrs Maybury. Our son is complying with his part of the deal so that just leaves you," Jim told her getting to his feet.

"And you," Tasha replied gazing up from her seated position with an unintentional pout.

"A pout, honey? And I am certainly keeping my end of the plan up," Jim told Tasha as he reached for her hand to pull her to her feet and as his lips lowered to hers he placed the hand within his against his own crotch.

"Oh," Tasha moaned as she felt the flexing erection behind her husband's jeans.

"Just for you, Tasha. Only ever for you," he told her as his lips rested against hers, ready to breach them.

"James," she gasped in response.

"Yes, baby? What do you want?"

"It's more what I need." Tasha attempted to pull back a little.

"And what's that? What do you need?"

"Please, James," Tasha pleaded.

"Tell me, Natasha."

"I need you, to fuck me, to make me come." She scraped her teeth over her bottom lip as a flush crept up her neck and face.

"Go into the bedroom and wait for me and maybe if you're a very good girl you'll get to come and be fucked."

"What about Connor?" Tasha asked with a concerned look across at her son.

"I'll make sure he's settled and then I'll put him down, okay?"

"Yes." Tasha placed a gentle kiss to her son's forehead before heading for the bedroom, to wait.

Epilogue

Four Years Later

"Hey," called Bria as she settled between her brothers in the garden at the vineyard. "Some of us are going to have to buy bigger houses for Fourth of July celebrations if anybody else has more kids." She grinned.

Laughing, Jim and Bobby looked around at the increasing numbers of people in their family. There were people everywhere, adults and children. Neither of his sisters had added to their brood but most of the older ones had boyfriends or girlfriends now.

Bobby's family had increased significantly; upon returning from London, Jim and Tasha found that Bobby and Abby had decided to have another baby using a surrogate and had found one quickly who had conceived their child, Dee Dee, Dakota, almost immediately. Within a month of discovering that Dee Dee was on her way, Abby discovered she too was pregnant with another daughter, Jo Jo, Jolie, and now Abby was pregnant again with a boy.

Jim's own family just kept getting bigger too; Lizzie was dating a model, another Dylan. The original Dylan was now racing cars professionally while Lizzie had rethought her modelling plans and was now a photographer for a fashion magazine. Philip and Juan had separated by the time Tasha and Jim had returned from London, but within six weeks had reconciled and were due to marry in a few weeks' time. Dan had relocated to L.A. a few weeks after he'd arrived and still lived in the huge apartment he shared with Travis over at the stables and seemed to be enjoying life to the full judging by how many pretty girls passed through. Pippa had been offered some work about a year after Dan relocated. That had only left Paul and Celia in the U.K. and they'd sold their business and retired to Florida, with Banksy.

When he first met that pretty English girl with the long, shapely legs he couldn't have imagined she would change his life like this, but she had completely turned his world upside down. He had never imagined having children beyond Lizzie and Philip, but now, they were everywhere, or at least that's how it felt.

Philip and Juan still lived on the estate, but the house they'd previously occupied had been completely gutted and renovated as offices for the charity Tasha had founded and launched three years ago. The charity provided support for current and previous victims of abuse. Lizzie lived with her boyfriend in a house not that far from his own, on an exclusive, private estate having turned down her father's offer to live on his estate too, although he suspected that had probably been Dylan's decision. Lucy, Tasha's best friend was almost a permanent fixture in their life, having settled into the L.A. lifestyle with Ryan and Skye and had added a son, Jude to their family a few months after Skye's first birthday.

Bria was right about bigger houses, although his was more than big enough for his increasing family.

There had been him, Tasha and Connor when they'd returned from London four years ago, or so they'd thought. However, unable to resist the temptation of his wife and a private plane complete with a bed, they had renewed their membership to the mile high club, twice, resulting in the birth of their daughter, Aimee, exactly nine months after that flight. A baby made possible by missing the pill during Connor's time in hospital and time differences that led to Tasha misjudging the twelve-hour window to take her pill, rendering it ineffective.

He smiled as he recalled her annoyance with him for doing this to her again, but she had readily accepted her second pregnancy in a way she hadn't with Connor. She had suffered less with sickness but indigestion and heartburn had been the bane of her life and his for much of the pregnancy along with her concern for her son with a new baby to accommodate, that and Tasha's insatiable sexual desires but that was in no way a burden for him. He remembered that after Connor was born he'd told her how enraptured he was by her body that pregnancy had improved if that was possible. Well, Aimee had only increased that to the point that Jim actually couldn't remember the last time a day had passed without them having sex at least once. He really couldn't keep his hands off her. With a frown he realised they hadn't had sex today, but he would rectify that as soon as they got home and the children were safely tucked up in bed. Hell, maybe he'd take her into his office.

"Daddy," cried Connor rushing across the lawn to find Jim ready to scoop him up into his arms.

"Hey buddy, how you doing?" He kissed the head of his son who had turned four a few months before.

"Okay, but the girls, they're bugging me," replied the little boy with big, innocent eyes making his father and his uncle smile.

"Yeah, they do that." Grinned Bobby.

"On that note, I am leaving you boys to it." Winking, Bria turned to Connor. "Grandma has made a chocolate cake, Connor, but she's hidden it so Auntie Bria is going to find it."

"Cool, I'll help you later," he said with a wide-eyed stare.

"Which girls are we talking about?" asked the little boy's uncle with increasing amusement.

He sighed. "Skye is chasing me and I don't want to run, but if I don't run she catches me. Then there's Aimee who thinks she can be with me all the time and she bugs me," he cried with a frown identical to his father's. "Jo Jo and Dee Dee follow Aimee so I have all three of them and then there's Lexi who is so bossy she is just a pain in my ass," cried the little boy seriously as his uncle and father laughed.

"Connor," came Tasha's cross mommy voice from behind them.

"Busted buddy." Smirked Jim.

"We don't speak that way," she told her son firmly.

With his mother's pout, Connor offered the only defence he had, "But Daddy says it about you."

"What?" Tasha stared at Jim.

"Yeah, Momma, before when you were telling Daddy about Auntie Angie's call he went to his office and called Uncle Marc and said that you were busting his balls and being a pain in his ass."

"Did he now?" Tasha glared at her husband with a disapproving shake of her head, but offered only a smile for her son who she was now reaching for.

"I really need to close doors behind me," muttered Jim to Bobby making his twin laugh.

Holding Connor against her front with his legs wrapped around him, Tasha looked over her son's shoulder and with a shake of her head directed her attention to her husband. "Really? You got that from his comments? This is not over, James."

"Didn't think it would be, Natasha, and maybe I need to teach my boy the guy code," he replied making her smile in spite of her annoyance.

"Mommy," interrupted Connor. "I'm sorry for making you mad."

Jim watched on, envious of his son's expert manipulation of his mother and if there was any doubt that this boy was smart beyond his years he dispelled it as he pulled her face closer by wrapping his arms around her neck and kissed her tenderly. "I love you, Momma."

Tasha was done for at that point.

"Sorry if you're in trouble, Daddy," the little boy said with a concerned smile in his father's direction.

"No problem, buddy," Jim told him with a reassuring smile.

Connor was still hugging his mother, teasing the ends of her hair between his fingers as he frowned at his dad. "Is that where I should have pleaded the fifth?" His question earned smiles from his father and uncle but they in turn earned a frown from Tasha.

"Really?" she asked her husband while she squeezed her son tightly.

She began to cover his face with kisses until he was giggling and flailing in her arms as he told her again, "I really love you, Momma."

"I love you too, baby boy," Tasha told him hugging him still. "Go and find Uncle Dan and see if he and Trav' will take you riding this week," suggested Tasha as she placed him on the ground.

"Will you come too?" asked Connor. "Nobody rides like you, Mommy," he told her making her smile so that her face was radiating with love for her son while Jim and Bobby merely giggled at the boys innocent comment.

"I'll try, but Mommy has to go to work for a few days this week."

Jim placed an arm around her middle, allowing his hand to rub a protective hand over her hip, then farther until it came to rest on her belly. He remembered with concern and sadness that just a year after Aimee's birth Tasha had *accidentally* got pregnant again. As accidentally as taking a child free holiday on a beach where you're permanently in a bikini but have unfortunately forgotten your birth control pills, which is exactly what had happened. The same accidentally that had Tasha saying, *don't worry, I'm sure it will be okay, please, just fuck me, I need you inside of me* whilst naked in a hot tub. The holiday was cut short after two days because Tasha missed the children so much and despite her assurances *it* hadn't been okay. She had got pregnant, but sadly miscarried about six weeks later leaving Tasha devastated and Jim sad, but more than anything concerned for his wife.

"How's the TV drama going, Tasha?" asked Bobby, referring to the medical drama Tasha was working on for Jim's studio and strangely enough she had been cast opposite a fellow Brit in the shape of Dean the lifeguard from a few years before.

"It's good, great and the fact that they're flexible with my schedule I still manage to get time at home with the kids," Tasha replied making her brother-in-law smile at seeing her so happy, although being the ultimate boss' wife might explain the show's bosses being willing to be flexible.

Connor suddenly tugged at Jim's hand and smiled up at him.

"I am really sorry if you're in trouble, Daddy."

"No problem, buddy. Momma doesn't stay mad with Daddy for long," he replied ruffling the little boy's dark hair.

"You think?" asked Tasha as their son ran off before she followed him in the direction of the house calling to Abby.

"You are screwed." Grinned Bobby. "The way that boy plays Tasha is beyond brilliant."

"Tell me about it." Laughed Jim. "But tell me you wouldn't love her if she was your mom."

"I get it, but I can't wait until his teenage years, when his testosterone is kicking in and he starts challenging you, but remains her little boy. If you piss him off, you'll be pissing her off more," laughed Bobby.

"He'll play us both, I'm sure, but he's her only son, mothers and sons and you and your three daughters will soon figure that once your only son arrives."

"Shit! We are both screwed."

"How's Tasha doing now? Abby was worried when the shit hit the fan back home again." Bobby gave his brother a disbelieving shake of his head.

"She's okay. It was all a shock but the truth is that none of them pose a threat any more. I think the fact that it all happened together knocked her on her ass and no matter what they did I still think she wanted them to show even a glimmer of decency by acknowledging it and being sorry somehow."

"I still can't believe the father thought he was up to dealing inside," said Bobby with another shake of his head.

"I believe it happens, but with Liam smuggling drugs in for the father to trade it was always destined to end badly."

"I know, but it ended with her father getting his throat cut with a shiv...that goes so far beyond badly, Jimbo."

"Yeah, well, I can't say I'm sorry and then for Liam to be found dead from an overdose the following day. It seemed almost poetic to me."

"But the mother. You can't have seen that coming, you nor Tasha."

"No, that was a bonus." Jim laughed, but with no amusement. "I don't think she saw it coming either until she was arrested as the dealer since all the drugs were found in her house."

"Do you suppose she knew the drugs had been cut with some nasty stuff that made it even more dangerous?"

"I don't know or care," Jim replied. "She is serving time and with the other two dead my wife is finally safe. Come on, let's go and join the others."

They moved towards a larger group where Aimee was sitting next to Jude and trying to hold his hand, attempts he was fighting off.

"Jude," she beseeched with a steely determination. "Hold my hand, now!" she snapped as she pulled his fingers.

"I don't want to," he cried and looked close to tears.

Jim looked down at his daughter who at three-years-old was far more confident and forceful than any grown woman he'd ever met, apart from her mother, but she certainly put Lizzie to shame. He smiled as he remembered when Lizzie and Aimee got into fights, which was often it was always Lizzie that would resort to calling for reinforcements in the form of a cry of *Tash* or *Daddy* followed by a *tell her*. He was certain that without intervention it would be Lizzie who ended up in tears rather than Aimee, which is how it usually went down with Connor.

She was a perfect replica of her mother, in miniature form. While that filled his heart with joy and pride, it also scared the shit out of him because that meant when boys did want her hand in theirs he would have to kill them, or lock her up.

Turning with a cut of her eyes identical to her mother's, she looked at Jude's almost blue hand then spotted her father, causing her look to soften, albeit slightly. "Hi Daddy." She grinned.

"Hi, baby," he replied leaning down to speak to her. "What you doing?" he almost sang.

"Holding Jude's hand. He's my boyfriend," she said seriously making him smile but knew that wouldn't always be the case when she uttered those words.

"No, I'm not," contradicted Jude who was looking at Jim with a pleading expression. "She's hurting me, Uncle Jim, and Auntie Tasha has already made her to let me go once," he said close to tears.

"Aimee," said Jim firmly. "Let go of Jude's hand, please."

"No. He's my boyfriend," she protested.

"Honey, you know Daddy doesn't work well with no and I don't think Jude wants to be your boyfriend and you're hurting him. Let go of Jude's hand, now," he said more insistently.

She looked ready to protest until her father's expression hardened further which is when she released him. Turning on Jude she told him, "You'll be sorry before I am."

Everyone around them stared at the undeniably beautiful girl standing now with her hands on her hips, some of them openly laughing.

"What?" she asked all the stares she was under. "That's what Mommy said when the guy at the club kept talking at her and trying to touch her. He got mean when she walked away, Daddy, and he said bad things, so she said you'll be sorry before I am," the little girl spoke with confidence, nodding her head. "I heard her talking about it with Juan and Philip. Philip said you'd go ape."

Tasha had just appeared and having gathered the gist of her daughter's revelation simply said, "It was a while ago and I too need to shut doors behind me."

"This is not over, Natasha." Jim repeated his wife's earlier words as he picked his daughter up and kissed her cheek.

"Didn't think it would be, James," she replied.

"And another time there was a guy and he wanted to get Mommy a couch, but she didn't want it and she told him to go and screw himself because he sure as hell wouldn't be screwing her," the little girl told her father with a wide-eyed stare and a little giggle as she shared the details of overheard conversations she didn't understand.

"A couch, baby?" Jim stared across at his wife before returning his undivided attention back to the little girl in his arms.

"Huh-huh. Auntie Abby and Auntie Lucy said it was a caster couch, and Mommy said you would flip if you found out." She giggled. "Flip like nobody has ever flipped before." She pulled her father's face towards her own with her hands gently cupping his face, much like her brother had done to their mother.

"Like you wouldn't believe, baby," he assured his daughter who was landing a gentle kiss on his lips.

"Momma said you were too much sometimes, and Philip said you only go bat shit crazy because you love us all so much. Juan didn't say anything though, he just told them that he was having nothing to do with it."

"I do love you all so, so much baby, but you shouldn't say some of those things, they're kind of rude."

"But Mommy and Philip..."

"Mommy and Philip will find out just how *too much* Daddy can be," Jim warned as Philip appeared with Juan.

"And Juan?" Aimee asked as Juan looked on with concern. "I love Juan. He's my best friend and he makes me laugh." She giggled.

"Yeah, baby, Juan is funny and always remembers not to cross Daddy."

Philip gasped with a horrified expression as the scene fully came into view before him. "Has she done it to us again? Jeez, Aimee we need to go over the importance of keeping sibling secrets," Philip told Aimee who shook her head at her biggest brother.

"Uh-uh, we don't keep secrets from Daddy, ever!" she exclaimed seriously.

"That's right, baby. Now go and say sorry to Jude for hurting him."

Compliantly, the little girl ran off to find her friend after kissing her father again.

"Jimbo, I know you shouldn't have favourites." Laughed Bobby. "But that kid is my favourite of all of your children. She has the unrelenting belief that she is always right, like you, but she also has Tasha's edge too. She is going to be a real ballbreaker, or an ace prosecutor." He laughed again before he called after his niece, "Hey, Aimee, wait for Uncle Bobby, I need to know more about this caster couch."

Pulling his wife close into his side, Jim leaned in and placed a delicate kiss on her ear and whispered, "I think you and I should meet in my office, later."

Turning to face him her eyes widened, her breathing hitched

as her face, neck and chest flushed with arousal making him smile.

"And we all need to close doors and choose our language more carefully," he added.

She smiled in response and knew that she really couldn't wish for anything else in this world or the next. She was happy, safe and content, as were all of the people she cared about and most of them were here. She had everything she'd ever dreamed of; a warm, loving family who loved and cared about her, friends she could truly trust, Dan and Pippa were safe from the harm she herself had endured and she had the best man in the world to call her husband, a man who loved her more than anything and wasn't afraid to show it. Together they had their children, all of them, Philip, Lizzie, Connor and Aimee. Four children when just five years ago she'd had no clue she would ever want any, but that was before she'd met James Maybury, before she'd become his Lucky Seven.

THE END

Keep reading for a sneak peek at Elle M Thomas' debut novel, Disaster-in-Waiting.

About Elle M Thomas

Elle M Thomas was born in the north of England and raised near Birmingham, UK where she still lives with her family. She works in local education and writes in her spare time with dreams of becoming a full-time writer.

Whilst still at school, and with a love of writing slightly risqué tales of love and romance one of her teachers told her that she could be the next Harrold Robins. Elle didn't act on those words for many years. In February 2017, with her first book completed and a dozen others unfinished, she finally took the plunge and self-published the steamy romance, Disaster-in-Waiting.

Elle describes her books as stories filled with chemistry, sensuality, love and sex that she always wanted to read and her characters as three dimensional and flawed.

You can keep up to date with all things Elle M Thomas on social media here:

Twitter – Elle M Thomas Author

Facebook – Elle M Thomas and Elle's Belles

Instagram – authorellemthomas

Goodreads – Elle M. Thomas

Disaster-in-Waiting

Have you read Disaster-in-Waiting by Elle M Thomas?

Chapter One

My friends, the ones I had at that point warned me that I was marrying my dad and I had no issue with that, none at all. Michael was older than me, by thirty years, but when I was twenty-three he seemed awfully exotic with his greater knowledge and experience of, well, everything. He represented all the positives of a good dad in my mind; he was caring, protective, and considerate of my needs and wants, and he offered me security and safety, although like an overindulgent father he did spoil me, showering me with gifts and material possessions. I smiled with a still disbelieving shake of my head as I remembered how he had once bought me a new car because my old car, which was less than a year old was dirty. But here I was almost six years later married to my dad, or at least a dad, a man who played golf, often, read, a lot and not even works of fiction, big books on real life, history, geography, architecture, things I had no interest in. That was fine though. He had no issues with my interests, not that I had many, so I reciprocated.

My issue was sex, or lack thereof. If memory served me right, which it did, it had been six months since he'd touched me intimately and another six months since we'd had sex, real sex and at twenty-eight I wanted sex. Needed it. Craved it. After a few health scares after hitting fifty-five Michael had lost confidence and stamina so he'd distanced himself from me

372

physically and as much as I wanted my needs fulfilling I didn't feel able to complain. Especially not as I knew how guilty my husband felt about his inability to satisfy my most basic needs.

He had been my boss, not my immediate boss, but my ultimate boss. He had owned the whole company I'd worked for, Stanton Industries, not that I understood what the business was, not really. I worked as a secretary for a middle manager in accounts on the seventh floor and Michael ran the whole shebang from his floor, the top floor, the twentieth where he occupied a corner office that looked out across the whole city. I didn't really know that when I was plain old Eloise Ross, although I was still Eloise Ross at work, having resisted the temptation to become Mrs Stanton in all areas of my life. Today I was to return there as P.A. to the new CEO having left my post there after marrying five years ago. I had been desperate to gain promotions and recognition in my own right, not for being married to the boss, which I'd done. Michael was no longer the boss, not since the downturn in his health when he'd made the decision to sell the company to a bigger conglomerate, Miller Industries.

"Darling, I've made you some tea. We don't want you to be late on your first day, do we?"

I smiled at my husband's kindness as I gave myself a final once over, dressed professionally in a black pencil skirt and a white silk blouse. I had opted for tights so I wouldn't be worrying all day that I was flashing stocking tops at my new boss, Denton Miller Snr who I had yet to meet in person. Along with commendations from my husband and a few webcam and Skype conversations I had decided that he was a boss I would enjoy working for.

Denton was of a similar age to Michael, but unlike my husband he had been married for thirty odd years to his teenage sweetheart and was living the American dream with his main home in California but numerous other residences around the world, seemingly in the cities that housed the offices of his vast business empire. Michael, by contrast had been married three times before me and I was the only wife not to have given him a child. Although sex would be required for a baby meaning that I was only a stepmother to four; two girls from wife number one, both older than me by a year and two years. His sons were aged twenty and fourteen with wives two and three respectively. God, I was like his middle child I realised with a smile, a smile that evaporated as I remembered I was also a step-nanny to three children under five and then he called me again.

"El, come on, Denton is a stickler for punctuality," he reminded me for the hundredth time causing me to bristle slightly.

"Yes, I know. I'm coming!" I screeched slipping black heeled shoes onto my feet but Michael laughed, annoying me further.

"If I was a jealous man those claims might offend me Mrs Stanton," he added as I appeared before him in the kitchen where my tea was waiting for me.

"What?" I asked impatiently, confused by his words.

"You shouted, *I'm coming.*"

Unsure how to react and thinking that if I did I might say something to open the can of worms that represented our lack of a sex life, I simply accepted the cup of tea and killed another ten minutes or so before dropping a kiss to Michael's head as I left the house.

****

Upon entering my former place of employment that was now my current place of employment I noted that very little appeared to have changed, except for the new signage.

"Hey there stranger," called the receptionist as I arrived on my new floor, my husband's old floor.

I spun to find a former colleague and friend, Maya, looking back at me with a grin spread across her face.

"What the bloody hell are you doing here?" I asked as I hugged the other woman, glad to find a friendly face. "Michael never mentioned you were back here."

"First day, babe. You remember I went to Provence with Aaron?"

I nodded, remembering her leaving a couple of years before with her boyfriend who had also worked for Michael but after his divorce was finalised decided to travel.

"Yeah, well that was great for a while, right up to the point

374

where I found Aaron was indulging in some serious online shenanigans."

"No way!"

"Way babe. So, I packed up, after paying the astronomical internet bill. My oldest sister still works here, in H.R. so she offered to put my C.V. forward and here I am, receptionist for the exec floor and I believe you are Mr Miller's P.A.?"

"Yes, first day too."

"So, you and Mr Stanton…"

I could see that what Maya really wanted to ask was, 'are you still married to the old man?'

"Michael is at home."

"Ah," she replied dropping her glance to my narrow gold wedding ring. "I heard he'd been unwell."

"Yes," I confirmed. "He had some heart trouble that required surgery, but he's on the mend," I added with a smile that not even I was convinced by. "Look, I should go, apparently my new boss doesn't like lateness."

"Okay, later, we'll catch up."

At ten o'clock I wondered if Mr Miller was one of those, 'do as I say, not as I do' bosses because he was a no show and I was over an hour and a half into my day. I considered calling Michael to ask him if I should be concerned, but decided against it. Another hour and then I would attempt to contact Denton Miller.

Another hour came and went, however as I was engrossed in a stationery delivery I was unaware of anything that wasn't made of paper until it was almost one o'clock when Maya appeared in my doorway.

"Do you want to grab lunch?" she asked as I stood up and faced her, still flushed from my exertion unpacking new paperwork.

"You'd have thought that such a forward thinking company would rely on electronic copies of this shit," I observed, opening yet another box of compliment slips.

"Lunch?" Maya repeated causing me to check out the clock on the wall behind my desk.

"No way, is that the time already? Where the hell is the boss?

375

I should call him, he could be ill or have had an accident." I panicked, grabbed the phone on my desk and hit the speed dial that had already been pre-programmed to my boss' mobile first, or cell as my directory had it listed as. Well, he was American I supposed as I heard the tone that seemed to ring forever before connecting to what I had anticipated being an answer phone.

"You've reached Denton Miller's den of debauchery and iniquity. Unfortunately Mr Miller is unable to come to the phone right now as he is busy between my thighs, can I take a message?" the voice asked, the voice of a woman I was fairly certain wouldn't belong to Mrs Miller, so who was she, with her soft and subtle American accent that sang with amusement?

"I erm, sorry, I'm, my name is P.A., well not, I, erm," I stammered while Maya watched on with a horrified expression that was in stark contrast to her grin. With a deep breath and a wipe of my free sweaty palm down my thigh I composed myself and tried again. "This is Eloise, Eloise Ross, Mr Miller's P.A. He was expected in his office this morning..." I allowed my voice to trail off so that my words might register when I heard another voice on the end of the line, a man's voice.

"Tia, what are you doing? How many times have I told you, do not answer my phone? That's not your place."

I glared down at the receiver in my hand wondering how my husband had got his views on my new boss so wrong. Arrogant prick I thought, except when I heard Tia giggle down the line and Maya stifle a laugh with a gulp, I realised that I had said it, out loud.

"It's your office, your P.A.," Tia explained. "Checking up on the boss."

This woman was also a pain in the arse, her and my new boss, maybe they were meant for each other.

"No, no," I stammered before I heard Mr Miller's reply.

"I don't need checking up on. I'm going in now, as per the email I sent to my P.A. Could this day get any worse?" he asked as I flushed crimson despite him being unable to see me.

"Did you get that, honey?" Tia asked still laughing.

"Yeah, got it, thank you, sorry, sorry to have interrupted your erm, sorry," I cried and hung up. "Oh bollocks, his day has nothing on mine!" I told Maya slumping into my chair.

"And you kind of hung up on him at the end there." She smiled with an accompanying cringe.

"Oh God! Why am I even doing this? He was so sweet on webcam," I said, thinking aloud.

"With Mr Stanton?"

I buried my face in my hands. "Shit, yeah. He was with a woman, maybe not his wife and like with her with her I think." My whispered realisation made Maya laugh loudly.

"So, to sum up, you have inarticulately interrupted a secret shag, somehow made it sound like he was a naughty boy by being late and then hung up on him?"

My horrified expression must have conveyed how awful I felt because Maya appeared before me on her haunches.

"It wasn't that bad babe. He'll be fine, I'm sure. Come on, lunch." Getting to her feet she pulled me to mine. "Come on, no arguments, we'll go to the pub over the road, no alcohol, just food."

Nodding, I grabbed my things and then quickly checked my emails, only to find an earlier email from my boss.

Morning Ms Ross,

I was hoping to be in before you this morning, but I had to change plans.

Will be very late afternoon so may not get to meet you until tomorrow as I have a busy day planned.

Regards,

Denton Miller
CEO Miller Industries (Europe)

"Oh," I whispered almost undetected as a second email hit my inbox.

Ms Ross,

Thank you for the nurse maid duties, however unnecessary they were. I am able to tell the time and arrive at the office without assistance!

After further changes to my first day I may not make it into the office at all today.

I shall expect to see you in the morning no later than 8 a.m.

Oh, and Ms Ross, don't ever fucking hang up on me!

Denton Miller
CEO Miller Industries (Europe)

"He's really got to be kidding me, hasn't he?" I asked pulling Maya to see my second email, but she literally just squealed with some kind of delight.

"I think I am going to enjoy working here, a boss that emails with swearing and a bollocking! Come on, lunch, I only have cover on reception for one hour, meaning we now have exactly forty seven minutes to be back here."

****

Every mouthful of my linguini that tasted like shoe laces rather than pasta got stuck where I imagined my gullet might be, even with the assistance of two glasses of a non-alcoholic beverage.

"Do you think he'll sack me?" I asked Maya who had no problems digesting her food that was a steak and ale pie with seasonal vegetables and seriously chunky chips.

"No, I wouldn't have thought the interruption of a mid coital rendezvous with his mistress would be classed as a sackable offence."

"Thanks," I replied, wondering what else I could say to that and decided there was no more to say.

I returned to my office, which was actually a working space within Mr Miller's office space. I suppose it could be seen that I occupied his vestibule or an atrium, the space between his inner sanctum and the world beyond, although as this space happened to be at the furthest point of the building everywhere else was the world beyond. I liked that a small amount of reworking had been done up here so I didn't mistake the office as Michael's, it was Mr Miller's and I couldn't, wouldn't forget my place. As well as my work space, this area also housed his reception area, the place where I'd be responsible for entertaining any visitors who were waiting for my boss. Maybe if he was finishing off Tia, or whoever.

With I sigh I observed the boxes of stationery that still littered my floor and decided to tackle them, get to the bottom of it all, just not yet. After a cup of coffee, if I could find where the coffee machine was housed. Yes, that was a plan. Coffee, and just in case my wayward boss turned up I'd take my photocopying down the hall with me and make myself look busy.

It was another forty-five minutes before I found myself back at my desk, with coffee and the photocopied proposals that Mr Miller would need later in the week. The mess on my floor was worse than I had remembered. Could this day get any worse I wondered once more as another email hit my inbox?

Ms Ross,

You appear to have littered the floor with semi-unpacked boxes of stationery, please resolve this issue. Also, why do we have such a ridiculous amount of compliment slips and headed paper? We live in an age of electronic communication. I think you may have overstocked somewhat. Again, resolve before tomorrow morning.

I am out for the day. In the event of an emergency, I repeat, EMERGENCY you may call me!

I take my tea with just a dash of milk, no sugar, and coffee no milk, one sugar. I drink tea until 10 a.m. and coffee thereafter, unless I instruct you otherwise.

Regards,

Denton Miller
CEO Miller Industries (Europe)

"Fucking numb nuts," I told him even though I was alone. The cheek of this man. "I have semi-unpacked the stationery that was ordered by someone else, not me, and I know we live in an age of electronic communications, so I have not overstocked anything and yet I am expected to sort it. I will call you when hell freezes over after my initial attempt at contact and on top of that I am now your tea girl!"

The sound of my phone's ring brought me back to the here and now, Michael.

"Hi, you okay?" I answered.

"Yes, just checking in. How's your day going?" he asked and as much as I wanted to vent I knew he wouldn't get it. He'd turn everything on its head and blame me. Not me personally, but my position, so I replied accordingly.

"The new boss had a change of plan. He appears to have popped in, a visit I missed and now he's not in until tomorrow, but things are fine."

"You don't sound sure? Maybe you should think about scaling back, love."

Oh my God! I actually wanted to scream at him because he was the retired one, not me, I wasn't even half way there. Why the hell would I want to scale back, but as usual he continued to speak.

"There's a group, at the hospital, a support group for families. You could help them out, or Johnny at the golf club was saying they're looking to take on a part timer to help with memberships…"

I cut him off, abruptly. "Michael, I don't want to scale back, nor work at the golf club, nor listen to people discuss how hard it is to, well, whatever. Denton Miller may prove to be more of a challenge than I had first imagined, but it's fine. What do you fancy doing this evening?" I asked hoping he'd say something exciting, different to the norm, maybe even dinner, alcohol, a bath and an early night.

"I'm easy, whatever you want darling, although there is a documentary on the demise of the bee on at half-past eight so I'd like to be done by then."

"And an early night?" I suggested, hating myself a little for pleading for his time, attention and his penis. This day really was turning to shit.

"El, I don't know, we'll see," he said, the dismissal obvious in his tone.

"I might be going out straight from work," I lied. "Maya is back here, she's the exec's receptionist now, so I thought we might catch up, in the pub, or a bar or something."

I was slightly disgusted with myself for lying so blatantly to my husband. Something I'd never done, about plans that didn't exist, but the mere thought of sitting and listening to a blow by blow account of why bees were disappearing made me want to cry. Almost as much as the idea of drinking cocoa before finding myself sitting up in bed reading stories of passion and romance while my husband slept next to me, snoring, having managed to fall asleep in the time it took me to wash my face and brush my teeth.

"Oh, okay, well let me know when you've decided what you're doing, and remember me to Maya."

"Okay," I whispered before guiltily but honestly adding, "I love you, Michael."

"I know darling, and I love you too."

Throwing my phone into my bag I felt shittier than I might have ever felt, but more than that I felt discontent, sad and restless, and possibly a little reckless.

Printed in Poland
by Amazon Fulfillment
Poland Sp. z o.o., Wrocław